Book I of The Lorn Prophecy

Fable

Book 1 of The Lorn Prophecy

By Lisa Fender
and Toni Burns

Djen-Works, LLC

Printed in the United States of America

First Printing, 2013

Djen-Works, LLC
PO Box 16951
Golden, CO 80402
www.LisaFender.com

Edited by

Adirondack Editing
Susan Uttendorfsky
Owner / Copy Editor
adirondackediting.com

Cover and Artwork by

Mike Kloepfer
www.mikeyzart.blogspot.com

ISBN-13: 978-1484143513
ISBN-10: 1484143515

Cataloging-in-Publication Data is on file with the
Library of Congress
1 – 1017762761

For Dad

John Lee Wright
(July 7, 1930 – April 28, 2012)

Mentor, supporter of dreams, and friend.

We miss you.

Acknowledgements

There are so many people I want to thank; I hope I don't miss anyone.

First, my friend and Author Lizzie T. Leaf, for mentoring me. When I met her and told her I had always wanted to write, she encouraged me to go for it. I'm glad she did. Next, my writing coach, Janet Roots. She took an amateur storyteller and molded me into a writer of novels. Her patience and understanding got me past the point of my low self-esteem to realizing I can learn and I will get it. I did. Of course, my critique partners with the Wanna-be-Writers group, Robin Calkins and Janet Baltz. They never let me give up and their honest and insightful critiques helped me all the way to the end.

After taking classes, working with a writing coach, and joining Romance Writers of America, I finally understood how to turn a story into a novel. My sister, Tanya (she took on "Toni" in the sixth grade, but she'll always be Tanya to me), came in the picture in the middle of all my learning to help edit, and she began to learn as well. We went through the book together and I realized she wasn't just editing, she was writing with me. I knew we were a great team, and she fell in love with the story. I made her my co-writer. It has been a wonderful journey together and we aren't finished yet. We have a lot of books still to write.

I don't want to forget my family and friends who were also so supportive through all this. My husband, Rick, my daughter, Brandie, my son, Travis, and my mom, Carol Wright, all read chapters when they were really rough and made suggestions or helped with editing. Then, my friend, Linda Armand, read the whole book in rough draft. My landlord, Gary Campbell, for his help with charting the west coast areas in the book, and, last but not least, Michael McFadden for offering to edit the entire book before it went to my Professional editor, Susan Uttendorfsky. Michael lives in another state, but he would call me and we would go through each page and he was wonderful. He really caught things I never would have. I couldn't imagine the complete manuscript without him.

Acknowledgements

I also want to thank all my blog followers and friends on LinkedIn who gave me support and commented on my blog. I hope that I didn't miss anyone.

Lisa Fender

I wanted to add a short "Ditto, sis!" to the above. Writing with my sister, Lisa, has brought us closer together than we ever imagined we could be. I joke that the two of us make one awesome writer. We complement each other's strengths and fill in the gaps in each other's weaknesses. I want to acknowledge and thank my husband, Scotte, for his patience through this process. He gave up evenings and weekends with me so that Lisa and I could bring her amazing vision to our readers. Of course, I want to acknowledge and thank Lisa for bringing me into her world and allowing me to make it mine, as well. Love ya, Sis.

Toni (Tanya) Burns

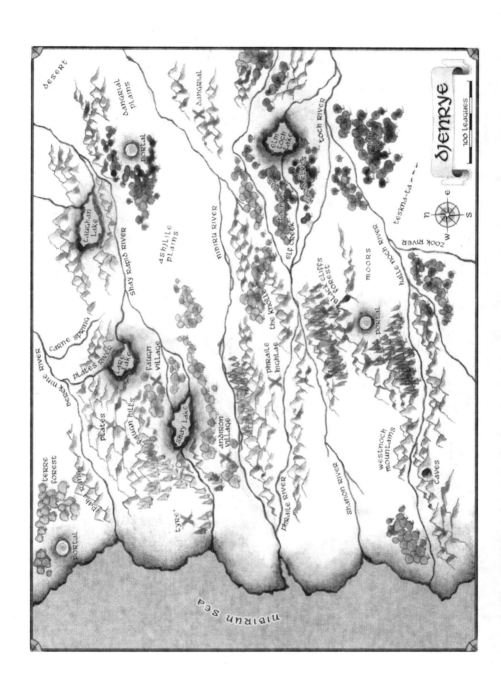

The Djen

The cool night air blowing
Leaves dance in its breeze
A backdrop of moonlight
Peeks through the trees

A glimpse of a sentry
A watcher stands alone
The hint of a beacon
A familiar glow

The ancient protector
A calm in the night
Blue beam of comfort
A trick of the light

A whisper in the wind
The fable is told
A faint trail of smoke
Prophecy unfolds...

Lisa Fender

PROLOGUE

Djenrye
18 Years Ago

The stone walls of the bed chamber trembled. A vase fell from the side table. Shattered porcelain, lilies, and water spread across the polished wood floor. Jolted awake by the vibration, Carlynn nearly tumbled from the window seat. She jerked her head this way and that, trying to locate the cause of the commotion. After a brief moment of stillness, came another tremor, followed by a distant war cry.

It could not be long past midnight, yet weak firelight filtered through the window. The bedroom was eerily illuminated. Goose bumps prickled Carlynn's arms and she instinctively wrapped them around her swollen belly. Squinting, she could barely distinguish the still silhouette of her husband in their bed, three long strides from where she sat. A thunderous noise rose again. When she opened the window outward, an undulating clamor passed beneath.

Torches glowed at the top of the hill where *Raile ai Highlae*, the Hall of Light, stood. Monumental in its height and girth, it blocked the light of the full moon. The torches at its base allowed Carlynn to glimpse hundreds of horses choking the long pathway leading to the Hall. Dismounted riders scrambled up the stairs and the hillside, attacking the posted guards.

On the path, three stories below her, a battalion raced toward the insurgents. The armored men rode Dangrial warhorses. Weapons drawn, ready for battle, they bellowed a call to arms.

The Warrior in the lead had short cropped hair in stark contrast to the unbound locks of the men behind him. Ghorgon, Master

Warrior of Phraile Highlae. He rode without the need of reins. In his right hand a sword, in his left an axe. Over the noise of the mêlée, Carlynn could hear his cries to his men.

"Guard the Hall," his voice boomed. "Death to the Rebels! Protect the Ortehlae!"

The Rebels mean to steal the Ortehlae!

She flew to the bed to wake the Guardian. "Raynok." She shook her husband fiercely. "Hurry, awake. Raile ai Highlae is under attack." His clear blue eyes fluttered open. She yanked at his arm in an attempt to pull him to a sitting position. Unmovable, he yawned, rubbing his face.

"Get up… Now," she shouted.

He opened his eyes to a squint, yet remained immobile. "What troubles you, my love? Did…" An errant arrow halted his query. It passed close enough to ruffle Carlynn's blonde hair, and speared the headboard by his left ear. Raynok pulled his wife over the top of him and to the other side of the bed. All weariness had left him.

"Stay down," he cried, bolting for the window.

Carlynn dropped off the side, keeping her head below the top of the mattress. Her elbow upended a longbow, propped against the wall. "Raynok …"

She slid his bow and quiver across the smooth planks. He grabbed for the weapons. She watched her husband move the lace fabric, trying to determine the direction from which the arrow had come. The warmth from the embers in the fireplace did nothing to stop the chill that ran up her spine.

Raynok backed away from the enemy's line of sight to lean against the safety of the stone wall. Using the top of his bow, he caught the edge of the latch and pushed the window fully open. He tucked a loose strand of hair behind his ear, retrieved an arrow from the quiver, and notched it. In one fluid motion, he moved from safety, drew his bow, and shot into the night.

Each arrow quickly followed the other—notch, draw, loose; notch, draw, loose. Carlynn knew most had found their mark from the screams below. Yet…no more entered from the outside. *It must have been a wayward strike.*

The bedroom door flew open and in raced a lean young man. He was clothed in the traditional black undershirt, wool breeches, and burnished chain mail vest of a Djen Warrior. His hand gripped the sword hilt at his waist.

Raynok turned on his heels, taking aim at the intruder. The scout staggered back, revealing the emblem of the City of Phraile Highlae on his left shoulder. The saber-toothed tiger's head, mouth open and snarling, and five orbs, representing the Ortehlae, formed a crescent above. It was all that stopped Raynok from ending his life.

"Lord Raynok, it is I, Warrior Creye," the soldier called out. "The Rebellion has infiltrated the Hall. The palace will be next. I am to escort you and your wife to safety."

Raynok lowered his arm. "Creye, do you have your bow? I need your aid."

"No, My Lord. We must leave. Now. The Rebels breach the palace gates."

Raynok looked back at Carlynn. "Make haste, my love. Get dressed. You need to leave quickly."

Carlynn nodded and hurried to the dark of the far side of the room. As she reached behind her wooden wardrobe, her hand brushed against soft lamb's wool. Even in the dim light, she knew this to be one of her favorite fall riding dresses. She made a mental note to bring her hooded overcoat for additional protection from the coolness of the night.

As Carlynn slipped into the dress, her thoughts mirrored the chaos occurring outside the gates. *How did the intruders manage to breach the city walls? The Rebellion has never been able to infiltrate the Raile ai Highlae. How did they increase their numbers without the Council's knowledge?*

Peering over the top of the screen, Carlynn watched Creye approach Raynok.

"Lord, you must come with us," Creye pleaded. "You know that the enemy cannot be allowed to apprehend you."

Raynok did not respond, but rather continued to rain arrows down on the Rebels. Backlit by the glow from the window, Carlynn could see the muscles rippling on his biceps each time he drew the bow. The outline of his virile form reminded her of stories of the War Gods of old—fierce, strong, and determined.

Creye grabbed his arm mid-draw. A bold move. "My Lord, need I remind you that you are the last Guardian? Your life is sacrosanct."

Raynok shook him off. "I cannot run like a scared rabbit while my men are left to fight and die."

"Yes you can, and you will," Carlynn called out, emerging from the screen, now clothed for travel. "If they capture you, our very existence will be in jeopardy."

"I implore you, My Lord. We have not time to defend the palace."

Carlynn moved to her husband's side, put a hand on his cheek, and turned him to look at her. "I need you with me. If you care not for your life, think of our child."

Without looking away from Raynok's steely blue eyes, she grasped his hand and placed it on her belly. The babe within kicked once, as if in agreement.

"I yield." He looked down. "To you both." Raynok raised Carlynn's hand to his lips, kissing it gently before releasing her.

Striding to the chair by the fireplace, he called over his shoulder, "I know a means of escape. A moment to dress."

Raynok grabbed his leather breeches off the chair. "Creye, my sword," he said, motioning to the bedside.

A thick long-sleeved shirt was hastily thrown over his head and he slipped into his boots. Completely clothed in black, the Guardian grabbed a doe-skin doublet in one hand and seized the proffered sword with the other. "Follow me," he ordered, buckling his belt and ushering Carlynn toward the door.

The echo of fighting surged in through the opened door. It could only mean that the Rebellion had breached the palace defenses. Carlynn trembled at the sounds of combat and groped for Raynok's hand. Her stomach recoiled from the screams of Warriors, the thick dull thud of axes splintering bone, the steel clanging on steel or stone.

Billows of black smoke rose from the stairs at the far end of the hallway, sucking at the oxygen and leaving behind a thick odorous stench of burnt leather, wool, and flesh. She swallowed against the sour taste in her throat and hurried after her husband and Creye, away from the attack.

Wanting to run, Carlynn felt her husband's hand on her forearm, holding her back.

"We must be stealthy," he said.

They crept down the hall, turned the corner, and quickened their pace. The torches remained lit, perched in their brass sconces, but burned low. Raynok approached a large portrait—a landscape view outside the city. The bottom of the tarnished bronze frame skirted the floor and the top was a head higher than Raynok. Running his hand along one side, he stopped. Carlynn heard a small click. The picture swung away from the wall to reveal an iron latch. Raynok pushed on it. Long unused hinges squealed, echoing back from the passage which had opened in front of them.

Carlynn stepped past Raynok, who then entered behind her, followed by Creye. The rock walls on either side were slick with moisture and she felt cold flowing out of the emptiness before her. She suffered a surge of panic when the door shut and plunged them into total darkness. One of the men brushed passed her. The familiar smell of musty sweat identified him as her husband.

He murmured, "Watch your step."

She could not see her hand in front of her face, let alone her step. Clinging to Raynok, she felt him hesitate as his hand pulled hers down slightly. *There must be stairs.* She shuffled her feet until she felt the edge of the floor and cautiously stepped downward. Running her hand blindly against the stone wall, she followed him onto a stairwell. It curved down and to the left—into nothingness. The mortar between the stones occasionally crumbled as her fingers slid over it.

In the blackness, time slowed to a crawl. Carlynn heard skittering and chattering above, below, and behind the walls. She imagined creatures with blind eyes and sharp teeth. They could be a whisker's distance from her hands, her throat, waiting for the right moment to pounce. Barely able to stifle the urge to run forward blindly, she called forth the Djen breathing techniques. Slow counted breaths, attention centered on something pleasant—her warm bed shared by her husband, and her attempts at slumber.

Earlier that evening, long after Raynok's breathing had become soft snores; Carlynn exchanged her comfortable cocoon for the solace of the window seat. The view onto the rooftops of Phraile Highlae always soothed her. This night she found her thoughts to be less on the town and more on the new life in her womb.

She recalled her worries that her child would never know the trials, or pleasures, of a simple townsfolk's life, such as the one in which she had been raised. Carlynn's life had truly been uncomplicated, despite hardships. That is, until she came of age and joined Raynok.

How could she hope for her baby to comprehend the struggles of the people when the child would live a life of privilege? A concern which no longer existed—the illusion of privilege and safety had been shattered as she now fled from her home.

Lost in thought, Carlynn bumped into Raynok's solid form. A spark. *Could it be a trick of the eye?* And then, a flash of light. Her husband held a torch that he lit with his flint. As her vision adjusted, she saw empty sconces and a narrow passage before them. Another torch lit and handed to Creye. With the illumination, they managed a faster pace through the passage to another set of stairs leading ever downward. At its crest, Raynok released Carlynn's hand. A determined look darkened his features.

Reading the expression, she pleaded, "No, Raynok," and clasped his forearm. "We need to continue on."

Raynok spoke to Creye over the crown of her head. "How can I? How can you expect me to desert my people knowing what is occurring?"

"If we lose you, we lose everything, My Lord," Creye reminded him. "At this moment, you are not a Warrior. You are the Guardian."

Raynok's shoulders slumped. Entwining his fingers in Carlynn's hair, he cupped the nape of her neck and bent to kiss her brow. His lips lingered for a moment and then he pulled back, took her hand in his, and drew her down the next flight of stairs. *How far under the palace are we?*

The air grew staler with each step. Even the torches did not flicker. Although cold, no draft arose from its depths. The escapees created their own breeze. Cobwebs and spider webs, disturbed by their passage, occasionally sizzled when errantly caught in the torches' flames.

These stairs dead-ended at a small landing enclosed on three sides by stone. Handing the torch to Carlynn, Raynok ran his hands along the edges of the uppermost stones. As before there was a click. Her husband pushed against the solid surface until an opening appeared. On the other side, he pressed hard and the stones melded together, leaving Carlynn staring at a solid wall. *All this time, I never knew this existed.*

Carlynn took a moment to catch her breath and get her bearings. The smell of death and despair hung in a cloud about her. The stench of decay, feces, and moldy garments was offset by the reek of urine. She assumed that they were in the dungeons. One area of the palace that she, gratefully, had never entered.

Resisting the urge to gag, she allowed herself to be pulled forward, past iron bars. The cells appeared empty, but she could not shake the feeling of dead eyes watching their escape.

At the end of the passage, they found another flight of stairs, leading upward. Fear, and the desire to leave this dismal place, urged her onward. *This is not how I want to remember my home.*

Three flights up, the air began to clear and Carlynn begged the men to stop. Her breath came in gasps and her legs burned. Creye clearly wanted to continue, but Raynok refused to move. Instead, he eased Carlynn onto a step.

"Just for a moment," Creye acquiesced, pacing up and down the stairs. His eyes continually darted to Carlynn, upward, and then back again.

And it was just a moment. Carlynn had hardly caught her breath before Raynok gently helped her back to her feet.

He encouraged her on with a whisper. "If I have to carry you, my love, I will, but we must make haste."

The devotion and tenderness in his voice gave her strength. She followed the men to the next doorway. An ancient metal and oak creation, it required the strength of both men to open.

Cool night air blew the stench and horrors behind them. In front of them was a cart path with deep wheel ruts that cut through the dirt and mud. Illuminated by the moon, the barred gate at the far end of the enclosed yard could be seen. That direction would leave them fully exposed. Rather than crossing the yard to the gate, Raynok skirted the wall to their right. They stayed in the shadows along the base of the battlement wall as it curved to the left, ending at an unused guard tower.

"Master Ghorgon provided me with the key," Creye said. He produced a piece of metal from inside his boot and slipped inside the tower, motioning them to follow.

"Worry not, my love," Raynok said. "If the Rebels knew of this exit, we would have seen some sign of them."

A short sprint from the tower and up a steep incline, and the safety of the forest appeared. By blind luck or a blessing of the Gods, they made it into the woods unnoticed.

Creye rushed into the dense growth. Carlynn and Raynok did not immediately follow. At the crest of the hill, they stopped and turned to see their city in chaos.

Torches were borne up the main cobblestone street by Djen, but these were not Phraile Highlae Warriors. They walked down the middle, five abreast, leaving substantial room on either side. They proceeded unchallenged by the townsfolk, who had either fled or hid in their homes. The Rebellion carried banners bearing the insignia of the enemy, two black gloved hands holding the Orteh, Élan-Vitál—the Orb of Universal Spirit. A crude parody of the stone sculpture at the entrance of their city honoring Élan-Vitál— two saber-toothed tiger paws raising the Orteh up to the Gods—the sight sickened her.

The cries of warfare, pain, and fear were unbearable. Her heart ached and she could not stop her tears. *What drives the Rebellion to destroy our way of life, our purpose for existing? They care not that they murder their own for the slim chance to destroy the Hundye, the humans, in the other dimension. No one knows what will truly happen if they set the* Ortehlae *in motion.*

Raynok's hand tightened on hers. Pain softened his rugged face, tears brimmed in his eyes. He turned his head away and, without a word, he and Carlynn followed Creye into the forest.

The harvest moon shone brightly through the treetops, guiding their way as they ran from shadow to shadow. A short time in, they paused, crouching behind dense foliage, peering into the dark for pursuers.

Creye whispered, "Ghorgon directed me to the old weapons shelter. We will hide there until our soldiers regain the city and he sends for us." Creye glanced up at Carlynn. "It would be quicker to move through the trees."

She shook her head. "I am sorry, Creye. It is not possible for me to run in the trees. I cannot risk it. Being heavy with child has adversely affected my balance."

Prior to pregnancy, Carlynn excelled in the inherent Djen skill of tree-running, moving through the branches as easily as sprinting on the ground. Through years of razor-sharp focus, and an innate ability to detect the next step, she had become the fastest tree-runner in Phraile Highlae.

Even when she was fully two-thirds through her pregnancy, she could still outmatch Raynok and Creye's strides, but now, it would be too dangerous. They would have to resign themselves to the forest floor.

"Actually, My Lady, I think a ground run would be unanticipated. The Rebels will be scouring the trees, while we skitter underfoot like silent mice," Creye assured her.

She hoped he spoke true. Capture would mean certain death for Raynok. Tied down, tubes inserted in his arms, his blood would be slowly drained into the heart of the Ortehlae. As he died, his power would also transfer. In this manner, the Rebellion would have power to control the elements through the Ortehlae and alter the balance of the Earth. But the horror of Raynok's death would be only the beginning.

The ensuing destruction from the power shift would be unfathomable. Great volcanoes that had slept for millennia could erupt, worldwide floods would occur, fault lines ripped apart, earthquakes strong enough to bring down even the largest cities, and hurricanes that would breach the coasts.

Carlynn knew the Rebellion's propaganda espoused the destruction of the Hundye dimension "for the sake of our planet."

Even the most learned of the Magi do not agree on what effect this would have on the Djenrye dimension. The Rebellion's true motivation for eradicating the Hundye is to bring the Djen out of hiding. Terra-hun, the plane of the Hundye, would be at the beck and call of the Rebellion—or so they hoped. Her heart froze at the thought of their lust for power and selfishness. *What if they are wrong and Djenrye comes to an end as well?*

Raynok nudged Carlynn forward from the safety of cover, bringing her back to the present. The growth became denser as they crept deeper into the woods. Creye occasionally motioned them to drop down, and then he would prompt them to scurry to the next bit of camouflage.

She could no longer hear the city. Instead, she strained to catch sounds of movement indicating the presence of the enemy. The three moved swiftly until they arrived at the weapons shelter. Creye signaled them to stop. If he had not pointed out the well-hidden structure, they might have slipped right by it.

Creye whispered, "Stay here and wait for my signal." He worked his way around the shelter. Anxiety engulfed Carlynn. She prayed to the Gods for their safety.

Movement drew her attention to the shelter entrance. Creye emerged from the surrounding shadows and motioned for them.

"Are you ready, my love?" Raynok asked. Carlynn nodded, grabbed his outstretched hand, and they prepared to run. A few steps from cover, an arrow whizzed across their path and thudded into a tree next to Raynok.

The two froze.

Creye cried out, "Stop—turn and run…"

Raynok grabbed her arms and yanked her behind the nearest pine. From the depths of the forest, a voice called Creye's name. Carlynn looked in the direction of the cry. Ghorgon materialized out of the darkness. He sped his horse toward them shouting, "Creye—get down…"

Creye turned to dive for cover and then collapsed face forward onto the forest floor. An arrow protruded from his back. Carlynn's hands flew to her mouth to stifle a scream.

Two enemy Warriors rushed from the trees. They headed directly for Raynok, who pushed Carlynn farther into the concealment of darkness and ran in the opposite direction. As he intended, the enemy did not see her.

Backing deeper into hiding, Carlynn's heel struck a root. Falling, she caught sight of Ghorgon speeding past. The enemy moved to attack her husband. Ghorgon unsheathed his sword. He rushed to Raynok's aid, cleaving one of the Rebels in two.

Carlynn squeezed her eyes shut and put her hands over her ears, but could not block out the sounds. Raynok uttered a battle cry. She risked a look.

The remaining Rebel Warrior vaulted from a fallen tree and leapt onto her husband's back, forcing him to the ground. Carlynn cried out in desperation, "Ghorgon, save my husband!"

She watched in horror as Raynok grappled with his assailant. He managed to grab him by the hair and land a few solid punches, but did not notice the knife until it slipped into his chest.

Her breath caught.

She physically felt her husband's pain and heard Ghorgon yell, "NOOOOOO!"

The scream sounded far away. Ghorgon leapt from his horse and brought his claymore down on the Warrior, full weight behind the blow, cutting off the assassin's head.

Crawling forward on hands and knees, Carlynn's anguish and swollen belly made it impossible for her to rise. "Ghorgon—help me," she wailed.

Rather than responding, Ghorgon knelt beside Raynok and eased the knife from his chest.

Carlynn cried out again. "Help me—I need to get to Raynok…"

Finally acknowledging her pleas, Ghorgon gently laid Raynok's head on the ground and went to Carlynn. He arrived at her side additional Rebels arrived from the direction of Phraile Highlae.

Ghorgon grabbed her arms roughly. "Come. Up on your feet. We must go. Now."

"I cannot leave my husband," Carlynn cried. She struggled, but Ghorgon managed to keep his grip.

"I give you my word, I will return for Raynok after I get you to safety." Ghorgon pulled Carlynn to her feet. The harder she fought, the tighter the Warrior held on. An arrow impaled the tree next to Carlynn. Ghorgon's eyes darkened and he rose to his full height— an imposing figure. Roughly wrenching her, Ghorgon half pulled, half carried her toward his warhorse.

"You will come with me, My Lady, willing or not," Ghorgon commanded.

"I will have you flogged," she spat, still fighting to reach her husband.

Ghorgon managed to haul Carlynn into the saddle. He swung up behind her with threats of tying her down. The admonition was unnecessary. The baby's movement stopped her cold—a potent reminder that she carried the last Guardian.

She cried out one last time, "Rayyyynokkk…"

Ghorgon wheeled the Dangrial warhorse, Abatos, away from the carnage. He turned the animal briefly toward the sound of renewed battle cries. Rebel Warriors flowed from the darkness in a tidal wave, weapons drawn. Arrows showered the trees around them. One found a weakness in Ghorgon's bracers. Blood ran down his hand and onto Carlynn. Another ripped the fabric of her cloak. A searing pain confirmed the tip had grazed her thigh.

Ghorgon yanked her close and shouted, "Hold fast!" Slapping Abatos with the reins, they sped off into the forest, death at their heels.

Chapter 1

Golden, Colorado
Present Day

Stevie threw her hands against the dashboard to keep from slamming into it. The black Mustang roared into the driveway.

"Watch out for my mom's flowers," Stevie cried. "And the new tree she just planted."

The car slid sideways on the gravel, spitting rock behind them. Stevie was flung forward as they came to a skidding halt. She turned to Jack. A huge "I just got a new car" grin formed across his face.

"Jack, are you frickin' crazy?" Stevie asked, cautiously releasing her death grip on the dashboard. "Mom's going to kill you...throwing gravel into the flower bed."

"Nah...it's just some little rocks. It'll be fine." Jack winked at her. His green eyes sparkled mischievously. "Besides, she'll still love me."

"Yeah? Well, I don't know if I will." She rolled her eyes and tossed back her long blonde hair. "So enlighten me. Your parents buy you a brand new car for high school graduation and this is the way you repay them? By breaking your word to be a careful driver?"

"Geez, Stevie—in total control. Just having a little fun."

Stevie silently collected the contents of her purse from the floor. She wanted to point out the stats on reckless driving and accidents, but she held back. She didn't want to bring up memories of his sister, Jennifer. Even after ten years, the loss still pained him.

Jack, never able to leave a silence unfilled, changed the subject to the concert. "So, you going to Red Rocks with me?"

"You're kidding, right? You know I have plans that night."

"Look…I already bought the tickets." He opened the console and produced an envelope. "Why can't you change your plans?"

"I don't believe you, Jack. I. Can't. Go. The Wild Earth Guardians only have two fundraisers a year. You know I promised I would run the donations table. Why don't you take Alyssa? I thought she was your BFF, too."

"Seriously? She hates that band. Come on. Please," Jack whined. He ran his hands through his wavy brown hair, pouting boyishly.

That was it. The last straw. "Damn it, Jack. Enough."

"Fine. I'll just give my tickets away. What's a hundred bucks?"

"Whatever you need to do," Stevie responded, crossing her arms.

Jack's jaw tightened. Fixing her with a fierce look, he said, "I can't believe that a bunch of mangy dogs, smelly hippies, and losers are more important to you than our friendship. Whatever happened to Best Friends Forever?"

"What? Now you're throwing my words at me? It's not like this is news. I told you weeks ago." Stevie got out of the car, slamming the door hard enough to rattle the window.

Without a glance backwards, she stormed up the porch steps. The sounds of a gunning engine and churning gravel followed her into the house. Banging the door shut behind her, she muttered to the dark, "Some best friend. After eight years, you'd think Jack would know me."

Too disgruntled to stop and turn on any lights, Stevie took the stairs two at a time. On the upper floor, she fumed down the hallway, pitched her purse into the bedroom, and stomped to the bathroom. She felt for the handle of the linen closet, grabbed a washcloth, and flung it into the basin. Turning on the hot water spigot, she wanted nothing more than to wash the makeup off her face and that stupid argument out of her mind.

At the sound of Tonka barking, she wrenched the faucet handle hard enough for metal to screech on metal. "What—really, Mom? Tonka's still outside?"

When no response came, Stevie poked her head out the bathroom door. "Mom?"

Wait a sec... The lights are off. Mom's not home?

She went down the hall, opened her mother's bedroom door, and turned on the light. It was empty. A quick walk to the window to glance at the driveway revealed the vacant space where her mom's SUV should be parked. *I can't believe I was so mad I didn't notice.*

She walked out of the room and absently flicked off the light. Her yellow lab was still outside and her mother nowhere to be found. The darkness of the house closed in around her.

Creeping back down the hall, she peered in to her room, and was relieved at the lack of movement and unfamiliar shapes. She tiptoed to the top of the stairs and looked down to blackness.

Tonka's barking stopped. Stevie strained to hear anything, but all was still. An uneasy feeling washed over her.

Spring nights usually brought the sounds of crickets, birds, and an occasional coyote howl, but never silence. In fact, the normal cacophony of nature's music frightened her "down the hill" friends the first time they stayed overnight. Comfortable in the symphony nature freely provided, Stevie would tease them about being "city kids".

But this quiet was complete. It created its own strange vibration. There is stillness, and then there is deathly silence. This felt like the second. Compounded by Tonka's sudden calm, the void was a weight pushing down on her. Stevie had never been claustrophobic, but a sense of being entombed and exposed at the same time unnerved her.

Quietly, she moved down the stairs, avoiding the middle one that creaked, afraid to bring noise into the void. At the landing, she turned right, in the direction of the kitchen. She passed the grandfather clock with its steady, rhythmic ticking, and glanced at the time.

Ten o'clock. Where are you, Mom?

Entering the kitchen, Stevie kept as close to the walls as possible, attempting to blend her five-foot-seven-inch frame with the shadows. Through the open blinds of the sliding glass door, a full moon cast weak light across the floor. Beyond the glass, Tonka's shape could be seen in the backyard.

Stevie inched across the pine floor. Again, careful to avoid the creaky joints, she positioned herself so that only her head would be visible to the outside.

The yellow lab stood at the base of the nearest cottonwood, front paws clawing at the trunk, attention completely focused on the branches above. Tonka appeared to be attempting to climb the tree.

A mountain lion? That would account for the silence, at least.

Living in the foothills, it was not uncommon for wildlife sightings, even bears or pumas. Stevie searched her memory, but couldn't remember when the last sighting had been broadcast. She leaned into the glass; hands cupped on either side of her face, and squinted into the night.

A tall figure stood on a thick branch, silhouetted by the moonlight. The way that it balanced on the tree, the easy athletic posture and height—it could only be a man. Tonka resumed her barking and the distraction drew her eyes downward. The lab's normally yellow fur glowed green. Straining to make out the source of the strange light, she looked again at the man-shape. A gasp escaped her lips and she jumped back.

What the hell?

Steady blue beams radiated from where his eyes should be.

Afraid to open the door, but more afraid for her dog, she reached for the latch. She unlocked it slowly, trying in vain to be quiet, but the lock clicked. The blue beacons turned her direction, and then winked out. Stevie's breath caught in her throat. She tried to locate the outline of the creature, but saw only the rustling of leaves.

"What was that?" she said to the dark.

Hoping the intruder had been scared away, she cautiously slid the door open, barely wide enough for her head. "Tonka, to me," she called in a loud whisper. The lab's head turned. One last look up the tree, and Tonka came bounding across the yard. She leapt onto the deck and pranced into the house, tail wagging as if nothing was amiss.

A quick close of the door, latch of the lock, draw of the blinds, and two shaky steps to the kitchen table, then Stevie collapsed in a chair. Within half a second she was up again, vaulting for the switch to flood the room with light.

Trembling, goose bumps rising on her arms, she hugged herself and backed deeper into the kitchen by the breakfast bar—as far away from the glass door and mysterious shape as possible. Tonka followed her, bumping her hand with a soft wet nose, but Stevie's focus was on the stranger outside.

He must not have known I was here. But the car—he had to hear Jack speeding away. Who is he...or what is he? Was it my imagination? No, that can't be right... Tonka was barking at him before I saw anything.

Gathering her courage, she returned to the door and peeked through the blinds. The yard and trees appeared empty now. *Should I call the cops? And what, girl? Tell them you saw a guy in a tree with glowing blue eyes? They'll think you're nuts. Damn...where's Mom?*

Stevie's cell phone was upstairs in her purse, but nothing short of cannon fire would compel her to go back to the darkness of the second floor. *What if he comes in through a window?*

With five acres surrounding the house and the backyard ending at the mountainside, she normally felt sheltered and snuggled in the wilderness. Now, the isolation terrified her. Unable to see her neighbors or the road, she did not dare leave the house for fear of being ambushed. By what, she feared to guess.

Too afraid to move the few steps to the cordless phone hanging on the kitchen wall, Stevie slid open the drawer closest to the stove. She pulled out a large butcher knife. The razor edge and weight in her hand made her feel safer. Leaning against the stove, she looked to her left and found that the blinds for the window above the sink were open. *He can probably see everything I'm doing.* Quickly, she closed them, too.

Finding courage, she stepped toward the phone, but a faint noise startled her. She held her breath and listened. A clinking sound came from the corridor leading to her mom's office.

There's nothing else back there but the laundry room and...the back door off the mudroom. When was the last time we locked that door?

Stevie clutched the knife in both hands and tiptoed out to the main hallway. To her left was the unlit corridor that led to the back door. Afraid to announce her presence by turning on the light, she instead tried to determine the sound's origin. The clinking stopped. She passed her mom's office door and hesitated outside the laundry room. Moonlight filtered through the curtains. The room was empty.

The window latch was locked. Skittering past the archway, she pressed her body against the wall. Faux sword against her chest, she peeked around the corner of the mudroom.

Whew...nobody here.

She sprinted to the door and bolted it, accidentally stabbing the drywall in the process. Stevie suppressed an uneasy laugh. *At least I wasn't running with scissors.*

The empty rooms and secured door quelled her fear. Feeling a bit foolish, Stevie headed toward the kitchen and the light. As she passed her mom's office, the clinking sound returned. She froze in front of the office door. Putting her ear to the smooth pine, she confirmed that the clinking was in there. Stevie reached for the handle and halted.

Isn't this where the girl gets killed in the movie?

She fled back to the kitchen, dropped the knife on the counter, and snatched the phone from its holder, her fingers clumsily pushing the buttons.

Please answer, Mom.

Instead of her mom's voice, she heard one ring followed by another.

Hanging up without leaving a message, she then tried to call Jack. The sight of headlights reflected in the front hall mirror stopped her. Phone in one hand, knife back in the other, she snuck down the hall to the front entrance. Tonka must have sensed her fear and stalked behind Stevie, nose pressing against the back of Stevie's legs. The long window flanking the door was beveled, obscuring her view of the vehicle and making it impossible to tell if the headlights were from her mother's SUV or some other vehicle.

Gripping the phone in her teeth, Stevie turned the deadbolt and moved out of view from the side window. With the butcher knife clutched tightly to her chest, she listened for movement on the porch. The knob turned left, then right, followed by a knock.

"Stevie, can we talk? I got halfway home before I chilled enough to realize I was being a jerk."

Jack's voice was a welcome relief. The phone dropped to the floor. Her hands shook badly. It took two attempts to free the lock. She swung open the door, arms outstretched to embrace him. "Oh, thank God it's you, Jack," Stevie cried, completely forgetting about the deadly blade in her hand.

Eyes opened wide, he stumbled away from the butcher knife into the screen door, slamming it hard against the frame. "What the heck... Stevie, what's with the knife? I know you're mad, but I'm not worth a murder charge."

"Jack, I'm so sorry. It's just..." Stevie's arms dropped to her side. The adrenalin subsided and, with it, her strength. She headed for the stairs, needing a place to sit down before collapsing. This time, Stevie remembered to flip on the hall light as she passed. Easing onto the third stair, she set the blade within easy reach and watched Jack approach. His lanky frame moved fluidly as he knelt silently in front of her.

"There was some man out back in a tree earlier and I was freaking out...then I heard noises inside the house." She covered her face with both her hands, and then ran them through her long hair.

Jack lifted her chin, focusing her attention on him. "I'm here, now. You're safe. Relax and tell me what happened."

"The man was in the backyard…"

"What? Where?" He marched into the cavernous kitchen and to the sliding door. Holding the blinds back with one hand, her friend-turned-protector glanced briefly through the glass. Tucking a stray lock of wavy brown hair behind his ear, he returned his attention to Stevie. The slats rattled back into place when released.

"Stevie," he said, retrieving his cell phone from his pocket. "You want me to call the cops?"

She had followed him as far as the kitchen table, keeping it between her and the door. "I don't think you need to, Jack—I think he's gone. He disappeared once he saw me."

"Are you sure he's gone? You did say you heard noises in the house." Jack slipped the phone back in his pocket. He crossed to the refrigerator and grabbed a can of soda. He held it up toward Stevie, and she responded with a shake of her head. "And where's your mom, by the way? She go out or something?"

"I don't think she's been home, but she didn't say she would be late and she hasn't called."

A horrible image of her mom being attacked and lying injured formed in Stevie's mind. Jack must have seen it on her face. He rushed to her side, spilling soda all over his hand.

"Stevie. What is it?"

"Jack, the noises I heard came from Mom's office. You don't think?"

"Nah, I'm sure it's nothin'." Jack sat the root beer can on the table, wiping his hands on his jeans. "I'll go see. You want me to check under your bed, too?"

Stevie punched his well-muscled arm as he walked by. She felt safe with Jack, the brother she never had. He had grudgingly accepted the role after an awkward moment in junior high. He had professed his love and tried to kiss her. She still sometimes wondered if his over-protectiveness stemmed from brotherly love or something else.

Regardless, she was grateful he was here for her. Not wanting to follow him down the hall, but too shaken to stay alone in the kitchen, she reluctantly shadowed her friend. Jack slowly opened the office door. The rusted hinges creaked softly and he turned his head toward her, lifting one eyebrow. Stevie mouthed angrily, "That wasn't the sound."

Jack slipped his arm into the dark. A light flickered on, illuminating Jack's face with an incandescent glow. He froze. His eyes opened wide. Jerked halfway into the room, he screamed. Stevie screamed, too, and lunged for her friend, grabbing him by the waist to pull him back. What she retrieved was a tall, wiry teenager with tears of laughter streaming down his face.

"Damn you, Jack," Stevie said, pushing past him into the room. With the overhead now on, the source of the clinking sound became clear. Her mother had hung a wind chime next to the opened office window. "I swear that's new." She pointed at the chime.

"Anything you say, Baby Doll." Jack smirked and reached for the latch. "There you go. I have vanquished your foes, my lady, with nary an injury."

"That's not funny, Jack. There were prowlers in my yard and you're making jokes." Stevie led the way back to the kitchen and plopped down on a stool at the breakfast bar.

"I'm kiddin', Stevie. You're just too easy. Okay, serious now… So, what did this guy look like? Did he come after you?"

Stevie roughly shrugged his hand off her shoulder, but decided to answer. "No, he was just standing on a branch with Tonka jumping up and barking away. I don't know, maybe Tonka scared him. I really couldn't get a good look at him, I don't even know for sure it was a 'him', it was too dark. Well, except for the glowing blue eyes."

"The what? Stevie, are you punkin' me?" Jack moved to the other side of the counter, his forearms resting on the cool granite surface as he leaned closer to her.

"No, Jack—would I stand behind the door with a butcher knife as a joke? Yah, well, you might. But me? Hell no. Yes, his eyes glowed."

"Were they as beautiful a blue as yours?" Jack rested his chin in his hands and batted his eyelashes.

"You're a laugh a minute, aren't you?"

Smiling, he said, "I'm not kidding. You do have beautiful blue eyes." Jack had enough sense to stop joking. "Sorry. Maybe you were staring at the moon. When you looked away, you could of had the image in your eyes. You know, like when someone takes a flash picture and you see spots?"

Stevie cocked her head to the side. "Then Tonka must have been seeing the same spots. She was practically climbing up the trunk."

"But glowing eyes?" Jack paused. "Maybe he had a flashlight up next to his face and was shining it out?"

"That could be, but why a blue bulb?"

"Blue? You're totally, positively sure?"

"Yeah, it turned Tonka green."

"Oooookay..."

"Damn it, Jack. Yellow and blue make green. His eyes glowed blue. You don't think that's frickin' weird?"

"Yeah, but it was dark. Your mind coulda been playing tricks on you, just like the noise you heard in the hallway—something simple blown out of proportion by fear."

"When have you ever known me to..." The phone rang and Stevie jumped. Jack barked out a laugh. Embarrassed, she ignored him and jogged down the hall to retrieve the phone from the floor.

"Hello," she said into the mouthpiece before she got it to her ear. "Yes, this is Stevie Barrett."

"Miss Barrett, this is Officer Murphy of the Golden Police Department. There was a break-in at your mother's spa and she was injured. We don't think she should drive. Are you able to come down and pick her up?"

Stevie glanced at Jack, feeling the blood drain from her face. "I'm on my way."

Dropping the receiver, she could only say, "Mom's been attacked—we gotta go."

She called over her shoulder, "Now!" as she bolted up the stairs to snatch her purse. Within seconds, she returned, nearly beating Jack to the front door. "Hurry," she demanded and shoved him outside.

Chapter 2

The car slowed once Jack turned onto Washington Avenue, Golden's main street. Nestled in the heart of the town, the spa sat between the local ice-cream shop and a Starbucks. Police surrounded the area. An ambulance was haphazardly parked out front, blocking the northbound lane of traffic. Emergency flashers lit up the scene with a sickly red and yellow glow.

Jack parked the car on the curb. Stevie's feet hit the pavement before the Mustang came to a full stop.

"Wait," Jack called.

He caught up with Stevie, who had outdistanced him despite his long strides. A uniformed officer stopped them at the spa's entrance. Stevie begged him to let her pass, saying that she was Jan Barrett's daughter. The officer checked her ID before lifting the yellow crime scene tape. Jack stayed close to Stevie's side and she clutched his hand tightly as they entered the spa.

They were met with chaos. The normally pristine reception area was in shambles. Couch pillows and travel magazines were strewn about. The overstuffed chair was upended, and flowers and shards of glass littered the floor. A pool of blood stained the carpet, filling the space where the chair had been. The desk and wall, splattered in red, continued the theme of violence.

The attack on her mom, coinciding with the strange man in their backyard, sent shivers down Stevie's spine.

A tall figure stepped in front of her view. She looked up at the sun-wrinkled face. The man's unkempt wavy brown hair and five o'clock shadow gave him a rough look, which was softened by his kind hazel eyes.

"I'm Detective James Wood," he said, extending his hand from the sleeve of a brown tweed jacket.

Stevie shook it, holding on in an attempt to ground herself in reality. "Where's my mom? Is she okay?"

"Yes, she'll be fine. She's in her office. Follow me."

Stevie noticed his attempt to shield her from the investigators milling about, but she had already seen the blood. She prepared herself for the worst as she hurried down the hall.

Two uniformed officers stood next to her mom's desk. Jan sat in the office chair, answering questions as an EMT knelt beside her, tending her wounds.

The woman bore little resemblance to the person Stevie called "Mom". Normally, Jan's attire would be pressed and crisp, every seam and button carefully aligned. The auburn hair styled in a layered bob with a skillfully crafted hint of curl. Make-up colors perfectly coordinated to her skin tone and the outfit of the day.

What slumped in front of Stevie was a mass of blood and bruises. Jan's split lip and battered face looked as though she had lost a boxing match. A bandage covered her left arm. The EMT had her right arm in the air, inspecting it for injuries. Jan's hair, in complete disarray, covered her deep brown eyes. The left eye was blackened and swollen nearly shut. The right glistened with tears.

"Mom," Stevie cried, running past the officers on either side, forcing them out of the way. "Are you okay?" She leaned over and threw her arms around her mom's neck. Jan returned the embrace and began to sob, losing whatever composure she had managed to salvage for the sake of appearances.

"It's okay, Mom… I'm here to take you home." Stevie helped her to her feet, Jan wincing in pain, but they were stopped by a gentle touch on Stevie's elbow. She glanced at the white shirt bearing a red patch with a snake wrapped around a staff.

"Sorry, Miss, but we need to take your mother to the hospital," said the EMT. "That cut on her arm needs to be stitched and we have to make sure she doesn't have a concussion."

Detective Wood interjected. "I would like to get her statement first, while it's still fresh in her mind. If that's okay with you?" he asked the technician.

"If you can be quick about it," said the EMT. He turned to Jan. "Mrs. Barrett?"

"I'm good with that. I'm happy to put off going to the hospital as long as I can." She sat down, her attention on the detective.

The investigator pulled up a chair. Taking out a pad and pen from his shirt pocket, he sat on the edge of his seat, leaning in slightly. "Tell me what you remember."

Jan nodded. Stevie could see the fear and pain in her eyes. The battered face had her wanting to burst out in tears, grab her mom, and hold her tight.

No. What Mom needs now is for me to be her strength, not some teenage crybaby.

Stevie leaned on the edge of the desk and reached out for her mom's hand. She needed her mom to know that she could lean on her daughter for a change. Jan clasped Stevie's hand, her grip tightening as she relayed the story.

"After turning out the lights for the night, two men attacked me. I don't know...they might have been hiding in the spa closet." She pointed to a door adjacent to the reception area. "I remember being grabbed from behind, spun around, and hurled to the floor." Gingerly touching her swollen cheekbone, she continued. "That's where this came from. My face hit the coffee table on the way down.

"I was too dazed to rise. I tried to push myself up, but they knocked me back down and kicked me when I tried to roll away. It was awful. They were both yelling at me in some strange language." She paused to take a deep, shaky breath, wiping away tears with a tissue. Jan squeezed Stevie's hand before returning her attention to the detective. "I somehow managed to get on my feet and run for the desk, but one of them caught me by the arm. I don't recall how, but all of a sudden, I had a letter opener in my hand. I whirled around and stabbed. The man that had my arm screamed and fell back... Blood spurted out of his chest."

The detective interrupted her. "You stabbed one of the assailants with a letter opener?"

"Yes. It's styled like a dagger, but doesn't have an edged blade. It does, however, have a long pointy end."

"Evidently." He nodded and motioned her to go on with her story.

She cleared her throat. "The other one rushed at me. He moved in a blur and had me by the wrists before I could react. I tried to break his grip, but he was too strong. He was growling that bizarre language, and then threw me back against the desk. The next thing I knew, he was slashing my arm and repeating something that sounded like 'shy lay' and 'gry' or 'grey owls' and 'frail high lay'."

"Excuse me?" said the detective, lifting his right eyebrow.

"I know. It's nothing I've ever heard, but it had a rhythmic quality to it, kind of like a Native American or African dialect. Truly, I don't know."

"Were they dark skinned?"

"From what I could see, I'd have to say sort of olive skinned—along the lines of Mediterranean—but with a sorta golden sheen." She paused, her eyes closed as if trying to picture the scene. "It could have been a reflection from the streetlights."

"Got it. Now, Mrs. Barrett, how did you manage to set off the alarm?"

"After the one man cut me—I didn't even know I was bleeding until later—he shoved me and I stumbled, landing behind the desk. I spotted the alarm button and hit it. It's a silent alarm, so he must not have known what I had done." Jan paused for the detective to finish writing.

"Please continue."

Jan nodded. "Well, there's not much more to tell. He just kept hitting me. I remember him grabbing me by the hair and dragging me out from behind the desk toward the front door. The one I stabbed managed to get back on his feet, but lurched over the chair. I don't know how he got up again, with all that blood loss, but he did, and he was furious.

"He ripped my hair from the other man's grip and put a knife to my throat, all the while screaming and trying to jerk me to a standing position. That's when I heard the sirens and saw the lights flashing down the street."

Stevie offered her mom a drink of water. Jan responded with her famous you-can-read-my-mind-sweetheart look and took the glass.

After taking a sip, Jan continued. "The one that I'd stabbed released me and they ran out the door. I fell backward onto the couch so I couldn't see which direction they went, but it seemed as though they disappeared in a flash—literally. One minute they were there, and the next they vanished."

Detective Wood had stopped writing. The pen poised above his notebook, he stared blankly at Stevie's mom.

Jan must have noticed the look. "I know it sounds strange, but that was nothing compared to their eyes. Their eyes shone—actually cast a light—and they were a gold color…"

Stevie and Jack gasped and Stevie yanked Jan's hand. "OMG, Mom, you mean their eyes shone out—like beacons?"

"Yes. I know, it sounds odd, but… What? What is it?"

Detective Wood stood abruptly, chair legs screeching as they scooted across the hardwood floor. His focus shifted to Stevie. "Young lady, if you have any information that might lead to the apprehension of your mother's attackers, now would be a good time."

"Well…yeah…maybe. Tonight—when I came home—there was a man in the trees behind my house and his eyes shined out, too. But they were blue not gold." Stevie turned to Jack. "See, I wasn't losin' it. It was real…"

"Wait." The detective held up a hand, shaking his head as if to provide room for this new, bizarre bit of detail. "You mean to tell me that their eyes were creating, not reflecting, the light—like a flashlight?"

Stevie nodded enthusiastically. Detective Wood lurched as though he had been jolted by electricity. An undertone of strained calm reflected in his voice, but his entire body seemed to reverberate.

"Hold that thought. I think my partner should hear this." He rushed from the room.

Stevie sat dumbfounded. She was sure her face mirrored the look of shock on the faces of her mom and Jack. "Is it just me? Shouldn't he have thought we were crazy, rather than getting jazzed at the idea of guys with flashlight eyes?"

Jack chuckled, but Jan's lips pursed together.

"I agree...that was peculiar," Jan replied. She began to cross her arms, winced, and then returned them to her side. "I don't think I want to go home right now."

The EMT reminded her, "Mrs. Barrett, we cannot let you go home until they check you out at the hospital."

"Understood." She gave the paramedic a sigh. "I meant after they release me."

"I'm with ya, Mom," added Stevie. "What if the guys that attacked you are in with the blue-eyed one and they're waiting for us on the mountain or something?"

"Don't worry," said Jack, moving toward them. "I'm sure the cops will check out the house, and I can stay over." He placed his hand on Jan's shoulder, squeezing gently.

Jan patted it. "Thank you, Jack, for being there for us. I truly appreciate that."

At that point, Detective Wood returned, accompanied by a slender, neatly dressed woman. She wore her blonde hair cropped and spiky. A badge hung from her belt and the butt of a gun poked out of her open black jacket.

"This is my partner, Detective Drake," Wood said. "I've given her a brief rundown, and she has a few more questions for you. Also, we've agreed that it would be best to have officers search your house and the surrounding area for any signs of the suspects. I'm afraid it won't be safe to go home until we're absolutely sure it's clear."

The tall, composed woman nodded at Wood and then acknowledged Jan. "Hello, Ms. Barrett," she said, her hand outstretched. "I'm hoping the officers can finish up in a couple of hours, but honestly, that's not likely. It's a large area to search, especially in the dark."

"So we may not be able to go home tonight?" asked Stevie, frowning.

"I don't think it's a good idea, do you?" replied Wood. "You stated that the man you saw had similar characteristics to the men who attacked your mother."

"Where are we supposed to go? And what about Tonka?"

"Even if the police give us the thumbs up, I really don't feel comfortable going back there tonight, Stevie," Jan said. "Maybe we can go to a hotel? We'll find one that's dog friendly."

The EMT spoke up, again. "Mrs. Barrett, you are going to the emergency room."

"I know, but afterwards we can check into the hotel until the officers give us the all clear."

"Let's not get ahead of ourselves. We'll see what the doctors say first," said Detective Drake. "Before you leave, I do have a few questions for you." Drake looked at the EMT. "I promise I'll be brief." She returned her attention to Jan. "One description you gave of the men who attacked you was that they had...umm...and these are apparently your words—shining gold eyes. Is that correct?"

Jan nodded.

"All right. Well, we'll leave that be for now. Is there anything else you are able to remember about them? Height, weight, build, hair color?"

Jan fidgeted with the hem of her blouse, which must have come untucked from her skirt during the attack. "It was dark, but I think they were at least a head taller than me. Maybe six one or six two? I would say maybe two hundred fifty pounds, but the way they threw me around like a rag doll, I'd guess it was all muscle. Oh, and they had on some type of costumes."

"What do you mean 'costumes'?"

"They dressed like, well, like in the movie Robin Hood—heavy, dark, loose-fitting pants, and leather vests of some sort. They wore beads in their hair and large stone or crystal pendants around their necks." Jan turned to Stevie. "Did you see what the man in the backyard looked like?"

Stevie shook her head. "It was too dark, Mom. All I saw was his outline and the blue eyes."

The detective closed her pad and said, "Thank you, Ms. Barrett. I know this has been difficult." Leaving the room, she stopped near Detective Wood, who had been listening intently by the door. "Time to head to the house and check it out. I'll call and let you know what we find."

The look that the female detective gave her partner did not slip past Stevie. *That woman thinks we're crazy.* Instead of voicing that thought, she asked, "If Mom has to stay at the hospital, where am I supposed to go?"

"Is there someone, a friend or family member, you can stay with?" Wood asked.

"Not really. Oh, wait—Lissy. I can call her."

"Lissy?"

"Alyssa Brier. She's my other BFF."

"Give me the address." He jotted it in his notebook. "Would you like me to bring your dog by—she's friendly, right?"

"Very, especially if you have food." Stevie squeezed her mom's hand. "Jack can run me over to Lissy's if you have to stay at the hospital."

Jan nodded and Stevie moved aside for the EMTs, who slowly led her mom out from behind the desk. They placed her on a waiting gurney.

"Is this really necessary?" Jan asked.

"I'm afraid so, Mrs. Barrett. We need to keep your body stable during transport."

"Can I ride with her?" asked Stevie.

"Of course you can." The taller of the techs smiled at her as he pushed the gurney out of the office.

Following behind, Stevie risked one last glance at the reception area. Investigators were taking pictures of the scene and placing small yellow tents everywhere, presumably to mark the evidence.

The sight and coppery smell of the blood made her stomach queasy. To keep from losing her dinner, she looked away and focused her attention on the backs of the EMTs.

At the ambulance, Detective Wood spoke to Stevie. "I will meet you at the hospital." She nodded and climbed in to sit near her mother.

Jack called out, "I'm right behind you guys."

Stevie turned and waved. As the rear doors closed, she leaned forward in the flip seat next to her mom and gently stroked her forearm. The tall EMT secured the straps around Jan's midsection and worked on getting the blood pressure cuff around her left arm. Eyes shiny with tears, her hand whipped out and grasped Stevie wrist—hard. Stevie was pulled down close.

"If I have to stay, I need you to call me the second you get to Alyssa's. Promise me. I need to know you're safe."

"I will, Mom. Don't cry, everything will be okay." Stevie didn't know what was more disturbing, the extent of her mom's injuries or this uncharacteristic display of weakness. Jan was the glue holding them together when Stevie's dad had died suddenly. Although her mom was strict, Stevie saw her as a friend. Someone she could go to for advice and a hug when things really sucked.

The confusion must have shown on Stevie's face, because Jan released her grip slightly.

"Don't worry, Stevie. I'm just a little shaken. You seeing that man at our house...I can't help but worry about you, too. You're all I've got."

"You mean, we're all we've got." She leaned over and kissed her mother's wet cheek.

Jan pulled Stevie in closer. "I thought this was it, Stevie."

The grip on Stevie's hand lessened and she was enveloped in a tight hug.

Her mom whispered in her ear, "I really thought I was dead."

Stevie felt her mother tremble. The fear from the last few hours caught up with them. There was no hope of holding back any longer. Stevie's composure crumbled. She sobbed against her mother's shoulder; their tears converged as one.

Chapter 3

A sea of green flooded her vision. Terrified and exhausted, determination driven by fear, her legs pumped hard, feet pounding against the forest floor. Riddled with panic, she dodged left, and then right, as an arrow whistled past her shoulder into the dark. Even with her speed, the pursuers were gaining. The large trunk of a Sitka spruce caught her eye. She darted behind it for cover, struggling to catch her breath.

Momentarily paralyzed by horror, an arrow struck within an inch of her hand. A shot of adrenaline pushed her onward. Arrows flew all about her. Their deadly metal tips were illuminated by a fiery glow in the forest background. The densely packed trees took the majority of the damage, but her arms and legs stung from a multitude of glancing blows.

She tripped on a tree root, caught her balance, and forged ahead, driven by the instinct for survival. Not understanding why she was being pursued, she knew, deep down, they wanted to kill her.

She sensed someone close to her and she glanced to her left. Matching her stride, a man ran beside her. His outstretched arm compelled her to trust and accept him. Not knowing who he was, she nonetheless took his hand. With staggering acceleration, he pulled her along. Her legs burned in agony, yet he pushed her harder, faster. Her heart pounded, threatening to explode out of her chest. She risked a glance at him. His smile and penetrating blue eyes captured her and the world slowed for an instant. He seemed to see into her soul.

Crack! The piercing sound shocked her to an abrupt halt. She turned to him, but he was gone…

A crack of lightening jolted Stevie awake. Frightened, covered in sweat, her breath held, she frantically scanned for pursuers. No forest, no arrows, no beautiful young man with piercing blue eyes. Another flash of light illuminated her nightstand and dresser. The thunder clap on its heels caused her to jump, but in the familiar surroundings of her bedroom, she knew it had been a nightmare.

Relieved, she eased back into the comfort of her bed and tried to recall the dream's details, but they were already fading.

"This dream is driving me crazy," she mumbled sleepily to the dark.

She had had this dream before, but tonight it felt like a memory, without the surreal elements of a dream—no trees turning into man-sized rabbits or falling down cliffs or flying as if she were a bird. It was as if it the events were actually happening.

Reaching over to click on her bedside lamp, she squinted to see the time. *Five thirty in the morning? Man, why does this happen so damn early?*

Stevie peeled away her blanket. Sitting up, a bead of sweat trickled down the side of her face. *Might as well get up.* She rose and tiptoed to the bathroom down the hall, trying not to wake her mother, who had finally fallen asleep.

Yesterday had been rough, what with bringing Jan home that morning and getting her situated in her bedroom. Every step seemed to pain her mother, but she remained restless and unable to relax. Stevie hadn't slept much herself. Her mother's moans had continued late into the night.

Closing the bathroom door softly, Stevie ran hot water over a washcloth. The heat calmed her nerves. She sat on the ledge of the tub, the cloth resting on the back of her neck. *What's wrong with me? Why do I keep having these awful dreams?*

Flashes teased her mind, but new details began to surface. She was in the woods running with someone. Tonight, she saw him clearly for the first time. And the light around them… Odd. She was certain it was night, but there was a glow in the distance—maybe behind her? If not the sun, what was the source?

And what's with the arrows? Stevie shook her head as if doing so could shake the dream out of her brain. It didn't.

Returning to her bedroom, the open blinds confirmed that the storm that awakened her so violently had moved on. In the wake of the rain, a breeze rustled the tree leaves. The remaining clouds turned from grey to white as the sun's rays broke through and cast a golden glow across the yard.

Sitting on the side of her bed, Stevie thought back over the past few days. First, the sighting of the man with glowing blue eyes: *What was he...an alien? What exactly did I see?* Then the memory of the attack on her mom flooded back and she winced as pictures of her mother's injuries surfaced in her mind. Stevie had hated to leave her alone at the hospital overnight. So much so that the moment the police gave the "all clear" on the house, Stevie was at her mom's bedside, ready to bring her home.

Once home, Stevie had marched her mom straight to bed (at least it wasn't a hospital bed). While she played nursemaid, two police officers stood sentry—one stationed outside in a patrol car and one inside the house. Detective Wood told her of his concern that the attackers might return. When she inundated him with questions, he admitted to fronting the cost of the off-duty officers out of his own pocket.

Stevie hated the invasion. Still, in her heart, she knew that a few days' disruption was a livable trade-off for their safety. It was hard enough to take care of her mom, what with preparing meals and keeping the house clean. On top of that, she felt obligated to make sure the cops were fed, too. *At least Lissy took care of me while Mom was in the hospital.*

Alyssa had baked frozen pizza and served it with Doritos and cherry coke, Stevie's favorite. It was nice to be spoiled and consoled by her friend. She listened intently to Stevie's tale of the man in the yard and the attack on Jan while they sat on the living room floor, Tonka nestled between them. Lissy's almond-shaped eyes alternately opened wide in shock and then squinted with concentration. The petite girl's frame leaned in for every detail, but that didn't prevent her from throwing her hands over her mouth to stifle the occasional gasp. Tonka had remained unfazed by Lissy's reaction. That is until Lissy grabbed her, burying her face in Tonka's neck when Stevie told her about the glowing blue eyes.

Stevie had to reassure her friend several times that whatever was happening was not supernatural. Raised by a superstitious Chinese mother, Lissy would get a panic attack at even the mention of ghosts or demons.

The talk that evening eventually circled around to Stevie's dream and how more details were emerging. The terror Stevie always felt after waking from the dream would subside, giving rise to curiosity. But she didn't see Lissy handling it that way. She tried to hide her anxiety, but the more they talked about it, the more Stevie sensed Lissy's fear increasing. Her friend's habit of twirling a lock of her dark hair when nervous intensified as they mulled over the events.

My dreams are frickin' weird. I wonder what they could mean? Stevie again glanced at the clock—not even six yet. Deciding to lie back down, she reached up to close the blinds and block out the morning sun.

A trail of smoke drew her attention. It blew out from behind the large cottonwood at the tree line, and then disappeared. *What...is the tree on fire?* She stood to get a better view, but saw nothing more. *What's up with that?*

Stevie stood motionless watching for a few moments, before deciding it must have been a trick of the light. One last glance—no flames. No more smoke. She sighed, closed the blinds, and cuddled under her blanket.

Her dreams, her worry about her mom, and the chaos of the last few days were wearing thin. Lissy and Jack would be over later to help put together the packets for the fundraiser and she would have to take care of her mom, too. Stevie closed her eyes and silently prayed for a dreamless sleep.

The brochures and flyers for the Wild Earth Guardians were spread across the dining room table. Stevie tried to keep them in some semblance of order. Jack and Lissy had knocked over several of the stacks with their roughhousing. The sandwiches and drinks perched on a small space on the corner also threatened to spill. As usual, Stevie stayed out of the fray to avoid the possibility of an accidental slip and an inappropriate touch. Lissy never seemed to mind. After all, she was the one who took the first playful swing at Jack.

Stevie had started the playful teasing with Lissy. Her reaction to the story of the man in the yard and the attack at the spa had sent Jack into fits of laughter.

"It's not that funny," Alyssa whined, punching him in the arm. "I mean, Jan got hurt and Stevie was really scared."

"I know, I know… But you should have seen the look on your face." Jack tried to suppress his laughter by sticking a sandwich in his mouth. Or perhaps to stifle his standard "Such a girl" comment.

Where Alyssa was frightened, Jack was intrigued. *But I guess when your goal is to be a writer, you love interesting stories—even if one of them is your best friend's nightmare.* That's what made him a perfect third point in the BFF triangle. Lissy was the heart, Jack was the intellect, and Stevie… *What am I? The punch line?*

Stevie had known them since grade school. From the moment Stevie and Lissy met, they became inseparable. Jack, however, was another story entirely. He was the typical boy who reveled in teasing girls. He would make faces in class and say really stupid things to impress his friends. Stevie initially thought him so annoying that she avoided him and his buddies like the plague—at least until halfway through their fifth grade year. That's when Stevie's dad died.

Stevie would always be grateful to Jack for abandoning his class clown attitude to be with her through the funeral and wake. *He never left my side. He held my hand and just let me cry on his shoulder.*

Months later, Stevie had learned that Jack's keen empathy with her pain came from the loss of his older sister, Jennifer, who had been killed in a car crash barely a year before. It was a stupid accident caused by her inexperience and by driving too fast in a snowstorm.

Alyssa had accepted Jack as part of their little clique immediately. Eternally openhearted, she also thought he was cute— a secret that Lissy made Stevie promise never to tell.

Jack still annoyed Stevie sometimes, but she loved him like a brother. With pinky swears all around, they agreed that no matter what, they would be there for each other.

Refusing to give Jack the last word, Alyssa dove at him, knocking him back against the wall.

He choked on his sandwich and sputtered, "Hey. You coulda killed me. Don't do that again unless you know the Heimlich maneuver."

Stevie laughed, slapping him hard on the back. "How's that, Jack?"

Officer Manderly entered the dining room and interrupted the hijinks.

"I checked the backyard and the trees like you asked, Miss Barrett. I didn't find any sign of fire. Thought you'd want to know." His tone was flat and he had the look of someone who would rather be chasing down suspects than babysitting a group of teenagers.

Stevie glanced at the cop. He couldn't be more than twenty-five, but his smooth features, ebony skin, and clean-shaven face made him look closer to twelve. "Thank you for doing that. I just had to make sure."

Manderly towered over her, his eyes straying to the sandwich in her hand, and nodded. "Is there any chance?"

"Of course," Stevie said. "I made sandwiches for you and Officer Buckner. They're on the counter."

The officer grinned. The promise of food seemed to brighten his mood. "Thanks." He passed by them and on to the kitchen. His voice echoed. "I'll take Jimmy's out to him."

"I thought the smoke was just your imagination." Jack said. "You actually sent the cops to check it out?" He moved to the window and pulled back the blinds.

"Well, luckily it was nothing. In case you haven't noticed, Jack, I do live on the side of a mountain. I didn't want to deal with a forest fire along with everything else."

Lissy seemed to miss the tone and said straight-faced, "That's true…a burnt down house would suck."

"I give." Jack unceremoniously plopped down on the dining room table, his feet taking up the area on the chair where his butt should have been. "Not to change the subject, but I've been thinking about Stevie's dreams. You said they seem real now. What do you mean by that?"

"What I mean is that my senses kick in. I can hear the arrows and feel the breeze when they pass."

"For real?" asked Jack.

"Yeah. There's a musty smell and the air feels damp. Not like here, where it's dry and the woods are full of evergreens."

Jack chewed on his lower lip. "I've never had a dream with so much detail. Lissy, what about you?"

"Well," Alyssa began, her voice quiet and an octave lower than her usual high-pitched tone. "Stevie's not having normal dreams. They sound more like visions. In Mom's folk stories, witches have visions, and I think they're real—the visions, I mean—not that you're a witch," she added hastily, as she nervously straightened her blouse.

"Seriously?" Stevie stared at her friend.

"That's whacked." Jack looked at both girls. "But it makes a weird kinda sense. You think these could be visions of the future?"

"If they are, that means someone with arrows will be shooting at me. That's messed up."

"Why?" asked Jack. "Hunters use arrows all the time. Arrows are silent, unlike gunshots."

"Thanks, Jack. So, someone wants to kill me? Wow, thanks for dishing me up a big bowl of I-feel-a-whole-lot-better-now."

"I'm just sayin'."

"I get it. But why would anyone come after me? I haven't done anything."

"I don't know—all that global warming and hippy stuff you're into. Maybe some pissed-off hunters are in your future." Jack drew back an imaginary bow and pointed it at Stevie, laughing.

"Oh, bullshit, Jack," Stevie said, punching him hard in the arm. "Seriously, if someone were trying to kill me, why would they use an arrow?"

Jack shrugged. "I have no idea, but they're your visions, not mine."

"So, now you've decided that they are for sure visions? Come on. I'm probably just stressed out with graduation so close and the event with Wild Earth."

"Okay, but you're the one that's fixated about the dreams and keeps telling us about them. Maybe deep down you know Alyssa and I could be right."

Stevie picked at the edge of her sandwich as her friends returned to stuffing information packets. Jack's words weighed heavy on her mind. Even as a joke, the implication scared her. Maybe her friends were on to something. But how could she protect herself from a vision?

Startled by the sound of a throat being cleared behind her, Stevie looked up to see her mom standing in the doorway, wearing a chenille robe and bunny slippers.

"Oh, hi, Mom. You need something?"

"No, I'm good. Actually, I am feeling a lot better today." Jan's smile at Stevie disintegrated into a glare directed at Jack. "Get off the table, young man."

Jack coyly slid off and took a seat where his feet had been. "Sorry, Mrs. Barrett."

"Why is it you call me 'Mrs. Barrett' only when you're in trouble?" Jan walked over and ruffled his hair. "What are all of you up to today?"

Stevie looked up from the papers. "Not much besides getting ready for the fundraiser."

"Oh, right. I've decided to give my nursemaid a night off. I'm going to make dinner tonight." Jan turned and headed to the kitchen, calling back, "Please make sure all of this is put away by the time dinner's ready."

"Mom, you don't have to—I can make it," Stevie said, twisting around in her chair.

"No, I'm good," Jan replied. "Besides, I am making my marinara sauce and I add the ingredients by sight."

When Stevie turned back, Lissy had a wide-eyed look of shock on her face.

"What?" Stevie asked in a whisper.

"OMG… I had no idea that your mom got that beat up. She looks like a truck hit her," Lissy whispered back.

"I know, and believe me, she looks better today than yesterday. I wish she would just relax and let me handle things. You know Mom. She doesn't like feeling helpless, and she's getting bored of just sitting around."

"Let her do it if she wants," added Jack. "I wouldn't dare argue with her. Besides, I love her spaghetti."

"Are you talking with your heart or your stomach?" Stevie paused. "Okay, you're right. I just hope nothing else happens. I can't wait for the cops to leave so our lives can return to normal—at least as normal as it gets around here," she said with a giggle.

Chapter 4

It had been a busy Sunday. Stevie, with the help of her friends, had managed to get all the packets stuffed and ready. Then she took over dinner—Jan lost her energy right after she finished the sauce—and cleaned up. Stevie was tired, but happy. She only had school until Wednesday and then graduation on Saturday. Bounding upstairs, her thoughts took a turn. Out of nowhere, the looming question hit her: Then what?

Stevie had no idea what her future would hold. Lissy looked forward to a full ride for gymnastics at the Colorado University in Boulder, and Jack would be going to the University of Denver to study journalism.

One of Stevie's options could be a path toward preserving wildlife, or she could look into becoming a "green" engineer. *Man, how I wish I had been accepted into the School of Mines.* It wasn't for a lack of trying. She'd sent applications to several of the big name schools anyway, but the two that had responded, denied her. Her 3.0 GPA and SAT scores were good, just not good enough. *I feel like the black sheep.*

Contemplating her future, she brushed her hair and got ready for bed. A sudden sharp pain caused her to drop the brush. The sensation centered on the location of her birthmark. She grabbed the hand mirror off the vanity to position it over her right shoulder. Trying to see what had pinched her so violently, she wriggled this way and that, slipped the strap of her pajama tank-top off her shoulder. Finally, she got a clear view—one that made her drop the mirror.

A chill ran up her spine and her whole body grew cold. The birthmark had changed. Inexplicably, it had developed color...not any plain old color, but gold. It shone as though metal had merged with her skin.

Over the years, Stevie had become used to the changes in the mark. It had slowly increased in size and the outline gained definition. It seemed as if time filled in the lines but now it looked more like a tattoo than a birthmark.

The small mark she had as a newborn had developed into a two-inch gold circle with a cross protruding out of the top. Not an actual cross, but more along the lines of four thin, elongated diamonds forming a plus sign, balanced delicately on top of the circle.

"What the hell?" Stevie said out loud.

Her mother's head popped around the corner. "What is it now?"

"Look at this, Mom, it's getting color. I swear my birthmark now has color to it."

Jan squeezed into the bathroom behind Stevie and carefully examined the mark. In the mirror above the sink, Jan's reflected brows rose and then sank into to a deep furrow.

"I think you need to have the doctor look at this."

"Which one?" she asked. "Remember the first time it started to change? We went to how many specialists?" Stevie emphasized the word *specialist* with air quotes. "None of the doctors have ever been able to figure out what this is."

"What if it's skin cancer?"

"Seriously, Mom? Besides, skin cancer looks like a sore, right? Not an über-cool tattoo."

"I still think you should have it checked. I'll set an appointment for later this week."

"If it'll make you feel better, but I doubt what's happening is something the doc can puzzle out." Stevie had not thought about her birthmark in years, but its rapid change coincided with her recurring dream and the presence of the strange men. "I sorta have a feeling that my birthmark has something to do with…with everything that's been going on."

"How so?"

"You know, the man in the trees, your attack, my dreams—maybe all these things are somehow linked."

Jan stared at her, unblinking. The corner of her mouth twitched slightly, as though trying to suppress a smile.

Stevie crossed her arms defiantly. "What, you think I'm nuts now?"

"No..." Jan drew the word out slowly. "I think you have a vivid imagination."

Stevie stuck her tongue out at the mirror as her mother turned away, and she picked up the brush. "Thanks for the props."

Jan shrugged and strolled from the bathroom. Stevie watched the reflection until it moved out of sight. *It does sound nutsoid...but now that I've said it out loud, I can't shake the feeling of being right on.*

The pain stopped completely by the time Stevie finished with her hair and brushed her teeth. She meandered about her room for a few minutes, flipped through her cell phone for messages, picked up a book and briefly thought about reading, but in the end decided it best to climb into bed.

As her hand touched the bedside lamp, a rustling noise drifted in from outside. *Must be the wind.* But when she turned off the light, the sheer curtains became awash in a blue glow. Stevie bolted upright and crept to the window, keeping below the sill. Leaning close to the wall, she slid to the right side of the window. With one finger, she parted the lowest slat of the blinds, scanning for the source.

The radiance seemed to emanate from the tree closest to the house. Behind the light, higher up in the branches than before, a man's silhouette was outlined by the moon. The same one she'd seen Friday night. Without warning, the light flickered out and with it, the stranger.

Stevie opened her mouth to call for Officer Manderly, but thought better of it. What would she call the officer for...to look at an empty tree? *Right, and give him more ammunition to tease me...after the smoking tree incident? With the cops everywhere, this man surely won't try to break in.*

As she lay back down, now more curious than afraid, she tried to piece together all that had happened over the past couple of days. *I wonder what he wants? He's going to a lot of trouble and taking a ton of risks if he's just a peeping Tom.* Stevie giggled softly, picturing a monkey man stalker. *But wait. What if he's somehow connected to the men who attacked Mom? Their eyes glowed too, except gold. His are blue. Maybe he's not a peeper. Maybe he's not watching us, but watching over us? Like a protector. But why?*

What the hell is going on?

Arriving at the corner of Twenty-Fourth and Jackson the next morning, Stevie spied Jack at the top of the hill near the school entrance. As usual, he played on his cell phone, joking around with his Internet gaming buddies. He stood a head taller than the guys around him. Where the other boys were awkward and looked the part of hippie-wannabes, Jack dressed in boot cut jeans (belted at his hips, not below his boxers). A fitted cotton shirt with the top three buttons undone accented his slim frame better than the oversized heavy metal band t-shirts worn by his friends.

Stevie bypassed the sidewalk that wound its way around the landscape and headed straight up through the grass. "Jack, we need to talk." Her sandals slid across the wet grass. By the time she reached him, the hems of her jeans were damp as well.

He smiled and grasped her hand as she approached. "What's up?"

Without a word, Stevie dragged Jack toward the school and away from his friends. He called over his shoulder, "What can I say, guys? The ladies love me."

Laughter and catcalls followed them around the corner of the building. Stevie stopped at a cluster of purple smoke bushes, her eyes darted about for anyone within earshot. Seeing no one, she proceeded to tell Jack about the latest sighting of the man in the trees.

"What? And you didn't tell the cops? Stevie, they were right there."

"Well, my brain's been riding a different rail."

Jack's brows meshed together. "Like, to where? To Dumbville? Two of them attacked your mom. They. Are. Dangerous," he said pointedly.

"I know they're dangerous. But the other one… It's just strange that he showed up again, knowing cops are watching the house. Have you ever thought that maybe he's protecting us from the others?"

"Oh, coz his eyes are a different color, is that it? My eyes are green and yours are blue. Does that make one of us a bad guy and the other good? Stevie, you're nuts if you trust this guy."

"I didn't say I trust him—I don't even know who he is. It's just a feeling I have. I can't explain it. A little more understanding and a little less judgment would be nice." Stevie tried to stomp past him, but was caught by the waist, spun around, and gracefully swooped into a dip.

"Hey, girl, don't worry," he said, lifting her back up. "There's gotta be a reason for all this, and if you can't figure it out alone, the three of us will."

Stevie smiled unwillingly, her anger fading. *Leave it to Jack.*

Offering the crook of his arm, Jack said, "Let's go find Alyssa."

They located the third point of the BFF triangle sitting alone on a bench in the courtyard, her expression contorted with concentration as she played a game on her cell. At Stevie and Jack's approach, she looked up from her phone. With no need for words, the three moved in concert to the picnic table farthest away from the other students. Stevie filled Lissy in about the blue-eyed man. Halfway through the account, her friend's creamy skin turned a prickly white.

"Demons," she whispered.

"Say what?" Jack turned sharply to face her.

"Nothing. I was just thinking about my mom's stories. Dark shapes in trees…glowing eyes…" Alyssa's voice faded.

"No worries, girlfriend." Stevie wrapped her arms around the slim figure, sorry at having upset her. "I'm sure it's not a demon. Besides, the cops are still there and I'll give them the skinny when I get home. If that makes you guys feel better."

"Makes *us* feel better… WTF, Stevie? What about your mom?" Jack's voice grew louder with each word.

"I know. I hear ya. I'll tell Officer Manderly, but I'd rather not tell Mom, at least not yet. I don't want to freak her out any more than she already is."

"Pinky swear?" Jack held up his right pinky finger, and so did Alyssa. Stevie laughed and wrapped her small finger around theirs.

"Swear," they said in unison.

The bell rang and they jumped. Three minds thinking as one, they raced to the door, realizing their books were still in their lockers. Jack arrived first, darted inside, and held the doors closed. The girls shouted curses about being late and tried to push the doors inward, but laughed so hard they couldn't get traction on the concrete stoop. The whole episode ended abruptly at the appearance of old Ms. Starkley, the English teacher.

Jack and Stevie were seniors, so they finished with classes early. It was a perfect excuse for a late lunch at the local hangout, the diner across the street from the school. The lunch crowd had died down a bit and Jack found an empty booth in the far corner. He ordered his customary burger and fries and Stevie added, "Make that two." When the waitress left, Stevie turned her attention to Jack, to find a grin had formed on his lips.

"What's up, Jack?"

"Nothin' really—just, my mom let slip that I'm getting an iPad for graduation."

Stevie fidgeted in her seat. "Wow, an iPad? I thought your new car was your graduation present?"

"I thought so too, but I guess my dad is over the top about me being accepted to DU." He shrugged his shoulders. "Besides, I think I did good."

Stevie giggled. "Of course you did…but, can you say spoiled?"

A sharp pain between her eyes stopped her before she could continue. "Ow!" She slammed the palms of her hands against her forehead. A wave of vertigo overtook her. Opening her eyes to a slit, she saw Jack's lips moving, but his voice was faint. He seemed far away. Everything went dark. Stevie felt herself being wrenched backward—the sensation of falling from a great height—and then forcefully dragged forward, as if on the end of a bungee cord now retracting. A sudden halt forced her eyes open. The pain in her head was gone, but so was the restaurant.

A forest replaced the vinyl and chrome booths. She closed her eyes, and shook her head vigorously, but when she risked a peek through squinted lids, the scene before her had not wavered. The hair on the back of her neck stood up.

The ground began to vibrate below her feet. A thunderous sound arose—hooves approaching rapidly. Stevie managed to back against a tree before fear immobilized her.

A massive black horse sped past, its feathered fetlocks kicking up a great dust cloud. It bore two riders—a man with a very pregnant woman seated in front of him. Stevie stared in disbelief. She blinked and, without warning, found herself in the saddle watching the trees fly by in a blur.

At the unexpected change in location, Stevie grabbed the pommel in panic, a panic that increased when she found herself reaching over her now swollen belly. Turning her head slowly to avoid losing balance, she managed a glimpse of the man behind her, but his focus remained on pushing the horse faster.

"Stay covered," the man yelled above the sound of the wind and hoof beats. "I will lose them in the forest."

Ghorgon. His name is Ghorgon, and he is trying to protect me.

Stevie let herself meld into the woman's body. The Stevie part of her fell away and she became the woman. *Her name is…my name is…Carlynn.*

Bile rose in Carlynn's throat. *How could they have found us already?*

Ghorgon abandoned the trail and pushed his horse to full speed, weaving quickly between the trees. Arrows struck the pines around them, missing her only because of Ghorgon's skill and Abatos' agility. Carlynn grabbed the warhorse's mane, holding on for dear life. They leapt over fallen logs and darted left, right, and right again. At Ghorgon's command, she ducked, her head barely missing an overhanging branch. The crack of wood and curses behind them told her that at least one of the pursuers had not been so fortunate.

At the next sharp turn, the clamor of breaking limbs and thundering horses faded. As they rode on, Carlynn relaxed slightly in the saddle, beginning to believe they had outpaced the Rebels. Then, Ghorgon pulled up hard. The path ended at the precipice of a cliff.

Craning her neck forward, she spied a narrow deer trail meandering down the cliff-side and was horrified when Ghorgon turned Abatos in a circle and lunged toward it.

"Hang on," he roared. They plunged over the edge.

Carlynn screamed.

The next sound she heard was Jack's voice. "Stevie, what happened? Are you okay?"

She tried to focus on the surroundings. The florescent lights hurt her eyes and the glare of the TV on the wall cattycorner made her head ache.

An uncustomary silence and the curious stares of the customers greeted her. In a daze, she covered her face and rubbed her eyes.

Jack pulled her hands down and held them tightly. "Stevie, you with me?"

Before she could answer, the waitress rushed over.

"Sorry," Jack grinned disarmingly. "I was telling her a scary story and kinda freaked her out."

The waitress raised one eyebrow and said, "Kids," as she walked away, shaking her head.

"I was telling you about my iPad, and then you grabbed your head. The next thing I know, you're all zoned out, and then you're screaming."

"I screamed? Wild." Stevie pried her hands from Jack's and leaned back in the booth. "I don't know what happened. One minute we were talking and the next I was on this horse, with a man riding behind me. And what was really strange is that I was someone else—Carlynn—I was watching through her eyes. I felt the pain of riding, the baby kicking in my belly—I *was* her. I also knew that the man with me was named Ghorgon and we were running from our enemies."

"What! Are you punkin' me? You were pregnant—on a horse?" Jack shook his head as if trying to clear it. "Hold up, Baby Doll. What you're describing is some sort of waking vision. Wow, that's way over the top."

"This is embarrassing," Stevie leaned over the table, whispering. "Can we go and talk somewhere else?"

Stevie slid out of her seat, shaking, stifling an urge to run for the door. Forcing herself to walk at a normal pace, she felt the weight of the stares as she passed. Jack stayed right behind her as she approached the car. Once safely on the road, Stevie said, "I don't know what happened to me."

He patted her on the leg. "It's okay. Actually, it's kinda cool. We can sort this out at your house."

She nodded and turned to stare out the window, seeing nothing but the vision replaying in her mind. *It felt so right, so natural to wear Carlynn's body—to be Carlynn.*

They entered the house. Stevie headed straight to the family room, as far out of earshot as possible from her mom upstairs. Jack joined her on the well-worn leather couch.

After Stevie rehashed the vision, she ended with, "Hear me out on this and try not to freak. It's not having the vision that scared me or even what happened. I'm afraid at how something so weird felt so normal." She folded her arms close against her chest to keep from shivering. "Am I losing my mind?"

Jack stood up and took her hands. For once, she allowed herself to be enfolded in his arms. "You're not crazy, Stevie...at least no more than usual. I promise, we'll figure this out."

Cocooned in Jack's embrace, she let him soothe her fears. She was overcome by a feeling of everything being somehow connected—the dreams, the vision, her changing birthmark, the stalker, the smoking tree (that made her smile a little)—all of it.

Not knowing how the pieces fit together frustrated her. *But I will figure it out.*

As the mark on her body clarified, her dreams had become more detailed. It reminded her of a picture or event gaining focus through a camera lens. But if her dreams and visions were one and the same, then her immediate future would not be planning for college. It would be to find out why she—as Stevie, and as Carlynn—were being hunted, and what she needed to do to stay alive.

When Stevie crawled in bed that night, the memory of the vision continued to haunt her. Despite her best efforts to be secretive about the vision, her mom had noticed something was wrong. The moment Jack went home, she questioned Stevie relentlessly. The story eventually flooded out. Rather than being a relief to tell the truth, it turned out to be a waste of time—her mom didn't believe a word of it and chalked it up to an overactive imagination.

Now, after half an hour of tossing and turning, she realized the uselessness of trying to sleep. She thought about the conundrum of the unbelievable being real. Had it not happened to her, she wouldn't believe it either.

Stevie sat up to look out the window near her bed. Most nights it remained open to allow the night smells to saturate her room. Remaining seated on the bed, she leaned her forearms on the windowsill, nestling her chin where they crossed. Wind blew softly over her bare arms and face. Breathing in the scents of fresh pine, lilac, and grass, she stared blankly ahead. Maybe she could find answers in the darkness. The sky, clear and littered with stars, held the waning moon poised directly above her backyard. The tops of the trees were bathed in moonlight, and she could see the leaves dancing as they swayed in the breeze.

Movement in the middle of the nearest grouping of trees caught her eye. Stevie lifted her head and squinted, trying to discern the source. A gust of wind moved the uppermost branches. A silhouette came into view. The glow of blue illuminated the leaves. She had a desperate need to see him.

"I know you're there, I can see your eyes." And then the blue light winked out.

Damn it. She scanned the trees, but could no longer locate his outline. Frustrated, Stevie fell back on her pillow, pulling the covers up to her chest. She twirled the blanket between her fingers, trying to figure out how to talk to this man without scaring him away.

Drawn back to the window, she squinted into the night. *Who are you?*

Stevie searched the tree line again. The backyard began to darken, as though a cloud had moved over the moon. The landscape shimmered and moved in waves like being viewed under water. Blackness crept in peripherally until her sight narrowed to a pinprick. Before complete darkness enfolded, the center of her view opened.

Stevie blinked against the bright daylight and reached down to brace herself against the bed, but found only air.

Chapter 5

No longer in her room, Stevie stood in front of a pristine lake. Trees dotted the landscape and snowcapped mountains created a backdrop to the valley. The smells had changed from the warming springtime of Golden to a crisp fall air filled with the scent of evergreens and earth. She looked at the crystal blue sky above her—awed at seeing the sun in place of the moon.

Sensing a presence, she turned her head to the right. Not ten feet from her, a man stood on the lowest branch of a ponderosa pine. His steely blue eyes, long raven-colored hair, and the way he smiled caught her breath. She blinked once and he was gone.

No. Wait, now he was in the tree to her left. He leaned back against the trunk long enough for her to get a clear view of his archaic clothing—dark breeches, deep brown leather vest over a rough-spun shirt, and fitted knee-high boots of some sort of animal skin. A two-inch pendant of blue lace agate, encircled in silver thread, hung about his neck and the sunlight glinted on the sword hilt peeking out from behind his right shoulder. Then he disappeared again.

Enjoying the game, Stevie glanced this way and that, trying to guess where he would reappear next. When the familiar dimming occurred, Stevie fought to stay in the vision, but it was useless. She found herself back at the window sill.

What happened? Who was that? Stevie sucked in short bursts of air as she leapt from her bed to turn on the lamp. With her room awash in light, she paced back and forth, struggling to remember the details of the waking vision. Glimpses of a lake, pines, mountains— and that perfect, sensual smile—came to mind. If she was to have any hope of recalling the full memory of him, she would need to calm her mind.

Stevie eased into a cross-legged position on the floor and filled her lungs with two long, deep breaths. Then she began counting. *Breathe in—one, two, three, four; breathe out—one, two, three, four; breathe in—one, two, three, four, five; breathe out—one, two, three, four, five*. In this way, she cleared her mind.

Within minutes, details of the vision flooded in, as did the realization that the real man in her physical world was the same as the one in her visions. *Did he hear me earlier? Did he somehow send me the vision as his way of showing himself?*

The clothes he wore came into focus, as did his silky hair and blue eyes. *And was that a sword on his back?* The more she thought about it, the more she became intrigued. Stevie considered this thousand-piece puzzle. She could see every piece clearly, but was unable to fit them together—yet. There were too many questions and no answers.

Time for bed, but Stevie knew that sleep would not come easy. Hoping for a distraction from the weird events and visions, she removed an unopened book from the shelf and nestled back into her pillows. *It's going to be a long night.*

The last two days of school seemed more like a month. Tomorrow would be Stevie's first day of real freedom. No more high school, no more boring lectures or homework, just free—through the summer, anyway.

Stevie had not told the police about the new sightings. She felt certain the man in the trees would not hurt her. At school, when Jack found out, he went off, again. *Maybe I shouldn't have told him, either.* It didn't matter the deed had already been done. At least he promised not to say a word to the cops the next time he came over.

Her friends had tried to talk Stevie out of any further investigation of the mysterious blue-eyed man. But now home from school and with Jack and Lissy off on their own errands, the need to know more ate at her. She couldn't wait for her friends to decide to show up. Taking Tonka, she headed up the mountain to search for signs.

Deep in the trees, Stevie scanned the area around her, feeling more nervous than she had anticipated. The thick foliage would make it easy for even an inexperienced camper to hide. She watched Tonka for clues, but the lab seemed content to push her nose through the tall grasses and do her doggy business.

She wondered how she would handle it if he did show himself. Would she run? Would she confront him? *Of course I'd run. I don't know what he wants or who he is. Then again—that smile...*

As they neared the top, Tonka disappeared behind a large outcrop of boulders. After multiple calls, Tonka finally reappeared, a leather pouch swinging from her jaws. Stevie commanded the lab to drop the item in her hand and followed the dog to find out what she had gotten into.

The outcropping of rock hid a small entrance in the mountainside. Surprised that she had never before come across this opening despite many years of hiking in the area, she ducked her head inside. The narrow mouth opened into a large cavern. Sunlight illuminated the first few feet of the entrance, providing enough light to see a rolled up wool blanket, more leather pouches similar to what Tonka had retrieved, a knife, an apple, and a sewn-together booklet.

Intrigued, she picked up the booklet and moved closer to the light. The cover had the feel of supple leather. It appeared to be handmade, and the front was embossed with a circle ringed in silver, like a pendant. She ran her hands over the silver inlay, remembering the agate pendant the man wore in her visions. Opening the book, Stevie gingerly turned to the first page. The paper had the textured feel of parchment—thicker, but more translucent than normal writing paper. The book was filled with drawings and a language she had never seen. Although beautifully rendered, Stevie was unable to comprehend the meanings, and then halfway through, she saw something familiar. Flipping back a few pages, there it was—in full color, bold as can be—her birthmark.

How can this be? Scanning the pages again, Stevie hoped to find some hint, but found nothing. Undeterred, she flipped back to the beginning for a more careful review. A cold wet nose nuzzled her arm. Stevie had all but forgotten Tonka. The light had crept a foot or more farther into the cavern. *I've been here over an hour. He could be back any minute.*

Hurriedly, she returned the book where she found it, but had no idea where to lay the pouch. Opting for tossing it near the other items, she called for Tonka to leave.

Stevie looked about as she exited the cave. Not seeing anyone, she couldn't shake the sensation he was nearby—hiding—watching her. Fear of being caught snooping through his belongings pushed her to race down the mountain.

That night, Stevie dreamt again of running through the woods, but this time there was no fear, no pursuit. The mysterious man ran with her. It felt right with him at her side, as though this was how it should be. They stopped at the precipice of a cliff. Stevie could hear rushing water below. A valley opened up in front of her. On the farthest side, breathtaking wooded and snowcapped mountains rose and continued on as far as the eye could see. A cloudless, vivid blue sky provided a backdrop for the surreal landscape.

The land appeared untamed and beautiful—Stevie felt the same way. Her hair blew back softly in the wind and she inhaled the crisp clean scents of pine needles and wildflowers. In awe, she watched the setting sun turn the scene to gold, then orange, and dark amber as it slipped behind the mountains. The world felt peaceful. Evening sounds of crickets, birdsong, and wolf howls in the distance synced with the breathing of the man beside her. Slowly turning to look at him, Stevie was met with a wink and a smile.

"I love you, Shylae." He clasped her hand, and together they leapt off the edge of the cliff and into the river, twenty feet below.

Startled awake by the sensation of being pulled back, Stevie's mind raced. *Is he here?* The dream felt real. She sprang to the window in search of her sentinel. Why had he called her Shylae?—a name unknown to her, but somehow familiar.

The night remained calm and quiet as she looked through the trees. She saw no one, but felt a reassuring presence. She climbed back into bed and closed her eyes, feeling safe for the first time since her mother's attack.

The man was here to tell her something. What that something was she had no idea, but she knew it would be life changing.

"Morning, Mom," Stevie said as she entered the kitchen. The smell of warm bread and brewed coffee made her stomach growl.

"Morning, honey. Did you sleep well?" Jan lifted a whole grain bagel out of the toaster to slather butter and jam on it.

"Yeah, I guess—I did have another weird dream, though." Stevie reached for her favorite cereal, Fruit Loops. "This one wasn't scary, but the strange man called me a different name…Shylae." She sat at the kitchen table in her usual spot close to the sliding glass door, absentmindedly watching Tonka chase a squirrel up a tree.

"Shylae? That's odd… I could swear I've heard that name somewhere before. Strange." Jan joined Stevie at the table. "After all the excitement Monday, I forgot to mention that I scheduled your doctor's appointment for today."

"I really don't think he is going to know what's up with my birthmark. I mean, he hasn't before." Stevie stood, tucked the bottom of her black t-shirt in her jeans, and went to the refrigerator and grabbed the juice. "Besides, I am going to the mall today with Jack and Lissy."

Jan's brows meshed. "I know you have two free days before graduation and want to have fun, but I would feel better if you kept this appointment. It won't take long, and you can hang out with your friends beforehand." She took a drink of her coffee and a bite of her bagel, chewing slowly while waiting for an answer.

Stevie gazed at her glass of juice to avoid the "mom" stare. "Okay. What time is my appointment?"

Jan swallowed. "Three o'clock, and tonight I would appreciate you being home for dinner. We need to talk."

Stevie stopped in mid drink. "About what?"

"About all the strange things that have been going on."

"Well, can't we just talk now? I mean, after the mall we were going over to Lissy's for a while..." Stevie paused, noticing her mom's slacks and silk burgundy blouse. "You're going to work today? No. Really? You're still recovering."

"I don't have time to talk right now. Kate is picking me up and I have to finish getting ready. So, yes, I am going in to do inventory and catch up on paperwork, but I'll be home early."

"Has she seen you since the attack? Is she okay with this?" Stevie knew that her mom's best friend acted more like a big sister. Kate would never agree to drive Jan to work if she had seen her injuries.

Jan finished her breakfast and put her plate in the sink. "No, but I warned her how I look. And, yes, despite her mothering attitude, she's my friend. Besides, *she* respects my decisions."

Knowing it was a battle she wouldn't win, Stevie changed the subject. "Where's our temporary houseguest, Officer Manderly?"

Jan leaned against the door frame, folding her arms together. "I decided to send him home. I'm sure he would rather be spending his time more productively."

"So, there's no cops watching the house?"

"No." Jan turned to leave, and called over her shoulder, "Nothing's happened in the past few days and we need to get back to normal."

Jan walked out of the kitchen and out of sight, leaving Stevie sitting alone, dumbfounded. *Normal? Nothing but another visit from the strange man and the visions.*

She rinsed her bowl and put everything in the dishwasher. *Something's up.* She wondered if her mom had been keeping secrets, too.

After a morning at the mall with her friends, Stevie drove to Dr. Cain's office on the other side of the city. They had all promised to meet at Lissy's house when she was through with her appointment.

Small but cozy, Dr. Cain's waiting room compelled quiet. Stevie, not immune to the spell, whispered her name to the receptionist when checking in.

A pale, blonde little boy mumbled to the young woman beside him about his sore throat. The haggard-looking mom occasionally nodded or patted his hand, but remained engrossed in old fashion magazines.

When Stevie met the boy's stare, he edged his way closer.

"What's your name?" he asked. "Are you sick, too?"

Without raising her head, the mother peered over the top of *Vanity Fair* to tell the child to be still.

"It's okay, ma'am. He's no bother," Stevie assured her.

"Will you read me a story?"

A nod was all it took for the child to lead her to the children's area. She located a popular book on the child-sized bookshelf fit the bill. Stevie sat cross-legged on the floor, unable to fit in the little chairs.

As she started reading, the boy's green eyes lit up and he chimed in with the familiar story. By the time they the third page, the child had climbed into Stevie's lap.

After a duet of the final phrase, Stevie and the boy closed the book with a great flourish. As if on cue, a young woman in yellow ducky-covered scrubs appeared from the hallway and called, "Sam McIntyre?"

The mother put down her magazine and headed toward the examination room.

Stevie cocked a brow. "Sam?"

"I am," he croaked. Jumping up, spinning in a half circle, he threw his arms around her neck. While he held on, prickles of electricity surged through Stevie's body—a vibration hummed inside her as if waiting to arc into the nearest ungrounded object.

Sam pulled away, his eyes wide as saucers.

He must have felt it, too.

"Mommy," he called in the clear ringing voice of a five-year-old, "my throat quit hurting!" He grabbed his neck and rubbed it.

"Uh huh. Come on, Sam."

"No, really, Mommy. It doesn't hurt any more." He tugged on his mom's hand and with the free one pointed to Stevie. "She hugged me and made it all better."

Stevie shrugged shyly and slowly stood, straightening the creases in her jeans. "All I did was read him a story."

Sam looked over his shoulder as his mom pulled him down the hall and waved enthusiastically. "Thanks, Lady."

The mother shot Stevie a glare and pulled her son protectively to her side. They disappeared into the first examination room.

An echo of the tingling remained as Stevie slid back into her chair. *What just happened?* The hairs on her arms stood up and she instinctively smoothed them back down.

A small, dark-haired, freckled woman interrupted Stevie's musings. "Stevie, you're up," Nurse Connie announced.

She chatted amiably with Stevie as they entered the second, and last, exam room. The scent of rubbing alcohol and antiseptic cleanser greeted her—a crisp, comforting smell.

The room, along with Nurse Connie, had changed little over the past eighteen years. The same Norman Rockwell pictures and a quilted baby blanket hung on the walls.

Dr. Cain walked in, looking as though he just stepped out of one of his own Rockwell prints—the same bald head, rosy cheeks, and bouncy step.

"Hi, Doc, how've you been?"

"Can't complain, my dear, can't complain. And what brings you here today?" he asked with his comforting country doctor grin.

"Remember my birthmark?" Stevie pulled up the back of her shirt to expose her right shoulder blade. "Well, it's changed. Or, more like it colored itself in. You know, like a tattoo or somethin'."

"Hmm," he said, peering over the top of his glasses. "Well, let's have a look."

Several minutes of poking and prodding followed, punctuated by, "Hmm, isn't that interesting?"

Dr. Cain looked puzzled and his brows knitted together. "I cannot think of a single skin disorder that would cause the epidermis to turn the color of gold." He paused for a moment. "I think we should do a surface biopsy and have the lab look at it. I'll have Connie bring you a gown."

"Ok…but what do you mean exactly? Do you think it could be skin cancer?"

"That would be unlikely at your age, but honestly, I've never seen anything like this before. To start, we'll look at a few skin cells."

Stevie nodded nervously.

Connie came in with a gown and a needle. "Don't worry, honey. It's just a little Novocain. I'm only going to inject it under your skin. Nothing scary."

Once the area was numb, Dr. Cain slipped behind Stevie. She felt a bit of pressure and then he moved away. He placed the specimen on a glass slide. It left a discernible sheen of gold.

"All done. No harm, no foul. It's bleeding a little, but nothing a bunny bandage won't fix." He turned his back to her and fumbled around in one of the drawers.

"Ok, Doc." The electric tingle began again, but mostly in her scalp. *Weird…* She sat on the table, trying to decide whether or not to mention it.

He turned, opening the bandage, and went to place it on her back. A strangled wheeze came from behind her.

"Doc? Is there something wrong?"

"Remarkable," he said. "It looks as though I never took a sample." He dropped the bandage on the exam table.

"What?" exclaimed Stevie.

"I…I just don't understand." Then he muttered something under his breath, which could have been, "Never in my life…"

Chapter 6

Stevie climbed into her Jeep and started the engine. Leaving it to idle, she slammed back against the driver's seat. "What the hell is going on?" she shouted then looked around the parking lot to see if anyone had noticed.

One more piece of weirdness to add to my list.

The doctor appointment had taken longer than anticipated. Her mom would be home soon to start dinner. Stevie retrieved her cell from her purse, dialing her friends. Better to have them meet at her house instead and they could hash everything out—with her mom.

She said she wanted to talk, so we're gonna talk.

While they waited for Jan to arrive, Jack rummaged in the pantry. Finding a bag of Doritos, he held it high over his head and shouted, "Treasure. I have found treasure."

Stevie rolled her eyes and continued gathering the colas while Lissy grabbed the glasses. All three settled around the kitchen table and Stevie laid out the list she had compiled of the past week's events.

Her friends leaned over the table, staring intently at the paper:

➢ *Man in tree/Blue beams for eyes*
➢ *Mom attacked/Gold beams for eyes*
➢ *Dreams of running/being chased – scary, but Man in tree was there to help me*
➢ *Smoking tree*
    o *Same tree Man was in before*
➢ *Waking vision*
    o *Carlynn? I was Carlynn*
    o *Running/escaping again*

➢ *Another sighting of Man in tree*
  o *Waking vision of a lake/Man moved freaky fast*
  o *Clear view of Man (yummy)*
    ▪ *Odd/Renaissance style clothing (similar to what Mom saw?)*
    ▪ *Long shining black hair, past shoulders (tasty)*
    ▪ *Pendant – blue agate surrounded by silver*
➢ *Hiked up mountain – found cave w/stuff*
  o *Book – has picture of birthmark*
➢ *Dream – sleeping vision? – Man (yummy) calls me Shylae*
➢ *Doc's office*
  o *Tingling (related to healing Sam?)*
  o *Mark heals after biopsy – no sign of being scraped (tingling again)*

Alyssa sat back, loudly crinkling the bag and stuffing chips into her mouth. Jack was more vocal, but his comments were accusatory. "Geez, girl, half this stuff is new to us. And what's with not calling the cops to investigate the cave?"

"Drop the cop thing, okay? What's done is done. Can we just stick to figuring out what the hell is going on?"

The last mouthful of chips swallowed, Alyssa piped up in her small high voice, "I don't really think the cops would have done anything anyway, do you? Besides, I want to hear more about this mysterious guy." A mischievous grin played at the corners of her mouth.

Jack threw up his arms in exasperation. "First, the cops are professionals—and I don't mean at picking the best donut shops. Stevie, you are not qualified to play a frickin' detective. Second, I don't like this guy. You make him sound like a dessert topping."

A wink from Lissy and then the comment, "Dessert's the best part of the meal."

He shot her a glare, making Stevie want to laugh. She held herself in check, realizing the seriousness of the situation she was in. *I'm lucky to have friends who believe in me, but Jack's acting like my boyfriend instead of best friend.*

"Jack, you sound jealous. Seriously—look." She grabbed the list off the table and shook it inches from his nose. The paper made an angry rustling noise, giving sound to her frustration. "Whatever is going on doesn't make logical sense. The cops will take one look at this and send me to a shrink. I'm just trying to figure this out by writing down the facts."

"Well, the facts are that this is bullshit—and why haven't you ever shown me your birthmark? I want to check it out," said Jack.

"Ditto. I haven't seen it since we were kids."

"You've seen it?" Jack asked in disbelief.

"Well, yeah," Lissy said. "When we played dress-up."

Feeling the need to clarify, Stevie said, "I've never shown it to you 'coz, well, because you're a guy."

"Oh my God, Stevie, it's on your back."

"Yeah, but." She felt a little embarrassed, remembering she had put on a pink lacy bra that morning, but pulled up the back of her t-shirt anyway.

"Wow," exclaimed Jack.

Please let him be talking about the birthmark.

"It does look like a tattoo."

Lissy whistled and interjected, "And those colors are cool."

"You mean color right?" Stevie craned her neck over her shoulder. "It has one color, gold, in the circle."

"No, girl, the arms are like a royal blue and the lines in the middle of the circle have a silvery blue tint," Jack confirmed.

The sound of someone clearing their throat had the friends turn toward the hallway. Jan leaned against the wall, arms folded across her chest, one eyebrow arched. "Am I interrupting something?"

Stevie felt heat rise all the way to the top of her head. She pulled her shirt down quickly and Jack nearly fell over a chair, backing away. Lissy's hands flew to her mouth, but the giggle still managed to escape.

"Hi Jack. Alyssa," Jan said, crossing the room, her high heels clicking on the pine floor. "I didn't know we'd have company for dinner," she added, giving Stevie a quick hug.

The scent of her mom's floral perfume and hair spray lingered even after she pulled away. "Yeah. I thought we could all discuss what's up together."

"You did, did you? Well, luckily I was planning on reheating Sunday's spaghetti, so two more mouths—even Jack's—will be fine."

"Mom, I have to tell you what happened at the doctor's office."

Jan stopped in her tracks, face slack. "Stevie?"

"No, no, Mom. It's not bad. The doc took a biopsy, but that wasn't the weird part. The skin healed. Like—right away. And before that I fixed Sam's throat. And my birthmark is even more tattoo'y. And..." Stevie knew she was rambling, but once she started to talk, the words rushed out in a flood.

Jan help up her hand, "Sam? Biopsy? Stop. You're not making any sense, and this is sounding like a long story. Let me get dinner started, then you can tell me all about it."

"K." She sighed. "We'll get out of your way."

Stevie headed through the kitchen to the dining room, her friends close on her heels.

Once seated around the formal dining room table, Lissy said, "Stevie, I am really worried about all this, and what about that little boy?"

"Sam? Oh yeah, that was über-weird, but not any more than anything else right now."

"Still, what if you do have an ability to heal people and you don't know it?" Lissy's voice dropped to a whisper. "And maybe that ability could be used to hurt people, too?"

"What?" exclaimed Jack. "Are you out of your mind, Alyssa? You might want to watch a little less SyFy and a little more Discovery Channel."

"You are such a hypocridiot, Obi-Wan. I'm not the one who's watched all six episodes of *Star Wars* ten times...in succession. Besides, I don't watch sci-fi."

"No, you watch marathons of *The Universe* and *Through the Wormhole* reruns," Jack retorted.

"Leave her alone," Stevie said, coming to her friend's defense. "She's just trying to look at the whole picture, unlike you..."

The discussion collapsed into joking, interrupted by a call from the kitchen that dinner was ready.

As they ate, the conversation revolved around upcoming graduation, the weather, how repairs to the spa were coming along, and other small talk. Afterward, the normal routine ensued of Alyssa clearing away the plates and Jan telling her not to worry about them. Jack watched the scene, leaning back on two legs of his chair, and Stevie put away the leftover leftovers.

"Now," Jan began. "Tell me what happened at the doctor's."

Stevie recapped the events of the afternoon and the past few days, concluding by presenting her list.

While Jan read, Stevie held her breath. The only sound in the kitchen was the soft ticking of the wall clock and the *swish-swish* from the dishwasher.

Jan set her reading glasses down with the paper. "Hmm...interesting."

"Mom, 'splain?"

Inhaling slowly, Jan said, "Stevie, you know I've been behind you—always. But, this...well, this sounds more like a fairy tale than reality. It's as though you've let your imagination get the better of you. Still..."

"Really? You know me, Mom. Have you ever heard me make up stories or go off on wild goose chases? You always said I had a good head on my shoulders. Well, this is what's been happening. No exaggerations. No wild embellishments."

Silence followed, either because Jan didn't know what to say or because she didn't know how to say it.

"Umm," Alyssa cleared her throat, breaking the silence. "I've known Stevie since we were little and I don't believe she's making any of this up. I mean, Jack saw her go into the waking vision. She sees things. And all this stuff..."

"I'm sorry, Stevie, but this sounds too much like the mumbo jumbo I was given when your Dad and I adopted you."

"What do you mean? What mumbo jumbo? What haven't you told me?" She felt goose bumps prickle her arms.

Shaking her head dismissively, Jan said, "Honey, I never took it seriously. It's just that the director of the adoption agency was a bit...let's say, 'cryptic'. She relayed a message to me, presumably from the man who brought you to the agency, a Nepalese Shaman."

"A Shaman took me to the adoption agency?" Stevie jumped out of her chair, tingling with excitement. "What did he look like? Where was he from? Did he say anything about my birth parents?"

"Relax. Sit. I never met him. All I remember is that the director said that the Shaman believed you to be special and in need of protection. He made her swear to place you with a loving and...understanding, open minded... I can't remember the exact words, but something like that. Because, you are a unique child with peculiar talents." Jan moved toward Stevie and wrapped her in a hug. "Honey, I've always thought you were unique and beautiful. Except for your strange birthmark, which so far has not proved to be life threatening, you were a normal child."

Returning the hug, Stevie looked over her mom's shoulder at her friends. She was elated at another glimpse of where she might be from and the chance that someone might know all the answers. Stevie could almost see the pieces fitting together, but the final picture eluded her.

Jack's lack of smart aleck comments drew her attention. He had been staring at the list during Jan's admission.

"What's up, Jack?" Stevie asked.

"Hmm... I guess I'm just as crazy as you now. Some of this is looking pretty familiar."

"I know. It's like it kinda makes sense..." said Stevie.

Alyssa chimed in and they both finished the sentence with "...but it's just outta reach."

"Maybe, maybe not. Hang on—I remember reading something." Jack pulled his new iPad out of its sling bag.

"Wha..." Alyssa's question was silenced with a sharp "ssshh" from Jack and his fingers flew over the tablet.

Minutes ticked by. Jan left the table to let Tonka out. Stevie paced the kitchen, chewing her lip impatiently, while Lissy leaned over Jack's shoulder.

"I think I found something. Check this out," he announced.

The three squeezed together behind him, their eyes scanning the dozens of windows on the iPad.

"I remembered reading something a while back about the connection between mythology and history. I thought if I could pull up some research on myths."

"Like what kind of myths?" asked Alyssa.

"You know, like fairies and elves…stuff like that. Here." Jack tapped one of the windows and it opened to an article about genies in Arabic and Hindu lore. "Stevie, you put on your list the smoke behind the tree, right?"

"Yeah, but that's crazy. Genies are in bottles and I'm sure I didn't see anyone rubbing the tree like a lamp."

Alyssa giggled. Jack leaned back, tipping the chair onto two legs, his arms folded across his chest. "Well, according to this man in India who claims to know about genies, or Djinni, he actually talked to one. They're not like the fables we grew up with. He said the Djinn can help people if they so choose, but that they don't grant wishes. They only show themselves when they want to be seen. Oh, one more thing, when they disappear, there's smoke."

Moving around until she squarely faced Jack, her hands on her hips, Alyssa retorted, "This is nuts. There's no such thing as genies, or the Easter Bunny, for that matter. What are you? Three years old?"

He stood, towering over the petite, dark-haired girl. "Myths come from somewhere, and usually have some basis in fact or history." He started pacing back and forth in front of the table. "That's what the article says—if you peel away the exaggeration, you often find the facts."

"OMG, are you saying you believe there is truth behind the fairy tales we grew up with?"

Shrugging his shoulders, Jack responded, "Yes. Look, after what I saw on Stevie's list, I have to admit that something is going on that we can't explain."

It was Jan's turn to pipe in. "Tell me you're not serious." She took a step back and rolled her eyes. "I think you—all of you—have pretty wild imaginations. It's a big jump in logic to take the surreptitious hints of Stevie's heritage to a belief in genies of all things."

"I don't know, Mom. How far a leap is it to believe that an all-American kid from Golden, Colorado, was born in a Nepalese village and has healing powers?"

"You don't really believe that you healed that little boy, do you?" Jan asked.

Ignoring her mother, she instead returned her attention to the iPad. "Actually, a lot of this makes sense, but still, Jack—genies?"

"Yeah, genies." He paused for a minute, and then continued. "I found more lore from other countries and cultures. I've seen stories about the genies not existing in the same 'dimension' that we do. That's why they're not visible to us."

"Well, then, how did that man from India see them?" asked Stevie, repositioning herself to view the tablet.

"Remember, the first article said they only show themselves when they want to. Think about the way Stevie described the way he dressed; don't you think that's weird?" asked Jack.

"Yes, I do," Alyssa agreed hesitantly. "But…"

"Wait a minute." Jan threw up her hands, motioning the conversation to stop. "The way my daughter described this man's clothing is frighteningly similar to what the men who attacked me were wearing. I think we need to worry more about who they are than what they are. Enough wild ideas." She began to walk toward the kitchen phone. "I'm calling the police."

Stevie ran around the table, blocking her mom's way. "Mom, wait. Before you call Homeland Security, I need to make you understand that this man is different. Not only his eyes, but he hasn't attacked me. He's watching me… Hell, he might even be protecting me from the ones who beat you up. Besides, exactly how are you going to explain this to the police?"

Hesitating, Jan's eyes moved from Stevie to the phone. Finally, she said, "Point taken. But whatever circumstances lie behind the recent events could be something dangerous and you need to be careful. You can't expect me to sit back and do nothing while my daughter is in danger."

"No, Mom, I don't. But nothing else makes sense. The only other thing I could think of was aliens, but no one's seen bright lights in the sky."

This time, both her friends giggled. Jan's brows meshed together and Stevie saw anger brewing in her eyes.

"Mom, look at me… I'll make you a deal. Give us a couple of days to do a little more research, and I promise I'll call the police if anything else weird happens."

Shoulders slumped in resignation, she said, "Okay, Stevie, but don't limit your search to the supernatural. Promise me you'll expand your search to articles and stories about cults or similar crimes, and I'll do the same."

A squeeze from her mom's hand and Stevie knew that she would refrain from calling the cops…at least for now. On impulse, she pulled her mom close into a hug and willed the electric tingle to return. It was as though they were standing in the middle of a substation, surrounded by energy vibrations.

Jan gasped and pushed Stevie away. "What was that?"

She watched as Jan's black eye faded, along with the bruises on her face and arms. Her mom swayed on her feet, looking as though she might faint. Jack had moved close enough to catch and steady her. Seizing the moment, Stevie clasped her mom's wrist and led her toward the hall mirror, her friends trailing behind.

"Look."

Jan stared at her reflection. Except for the shocked expression, her face was back to normal. She slowly unwrapped the bandage on her arm. "Stevie? How?"

Stevie ran her fingers over the unbroken skin. Even the stitches had disappeared. The room was still, and she looked from her mom to her friends. Their faces changed from shock to awe.

It really worked. I can really heal with a touch.

Chapter 7

Graduation day found Stevie in the locker room, primping with the other senior girls. Jan popped her head in and loudly announced that it was time to get in line.

Outside the gym doors, students milled about nervously. Stevie waded through them to find Lissy.

"I can't believe we are finally done." Alyssa excitedly hugged Stevie.

"Me, too. I'm so proud you scored that scholarship to CU. You are such an awesome gymnast. And brilliant, and funny, and cute..."

"Stop!" Alyssa blushed bright red.

Signaled by the start of *Pomp and Circumstance*, the students lined up and marched to their seats on the floor of the gym. Stevie looked around at the banners lining the walls. There was one for the Demons taking State in football and, of course, this year's gymnastics championship. Stevie could just make out Alyssa's name in the list of the girls who took Nationals.

An unexpected melancholy settled over her. *This is really it.* She was torn between happiness at high school being over and the realization that she might actually miss her school. A feeling of loss crept in with the thought of no longer seeing the paintings hanging on the walls outside the art room and hearing the chatter in the cafeteria from all the gossiping students. Even the bustle of the crowds in the hallways between classes and the boring lectures by her teachers were fading to memories.

Stevie's mom had told her that someday she would yearn for her high school years. *She was right. I already miss it.* A tear welled up in her eye when she glanced at the parents sitting in the bleachers. Some waved, some clutched tissues and cried, and others talked to their neighbors.

As Stevie searched for where her mom was sitting, she saw him in the farthest corner of the gym where the ceiling sloped down to meet the wall. It was the man in the trees, standing in the shadows. Florescent light reflected off his sword hilt as he shifted his weight. His long black hair fell over a tanned leather vest and broad shoulders. Stevie reached over the girl sitting next to her and roughly grabbed Alyssa's thigh.

"Lissy, look." Stevie pointed up to the bleachers and glanced at her friend. "There's that guy that was in my back yar..." But he had disappeared—again.

A second. I only looked away for a second.

"He's gone! Who is this guy, Houdini?"

"Where?" Lissy leaned toward her, clearly distressed. "I don't see him."

Why would he come to see me graduate? Is he looking over me like Dad? Gawd, I hope not. He's way too hot to be a dad... This doesn't make any sense.

Stevie realized, apparently at the same time as Lissy, that they were practically lying in Robyn Brand's lap. Simultaneously, they looked at Robyn and apologized, sitting back in their seats.

"No worries," the cheerful redhead said, squinting at the upper bleachers. "Look at that. Can you believe that someone has the nerve to light up in here?"

Sure enough, a faint trail of smoke lingered where Stevie had been pointing.

The man...the trees...maybe he is a genie? Dazed, it took a nudge from Robyn before she noticed that the students in her row had left to receive their diplomas.

After the ceremony, the graduates gathered with family and friends for pictures and good-byes. Locating Jack, the girls told him about seeing the strange man and the puff of smoke.

"What? Stevie, you promised to call the cops." He stomped, jaw clenched, and ran his hands through his hair showing his frustration.

Does he think anything through? I'm not scared. I love Jack, but man, he's being overprotective. He's supposed to be my best friend, not my dad.

"I'm supposed to call the cops and say what, exactly? I saw a man in the stands that I've seen before, but don't know who he is. And don't worry about looking for him, because he disappeared into thin air," said Stevie. "Oh yeah, and stop graduation in the process?"

Jack shrugged his shoulders. "But still, Stevie, this man is stalking you."

She started to disagree, but was cut short by a tap on her back. Turning around, she was faced with her mother, arms crossed, lips pursed, and eyes glaring. Behind her mom were both sets of grandparents. This discussion would have to wait.

"Oops—sorry, guys. Family first," said Stevie. "Catcha later, K?" She put on her best happy-to-spend-time-with-my-family face and left.

Dinner with her grand folks followed the ceremony. She dreaded the inevitable questions for which she did not have the answers: What college did you decide on, dear? What are your plans for the future?

The only reprieve of the evening came from Grandfather Barrett, who defended her apparent lack of direction. So like her father, not only in his facial features, but in his gentle and comical nature. His parting gift was to express how proud he was of her and his belief that she would figure out her place in the world. He surreptitiously slipped an envelope into her hand, kissed her on the cheek, and headed out the door.

Totally exhausted, Stevie crawled into bed that night, her thoughts returning to the mysterious stranger. She felt a twinge of guilt at not telling her mom about seeing the man at the ceremony.

With everything I'm asking her to accept, it wouldn't be fair. She would freak if she knew he was in the gym.

He had remained visible longer this time. How nobody noticed him standing at the top of the bleachers dressed like he had stepped out of a twelfth century forest puzzled her, but he was in the farthest corner.

Closing her eyes, his image floated in her mind and calmed her as she drifted off to sleep.

That night she dreamed of a city high on a cliff. She viewed it from an adjacent mountainside and, as the sun rose behind her, details of the scene were illuminated.

At the highest point rose an imposing rectangular structure. The white granite from which it had been constructed caught the sunlight, reflecting it back over the town below. *It looks like a tomb.* Stevie guessed it reached five stories high, topped by a glass dome, but she could not see the base because a palace blocked her view.

The palace had been built with massive symmetrical stones of a softer, earth-toned granite. The ivy and moss climbing up the three stories gave it a familiar homey feel. The architecture mimicked that of the homes and shops below, and bore a sharp contrast to the white monolith, which towered above all.

The entrance to the city stood back, roughly a hundred yards, from a cliff. To her right, a massive waterfall cascaded from the mountain and fed the river far below. To her left, a bridge spanned the canyon that separated her from the town.

The bridge opened to a road that led to the city. The road split into two stone paths when it reached a courtyard, flanking it on either side. Surrounding the courtyard were tall columns, similar to ones from an ancient Greek temple. These and the floor surface appeared to be made of the same white granite as the tower on the hill.

In the center of the courtyard stood a massive orb of polished gold a good twelve feet in diameter. It hovered six feet or more off the ground, supported by what looked like claws of a large feline.

Whatever the orb symbolizes must be of deep significance to these people.

Her vision moved down to the bottom of the bluff. The river, churned white by rapids, roared through the canyon. Beyond the metropolis valleys and meadows spread out, bounded by majestic snowcapped mountains with unforgiving summits.

Looking back at the entrance, the sun's rays had begun to move across the surface of the orb. It gleamed with a multitude of changing colors: blue, purple, yellow, and pink. The surreal beauty calmed her.

Sensing a presence beside her, she turned and there he was, smiling at her.

"Isn't it beautiful?"

She nodded. "What is this place?"

"Your home."

Her heart began to race. *Home?*

Stevie woke in a panic. She hurried to the bathroom to splash cold water on her face. She sat on the edge of the tub to catch her balance. As her heartbeat slowed, a searing pain exploded on her back, as if her birthmark had caught fire. Her hands shaking she grabbed the small hand mirror and positioned it over her right shoulder. An intense, reflected light blinded her. A sensation of being stabbed forced her to her knees. The torturous burning intensified. It knocked the wind out of her and she dropped the mirror. Her throat constricted in pain. She feared that the skin on her shoulder would burst into flames and she crawled toward the tub. Before she reached the cold water handle, the pain paralyzed her.

Terrified, she tried to call out for her mother. But the abrupt cessation of the burning silenced her cries.

Shaky and clammy with sweat, Stevie pulled herself slowly up from the floor. With hands on either side of the sink, she tried to steady herself. The pain was a memory, but the terror remained. Tentatively lifting her head to look in the mirror, she saw ice-blue light emanating from her eyes. Behind her, reflected in the mirror, a stained glass spotlight of her birthmark projected on the wall.

"Oh my God!" Stevie cried out. Her hands throbbed from clutching the sink and she forced herself to relax. As she released her death grip, her mind cleared for an instant, allowing in the realization of her connection to the man in the trees. *I'm one of them.*

She staggered into her bedroom and cried out the window, "I know you can hear me. I need to know. I need to know everything!"

Her eyes darted around wildly, Stevie's panic returned. Her shining eyes flashed blue light on the trees. Throwing her hands over her eyes, she flung herself onto the bed, crying hysterically.

Without warning, Stevie found herself running down a hallway, the smells of burning wood and cloth assaulting her senses. She choked from the bellowing smoke. Two men pulled her along—they were escaping.

A moment later, her mother's arms embraced her. "Stevie, what is it? What's wrong?" Jan asked.

Before she could answer, she was pulled into another vision. This time, she ran through a dark forest. The same two men flanked her. They ducked under brush and one of the men tried to ask her something, but she couldn't understand him. Fear engulfed her. As quick as the vision came, it left, and she found herself back with her mother.

Jan shook Stevie, her face awash with fear. "What's happening? What's wrong with your eyes?"

Stevie looked at her mom and for a brief moment, the panic subsided, along with the light from her eyes.

"I don't know what's happening." Stevie shook her head, and then the fear reclaimed her. "I think I'm like them!"

A second later, she was surrounded by pine trees. The scent of pine and earth, mingled with the smell of blood and fear overwhelmed her. A bear of a man stood not five feet from her. His sword raised in the air. He brought it down swiftly and cut a man in half. She turned away from the bloody spray. The carnage horrified her.

A cry forced her to turn back and witness another man jump onto one of her companions and stab him in the chest. Empathic pain surged through her, but not her chest. Rather, in her back…her birthmark. Then, the bear-man rushed at the attacker and decapitated him. She recognized the bear-man…*Ghorgon*.

As fast as before, she was back in her room with her mother, who was crying hysterically. The rapid transitions between her world and the other continued. Glimpses of arrows—her mother shaking her—the man who'd been stabbed lying dead on the ground—Jan's confused words. Unable to fight any more, she gave in. The vision had control.

Then it stopped.

The only sounds remaining were her mother's sobs and her voice begging for answers. Stevie wiped away her own tears.

"I don't know what just happened to me." She pulled her mom in close. "I think it's over."

After several moments, her mom's cries turned to whimpers.

Jan glanced at Stevie. "I don't understand," she said and began to cry again.

"I don't either. I may be one of them, but I don't know what that means." Stevie released her mom and went to the window, scanning the tree line. "He has the answers. I know it."

"Who? Who has the answers?" Jan called out.

Stevie didn't respond. Her mind was bent on picking out details of the visions or flashbacks she had just experienced. *I remember seeing those images before.*

It hit her.

Several months ago, she had a dream similar to these visions. She had forgotten it, because most of the details had faded once she woke up—except for the one horrific moment of the man being stabbed.

The sounds of her mom pacing the room and sniffling flirted on the edge of her thoughts, but Stevie's mind focused on the vision. Carlynn was there. *No, wait. I think I was Carlynn again. I didn't*

completely join with her, but I saw through her eyes. Who was the
man that had been stabbed...the one that Ghorgon tried to save?

An insistent shaking forced her attention back to her mom. "I'm
okay."

"Well, I'm not. How can I protect my girl when I can't make
sense of...of any of this?"

"Let's be honest here. We know what's happening. The only
question is why? My experiences are not of this world and we have
to face that I may not be of this world, either."

"I don't believe that. I won't believe it." Jan twisted the sleeve
of her robe. "I wish your dad was here. He'd find a way to make
sense of this."

Stevie gently touched her mom's hands. "We can't make sense
of this. We're outta our league. That's why I have to talk to the man
who's been watching us...watching me."

"I don't want you going near him," Jan barked. "They attacked
me—the ones that look like him."

Frustrated, Stevie took a step back. "They aren't the same."

"You don't know that."

"Yes, I do. If he wanted to hurt me, do you really think you, the
cops, or anyone else could stop him? No. He's here to protect me. I
can feel it."

Jan shook her head. "I can't do this now, Stevie. I'm too tired
and too scared."

"Me, too." Stevie approached her mom, who grasped her hands.

A weak light came through the blinds, signaling the dawn.

"I have to go in to work today," Jan said, glancing at the
window. "I have no choice. Will you let me call Jack to stay with
you? I can't bear the thought of you being alone if it happens
again."

Stevie mustered a smile. "Sure, Mom, but I'm in overwhelm
mode. If I don't lie down, I'm gonna collapse. Would you wait an
hour or so to ask him?" Yawning, she returned to her bed and
wiggled under her comforter.

Jan leaned over, kissed Stevie's forehead, and whispered, "If you need me, call me."

"K…" Her eyes closed as the door shut. Before drifting into sleep, her last thoughts were of what the stranger had said. *My home.*

Colton balanced in the uppermost branches of the cottonwood tree. From this vantage, he was able see Stevie with little fear of being discovered. *Stevie… I care not what name they give her in this world. She is Shylae to me.*

The terrain around the house gave him an excellent advantage for surveillance—an advantage he had used wisely for nearly two decades. Summer or winter, the variety of foliage provided by the ponderosa pines, spruces, aspens, and cottonwoods offered an assortment of hiding places in the trees, allowing him to remain virtually unseen.

Shylae had seen him earlier, during the daylight, but that was no accident. Allowing her that glimpse had broken one of the laws he had sworn to obey. But by the Gods, his patience was wearing thin. How long could he be expected to wait and hide in the shadows? Especially with his feelings moving beyond those of a protector. He wanted to be near her—to be seen by her, to exchange words…and touch.

Her graduation from the Hundye schooling was complete. Colton's elation grew, knowing that soon their lives would intersect. Recently, he had risked creeping closer to the house than normal. While he sat under the kitchen window, petting Tonka, he listened to the conversations of Shylae and her friends. *They have surmised much, but understand little.*

Tonight, Colton had witnessed Shylae's eyes washing the trees in a blue light. He knew her mark had come into enlightenment and heard her call out to him. Much as he desired to ease her pain, he could not go to her with Jan Barrett in the house. From this moment forward, Shylae's senses would become acute and her visions would gain frequency and clarity. All was as it should be. Yet Shylae knew nothing of her Guardian birthright and would be frightened.

It is no longer safe to wait. Tomorrow eve, I will go to my Shylae.

From an early age, Colton's sole purpose had been to protect his charge from detection by the Rebel forces. Her mark would now act as a beacon for the Rebels, increasing the danger ten-fold. If the Rebellion were to capture her, she would be taken to the Raile ai Highlae, the Hall of Light, her blood and her power drained. This could not be allowed. She was the last Guardian. The death of her would mean the death of both worlds.

Colton slipped deeper into the tree line, still within sight of the house. Fighting Rebels was of little concern. Time and again he had proven himself to be the greatest Warrior in his world. He was Djen—strong, brave, honored, and undefeated. Unafraid, at least for himself, he would not permit anything to happen to Shylae.

His mind worried over how to reveal himself. Her mental and physical training would need to be conducted with more haste than would be prudent. Yet he had great confidence in her ability to learn quickly. Of greater concern was the inevitability of Shylae leaving the mother and the world she had come to know as her own.

Would that I could keep her safe without burdening her with the knowledge of her heritage... I know not how she will react. Anger? Grief? Excitement? Will she accept me? Regardless, he had no choice.

Chapter 8

Detective James Wood sat at his desk, reading over the file on the Barrett attack. He grabbed the pack of smokes and got as far as putting one in his mouth and a flame on the lighter before remembering. *Damn it.* He tossed the lighter back on his desk, but left the cigarette perched between his lips. Even after five years, old habits die hard. *Stupid, stupid, smoking ban.*

Turning back to the file, he couldn't get past the descriptions of the suspects. Their clothing, their eyes, and how quickly they moved. *Mrs. Barrett thought they disappeared, but maybe they left so fast they seemed to vanishd. That must be it. But, then again, maybe not.* A weird feeling gnawed at the corner of his mind, despite his best efforts to ignore it. He whispered at the file, "What if they are aliens from another world?"

There, I said it. Rather than making him feel better for giving voice to his thoughts, the words nagged at him, and he tried to push them aside as a product of an overactive imagination. His last unorthodox thoughts, although right in the end, almost cost him his career.

Close to ten years ago, Wood had come to Colorado with his wife and kids. Sick and tired of the violence in New York City, he had become so jaded he feared he was losing himself, and was in danger of losing his family.

Wood's first real case with the Golden police force involved a series of murdered women in the Wiccan community. The women had been killed and placed on makeshift stone altars in the woods off Highway 72. Believing the murders to be some kind of satanic ritual, the task force went on a witch hunt. They had treated the Wiccans as suspects, rather than victims. He took a different tack.

Wood researched the religion, the practitioners, and even attended a few ceremonies to understand the victims, in hopes of understanding the perpetrator. He came to the belief that the murderer was more likely to be anti-Wiccan, rather than being a Wiccan. What with this unorthodox idea and being the "new guy", he had to suffer jokes from the other officers. They left miniature broomsticks in his desk drawers and hid his dress uniform cap, replacing it with a black pointy witch's hat.

His new partner at the time, Sarah Drake, ignored the jibes and teasing but didn't completely let Wood off the hook. Every "out of the box" idea he had, she would fastidiously break down, forcing Wood to give her concrete reasoning for his arguments. Between the two of them, and with a lot of hard work, they uncovered the identity of the serial killer. He turned out to be a fanatical charismatic Christian who used the Biblical reference in Exodus 22:18, "thou shalt not suffer a witch to live", as justification for the murders. The murderer carved Wiccan symbols on the bodies as a sick joke and to degrade the women and the religion.

But a belief that aliens could be involved in this current case was miles apart in reasoning from defense of an earth-based religion—maybe too distant to convince his partner, or anyone else, for that matter. Except for an occasional side comment to Drake, Wood kept his belief in the existence of aliens to himself. That belief had begun during a weekend fishing trip with his dad.

On that particular excursion, they went up into the backcountry of the Adirondacks. James, a teenager at the time, had only been camping there once before and looked forward to the time alone with his dad.

They stayed in Uncle Jeff's cabin on the edge of a lake. The second night, after stuffing themselves with German sausage and potatoes, James' dad, Josh, suggested they take the boat out. It was dusk. The mosquitoes were as big as houses, but the insect repellent seemed to work—mostly.

As the sun descended, his dad spotted a light in the sky. They both watched as it came toward them. The orb grew in size as it approached. Then it disappeared.

His dad looked at him with a puzzled expression. "Did you see that?" he asked as he pointed at the sky.

James shrugged his shoulders. "Yeah. Kinda looked liked those old pics of foo fighters from World War II."

"You mean like a UFO?" Josh asked. "Fowget-about-it."

The instant he finished the sentence, a beam of light appeared not more than fifty feet directly above them. It lit the entire lake with an amber glow. James' dad glanced at him and, with speed born of panic, rowed the boat back to the cabin. The beam remained focused on them all the way to shore. Once James stood, the light lifted higher into the sky. He looked up and watched as it shot straight up into the night. The farther it moved away, the easier it was to see the outline of the source.

Then the beam blinked out, leaving a circular object hovering above them. Multi-colored lights illuminated the outer edge of what he believed to be a ship. As he began to discern the details of the object, it tore away—a shooting star racing up rather than across the night sky.

Wood never got over that night. He developed an interest in aliens, feeding his need for understanding with books, documentaries, news articles—anything he could find on the subject. He and his father had recounted the story so often, the excitement died down until it became nothing more than an anecdote and inside joke within his family.

Deep in his thoughts, Wood barely registered Detective Drake's entrance into the office. The sloshing sound of her pouring a cup of coffee brought him back to the present. His eyes wandered to her. She stood by the dented metal filing cabinet in the corner, the top of which held the coffee maker.

Turning to Wood, she held up the glass carafe, stained brown from years of use that even bleach could not clear. "Care for some?"

He looked up. "Sure." He returned his attention to the file, but not before catching the disapproving glance from his partner. Her eyes focused on the cigarette in his mouth. He held it up between two fingers. "Not lit. All right?"

She shook her head and grabbed his mug.

"Drake, what do you make of the descriptions of the suspects in the Barrett case? Let's start with their clothing. Don't you find it strange? It reminds me of the costuming on that TV show, *Legend of the Seeker*."

Drake set Wood's coffee on the desk. "Only knowing about it from you—I'm guessing you mean a woodsman-Renaissance-style-by-way-of-Native-American garb kind of clothing? Strange? Yes. But no more so than the cross-dressing, door-kick burglars last month."

"Okay, I'll grant you that. But what about the glowing eyes?" He gazed up, looking for any sign of agreement.

"I have no idea. Maybe it's some kind of new contacts. You remember the ones from the eighties and nineties that looked like cats' eyes, or the ones that were purple, or the ones that glowed in the dark?"

"Listen, Detective Logic, I researched that line of thought, including checking with that new novelty store on Washington Avenue. The owna had never heawd of any type of 'flashlight' lenses." Wood smiled and added, "But he did offa to pay tawp dolla if we could appropriate 'em."

Drake propped her hip on the edge of Wood's desk, clasping her drink in both hands, alternately blowing at the steam and speaking to him. "You do realize that when you get excited, your East Coast accent gets stronger?"

Wood laughed. "Fowget-about-it."

"Anyway, I checked out costume shops, theater companies; I even spoke with some of the Renaissance and Trekkie weirdoes."

"Watch it." He wagged his finger at her. "That's not politically correct."

Rolling her eyes, she continued. "...as well as speaking to our confidential informants on the streets and looking up an old Ute friend of mine, but they've never heard of or seen anything like this. As of now, we're out of leads." She paused, taking a sip of the coffee. "Have the Barretts reported any more sightings?"

"No. In fact, they've cancelled the police security. I'd still like to drop by and talk with the both of them. My spidey senses are tingling like mad." His daughter, Beth, had given his gut feelings the moniker of "spidey senses" when they were still living in New York, and it had stuck.

"I know all about your spidey senses, Mr. Detective Fox Mulder. Let's take this slow. We'll both pay a visit to the Barretts. If nothing comes of it, you and I can still watch the spa and house—discreetly."

Detective Wood fingered the papers in the file. *What is the motive behind the attack on Jan Barrett, and why would they try to kidnap her?* This past week, both he and his partner had interviewed most of Jan's friends, acquaintances, and customers, but turned up nothing. She was well liked, respected by other business owners. By all accounts Jan appeared to be a dedicated mom and all around nice lady. *But what about the daughter? She claims to have seen one of the assailants in the backyard, but he didn't break into their house—didn't even try. What about their eye color differences? Is that significant?*

Wood closed the file and stood, rubbing the kinks out of his lower back. "Well, we can't just sit here all day. Let's head out. Do you want to start at the spa or the house?"

"How 'bout we call first so we're not running all over Golden?"

Wood flipped back through the file to retrieve Mrs. Barrett's contact numbers. Having no luck at the spa, he called the house. Jan Barrett answered.

"Hello, Mrs. Barrett. This is Detective James Wood."

"Yes, Detective?"

"My partner and I would like to come over and talk with you and your daughter today."

"About what? We've told you everything we can remember. What more is there?" The voice on the other end of the line sounded aggravated.

"Maybe nothing—but you might be able to remember something new if we go over the details again. I understand your frustration, but this could help us to find and catch the men who hurt you."

"All right, Detective. But, could we possibly do this tomorrow? I am on my way to the spa and Stevie is not feeling well."

"Sure." He set the meeting for ten the next morning before hanging up the phone.

"So what now, Wood? Should we watch a few episodes of *Ancient Aliens* as research?" Drake quipped.

The sarcasm annoyed him, but less than her insight. "Hey, I never said I thought they were aliens." *How does she do that?*

"I know you all too well, James Wood. You are intelligent and resolute in your convictions, but we both know you have a vivid imagination. Don't forget, that's hurt you in the past."

Wood opened his mouth to respond, but thought better of it. He was in no mood to hash out the reasons for his ability to generate alternative theories. Angering Drake would not help. Although tolerant of him out of respect for his years of service—twenty and counting—and his gut instincts, she could no more relate to his style of police work than to his way of life.

For example, she did not like bars, but she seemed to endure the whining about his head hurting and needing a pot of strong coffee after an especially fun night. Even so, he could swear that on those mornings, she had a tendency to talk loudly and slam doors and files around.

With Wood's divorce four years ago, he and Drake had less in common. Her first and only marriage, a sixteen-year-old son, Cody, and a family orientation differed radically from Wood's bachelor life. Not to say that she wasn't driven.

Wood had been impressed that at the age of twenty-eight, she had become a detective two years before the male officers who had been hired with her. *Gawd, was that really ten years ago?* An athletic five foot ten, she had emerald green eyes that reflected the fire inside to be the best at everything. Intelligent and inquisitive, she kept Wood's focus on the facts and grounded him. He could forgive her dogged skepticism because she was his loyal and steadfast proponent.

Drake broke the silence. "I'm in no mood to hash out your wild theories right now."

"Neither am I. You are more than welcome to stay here when I go over tomorrow."

"Not on your life. Someone needs to hold onto your leash."

Detective Wood laughed. "Yeah, and that someone is you—whateva, Drake. We'll see."

"Yes, yes, we will."

Stevie and Jack sat on opposite ends of the overstuffed couch. His idea of keeping her company involved surfing the daytime TV channels and raiding her fridge. Stevie assumed he must be trying to find something to take her mind off the previous night's events. Stealing glances at him for any sign of fear or apprehension in his expression, she found none. He seemed the same old, normal Jack.

Does he think I'm an alien? Is he scared of me now?

"Whatcha wanna watch?" he asked. "I'm drawing a blank here."

Stevie rolled her eyes. "I don't care. All I want is answers."

"Come on, at least try to take your mind off things. Dwelling will get you fitted for a straitjacket."

He scooted closer and reached out for her hand, but Stevie rose instead. Her stomach was tied in knots and her mind whirled. How could she find answers when she didn't even know what questions to ask? The erratic sounds of the TV followed her to the family room window, where she stopped to peer into the trees, searching for her sentinel.

Without turning around, she asked, "Are you scared of me, Jack?"

The noise of the channels stopped and she heard approaching footsteps.

"Of course I'm not scared of you," he said, placing a hand on her shoulder to turn her away from the window. "You're my best friend. I could never be scared of you."

"But I feel like some kinda freak…and now I'm starting to look like one."

"If you're talking about your eyes changing since last night, I think it's kinda cool. You look like one of those anime babes, with your irises crystal blue and that bitchin' black ring around them now."

Stevie couldn't help herself; she laughed. "Only you would think that it's cool."

"No, I'm serious," he said, taking her hand before she could protest and leading her back to the couch. "You were always pretty. Now you're smokin'. A hot babe with powers. Just think of the possibilities…"

"Don't be silly." Stevie nestled down into the cushions, wishing she could burrow out of sight. "Besides, I've never had powers before… Why now?"

"Maybe you grew into them? You're eighteen and a grown woman. Everyone knows that's when abilities mature." His wore a serious expression, but Stevie glimpsed a nearly imperceptible curve at the corner of his mouth.

"I can see where Alyssa has the idea that you watch too much sci-fi."

"Ha…yeah, you both are comedians," he deadpanned. "No, for real. What is happening to you is beyond the norm, beyond nature…you know, *super*natural."

A wisecrack dangled on the tip of Stevie's tongue, but before she could let it fly, Tonka's head plopped onto her lap. She rubbed the lab behind the ears, her mind racing with the possibilities.

Scenes from a scattering of movies came to mind—images of wizards, sorcerers, witches, an old crone at a caldron, a white-bearded man on a mountain with electricity exploding from his upheld staff. Her apprehension began to morph into excitement.

Turning to her friend, she needed to express this sudden elation, but was unable to find the words. Her eyes felt as though they were twinkling, and her vision clarified to the point of distraction. She could individually count the hairs on her father's head in the family photo, a good ten feet away. A soft blue glow blanketed the room.

The spell broke with Jack's gasp. "Your eyes are shining…like that man in the trees." His face, a mixture of shock and amazement, propelled her off the couch and into the adjacent bathroom.

"Oh no, I actually felt it happening," Stevie called out, transfixed by her reflection in the mirror.

Lightheaded with excitement, Stevie slowly returned to the family room. Leaning heavily on the arm rest, she eased down onto the couch. The tingling in her eyes subsided, and with it, the blue light. Her head spun and she was forcefully pulled through the couch. This time, there was no fear. She recognized the signs of a waking vision.

She found herself in a forest again, but this time winter had arrived. The leaves that remained on the trees glowed red, brown, and gold, with frost giving the bark the look of glass. Icicles hung from the highest limbs. Newly fallen snow sparkled with crystals across the forest floor, and the beauty of the untouched landscape caught her breath.

Whinnying horses and voices could be heard just beyond where Stevie stood. Letting the sounds guide her, she trudged through the knee-deep drifts and into a small clearing. A man, who could have been mistaken for a great furry beast, helped a woman down from her horse. The man stood a good six and a half feet tall, was broad backed, and a thick fur cloak hung from his shoulders. Two men on horseback flanked the couple. By their size and imposing stature, Stevie guessed them to be soldiers. One wore a cloak, which bore an insignia of a saber-toothed tiger with five orbs above its head. Unlike the man on the ground, the faces of the riders were hidden behind helms, and swords swung at their sides.

She recognized the woman—Carlynn, and the man helping her dismount—Ghorgon. When Carlynn turned in profile, a baby rested in her arms. Ghorgon led Carlynn into the woods at the far side of the clearing, but the soldiers did not follow.

Fearing losing sight of the two, she tried to run. Her spring outfit of jeans, tank-top and sandals impeded her advance in the deep snow. "Wait," she cried, but they continued without slowing. The harder she struggled, the farther away they seemed to get. Her lungs raw from gulping in freezing air, legs cramped and shaky, she realized she could not continue. Leaning against a tree, tears burned on her chaffed cheeks. *I must catch them.*

Stevie closed her eyes in resignation. When she opened them, she stood in a cave. A soft wool cloak brushed her legs and the riding dress she wore helped to keep out the damp chill. It took a minute to adjust to the dark. As her vision became more acute, she melded into being one with Carlynn once more.

Cold permeated the cave. Water glistened on the walls and flowed down, creating little streams which trickled out of the entrance. Carlynn was careful not to tread in the freezing puddles and headed for an adjacent wall that held an oval-shaped doorway. In front of the opening, some type of liquid was suspended, composed of a multitude of colors swirling together—a portal entrance. Carlynn reached into her cloak and pulled out a bottle of red liquid. She sprinkled a small amount onto the portal entrance and stood back. The colors twirled faster until they blended into a shining grey-blue, reminiscent of the color of the sea after a storm.

Ghorgon moved to Carlynn's side and offered his arm. The moment they passed the threshold, the three were wrenched forward, as if grabbed by an unseen force. Violently spun around, dizzy and nauseated, Carlynn lost all sense of bearing. Then, without warning, the movement abruptly ceased.

On the other side, a blast of blowing snow nipped at her bare cheeks and forced her to turn away. Carlynn checked her babe, still bundled safe and quiet, and pulled the blanket across the infant's face. Ghorgon, at her side, rubbed his temples. They stood precariously on a path high up on a mountainside. Across from them rose jagged cliffs, at the base of which was a snow-covered valley.

She squinted against the bitter wind to see if she could spot Ni-Tu coming up the path. Covering her head with the hood of her cloak, she moved toward the shelter of a nearby outcrop. Movement on the trail below caught her attention.

A small man ascended with a donkey in tow. He had covered himself from head to foot in fur, with nothing visible but the area where his eyes should be. This, however, had been hidden by a strange, glass-like shielding. To Carlynn, he looked like an animal with large black eyes and for a moment, his appearance frightened her. Once he reached them, he removed his hood and the dark shield to reveal a gentle face and a balding head spotted with wisps of salt-and-pepper hair.

"Greetings," said Ni-Tu in the Djenrye tongue. He bowed his head slightly. "I apologize for my delay. The snow slowed my climb. You must be the Lady Carlynn," he said. "Your husband was a good man. The news of his passing brought me great sadness."

Carlynn did her best to smile at the little man. "Thank you kindly."

Ni-Tu gestured toward the path. "I am sure you have many questions. Please follow me to the village and we can discuss your baby's future."

Before answering, Carlynn turned to Ghorgon. "Is there time for us to go to his village before the sun sets in Djenrye?"

"Yes." He motioned Ni-Tu to lead the way.

As Ghorgon helped Carlynn onto the donkey's back, Ni-Tu must have sensed her unease.

"The beast is surefooted and it is safer for you to ride than to risk the icy path on foot with the young Guardian in your arms."

The child, buried in the folds of the cloak, did not stir while the travelers headed down the path toward the meadow far below. As they neared the village at the base of the mountain, shielded on all sides by the imposing peaks, the wind subsided and the air seemed to warm. The terrain reminded her of Phraile Highlae—mountains and cliffs with streams and forest as far as the eye could see.

Carlynn thought that at least Shylae would be raised in a simple life, close to nature.

Shylae?

Stevie's head swam at the pronouncement of the name. Jerked forward abruptly into her own reality, speckles of light danced before her eyes. Someone shook her, making the lightheadedness worse. A rough pink tongue licked her cheek. Her focus returned. Tonka had jumped on the couch, and whimpered softly in Carlynn's ear. *No. Wait. I'm Shylae... I mean, Stevie.*

Stevie pushed both Jack and the dog away and sat up. She rubbed her face and reached for the glass sitting on the coffee table.

"What happened?" cried Jack. "Did you have another vision?"

A couple sips of water and Stevie could finally make out her friend's face.

"Yeah." Stevie cleared her throat. "I can't believe what I just saw."

"Tell me." Jack peered at her intensely, his green eyes darkening.

"I saw my mother—no, I was my mother—Carlynn. She was taking me through a portal to this side. I actually saw the man my mom—I mean my mom, Jan—spoke of, the one who took me to the adoption agency."

Stevie stood and touched her wet cheek, only now realizing she had been crying. Turning away from Jack, she moved to the window to look out at the backyard and the woods beyond. Leaning against the frame, her forehead on the cold glass, she wrapped her arms protectively around herself. "I could feel her pain from letting me go, but also the strength she possessed." Stevie glanced at Jack.

With his mouth dropped open, he seemed to be struggling to find the right words to say. Stevie returned to the couch and collapsed into a pool of tears. Without speaking, he pulled her into his arms. For the second time in the past eight years, she allowed him to hold her while she sobbed.

Chapter 9

Heart and mind numb, her eyes burned from crying, thoughts scattered, Stevie sat at the kitchen table. She stared blankly at the yard through the sliding glass door. Jack, as usual, had found chips to munch on and soda to wash them down. At one point, she had run into the backyard yelling for the mysterious man to come down the mountain, but she received silence in response. All she could do was to wait for him to decide to show himself.

The sound of gravel crunching in the driveway announced her mother's return. Goose bumps rose on her arms, despite the summer weather. *Now or never.* She had to tell her mom about the new waking vision and beg her not to tell the cops anything. Somehow, she needed to convince her mom that protecting the man in the trees, would also protect her. Thoughts of being whisked off to a secret government facility to be poked and prodded as though she was an alien caused her stomach to tighten. Perhaps that was one of the reasons the man outside stayed stubbornly hidden.

"Hi, Jack." Jan walked into the kitchen and sat her purse and keys on the table before noticing Stevie's face.

"What's wrong, honey? Why are you crying?"

"I'm scared. More scared than I've ever been. More scared even than when Daddy died."

She knelt beside Stevie's chair and pulled her into a hug. Stevie thought that there were no tears left, but still they came, saturating her mother's shoulder.

"Don't worry, honey. It will be all right."

"How do you know that? What if the cops figure all this out and lock me up in a cage somewhere to do tests on me?"

Jan smiled at her and brushed Stevie's hair away from her face. "You don't have to worry. I'm not going to tell them anything."

Stevie's words came out in hiccups, but she managed to ask, "You aren't?"

"No, silly. Even if they didn't lock you up for study, they'd surely commit me to an asylum for telling the same story."

Tears subsiding, Stevie threw her arms around this wonderful woman. "Oh, thank God. I was so worried that I would have to convince you to protect him."

"Wait. What? Are we on the same page? I'm talking about you, not the man stalking you."

"I think we've gotta keep silent about him, too." Stevie continued before Jan could argue, "I had another waking vision today." Try as she might, she could not keep the tremor from her voice.

"Honey…what is it? What did you see?" The concern on her mother's face contrasted starkly with the smile she had been trying to form.

"I saw—I saw my real mother… I mean, the one that gave birth to me. I watched her bring me through the portal to this world. I saw…"

Jan's facial expression changed from worry to confusion. "Wait a minute, a portal? This world? What are you talking about?"

Taken aback that her mother appeared more upset about the idea of another world than the mention of Carlynn, it took her a moment to continue. "Yeah, Mom, I was brought through some sort of a doorway that landed me in what looked like Tibet or some place. I even saw the man you talked about. You know, the one who brought me to the adoption agency? After that, I was pulled back here."

"You're serious, aren't you?" Jan stood up and moved unsteadily to the counter. Her hand shook as she poured a glass of water and took a sip. Turning back, she continued. "Do you really believe what you saw was real? Are you certain you weren't just dreaming?"

"I'm positive. Jack was with me. He saw me go into the vision."

Jack nodded. "It was just like the last time, Mrs. B."

After digging a tissue out of her purse, she offered it to Stevie, who blew her nose and wiped at her tears. Jack eased into the chair across from Stevie and clasped her free hand.

One more sip and Jan cleared her throat. "I think we should just have some dinner and try to take our minds off this for a while."

The thought of food turned Stevie's stomach. She didn't want food—she wanted answers. "I don't think I can eat anything right now."

The glass slammed down on the table, causing Stevie to jump.

"Damn it. This is too much for me. Can't we just pretend to be normal for a little while?"

A chink in her armor: I didn't think how all this talk of this weird crap would freak out Mom.

Timidly, Stevie agreed. "Dinner might calm us all down."

Glancing up, she caught her mom's expression—a mixture of shame and apology.

"Cool," Jack said. "How about we order pizza and a movie?"

Jan agreed.

Hours later, even with the distraction of Stevie and Jack's favorite, *The Lord of the Rings,* and a side of pepperoni, the evening dragged on uncomfortably. Jack seemed to be the only one actually watching the TV. The lack of conversation increased the awkwardness. Jan seemed detached, sitting in the recliner and fussing with her nails. Stevie, lost in thought, worried about meeting with the detectives tomorrow. *They're trained observers, after all, and I'm afraid they'll be able to see the hidden secrets in my eyes.*

All Stevie wanted to do was to slip away to her room. The man in the trees had revealed himself, at least a little, when she had been alone—at night—in her room. If she sat at her window, maybe he'd come and help her understand who she was. In her heart, she knew he would come to her…but when?

When the movie ended, Jack must have finally sensed the tension. Rather than staying and chatting, he gave a lame excuse of needing to get up early and headed for the door. Stevie followed him out.

He hesitated on the porch, and then turned. "You know this will all work itself out—one way or another—right?"

"Yeah, but I'm not so much worried about me. I'm worried about you guys and Mom. I've got the mysterious man watching out for me, but you don't have any protection."

Jack laughed, but it sounded forced. "We've got you, babe." And then he was down the stairs and in his car before she could argue.

Sleep would not come. On edge from the events of the last twenty-four hours, Stevie could only lie in bed and stare up at the night sky. A skittering sound outside distracted her.

What was that?

Something moved in front of her window, large enough to block out the stars. As her eyes adjusted, she could discern an outline. *He's here.*

Slowly, without taking her eyes off him, she sat up in bed. As she hoped, he did not disappear this time. She slid open the window. Nothing stood between them but the thin screen.

Gingerly touching the aluminum netting, she whispered, "Who are you?"

"I am called Colton. I am your protector."

"Did you attack my mother that night?" She was momentarily shocked at herself for being brazen enough to ask.

"It was not I, yet I know with whom they are aligned. I am deeply grieved that I was not in attendance to stop the assault."

"Why did they do that to her?"

"I believe they had hoped to find you." Colton paused. "Is it your intention to allow me entrance?"

The screen bulged out slightly as Stevie pushed her forehead into it. "I don't see a rope or ladder. How are you hanging on the side of the house like that?"

His leg must have slipped, because he dropped a few inches and scrambled for a grasp on the frame. Stevie quickly popped opened the screen and helped him in.

Once he was safely across the sill, she backed away a step. *I just let a strange man into my bedroom.* Her heart raced—whether from fear or excitement, she couldn't tell.

He stood before her, within a breath's distance. Where the moonlight caressed his raven-colored hair, it cast a purple hue. Bound in a half-braid, the loose strands cascaded over his shoulders in a silken flow. The descent ended at the bend of his elbow. His leather vest hung open, teasing her with a glimpse of his well-muscled chest. The only thing missing from the memories of her visions was the hint of a sword hilt above his right shoulder and the strap that held it.

His pants were the color of pine bark. They appeared to be canvas, but hung loosely from his hips, as though made of lighter cotton.

He looks like a hero of old—a majestic, barbarian warrior.

It took all of her courage to meet his gaze. Then, she knew. Her heart did not race from fear.

Lost in the crystal blue pools of his eyes, she wished to drown in them. The longer he held her gaze, the deeper she fell in—a glacier lake reflecting an unclouded mountain sky, veiling an unseen darker depth.

A deep blue-black ring encircled the iris, creating the illusion that his eyes were framed by…something more. She stood mesmerized, unable to speak.

"Shall I sit?" he asked, in a soft tone.

Able to muster little more than a nod and a sigh, she followed him to the edge of her bed.

"Will you join me?" he patted the bed.

Hell ya!

Wait. Snap out of it, girl. She sat down, keeping this strange beautiful man (and temptation) at arm's length. "I have tons of questions. And I'm thinking you're the one to answer them."

"There is much to explain, but I will do what I am able to help you understand." He smiled at her, the smile she remembered from her vision of him by the mountain lake. It affected her even more in person.

A deep breath helped to calm the electricity surging through her body. She asked about the most recent event first. "I have this birthmark that I think has something to do with what's been going on."

Colton nodded.

"I want to know what it is and why it lit up. Is this gonna keep happening? Coz it hurt like an SOB."

The bedsprings squeaked when he shifted position to fully face her. "The thing you call a birthmark is the mark of a Guardian. The firstborn of every Guardian bears such a symbol. The pain upon the initial shining is a sign of coming into enlightenment. Do not fear the process. It occurs naturally when a Guardian attains the age of manhood or, in your case, womanhood."

"What? You keep saying 'Guardian'. What is that?"

"There is so much you need to be told, to learn, to understand. We are Djen, you and I. I suspect you have begun to awaken to the understanding you are not the same as those around you." He paused.

Stevie wanted to respond, but kept quiet, trying to absorb the confirmation of her suspicions. *I'm not human... Now what?*

"The Djen are an ancient race charged by the Gods with the protection of the planet. The world in which you were raised, our people call *Terra-hun*."

Stevie felt faint, but forced herself to ask, "K, wait. So, I got that I'm not human. But...now you're saying I'm from another world? Like some kinda alien?"

At this, Colton actually laughed. "No, my Guardian. Our world, Djenrye, is parallel to this one, not on a separate planet. I believe the Hundye, human, word is 'dimension'. The worlds exist together, but remain unseen by the other. Crossing from Djenrye to Terra-hun is accomplished through a portal."

Excitement tingled every nerve. "So my visions were right on… I figured out the other world thing." She noticed the blue glow over Colton's face. *Geez, my eyes are shining again.* With a little concentration, the light dimmed.

His answers created more questions. She wanted to know about her home world—dimension—why her eyes shone, what the Djen were like, what this whole Guardian thing was… *Pick one, girl.*

She paused, looking for the right words. "Are you what we…what the humans…call genies?"

Colton's eyes lit up. "For countless generations, Djen have existed. It has been necessary to enter your plane from time to time to fulfill the charge given us by the Gods. On occasion, we have been glimpsed by Hundye. It is likely these encounters are the basis for the genie myths. Djen and Hundye alike create fables to explain what they do not understand."

It made sense to Stevie…for the most part. *That's what Jack had said.* But there was so much more.

"My visions. I'm having these waking visions—I think they're about the past. Is that normal for a Djen? It sure isn't for a human…umm, I mean, Hundye."

Shifting again, this time farther away from her, he responded, "I suspected your sight had begun. When did your first vision occur?"

"A few months ago. They started with the running dreams…wait… You were…"

Before she could finish, Colton interrupted. "Someone is coming."

"My mom! You gotta hide." Stevie leapt to her feet, pulling at Colton's arm. When skin met skin, a sensation of souls linking surged through her. Before she could speak, the connection broke and he disappeared into the closet. She dove under her covers. The closet door closed in concert with the bedroom door opening.

"Hey, honey. I thought I heard voices. Are you okay?"

"Yeah, Mom. I couldn't sleep and was listening to late-night talk radio."

Jan chuckled. "I doubt that'll help you sleep." She sat on the edge of the bed and stroked Stevie's hair. "I'm having trouble sleeping, too. I want to talk to you about earlier this evening. Not right now, of course, but maybe after the detectives leave tomorrow?"

"Sure, Mom. I want to make sure you're all right with all this."

Wrinkles formed on Jan's forehead. "Even if we figure this out, I doubt I'll be 'all right'. But I'll find a way to live with it. You're my girl, ya know?" She kissed Stevie's head before leaving. "Try to get some sleep."

"I will."

The door clicked shut, Jan's footsteps receded down the hall and Colton slipped out of hiding to return to Stevie's side. "Dawn threatens to rise soon and yet there is much for you to learn. For now, know it is you who are in danger, not Jan Barrett. When your mark shone, it created a way for the Rebellion soldiers to find you."

Stevie's face went pale. "Back up. The Rebellion?"

"A rebel force intent on destroying this world." He held his hand up before she could speak. "It is not through any fault of yours or the result of a wrong you committed. The Rebels search for you because of who you are. The blood of a Guardian—your life force—is required to control the Ortehlae in Raile ai Highlae."

She looked at him, dumbfounded. "Back up to the Guardian thing. What's an Ortehlae or Raile, whatever you said? How can I protect myself, and Mom, if I don't know what the hell's going on?"

"The Goddess Hel has nothing to do with this. The word Ortehlae means orbs in the Hundye tongue. Raile ai Highlae is Hall of Light." He paused. "The night grows too short. This you should know, and understand in your being—I am sworn to protect you. As long as I draw a breath, I will not allow you to be harmed." Colton rose and moved to the window.

"But wait, you can't go now... I have so many questions."

"Do not fear, I shall return." His lips brushed her forehead.

She rose up to meet him, but in a blur he left the room and raced across the yard to disappear into the tree line.

Colton returned to the cave—cold, dark, empty. The wood he had stacked against the wall made the preparation of a fire quick work. A few strikes of the flint and the flame took. Colton pushed at the logs with a stick. The fire blazed and the heat seeped into his bones.

There had been no sign of his informant, Marise, and he worried. She should have arrived by the new moon to report on the movements of the Rebellion and whether any additional Rebels had crossed into Terra-hun. Failed attempts to contact her could indicate she was injured or unconscious. *Or, perhaps, simply occupied and unable to respond?*

He prayed for sufficient strength to endure the challenges that lay ahead.

The threat has increased ten-fold now that Shylae has come into enlightenment. Her mark will draw the danger to her.

To protect her, train her, and teach her the meaning of being a Djen would prove difficult under any circumstances. Forced to fulfill these tasks quickly, his urgency was compounded by his need for answers. If he could not gauge the extent of the threat, he would not be able to engage it.

What delays Marise? If she did not arrive by the morrow, Colton would be forced to search for her instead of protecting his charge at this critical juncture.

Light broke through the blinds, waking Stevie. Her first thought was of him—her protector, Colton. *My God, he kissed me… Okay, my forehead, but it's a start.*

Stretching languidly, she recalled his eyes, his smile, his chest, and his muscular build. Her gaze settled on the clock across the room on the dresser. Seven fifty-five in the morning. *I can be lazy…*

I have all day. The only thing on her list was to gather the pamphlets for the fundraiser and load them into her mom's SUV. *And I can do that right after... Oh, damn, the cops are coming over. And they'll be here in a couple hours!*

Stevie jumped out of bed, threw on a robe, and ran downstairs to see if her mom had started breakfast. Reaching the hallway, she heard nails clicking on a keyboard. The door to Jan's office was open and Stevie popped in.

"Whatcha doin', Mom? You working this early?" asked Stevie, moving to the wingback chair in front of the desk.

Jan looked up from the computer and shook her head. "No, I was attempting to do my own research on what's been going on."

Breaking into a grin, she said, "Well, search no more. Last night, I met the man—Colton." She lowered her voice an octave. "I am called Colton."

"What? How?"

"He came to my window. He didn't stay long, but he did answer some of my questions and promised to tell me more soon. He also told me not to worry. He's protecting me."

"What questions did he answer? And protecting you? From what?" Jan rose and moved around the desk to sit next to Stevie.

"He said I am from Djenrye and I am a Guardian in their world. And he said…"

"Wait a minute—what? Where is this place? What's going on? Did you have another dream?"

"No, Mom, I wasn't dreaming. I told you before I came through a portal …"

Jan put her hands over her face, rubbing her cheeks and eyes as if doing so could somehow ground her in reality.

Stevie's elation subsided. She had hoped for a different reaction. *Maybe a little more acceptance?* Jan looked like she was teetering between crying and hysteria. "Mom? I thought with the portal and all, this wouldn't be so hard for you to believe. I even healed you. What did you think this man was going to tell me?"

Slowly moving her hands from her face, Jan met Stevie's eyes. "This is too crazy for me to absorb. You expect me to just believe you are from another world? Where did you say you're supposed to have come from… Gin-what? And they brought you through some doorway and this man is your protector? Really, Stevie?" She took in a deep breath and then let it out. "Look, I need some time to come to terms with all this. And the detectives will be here soon. Can we change the subject for now? Maybe to something more normal so that I at least try to look like I'm not hiding anything?"

"Sure." She stood to leave, her head lowered, feeling alone.

As she moved past, her mom grabbed her arm.

"What is it?"

"You're scared of me now, aren't you? You don't know what kind of freak you adopted."

"Stevie, that's not true. No matter what, you are still my child, the little girl I raised. Even if you are from—well, from somewhere else—that makes no difference."

Wanting to believe, Stevie lifted her head and nodded.

"I just need some time…that's all. Don't worry, honey. We'll figure this out—together."

Chapter 10

The Barrett house sat halfway up Golden Gate Canyon, a few miles west of Golden. Surveying the landscape, Sarah Drake commented on the denseness of the brush and trees. How the lay of the land, with its miniature valleys and berms, would make it easy for someone with a modicum of skill to elude detection while moving through the area or down another mountain, or even heading into town.

"Maybe we need to get the dogs out here," she said as they pulled into the gravel drive of the Barretts' home.

"Maybe…" said James Wood.

As they left the car, Wood scanned the trees. He spotted a mule deer peeking out from behind the rabbitbrush as they stepped onto the porch, but no other movement. Regardless, his eyes continued to search the perimeter until Jan answered the door, turning Wood's focus to the interior of the house.

Good light—although having windows in every room makes it easy for an intruder to see everything that's happening in the house.

Out loud, he commented, "I really do like your house. It's comfortable, homey…reminds me of the spa."

Sarah voiced her agreement as Tonka ran up to them, wagging her tail.

"Thank you," said Jan. She led them into the kitchen.

"Nice dog, too." Detective Wood bent down to pet the lab.

Detective Drake chuckled. "Not much of a protector, though."

"Tell me about it. The only thing you have to fear from Tonka is being loved to death." Jan motioned them to sit at the table. "Would you like some coffee?"

"Sure, love some," said Detective Wood as he surveyed the room. *Plenty of exits, but too many hiding places. Great view, but not much security.*

Jan interrupted his internal musings by handing him a cup.

"Mrs. Barrett," Wood began. "We wanted to follow up with you to make sure you're safe and to give you the opportunity to tell us anything else you might have remembered."

"I've told you all that I know."

"I'm sure you have. But going over the events again with you and your daughter may jog some memory. That is, if you feel up to it."

Jan moved to the stairs and called for Stevie. Pounding on the steps followed and a moment later, the two women entered the kitchen.

Pretty girl. How is it I never noticed her eyes were such an intense blue...and black rings around her irises. Is that new?

Wood motioned for Stevie to join them. "The reason we are here..." he nodded toward Detective Drake. "...is that we wanted to talk to both of you now that the dust has settled. We're hoping you might be able to remember additional details."

Stevie bobbed her head slightly.

"Do you have any leads?" Jan asked.

Drake took up the conversation. "We're working on a few ideas, but as far as identifying the men that attacked you and the one in your backyard, we've exhausted all leads."

Wood added. "Have you seen anything unusual or has anything else happened since we last spoke? The smallest detail could be helpful."

Stevie shrugged. "No, I haven't seen anything since the day I thought the tree was on fire, but it wasn't."

"Officer Manderly mentioned that. So, you haven't seen any more blue lights, or gold, for that matter?"

Stevie shook her head, looking at her hands instead of at Wood. She rose and headed for the refrigerator.

She's hiding something. He glanced back at Jan. "How about you, Mrs. Barrett? Have you experienced anything or had any more sightings of these men?"

"No, I haven't, Detective... and it's Jan."

"Jan, here's the conundrum. Generally, when an assault occurs randomly—call it a crime of convenience—even if the assailants are unsuccessful, it is unlikely that they will return. However, when there are other reasons behind the attack—such as a kidnapping—and the suspects are unsuccessful, they tend to try again. With no leads, we don't know the motive. But..." At this point he cleared his throat. "...I believe you fit into the second category."

"Is that so, Detective? And with all your interviews and contacts, you haven't found anyone who has seen them?" Jan asked.

"Nope. You two are the only ones." Wood gazed back over at the teenager, who leaned against the kitchen counter, intently focused on the juice in her glass. *She's still. Not like the fidgety kid we interviewed before.* "Are you sure you don't want to share anything else with us, Stevie?"

She looked up, and for a moment resembled a deer caught in headlights. "No, I told you all I know." Before Wood could follow up, she asked her mom, "Can I go now? I have a million things to do before tomorrow night."

Jan nodded. "Go ahead..." Then she addressed Wood. "I mean, if there isn't anything else?"

"No, that's fine," Wood replied.

Stevie strode from the room without a word. Wood glanced over at his partner for a reaction. Drake's face was a mask of composure, except for the hint of a crease between her eyebrows.

"Jan, thank you for your time today. I just need to ask one more thing, if I may," Wood asked.

The auburn head nodded.

"I have a feeling that your daughter knows something. Do you have any idea why she might withhold information?"

In a split second, Jan's expression flashed from shock to anger. "She's not hiding anything. Why would she? She is not a liar, Detective." She left the table and headed to the counter.

Wood was forced to talk to Jan's back as she poured another cup of coffee. "I didn't say she was. Look... I have kids of my own and pretty close to the same age as Stevie. Sometimes when kids think something is cool, they don't want to fill you in—if you know what I mean. My son, for example, the only time I hear from him is when he wants money. And my daughter, Beth, well, she hardly tells me anything, except that everything is fine."

"Stevie's not like that. She is responsible. Her mind is just on other things. That's all."

Detective Drake interjected. "Well, if she is so responsible, why is she trying to protect those men?"

Jan turned to face them. "I really don't think she is, Detective." The word "Detective" came out with a particular sharpness. "She has not mentioned that she knows them or has seen them since."

"Ms. Barrett... Jan, are you sure you're not doing some protecting yourself?" Drake asked.

Jan banged her cup on the counter, coffee sloshing over the edge. "I do not appreciate being accused of hiding information about men that attacked me. Who is the victim here?"

Wood rose, holding up his hands. "Now, now, no one is trying to accuse you, Jan. I just had a feeling that Stevie could be hiding something, that's all."

"Well, your feelings are wrong." The anger in her expression was accentuated by the sharpness of her tone. "You may leave now."

The detectives headed down the hallway, but before walking out, Wood stopped and turned.

"Just a reminder, we have no more leads. It is very important for you to let us know if you have any break-ins, strange phone calls, or even just a feeling that something is off. In the meantime, you get some rest." He paused. "By the way, you healed up fast. You look great."

Jan offered a tight-lipped smile. "Thank you, I appreciate that."

"Well, we'll be in touch."

Once on the road, Wood glanced at Drake. "Stevie is hiding something."

"Oh, most definitely. And, the mother knows what it is."

Wood smirked. "I believe so, too. And what about how fast Jan Barrett healed? In just over a week?"

"You know nothing about make-up. She owns a spa, for God's sake. One of her employees could have helped her cover up the bruising."

"Maybe, but I've worked domestic violence cases. That wasn't make-up. Don't you remember how beat up she was? I'm calling her doctor to see if she made it to her follow-up appointment."

Out of the corner of his eye, Wood caught Drake looking at him. "You and I both know her doctor isn't going to tell you anything. They have that privacy act thing."

"I'm not going to ask about her prognosis, just if she has returned. Besides, if the doc won't give me any info, I can use my boyish charm on his receptionist."

"Oh yeah, I'll warn the chief to expect a call on that one."

"You're quite the comedian, Drake."

"Seriously, I think we need to consider setting up surveillance; maybe under the guise of protecting the Barretts."

This time, Wood grinned. "Absolutely. I think something is up—the spidey senses are hummin' again."

Finally back in the privacy of her room, Stevie texted Alyssa and Jack. She felt relieved to be away from the pair of detectives downstairs, and now needed the support of her two best friends. Jack was at work, but Alyssa agreed to come right over. Stevie had a lot to tell her friend. Between working and gymnastics practice, Alyssa had been scarce, and Stevie missed her.

Hearing the detectives' car leaving, Stevie went downstairs to talk with her mom. When she entered the kitchen, she saw that Jan had moved out to the deck, her feet resting on the railing, a glass of lemonade in her hand.

"Mom," she said, closing the sliding door behind her. "How do you think it went? With the cops, I mean?"

Jan took a sip of her drink before answering. "I think they think we are hiding something. I don't feel as though they bought the whole 'we don't know anything' scenario."

Stomach knotting, Stevie tried to settle into the Adirondack chair next to her mom. "Oh, no…what's going to happen now?"

"Well, the next time you see this man… What did you say his name was?"

"Colton."

"Yes, well, the next time you see Colton, let him know that the police are probably watching the house again and he should stay hidden."

Stevie thought for a second before speaking. "Why would they watch our house? I mean, what do they care?"

"I think they care about catching the men who attacked me and have run out of ideas on where to look. And…that Detective Wood is a curious one. He is not going to let the matter lie."

Nestled deeper into the chair, Stevie tried to figure out Detective Wood. She agreed that he seemed overly engrossed, but to watch them—that didn't make sense.

We're the victims. Shouldn't he be trying to find the criminals, instead? With a shake of her head, Stevie decided she wasn't going to worry about it. Her main focus was to find out more from Colton. After last night, her curiosity was piqued and it needed satisfaction—badly. She wondered when he would show up again and prayed it would be soon.

Stevie got up and kissed her mom on the cheek. "I need to finish sorting the packets and Alyssa's coming by."

Jan nodded. "What time is the event tomorrow?"

"Six o'clock, but I have to be there by four thirty to help set up."

"I hope this helps you get your mind off things."

"Yup." Stevie walked back into the house and up the stairs to her room. Packets of papers lined her bed. Filling a box with several stacks, she headed out to load them into her mother's SUV. She would rather have driven the Jeep, but with the top off for the summer, there was no guarantee the papers would make it to the fundraiser.

Alyssa pulled into the driveway. She greeted Stevie with a hug.

"I've missed you. Is that your new car? How's work going?"

"Yeah, my graduation present. Not exactly new. But, hey, it runs, and I don't have to rely on anyone to get around. And work's good, as waitress jobs go. So what's up? You said that you have a lot to tell me."

Stevie nodded and led Alyssa inside. They loaded the SUV while Stevie relayed all that had happened since Saturday—the enlightenment of her birthmark, meeting Colton in person, and how her mom covered for her with the cops.

Her friend's silence during the tale was disconcerting. While carrying and loading the boxes, she kept her head down and wouldn't make eye contact.

Putting down her box, Stevie grabbed her friend by the shoulders, forcing her to look up. "Girl, you haven't said word one. Wassup?"

Hesitating for a moment, Alyssa slowly responded, "I'm jazzed that you've got this hot protector, but what about those other men? They've tracked you to your mom. How long before they figure out where you live?"

A huff escaped Stevie. *Holy cow, with everything else going on, that's your first thought?* Out loud, she said, "That's Colton's job. I've made it to eighteen, so he must be doing something right."

"Yeah, but didn't you say that he said your mark is some kinda beacon?"

"Again, Ms. Buzz Kill, Colton has my back. I'll be fine. But that is one of the things I want to talk to him about." Stevie closed the back door to the SUV. She followed Alyssa over to the porch and joined her as she sat on the top step.

Alyssa's face softened. "Okay. Reboot. Wow, Stevie. So he actually came to you...and he's hot, too. What more could you ask for?"

That brought a laugh. Stevie knew that her friend was trying to be happy for her. "Thanks. Yeah, he is all that, and a bag of chips." Not knowing how to ask the next question, Stevie blurted out, "So, umm, you seem to be taking this thing about me being from another world in stride."

"Sorta. I mean, it's way over the top. But I don't think it's sunk in yet."

Stevie took both her friend's hands in hers. "I'm just…well…kinda worried that knowing all this about me might scare you."

Alyssa smiled and hugged her. "No, of course not. I'd rather have you from another world than a demon."

"You have no idea how much better that makes me feel."

"Besides." A mischievous twinkle appeared in Alyssa's eyes. "We knew the outcome would be something strange. And this so-o-o-o qualifies as strange."

Returning the hug, Stevie said, "I'm glad. The last thing I want is to lose my best friend because of this."

"There is no way that's going to happen. Remember, BFF."

Stevie walked Alyssa to her car, a red Taurus. *Maybe a 2005?* No dings or dents and few scratches. "This is a nice gift you got."

"Thanks. What did you get?"

"Well, my grandpa gave me five hundred cash and my mom got me a new laptop."

"Sounds awesome!"

They chatted a few minutes more about nothing important before Stevie said good-bye. She waved at Alyssa as she drove away.

Elated that no one was freaking out about her being from another world, Stevie walked slowly up the porch steps. If she had lost her friends and family, she would be lost herself—they were her heart, her world. And now she had an added bonus in this tall, handsome protector. Just the thought of him made her skin tingle. *OMG, I hope he feels the same.*

Tuesday morning, Detective Wood drove to meet Drake at the Starbucks on Washington Avenue. The discussion would center on the surveillance they intended to set up at the Barretts'. He had found out that Jan's follow-up appointment with the doctor wasn't scheduled until next week. It truly did take all of his charm to persuade the receptionist to give him that little bit of information. Now the only thing he had going for him was a hunch, but at least he had Drake in his corner.

The job of a police officer in Golden tended to be slow and routine. But now, after ten years, here was another case he could sink his teeth into. A gut feeling told him something supernatural must be occurring, and he loved being in the thick of it.

Drake's usual scolding about his overactive imagination had been poignantly absent since leaving the Barretts'—maybe because this time he had some evidence. Still, he doubted her full readiness to admit the most fantastical possibilities. She would likely retain most of her skeptical self.

That would never change.

When he entered the coffee shop, he spotted his partner sitting at the back of the room, squeezed between two other tables, sipping her coffee and reading the local paper. She looked up and smiled. He waved before he made a quick stop at the counter to order a coffee.

"Mornin'," he murmured as he joined her. "Not the most private setting to discuss the case."

"And a cheery good morning to you, too. You look like hell. Didn't you sleep?"

He shook his head. "Actually, this case kept running through my mind. I think I finally fell asleep around one."

"Well, I am sure sitting in a car will make you nice and sleepy today. What brilliant plan have you devised?" Drake smirked.

Always the smart ass. "I'm thinking you should watch the spa, but not until they close. I'll set up surveillance at the Barretts' once Jan leaves for work."

"Not 'til nighttime? You don't think there will be any signs during the day?"

"Think about it… These guys, if they are going to at all, won't show until dark. There are too many people around during the day, at least at the spa, anyway."

Drake shrugged. "I agree, but we don't know what time those lowlifes snuck in. It was obviously before it closed."

"That's true, but I don't think long before that. Someone would have noticed—unless the Renaissance Fair unexpectedly came through town. The best bet would be for you to show up about an hour before the spa locks up."

She took a sip of coffee before asking, "So, you don't want me hanging out in the car with you at the Barretts'? It's going to get awfully lonely."

Wood grinned. "If you want, you can follow Jan home tonight and join me."

"K—I'll do that."

"I hope something comes of this. I know that girl is involved. I just don't know how…or why." Wood's daughter was close to Stevie's age and Stevie's body language mirrored Beth's when she didn't want to tell him the truth.

"What time are you setting up at the Barretts'?" his partner asked.

"I'll sign out the equipment when we're done he-a before headin' up Golden Gate. I have no idea if it might be too early to see anyting, but my spidey senses say udda-wise." Wood rose from the table. "I'll cauw you later to check in."

"Sounds good—albeit a bit New-Yorky. Don't forget I have to testify on the Reynolds' case today, but I should be done at the courthouse around lunchtime."

Detective Wood made it out the door before realizing he'd left his coffee at the table. Without lifting her head from the paper, Drake held it out for him as he returned.

Back outside again, Wood slid behind the wheel of his car. He'd earlier decided that using his own vehicle would be a better idea, since the Barrett women had ever seen it.

At the police station, he headed downstairs to check out the surveillance camera. It was a Sony Alpha DSLR-A900 with a 24-70mm f/2.8 zoom lens. Wood had been itching to try it out ever since the department had acquired the grant to purchase it last year. With that level of power, he would not need binoculars, but grabbed a pair anyway—for Drake.

Afterward, he stopped at the closest 7-11 to buy sugar and cream, to which he added thirty-two ounces of coffee and, of course, a side of chocolate donuts. Well supplied, he headed up the mountain to find a spot to watch the Barrett house.

During earlier runs, Detective Wood had discovered a dirt road that meandered up the hill around the backside of the Barretts'. Halfway up, he turned right onto a fire road that continued in for roughly a quarter mile before devolving into an overgrown walking path. Parked there, he was afforded a clear view of the Barretts' backyard, house, and driveway. This was unobstructed by the stand-alone garage at the west end of the property. The thick strands of pines and aspens would conceal his vehicle from anyone looking up the hill.

The day passed without incident or any sign of intruders. Clouds moved in and sprinkled a little, but the main storm moved on. Around five, he ran out of the last of his coffee and donuts and went back into Golden proper to pick up a cheeseburger and fries. He waited to eat until he returned to his perch on the hillside. Drake called shortly after to say that Jan had closed shop and was on her way. He knew that meant Drake wouldn't be far behind and was glad for the impending company; it had been a long day.

He had nothing to report to his partner other than the shifting weather, and that took a few short minutes. Stevie had not shown up all day. At least with Jan returning home, there was some movement.

Earlier misgivings about the exposure to the interior of the house from the numerous windows turned to relief. It certainly made Wood's surveillance easier. With a clear view, they watched Jan eat dinner in the kitchen. After she finished, the room went dark and a light came on in the living room. A short time later, Stevie drove up.

The kitchen was illuminated again as the athletic blonde came into view. Sandwich in hand, she sat down at the table, cell phone propped between her shoulder and ear. Half an hour or so later, she too left the kitchen. The next light to turn on came from her bedroom.

"This is boring, Wood. What do you expect to see?"

"You sound like a rookie who's never been on a stake-out. Of course it's boring, but you have to keep watching. You never know what's going to happen."

"I get it. But you forget, I'm usually the one doing web research and interviewing witnesses—and paperwork, yours and mine. Besides, other than that serial killer case ten years ago, when's the last time we had something happen that required surveillance?"

Wood just shrugged and offered her a cold French fry.

She declined with a shake of her head. "I'll hang out with you a little while longer. Then I need to head home. My son asked me to help him get ready for his new job tomorrow."

"Yeah, you mentioned that. His first one, huh? Well, there's no reason for us to both be stuck here." He picked up the binoculars and switched them over to the night vision setting. First scanning east, he swept back to the west side of the house.

Something caught his eye. There—movement in the overgrown lilac bushes next to the garage. Yes, a shape, but the heat signature from the gravel driveway obscured the image. Moving quietly and slowly, he eased open the car door. Drake made a sound, but he silenced her with a "Shh…" He pointed over toward the side of the house and handed her the binoculars.

Gingerly stepping out, he started down the hill with all the stealth he could manage through the thick foliage. As he entered the backyard, he tiptoed toward the garage. He knew Drake was watching him, even without being able to see her—he could feel the weight of her cynical eyes. Pressing his back against the garage door, he slid toward the bushes.

Within ten feet of the perpetrator, he sprang out of hiding and commanded forcefully, "Police! Come out slowly with your hands where I can see them!"

His stance was perfect. Feet firmly planted, gun drawn and steady; an imposing figure which any sane criminal would have quickly obeyed. And, indeed, he did instill fear in the perpetrator—a beige-colored streak, followed by a white tail, dashed out and across the yard.

Wood lowered his gun and cursed under his breath. "Shit… Damn it! A freakin' doe!"

Attempting to keep his anger and embarrassment in check, he walked stiffly up the hill, head held high. Slipping into the driver's seat, he glimpsed the ear-to-ear grin on Drake's face as she wiped tears from the corners of her eyes. *She's been laughing her ass off.* Saying nothing, he lit a cigarette and seethed. He felt like an idiot, and was certain that Drake thoroughly agreed.

Chapter 11

Up since dawn, Stevie worked on the tally from last night's fundraiser. She heard her name called from down the hall. As she rose from the desk, she closed her laptop, and headed to her mother's room.

"What's up?" She plopped down on the bed.

Jan emerged from the adjoining bathroom, wearing her blue-green robe and a white towel wrapped around her head. The morning sun shone in through the east-facing window, casting a soft light across the room.

"I wanted to know if you've let Tonka out."

"An hour ago. That's what you called me in here for?"

"Sort of. I also wanted to ask how your fundraiser went last night. You came in after I'd gone to bed and we didn't get a chance to talk."

"It actually went great. The hall was totally full and the founders of the Colorado Wolf and Wildlife Center brought two wolves. I'm working on the final numbers, but I think we raised a lotta cheese."

"Cheese?"

"Money, Mom. You know, moola, greenbacks."

Jan walked back into the bathroom, chuckling under her breath. "I'm glad to hear it was successful. Do they have a date set for the next one?"

"Probably six months or more. I'm not sure." Stevie paused. "You know, I heard one thing that was really weird."

When Jan returned to the bedroom, she had a comb in her hand. "What's that?"

"Well, one of the scientists who studies wolves told me he was approached right before the event. Some man accused him of being responsible for his livestock being killed. Of course, Dr. Klein told him that there aren't any wolves in Colorado, and I guess the man said that there must be because over the past month or so, he's lost some calves and stumbled across remains of an elk and a skinned bear."

"Hmm… That is strange. Did Dr. Klein have any ideas what it could be?"

"No, but one thing's for sure, a wolf did not skin that bear. I think Klein's going to investigate it, though." Stevie heard the hairdryer start up and figured her mom was in a hurry. The clock on the dresser showed seven thirty, the time Jan normally left for work. Knowing they'd talk again at dinner, Stevie headed back to her room.

Grabbing her laptop, she positioned herself cross-legged on the bed to surf her favorite sites: Facebook, Denver Green Streets, and some of the groups she worked with such as Wild Earth Guardians and Defenders of Wildlife. Stevie listened to U2 as images, updates, IMs, and emails flashed across the screen, but her mind was on other things. Last night, childhood memories of being different— odd—had surfaced and she couldn't shake them.

She recalled the day she rescued a mouse in one of her dad's traps. She had been very young at the time, maybe seven years old. She felt sorry for the little guy, lying there so still with droplets of dried blood on its fuzzy little nose, so she took it out of the trap. As she held the limp body, tenderly stroking the soft fur, it stirred. A moment later, the mouse rolled onto all fours, shook itself, and sat up on its hind legs. With its whiskers twitching in the cutest way, it looked right at her. She had lowered her hands to the floor and the little guy scampered off, just after he turned his head back toward her as if to say, "Thanks".

And then there was time she found an injured bird flailing about in the yard. She tried to pick it up to bring it indoors, but when her fingers brushed its wings, the bird flapped twice and flew away.

Back then, her healing abilities seemed normal. As she got older, they occurred less frequently, until she nearly forgot about them—at least until the incident with Sam.

She needed to talk to Colton and find out if he could explain exactly what her abilities were, and what she was meant to do with them. It was time to find him.

Stevie would wait until her mother left. *Until then, breakfast.* Less than two bites into a bagel, Jan passed her in the kitchen to say "bye" and kiss her on the cheek.

"Call me if you need anything. I won't be home until eight or so tonight."

Stevie nodded and listened for the sound of her mother's car pulling out of the driveway. She gulped down the remaining bagel and then raced upstairs to slip on her tennis shoes. At the last minute, she decided to take Tonka with her. The lab wasn't much of a watchdog, but she was still good at letting Stevie know if someone was near.

Stevie waited until she was a fair distance up the mountainside before calling Colton's name. Even so, there was no response. With no clear trail to follow, Stevie relied on her memory to find the cave entrance she and Tonka had discovered last week, now certain that it was Colton's encampment. Over the next rise, Stevie spied the familiar outcrop. The lab bounded ahead. Stevie reached the cave just in time to see a wagging yellow tail disappear through the entrance.

She followed, calling softly, "Colton…are you in here?"

The sun's rays did not penetrate deeply into the cave, but provided sufficient light to see Colton pushing Tonka off his chest and wiping dog kisses from his face. "How did you find me?"

"Actually, Tonka and I found you—last week."

"Last week?"

"It doesn't matter. I need to talk to you. A lot's happened, not the least of which is that the police might be watching the house."

"Accept my deepest apologies for not having returned to you. Know that I still stand watch, but from a greater distance. My informant continues to be absent and I must remain close to ensure I do not miss her arrival. She is my eyes and ears on the Rebellion's movements from our world into this one." He motioned for her to sit down. "Please…"

Stevie found a flat rock near the entrance and took a seat. Tonka joined her, curling up at her feet. "Look, Colton, things are coming back to me. Ya know, from when I was a kid. Weird things. I need to know what's going on."

"Speak to me of your recollections."

"I think…no, wait, I know I can heal people."

"Yes… That is a benefit of having the Guardian bloodline. Even those of us who are not Guardians, but are related by blood, are able to heal. You will find your dexterity, speed, and physical endurance to have increased far beyond what would be called 'humanly' possible."

Stevie felt her skin tighten and heart race. *Different. I always knew I was different, but this is more like being a superhero.*

"There is more. You have other, as yet undiscovered, powers that will awaken soon."

"But how is this possible?"

"To know this, you need to understand your people. The Djen are connected to the energy of the Earth in both dimensions on a level beyond current Hundye comprehension. The Djen possess an inherited gift to utilize this power by serving as conduits. In the early stages of Hundye development, they too had the capability— to a smaller degree—to experience and use the natural energy around them. However, long ago, whether from fear or disbelief, those on this plane shut themselves off from it.

"After a time, the loss created a need in the Hundye that could not be named. Rather than striving to reconnect with the universal energy, they filled the void with science. The possibility of reawakening their abilities in conjunction with their science remained beyond their reach."

Stevie could not speak. The realization of the vastness of her potential and the power she had unknowingly possessed was emerging. "But what about me? I was raised in Terra-hun, the human world."

Colton smiled at her. "You used your birth language. That is good. Remember, you were born a Djen. You may have experienced glimpses of your capabilities, but you did not fully come into your powers until recently. This is because in Terra-hun, you were neither trained in, nor lived with, an acceptance of these inherent abilities."

The need to understand, to learn more, became palpable, but Stevie found her thoughts shifting to concern about the cops finding Colton.

"But what about the detectives? I don't think that the one who keeps asking questions is going to let up. He's already suspicious, and if that flashlight-eye thing happens or I accidently heal someone else, he'll be all over me like wolves on injured prey."

"You will have to pretend innocence and ignorance. Try to avoid him so that he cannot bear witness to any of these occurrences."

That's easier said than done. "I know you're not from around here, but being distrustful is a part of being a cop. He's not going to just let things go."

Colton rose to his feet and strode toward her. Gently grasping her hands, he pulled her to a standing position and guided her out of the cave.

He lifted his face to the sun, and then rested his hand lightly on her shoulder. "All will be right," he said, turning her to face him. "Yet, my mind weighs heavy with the lack of contact from my informant. I fear she may have had an encounter with one or more of the Rebel forces, as she was due to report to me three sunsets past."

"Maybe she saw the cops too and is waiting."

"No…like me, she is able to cloak herself from the Hundye. That cannot be the reason for her delay."

Shuffling her feet, Stevie felt uncomfortable at the idea of his informant being a she.

"As concerns the police soldiers, you are certain they did not follow you here?"

She'd never even thought of that. Glancing around, she saw no signs, and Colton did not appear guarded. If they showed up, however, it would be better to be home.

Reluctantly, she called Tonka to her side. As she turned to leave, Colton instructed her to meet him by the trees behind her house at first light the following day. He leaned close enough to her to kiss, but instead turned and vanished into the cave.

Piecing her way between rocks and brush, Stevie's mind overflowed with thoughts of Colton. The way he looked at her felt as if he were peering into her soul. All she wanted was to wrap herself up in him—her warm security blanket—but she didn't know how to tell him how she felt.

Geez, girl, you sound like you're in grade school. Stevie scolded herself.

There had been one romantic relationship in her life. Not that she was a complete nun—she had dated several guys in high school, but nothing serious. The only guy she ever considered a boyfriend cheated on her. Feeling betrayed, Stevie vowed to never trust any man except, of course, Jack.

Now she might be falling in love, but with no idea how to deal with the feelings—on top of everything else.

"Alyssa, I'm telling you…I've never felt like this before." Stevie slouched on the couch, head on the arm rest, cell up to her ear.

"I think you should slow down. You don't know anything about this guy…except that he's smokin' hot."

"And—as far as I can tell—perfect."

"Are you seriously telling me that you've found someone who can live up to your expectations? What happened to 'I'll never trust any guy but Jack?'"

"I know, I know, but still, I can't help it. I'm doing the Wicked Witch of the West thing…. I'm melting here."

"Girl, you need to chill. Give it time."

Stevie moved the phone in front of her face and rolled her eyes. *Give it time...right.*

"I hate to do this," Alyssa added, "but I gotta go. I have to work tonight."

Hanging up, Stevie returned to surfing sites on the Web. Her eyes flickered with the movements across the screen, but her mind kept drifting back to meeting Colton at the cave.

Did I totally misread him? I thought for sure he was going to kiss me. After staring blankly at the laptop—long enough that the screen saver clicked on—she gave up. All she could picture was Colton's face. The way he smiled at her, the warmth of his lips when he kissed her on the forehead. *Damn it, Stevie. If it's meant to be, it will be.*

Stevie moved from the couch to the kitchen and grabbed a soda. The pop and fizz echoed in the empty house. Her stomach added to the odd orchestra with a gurgle. *When's the last time I ate?*

Too anxious to fix anything and feeling a little rejected by her protector, she meandered toward the back door. Tonka darted past her the moment the glass door opened and raced into the yard. Stevie watched to see if the dog would head for the tree...Colton's tree. But no—instead, Tonka began her standard sniffing patrol around the edge of the yard.

Staring into the forest as if willing Colton to appear, she felt silly, knowing she would see him in the morning. *That seems like years, rather than hours, away.* Why she already felt tied to him defied logic. But the feeling that they were somehow destined to be together could not be denied.

For now, though, I need a distraction. Returning to the family room, Stevie turned on the TV and shifted to the easy chair in the corner. A documentary caught her interest as she flipped through the channels. Two scientists discussed the most recent earthquake and the similarities to the quakes in Indonesia. Along with the statistics, graphs, and charts, the filmmaker showed numerous videos and photos of the devastation around the world. The images and magnitude of the destruction made her reel, tempering her normal fascination about the earth's cycles and causes, making her wonder if humans would be able to survive the ever-increasing catastrophes that seemed to be plaguing the planet.

Stevie accepted the teasing from friends and family, who considered her fixation on the natural order of the earth to be an obsession. For as long as she could remember, her greatest desires revolved around protecting nature. Her mom often joked that Stevie was born with a *National Geographic* magazine in one hand and a Greenpeace flag in the other.

Weather patterns also intrigued Stevie. For a time she studied meteorology, geology, and the history of tectonic shifts, out of some unknown drive to understand not only current events, but also how these were shaped by those of the past. The need to gain all available information seemed akin to an addiction. One she had been obliged to feed. With Colton's hints about the Djen, perhaps this insatiable need came from being one of them. *Do all the Djen feel the same way?*

Stevie struggled to refocus her attention on the documentary, but the more she learned, the greater her concern increased over the rapid changes besieging the planet. The scientists being interviewed surmised that several of the quakes may have shifted the earth a few degrees off its axis. *I wonder how the turmoil is being felt in Djenrye, or if it has any effect on that world?*

Stevie's curiosity about this other world, her world, created an itch she needed to scratch. Her brief glimpses, including those when she shared consciousness with her birth mother, showed a world untouched—pure and ancient. *But is it still that way? Have the earthquakes on this side screwed up Djenrye, too?* Stevie fervently hoped not.

The fact that the Djen still traveled on horseback rather than gas-guzzling, pollution-spewing vehicles delighted her. *And the city.* Not only beautiful, it looked to be thousands of years older than the timeline on this side of the portal. She pictured herself there, Colton at her side, a fairy tale in the making: A new past, a bright future, and sharing it all with a delicious man. It would be paradise, except for one little thing—she was being hunted by an enemy she knew nothing about. *Umm, wasn't I doing this to get my mind off Colton?*

The thud of a car door resounded through the window to Stevie's left. Craning her neck, she managed to glimpse her mom getting out of the car, pizza box in hand. *Woo hoo! This world has its own awesomeness.* She ran to the front door, wondering absently if they had pizza in Djenrye. The sliding door in the kitchen must not have been completely closed, because Stevie had to dodge the lab darting in front of her.

Jan laughed at Stevie and Tonka rushing her the moment she stepped over the threshold. Stevie grabbed the dinner from her mom and raced to the kitchen, Tonka at her heels.

"Wait for me," Jan called out as she dropped her keys on the hall table.

"Of course." She set the steaming box on the breakfast bar. "You wanna soda?"

"Sure," said Jan, her purse deposited unceremoniously on the nearest chair. "I rented a movie too. I thought we needed a girl's night tonight."

"You're the bomb, Mom—two nights in the same week. What's the occasion?"

"Nothing special, just wanted to spend a nice quiet evening with my daughter."

"Well, you'll get no argument from me. This is great." Stevie handed her mom a paper plate. The smell of green peppers and pepperoni wafted upward, answered by a rumble from Stevie's stomach; a reminder that she hadn't eaten since breakfast. Pizza and colas in hand, the two headed to the family room, with Tonka positioning herself between them. "What movie did you rent?"

"*I am Number Four.* I thought some earth-bound aliens disguised as teenagers battling a rival species bent on destroying them was in order."

"Really? Umm, Mom, just one thing…can you say 'a little too close to home'?"

Jan's face went blank for a moment, and then her eyes opened wide. Stevie could almost see the light-bulb turning on over her head.

"Oh geez, honey. I never thought…"

Unable to help herself, Stevie broke out in laughter. "No worries, Mom. I heard it was a good movie. Besides, we're dealing with another dimension, not another galaxy or aliens."

"You sure?"

"Absolutely." Stevie cuddled up on one corner of the couch while Jan put the movie in the player.

"I do want to talk to you about something, too." Jan sat sideways next to Stevie, remote in hand. "Don't worry. It won't take any longer than the previews."

This is perfect. Please don't let her start freaking out about everything. Her worry must have shown on her face, because Jan actually giggled.

"Don't look so grim," her mom said, playfully nudging Stevie on the arm. "I just thought that maybe you would like to come to work at the spa. Lilly is quitting and you could take her place as my receptionist, at least until I can find a permanent replacement."

Stevie straightened up and said cautiously, "Yeah. That would be cool. I've always wanted to work there, and it would be nice to have something to do and earn some money. But…" She paused, wondering how to phrase the rest of her thought. "…there is one problem."

"What? I think it's a great idea."

"Well, I do, too, except for the whole Rebel and Colton thing. I don't want to put anyone in danger."

"They didn't attack me when we were open and people were around. I think you'd be safer at the spa than alone at the house."

"I'm not going to be alone—Colton's been protecting me for years. Besides, my being at the spa could draw the Rebels back there."

"You could be right." Jan sighed, looking down at her hands rather than at Stevie.

"It's not personal, Mom. You know how much I've always wanted to work there...with you."

"I know, honey."

Jan dropped the subject, and instead leaned back on the couch and started the movie. Kicking off her sandals and folding her knees under her, she let the broomstick skirt flow over her legs as a makeshift blanket.

Jan looked as put together and chic as usual, but Stevie noticed creases around the corners of her eyes that had not been there before. *And are those silver hairs poking out of her bangs?*

With the excitement of the past week and looking forward to the adventures that lie ahead, she had not thought of the toll it might take on her mother. Although physically healed, Stevie wondered about her mom's unseen emotional wounds.

Stop it, girl. At least you have a nice night with Mom. Scooting across the couch, she snuggled against her mother's shoulder, enjoying the moment of closeness. Forcibly, she pushed away thoughts of leaving and the danger looming before her.

Chapter 12

Fried bacon smells like home. The sharp tang of freshly squeezed orange juice accentuated the taste. Outside, the sun warmed the landscape and a cool morning breeze drifted through the open door. *What could be more awesome?*

Stevie stuck a crispy piece of pork in her mouth and savored the salty goodness. Tonka's barking distracted her taste buds from their happy dance. Craning her head to peer out the sliding glass door, Colton's form came into view. He sat in the lowest branch of the cottonwood, grinning. One leg swung back and forth, the other wasfover did tucked beneath him.

Taking the pan off the burner, she walked barefoot onto the deck. The boards, still damp and cold from dew, chilled her feet as she crossed to the edge. The spring smells of pine, roses, and earth displaced the aroma of breakfast.

The sun hung low on the eastern horizon, shining through the branches behind Colton. Despite the glare, she could see him motioning for her. Stevie paused to scan the area, muscles coiled, tense, and ready. Seeing no one, she exploded across the yard, astounded at how swiftly she moved. The surprise compelled her to run faster, as if body awareness increased her agility.

Stevie glanced at Colton as she raced toward him. He stretched downward—arms just out of reach, a great grin across his face. She leapt to him with all her energy. Hoping to at least reach his waiting hands, she was astounded by landing instead on the branch above him. She swayed for a moment and then threw her arms around the trunk, looking at the ground fifteen or so feet below. "Oh my God...I did that?"

Colton laughed. "That feat is but a hint of your capabilities."

He helped her down to the limb on which he balanced. The rough bark created the sensation of a pedicure and pumice stones on the soles of her feet. Sliding next to Colton, her legs dangled in the opposite direction. The position had her hip-to-hip with her protector, allowing her to hold his gaze. "I'm floored. Why haven't I been able to use these powers before?"

"Your life thus far has been spent far away from the magic of your home world, but it was bound to come forth with your enlightenment. You are, after all, Djen."

They relaxed and talked about the other innate abilities that would soon emerge. "Would you like to go higher in the trees?"

The question intrigued her. *Can I really leap from tree to tree like a lemur or scurry to the top like a squirrel?* "Yeah, I'd like to try it, but take it easy on me. I'm kinda nervous."

With a nod, Colton stood and took her hand, pulling her to her feet. "You already have the power within you. Do not fear. With little effort, you managed this height."

His comment reassured her. He crouched slightly and, in a flash, he landed in an ash tree less than ten feet away.

"This is a good distance with which to practice," he called back to her.

Stevie looked down, and then back at Colton, steeling her nerves.

"Do not look down. Focus on me."

Barking from the ground drew her eyes down, nonetheless. Tonka bounded back and forth between Stevie and Colton. She seemed to be enjoying this game. *But her barking may attract attention.* Reluctantly, Stevie ordered, "House."

Ever dutiful, Tonka dropped her head and slunk toward the deck. She turned back once, perhaps hoping Stevie would change her mind, and then went inside.

With Tonka safely back in the house, Stevie jumped. Colton caught her by the arm as she passed him and pulled her back to the branch on which he stood. "I did it," she cried, taking a deep breath and then releasing it.

"You did, indeed. You nearly over did it. Have you the confidence to reach that one?" He pointed to an aspen a good fifteen feet away. Determined, she followed him, focusing on matching his reach. To her delight, she landed next to Colton. The moment she reached his side, he left for the next one. Without hesitation, she followed, tree to tree, laughing at the sheer joy of this newfound freedom. The last tree must have been at least thirty feet away. In this one, Colton stopped.

"You learn to tree-run quickly, but can you climb?" A quick grin and he headed up, without a look back.

Exhilarated, Stevie joined the race, bumping him when they gained the pinnacle of the cottonwood, a hundred feet high.

"It's so awesome up here!" Stevie spoke in short breaths, not from exertion, but from excitement. From her vantage point, she saw an ocean of trees. The panorama before them consisted of mountains rising in waves, dotted by the roofs of homes between them. A Golden eagle swooped low, close enough to touch. Her cheeks ached from grinning. "Look! You can see Denver from here."

The thrill, the speed, the flight—though strange and new—felt natural…a part of her. The ease with which she had mastered these abilities made her want to continue on, but Colton remained still.

"An excellent beginning. Now we must return."

Disappointed, but having no choice but to trust his judgment, Stevie followed as Colton retraced their path back to the original cottonwood.

"I can't believe how easy that was." She returned to her previous seated position.

"With practice, it will become as natural to you as walking." Colton paused. "Let us speak of Djenrye."

"OMG, yes. I have tons of questions." Stevie sat up, craning her head to look at him. "Oh, but did you ever hear from your informant? Is she okay?"

Colton nodded. "Yes. It is kind of you to ask. She arrived before dawn. Her delay was the result of evading Rebel soldiers so as not to lead them here."

"How many of them are there?"

"Close to a thousand. The young and discontented continue to flock to their cause."

"There're that many here? How come no one's seen them?"

"My pardon. Not here…few pass into Terra-hun. Their strength is in their numbers in Djenrye. The rarity of the blood required to enter the portal demands it be used sparingly."

"Wait. Reset button…what blood?"

Colton's eyes sparkled mischievously, but his smile was gentle as he looked down at her. "I spoke earlier of the portals between our worlds. They are known as *Ty Wanaji mánae*. The Gods created Ty Wanaji mánae as the sole manner of passage to ensure the Djen remain hidden from the Hundye. For this reason, they may only be opened with the blood of a Guardian. Unlike with the Ortehlae, living blood is not required. Collected blood suffices." He paused as he moved to sit next to her. "Each Guardian is bled a small amount every spring and that blood is put in safekeeping, to be used when needed. With all of the Guardians gone, the supply of blood dwindles. Therefore, it must be used sparingly."

"Well, then, how did the Rebels get the blood? Did a Guardian go all Darth Vader on them?" The curious look Colton gave her made Stevie clarify. "Switch-hitter. You know, go to the dark side?"

"No. That would have been the death of us all." Colton's face darkened, as if the mere thought of the Rebels enraged him. Stevie felt a flicker of fear. *I bet he scares the crap out of his enemies when he's really pissed.*

The flare of anger subsided and Colton continued on as if it had never happened. "Obtaining the blood was Torren's work."

"Torren?"

"A former leader of the Rebellion, raised in the palace of Tyré—one of our cities. His father, Larrik, was a noble and loyal Shield to Hayden, the Guardian of Tyré. I believe Torren's free access to the palace enabled him to discover where the blood was stored."

"Wait. Hayden? There's another Guardian? Where is he?"

It took a moment for Colton to respond. Finally, he said, "No one knows. Our world is not perfect. Before the Rebellion, the Djen and other races fought against the Jajing, a race of two-legged savage beasts. By the strength of our armies and the blessing of the Gods, they were defeated and banished. During the war, two of the Guardians took their families into hiding. Ephrum, the previous Guardian of Plates—another of the main cities—never returned. His body was discovered butchered, along with that of his family. It is feared that Hayden and his family did not survive, as no sign of them has ever been brought to light."

"There is so much to learn. It's a little freaky." Stevie ran her fingers through her hair, letting it fall to her shoulders, trying to absorb the information. The desire to know everything at once made her skin prickle, but she didn't want to barrage Colton with questions. "Okay," she finally said. "What do I need to do?"

Colton's knitted brow and the pinched expression worried her. "Our first task is to locate the Orteh they stole, and return it to Raile ai Highlae, the Hall of Light."

"You keep talking about the Ortehlae. What are they? Why does a Guardian's 'living' blood need to be used to control them? I don't get it."

"One question at a time. Orteh is the Djenrye word for Orb. They are gifts of the Gods, entrusted to the Djen for safekeeping. Five Ortehlae—the plural for Orteh—exist and through them the balance of *Tectrea*—the Earth—in both dimensions is maintained. Each Orteh controls a facet of the planet. Tecton is connected to the tectonic plates. Borvo controls all that is fire—volcanoes, lighting strikes, wildfires, even droughts, to some extent. Huana is the water Orteh, and has power over the seas, lakes, rivers, and rain. Avira is the Orteh of the air, which has dominion over tornadoes, trade winds, and the like. These four elements are independent, yet intertwined and linked to Élan-Vitál, the Universal Spirit. The balance of the Ortehlae controls the weather, volcanoes, earthquakes, and all other natural occurrences."

"Back up, cowboy. You have a God Orb, I mean, Orteh?" Colton looked puzzled. Stevie tried to clarify. "Élan-Vitál, the Universal Spirit one?"

Colton barked out a laugh. "It is true that the native peoples of this land sometimes use that term for God. There is no perfect translation into the Hundye language. Perhaps a closer phrase would be a connecting spirit, but not standing alone—all spirits being one, yet separate. The Hundye Buddhists speak of this."

"Gotcha. The Zen idea of being one with everything."

"You gain understanding. To continue... The Ortehlae are housed in Raile ai Highlae, located in *Phraile Highlae*, the city of your family. Just prior to your birth, the Rebels breached the defenses of Phraile Highlae and stole one of the Ortehlae—Tecton. I believe that its separation from the others, and the possibility it has been brought here to Terra-hun, is the cause of the inundation of earthquakes on this plane. My scout tells me that Djenrye is experiencing disturbances as well, but to a much lesser degree."

Stevie was dumbfounded. Of course she had an instinctive need to protect the planet and its inhabitants—it was in her blood.

"I was just watchin' something about the earthquakes and tsunamis. They're some of the biggest quakes ever recorded." Her scalp tingled with the feeling that the puzzle pieces were falling into place. "You still haven't told me... What's the plan?"

"First, you require adequate training—your mind and body must learn to work as one, without hesitation, to utilize your natural talents. As a Guardian, your connection to the Ortehlae is powerful and concentrated. This we may use to our advantage. With guidance, I am certain you will be able to discover Tecton's location." Colton's brows knotted, as though he was considering something more than what he was saying.

Colton glanced passed her and sprang to the balls of his feet so that he squatted on the branch rather than sat. "I must leave—I remained too long." Colton took her hand in his. "It is not safe here. I will return at the next sunrise to begin your training."

"Wait. I have so many questions. Don't leave."

"I must. Your police have returned and could be watching."

Stevie's eyes scanned the area. "Returned? I don't see anyone."

"Nor do I, yet I feel the change in the air and the scent of the curious one lingers in the wind."

Fearing that they were being watched and not understanding how he could know something he couldn't see, she simply asked, "Is there something I should do to prepare?"

"You require sleep to calm and clear your mind. Save your energies for the morrow."

As they both stood, Colton leaned in toward her.

Her breath held, eyes closed in anticipation, and his lips…brushed her cheek. Before she could turn her head and meet his mouth with hers, he vaulted to another tree and out of sight.

Stevie dropped lightly to the ground. Racing to the house, her feet barely touched the ankle-high grass, spurred faster by Tonka's renewed barks. *If I can run fast, I can move fast. Next time, he's not gonna get away with just kissing my cheek.*

Detective Wood lay prone under the bushes near Stevie's house, just inside the trees lining her backyard. The digital camera through which he had been surveying the encounter fell, followed by his jaw. He could feel the color draining from his face.

For the first time in forty-two years, I think I might faint. He had just witnessed amazing—no, not amazing, unreal—feats. The man sitting with Stevie vaulted into another tree a good fifteen feet away. And Stevie…she dropped twenty feet out of a tree, landing as easily as stepping off a curb, and then ran across the yard at lightning speed. *I knew their ships were fast, but had no idea how fast an alien being could move on the ground. Holy crap…and Stevie's one of them!*

He rolled back on his elbows, vision threatening to tunnel to black. He shook his head in an attempt to make sense of what he'd seen. Moments ticked by before he realized that he hadn't gotten it on video. *I have to get back to the car and call Drake. I hope to hell the pictures come out or she'll* never *believe this.*

Wood crawled backwards out of the bushes to avoid being seen, cursing himself for not having the video camera positioned and ready. The whole purpose had been to scout out the best place to set up the surveillance. He never imagined Stevie would be up and about this early. *And how could I have anticipated seeing her use her alien powers?*

When he had arrived just before dawn, the grass had been damp. He left to get coffee and give the sun time to dry the dew. When he returned, he decided to park the car up the road, rather than his earlier spot at the top of the hill.

Now he was glad that it was so close. His legs were rubbery. Still, once out of sight of the house, he found the strength to bolt to his car, dive in, and snatch up his cell phone from the front seat. He tried to catch his breath and calm down before he called Drake, but apparently failed.

"What's up, Wood, you sound winded?"

"You aren't going to believe what I just saw," Wood panted. He closed his eyes, willing his heart to stop racing.

"What is going on? Where are you? You were supposed to be at the station an hour ago. The chief's asking questions."

"Look, I'm on my way. I need to talk to you. And Sarah, I need you to promise you'll keep an open mind when I do." The sigh before the line went dead told him that she would try…as best she could.

The one upside to all this was that the man he saw in the tree fit the description of the men who attacked Mrs. Barrett. He wore the same twelfth-century clothing and headed up the mountain rather than toward the town. *Maybe he's camped there…somewhere. At least now I know why the daughter is harboring this guy. Still, I can't believe she's involved with anything that would hurt her mother. But then again, she's not Stevie's birth mother.*

Wood started the car and headed to the station. His plan would be to return and scout the area above the Barretts' home after filling in his partner. Maybe he could find where this guy was hiding. *I just hope Drake realizes that this is the first real lead we've gotten. I don't care if she thinks I'm nuts, as long as she has my back.*

Hands shaking, he barely saw the road. His thoughts scattered, he pulled the car onto the shoulder. Taking in a deep breath and then releasing it, the mountain curves began to come into focus. He shook a cigarette out of the pack and lit it. A bead of sweat trickled down his cheek and he rolled down the window to let the cool air in before feeling ready to continue.

I can hardly believe what I saw with my own eyes... Now, to get enough hard evidence to convince Drake.

Colton balanced on a rock, the ball of his left foot the only part of him in contact with the stone—a Warrior technique of extreme exertion of the body to free one's mind. He contemplated the appropriate method to teach Shylae the ancient ways of the Djen. *Training her will be challenging. She will have to strengthen herself physically and mentally. Our greatest obstacle shall be to keep the training secreted from the eyes and ears of the Hundye.*

Keeping the rest of his body motionless, he slipped the *Din Ashyea* from the pouch at his hip. He ran his hands over the leather cover, worn soft as silk through generations of use by *Ty Tesknata*, the Magi.

With reverence, Colton opened the book to the pages that described summoning the Gods to assist with the journey of the mind. He scanned them, stopping when he came upon the *Chatea*, the chant he must perform to aid Shylae with her visions. He would also require the help of fire, water, air, and earth combined to give the seer a clear path. Yet, he had no idea of how to bring these elements into the confines of Jan Barrett's dwelling. *I must convince Shylae of the need to go deep into the mountains to train. The perfect setting—all four elements in close proximity of each other.*

It became too dark to read. Colton unbound himself from the pose and rubbed the stiffness from his leg. As he leaned against the mouth of the cave, he knew he should rest. His mind must be clear and ready for the training ahead.

Marise waited for him by the fire inside the cavern. Crouched in a squat to allow a quick launch into action if needed, she warmed her hands. Ever watchful of the cave's entrance, she called to Colton as he entered, "Do you wish me to take the next watch? You should sleep a while."

Colton nodded. "I do desire rest. I have had precious little of it this past moon turn."

"You sleep; I have safeguarded her many times on your behalf. Trust that I will not let anything happen."

"Of course. My gratitude." Colton took off his boots and crawled under a bedroll. He watched as Marise strapped on her sword, bound the scabbard to her thigh, and tucked a small blade into her leather-laced boot. Her long raven hair, wrapped in a braid, brushed the ground when she reached down for an apple.

"I will wake you upon my return." The crunch of the apple punctuated the end of her declaration. The tip of her braid flicked to the side as she ducked out of the cave, giving the impression of a puma's tail when stalking prey.

He rolled onto his side, comforted by the sound of the crackling wood and the warmth on his face. Thoughts of the Hundye soldier, what they called 'police', slipped into his mind. The man had been close during his first instruction to Shylae. *How much had he witnessed?*

After Colton had returned to their dwelling, he and Marise spied the police soldier return to the area surrounding the cave.

Clearly not a scout, he had walked within three strides of their camp without discovering the cave entrance. Still, Colton decided it would be wise for Marise to shadow this man.

After the police soldier left, they agreed it best to cloak themselves to evade the Hundye, even within the wilderness.

"Prudent, yes," Marise had pointed out. "But such an illusion will not deceive the Rebels."

"You speak true, but I long for some manner in which to mislead our enemy."

In her practical manner, she ended the discussion. "With Shylae's mark now fully present, such thoughts are futile."

At Marise's arrival the previous night, her report had been unsettling. She detailed her discovery of a campsite, elk carcasses, and the skinned body of a bear little more than half a day's travel from the west. There had been no signs of bullet leavings or metal in the bodies. Rather, the wounds appeared to have been made by either arrows or razor sharp daggers.

The slaughter of the animals pointed to the Rebels. The bearskin taken, most likely for warmth, but the meat left to rot—skin and bones wasted. A life taken and not fully utilized—sins in the eyes of the Gods and a crime amongst the Djen.

Colton reined in his thoughts. With Marise watching over Shylae, he must fulfill the only duty left to him. Sleep. He began a breathing meditation. Instead of focusing on Élan-Vitál, as was his custom, he brought forth the image of Shylae and pictured her lying in his arms. With this as his last thought, he was able to drift off.

Chapter 13

With a shot of whiskey in one hand and a beer in the other, Detective Wood slouched on his favorite bar stool in his favorite bar—the VFW.

What did I see? Was it real, or have I finally lost it? Drake, of course, had not believed a word. Why should she? He had nothing except his story and a few pictures of Stevie and that man sitting high up in the cottonwood, and blurry pictures of what could be Stevie running. Still, he refused to dismiss what he had witnessed.

His frustration and the nagging drive to get to the bottom of it, whatever it was, created a bad tasting medicine he had difficulty swallowing. To clear the bitter taste, he slammed his shot and beer chaser, ordered another round, and then headed to the patio for a cigarette.

A chair in the far corner provided a good view of the street and the entrance back into the Post. He managed to light his smoke and take a deep drag before Drake emerged from the bar.

"I thought I would find you here. Are you trying to drown your imagination?" She smirked, nodding at his drinks.

"You know, Sarah, I think you missed your calling. You really should have been a comedienne... Not that you care, but I was contemplating my next move."

"Which is?"

"Tomorrow, I'm going to have a little talk with Mrs. Barrett."

The frown she gave him added ten years to her face. "Are you crazy? What are you going to do, demand to know why her daughter can jump down out of a tree?"

"Ahh...you are full of wit today. No, I want to know why she healed up so fast and what they're hiding. And yes, how Stevie can drop twenty feet out of a tree and just keep walking...or running, since that was the case."

His partner pulled up a chair at the same moment the waitress appeared. She ordered a Greyhound. His attention, focused on the hips of the departing redhead, was broken by a hand waving in front of his face.

"Hello? Earth to Wood? You cannot go to the spa, Ms. Barrett's business, for God's sake, and accuse her or her daughter of anything. She'll think you're nuts, and she won't be far off. Besides, she was the one attacked by these, these…men. Remember how angry she got last time you two had a 'little talk'?"

Wood shrugged. "I don't care if she gets mad. I want answers."

"What you're likely to get is a reprimand for harassing her. Perhaps you should change your first move to getting better pictures."

"I'm going to assume that was a constructive suggestion and not another dig." He took a drag, the smoke puffing out, punctuating his words. "But you're right about one thing. I'm not going to convince anyone of anything without proof."

"You're right about that," Drake said. "If you approach Ms. Barrett with nothing but a tall tale, she'll believe you saw something. If her past actions are any indication, she'll likely hide whatever or whoever it is."

"Good point. I knew there was a reason I've kept you on as my partner."

"Besides being the only cop in Golden who will work with you."

Wood ignored the jibe and stubbed out his cigarette as he rose. His partner followed him back into the bar. They managed to locate a couple of stools side by side.

"Seriously," he said, motioning to the bartender for another round. "Thanks for the insight. My mind was scattered after what I saw."

"I believe that *you* believe you saw something. On the outside chance it actually occurred, you're asking for a whole lotta trouble." Drake took a sip of her drink, shaking her head at the offered second round. "I'm talking FBI trouble—if you get my drift."

"I need to know what the hell is going on before that happens. The Feds would just muck it up. Or, worse yet, cover it up."

Detective Drake slid off the barstool, brushed the wrinkles from her slacks, and then patted Wood on the shoulder. "Well, good luck with that. I'm heading home." She set her half-empty glass on the bar.

Wood scowled. "I thought you were my pawtna?"

"I am. But you know me; I need hard evidence. Once you get it, I'm right there beside you...partner. Until then, you're on your own." She turned to leave, but not before tossing a crumpled five on the counter. "See you in the morning."

He watched her depart before turning back to his drinks. Downing the whiskey, he raised the empty glass to the bartender. *You want proof, you're gonna get proof...in spades.*

The sounds of forks clinking and mouths chewing proved that everyone enjoyed the burritos. It was one of the kids' favorite meals that Jan made. Jack certainly thought so, or he wouldn't have filled his plate with a third helping.

Alyssa and Stevie picked at their second burritos, and between bites teased Jack about being in love with his Ford Mustang.

"I can't believe you bought new mag wheels," said Stevie. "It's not like you're gonna be racing the car at Bandamere or something." The women laughed.

Jack mumbled, his mouth full, "I might...you never know."

"Yeah, right. Your parents would kill you," said Alyssa. "It must be nice to be rich."

"Hey," he said, swallowing his food. "I do have a job, you know."

Stevie laughed. "Yeah, a real productive member of society. Admit it, you're a spoiled brat."

Alyssa nodded. "I wish I had a brand new Mustang. I'd look hot in it."

"Yeah, you would, girl," commented Stevie. "In fact, I would, too." She gave Lissy a high five.

Jan interrupted. "Well, not to put a damper on this most interesting of conversations. But, Stevie, wasn't there a reason you wanted all of us together tonight?"

She pushed her plate away and nodded. "I wanted to fill you all in on what Colton told me about the Djenrye world."

"So, did you get all your questions answered?" asked Alyssa, leaning in.

"Not all, but enough to know that I have a very important quest."

"A quest? Who are you now, Frodo Baggins?" Jack joked.

Stevie playfully slapped his arm. "No, I'm serious, you guys. He explained about these Orbs that I am tied to by blood." She saw Jack roll his eyes and punched his bicep again, this time hard. "This is no joke. He said that one of these Orbs was stolen by the Rebels, and I have to train to see it in my visions and figure out where it is. And I have to be trained how to defend myself from them. The Rebels, I mean, not the Orbs." She paused to gauge their reactions.

Her mom was the first to speak. "I don't like this," she said, her face pinched. "Where is it exactly you are going to do this training? Someone might see you. Have you forgotten our inquisitive Detective Wood?"

"Colton thought about that already and suggested we start training in the basement. Once we move the furniture outta the way, there should be plenty of room."

"But what if the police see him coming and going?"

Stevie sighed. "They haven't yet. Besides, I think if he arrives before dawn, he's Ninja enough to sneak past them."

"Are you crazy? That's way too early," said Jan. "I'm not keen on the idea of getting up hours before I have to leave for the spa."

"We'll figure something out."

"Ahh, wait a minute," Jack said. "Are you telling me that it's just gonna be Stevie and the Fabio-wannabe in the house...alone?"

Then, squarely facing Jan, he added, "I think I should come over and supervise while…"

Stevie cut him short. "Geez, and who elected you my dad? I don't need a babysitter."

"She's right," Jan agreed. "Being left alone with this protector of hers is not what worries me. I'm more concerned about what all this is leading to."

Stevie tried to make light of the comment and focused the rest of the conversation on the positive information she had received about where she was from. Regardless, her mom's tone weighed on her thoughts.

They hadn't discussed the inevitable outcome of her training: that she might have to leave Golden and help Colton find the missing Orb. *Is that what Mom's worried about?*

Before Colton, her plans for the future were undefined—maybe go to college, and run the spa for her mom, with volunteer work on the side. Having a man in the picture had not been a consideration. But, as she told Alyssa earlier, Colton was not just any man.

Or is that it? Has Mom been relying on me so much that the thought that I've found the man of my dreams scares her? Or is it because he's not of this world?

Stevie awoke bright and early, elated at the thought of having Colton to herself all day. The aroma of fresh ground coffee brewing welcomed her as she entered the kitchen. Jan had positioned herself in the usual spot—the chair facing the sliding glass door. Stevie hurried past, grabbed the cereal box out of the pantry, and stuck it under her arm. She balanced a bowl between her chin and neck. With her free hand, she grabbed a spoon and then the milk from the fridge, juggling her treasures to the kitchen table. The resounding clank, clatter, and splash made Jan gasp.

"Slow down," she said. "You're making me nervous. I'm too tired to deal with all your extra energy." Jan wandered to the door to let Tonka outside. "Looks like rain," she mumbled absently.

Stevie plucked the newspaper off the table and skimmed through it, offhandedly listening to her mom ramble vaguely on. A comment about remodeling the kitchen caught Stevie's attention.

"Did I hear you say you want to fix up the kitchen? Are you warped? I have so much going on right now."

"I know it sounds crazy, but I have to do something mundane if I ever hope to feel normal again." Jan returned to the table and sat down. She sipped the coffee, peering at Stevie over the rim. "I have to ask. What are your plans with Colton?"

"OMG, Mom, are you asking me his intentions? When did we time warp back to the fifties?"

"He's going to be here soon to train you. For what? Battle? Certainly not for your undergrad degree. I'm worried you'll never go to college, or even have a normal life now. That's all your dad and I ever wanted for you."

In an attempt to close the physical and emotional fissure that had begun to grow between them, she took her mom's hand. "I wish I had an answer for you, but I don't. I'm playing this by ear myself." The warmth from her mother seeped into her fingers, along with a slight tremble. "I think the training is to make sure I can protect myself, and maybe you, if the Rebels show up again. And it's not gonna all be fantasy video game stuff. He's gonna teach me to control my visions."

Jan's head bobbed faintly.

"Since we don't know what the future's going to bring, let's enjoy our time together and see what happens, okay?" Stevie searched her mother's deep brown eyes for a hint of agreement. Instead, she saw tears.

"When did you become so grown-up?" Jan seemed unable to continue and turned to face the glass door.

"I'll tell you what, Mom. The next day you're off work, we'll go to the hardware store and get some paint and whatever else you want, and we'll work on the kitchen—together. Sound good?"

Jan nodded and moved to put her coffee cup in the sink. "Thanks, honey. I appreciate that. But right now, I have to get to work. Can we finish this talk over dinner?" Without waiting for an answer, she headed toward the door, and then stopped near the archway. Keeping her back to Stevie, she said, "I know you're of age and I do realize that this is not make-believe. But," her voice wavered, "I'm afraid you're going to leave and I'll never see you again."

Stevie moved with the swiftness of a cat. In the blink of an eye, she was at her mother's side to pull her into an embrace. "I promise you, Mom, that won't happen. But our world is in danger. You are in danger, and I am going to do whatever is necessary to stop these Rebels." Stevie paused for a moment. "Here's a thought. Why don't I invite Colton to dinner tonight? I think if you got to know him and gave him a chance to answer your questions, you might feel better about the whole thing."

"That's a good idea. In fact, why don't you ask Jack and Alyssa to come, too? They'll feel left out if you don't, and will likely come up with questions I wouldn't have thought of."

"Awesome. See you tonight."

Chapter 14

The warrior stood on the other side of the glass. He wore looser garb than before. He wore the same leather vest, but had changed into black cotton pants. Still missing was the sword across his back, replaced by a pack, although he still carried a blade at his hip. The morning sun behind him created a halo effect.

Stevie blinked twice, a deer caught in headlights—*beautiful, breathtaking headlights*—before she gained enough composure to wave him in. The sweatpants and loose t-shirt made her feel underdressed next to him. As he entered, she stood up. The world moved in slow motion. He stopped, inches from her, radiating strength and pride.

He spoke first. "Did you rest well?"

"Yes, I did, thank you for asking…" *Did that sound as stiff and formal to him as it did to me*? Her worry was laid to rest when he smiled.

"Good…let us begin."

Stevie led the way, stealing glances behind her as she headed down the stairs. The arrangement of the basement had not changed since her father had died, geared to watching sports with friends. Near the middle of the room sprawled an old worn couch, on either side of which were recliners, the leather faded and scarred from years of use. Taking up most of the far wall, an imposing, black, fifty-four inch projection TV lorded over all.

Colton surveyed the room. "The size should be adequate, if we are able to clear away the furnishings."

"We can put most of it into the storage room," Stevie said, pointing to a door at the opposite end of the basement. "It's pretty good sized, but the TV will have to stay."

With no need of further direction, he lifted one of the recliners as if it weighed little more than a folding chair. "The focus of your training today will be meditation. The sword-play shall consist of stance and balance."

After the furniture had been removed, Stevie's muscles felt as though she had already worked out. *He's not even breathing hard. This is gonna suck.*

The room now bare, Colton set out two swords, and Stevie caught a glimmer of metal when he opened the flap at the top of the bag. Unidentifiable shapes created bulges in the canvas, piquing her curiosity.

"Are you going to teach me to fight?" she asked, straddling the blades he had set on the cream-colored carpet.

"Among other things. Come." Colton motioned for her. "Sit with me."

Stevie faced him, cross-legged on the floor.

"Have you dreamed of your home, of Djenrye?"

"Yes. The first dream was a couple of months ago. In it, a man—Raynok—was killed. That same dream came back to me after my enlightenment. I've also dreamed of Carlynn. In several of them, I was Carlynn… Crap. I'm rambling aren't I?"

Colton's eyebrows rose ever so slightly. "You already know of Carlynn? How long?"

"A few weeks. And I know she's my birth mother." She waited for his reply, or confirmation, or…well…something, but Colton remained silent.

Steeling her courage, Stevie decided to approach the subject of dreaming of Colton before they met. "Then there is this one dream of me running for my life from an unseen enemy. I barely remember the first couple of times I had it, but with each successive dream, I recalled more details. One of the new details was…" At this point, Stevie no longer met his gaze, "…you. You were racing next to me, protecting me. After that, I started having visions when I was awake."

Crossing his arms over his chest, he looked Stevie up and down, an expression of knowing more than he let on glimmering across his face. "The first dream is reminiscent of the story your mother told of her and your father's flight from Phraile Highlae, and the manner in which your father was murdered."

"My…father? Raynok was my father?" The full impact of the statement smashed into her. "I saw my father's death?" Not able to fully wrap her mind around seeing her birth father being murdered, Stevie's thoughts frantically searched for something—anything—to ground her.

Colton.

Staring at his face, blocking everything else from her vision, she still could not grasp the calm she had hoped for.

He did not look at her. His attention seemed to be turned inward. "This is highly unusual, even unheard of—you weren't even born, yet you have seen the event?"

The words, the tone, and the reaction increased Stevie's anxiety. Did he think she was some kind of freak, even by Djen standards?

"What do you mean 'unheard of'? Like…'weird'?"

Finally, his attention returned to her. He uncrossed his arms and reached for her hands. "No. Not at all. 'Unheard of' refers to your powers being greater than any of the Guardians who have come before you. Not 'weird'. A more apt word would be…remarkable."

Her tension edged down a notch. *Well, at least All Powerful is better than Freakazoid.* Unable to stop herself, Stevie asked, "What happened to Carlynn?"

A shadow moved across Colton's face. He shifted, leaned forward, and with eyes downcast, his strong calloused fingers gently caressed hers. "After your father died, your mother knew of the danger in giving birth to you in Phraile Highlae. She was secreted away to Tyré…"

"By Ghorgon! I dreamt, or saw, him, too."

"Yes. Ghorgon was a Master Warrior who protected your family for several generations." Colton looked directly at her. "There is much more to the story, but know that your mother had a strength few possess. Her only choice to ensure your safety was to relinquish you…to hide you in Terra-hun in the hope of keeping your existence concealed from the Rebellion. At least, until you became of age to return to your home."

Colton seemed to be searching for the right words. After a few moments, he said, "She died returning from this difficult task at the hands of the Rebel soldiers. Even at the end, she did not give up the secret of your survival."

Stevie gasped. The recollection of Carlynn's pain when she had released her newborn to the Shaman, and the feeling of abandoning her child, was more than Stevie could bear.

The death of her dad, her birth father, and Carlynn compounded with the memory of Carlynn's pain. They loved and sacrificed everything for her. She began to weep. Colton released the grip on her hands and enfolded her into his arms. There they sat, Colton consoling her with a gentle embrace, as she sobbed.

Time passed, but Stevie did not notice until the sun rose high enough to cast beams of light into the darkened basement. Only then did her tears subside. It would take time to accept the deaths of the parents she never knew, but the sorrow must be set aside. She had so much to learn about who she was and the role she would be expected to play.

Sitting up, wiping her tears away with the backs of her hands, she managed to ask, "So, now what?"

"I knew the responsibility would fall upon me to inform you of the death of your parents, yet it grieves me to have caused you this pain."

"Thank you. I needed to know. It's gonna take some time, but it sounds like that's something we don't have a lot of right now. But, I don't understand why the Shaman didn't keep me."

"Do you not think a blue-eyed, blonde haired child in a village of dark-eyed, dark-haired people would have drawn attention? Especially given the village's proximity to the portal. It would have been akin to placing you directly into the Rebellion's hands."

"Good point." Stevie straightened, but remained seated. "Okay. I think I'm ready to start."

"As you wish."

Colton's expression hardened. She didn't think he looked angry. It was as if the friend had changed back to the teacher.

"The first step is to strengthen your seer abilities. It is your visions that will enable you to locate the Orteh, Tecton. By returning it safely to its rightful home, we will have retribution on those who destroyed your family and who threaten to annihilate the existence you have come to know."

Stevie shook her head in frustration. "You're Djen. Can't you find it with your special off-the-chain Djen sight? Besides, I've never seen any type of Orteh in my visions."

"It is complicated. Only Guardians have the ability of sight. They are able to travel through their visions into the past, present, and to some extent, the future.

"Outside of the Guardian line, a few Djen have been born with great aptitudes—perhaps at a young age they can will a toy to come to them, or push away a tormentor without touching him or her. These children are rare, perhaps only three or four born in every generation. With rigorous training and the use of spells and potions, they may develop a weak ability to have visions. The skills are learned when they are sent to *Ty Tesknata Halle*, roughly translated 'Magi House of Learning'. Even the most learned are limited. At best, their visions are flashes of insight, left to interpretation.

"Guardians, however, require no outside assistance and minimal training, being born with complete seer ability. It is in your blood. Where a Tesknata, a Mage, might be able to 'see' the Orteh in a vision, he or she would be unable to discern its surroundings or location, or even whether it is in the past, present, or future. Further, they are unable to—how would you say it—'pan back' on the image. Despite these shortcomings, we believe it was a tesknata who discovered that the Orteh had been removed from Djenrye and hidden in Terra-hun."

"Okay, hold up—a tesknata is a kinda wizard? Like guys in long pointy hats covered with stars?"

Colton broke out in a rumbling laugh so intense that Stevie feared he might hurt himself. Wiping tears from the corner of his eyes, he said, "Stevie, if I am to continue your teachings and training, you must forget all the misinformation taught in Hundye fairy tales."

The laugh broke through the remnants of her wall of grief. "I'm trying, but what you're telling me sounds like a fairy tale." She playfully punched him in the arm.

"One of the many reasons I am here is to teach you of the Djen ways." Colton straightened his posture, all business again. "Enough discussion for the moment. Now, we begin the training. First, a slow, deep breath…"

As she breathed in and exhaled fully, his voice lowered to a whisper. "Close your eyes and clear your mind."

Closing her eyes was easy, but her mind raced. Colton must have risen, because she sensed movement behind her.

"Relax." His word flowed soft as silk in her ear. Then his touch—light, but strong. He rubbed her shoulders. Her body tingled. Despite his closeness and an unexpected surge of desire, she nevertheless found herself beginning to relax. Her heartbeat slowed, thoughts stilled. She did not notice Colton had returned to a seated position in front of her until he took her hands in his. In less than a breath, she felt the sensation of being pushed forward as she entered a familiar dream.

She ran through the woods, Colton at her side. He pulled her out of the path of an arrow, causing it to impale a tree, rather than her. They raced across an expansive field flush with summer growth, vaulted into the adjacent Sitka spruces and Douglas firs and, without pause, continued—tree to tree—until a sheer drop halted their progress. Forced to a slower pace, they balanced their way along the edge of the cliff, coming at last upon a cave.

In the dim light of the cavern, Colton stopped and turned her to face him. "We need to get back, now."

She blinked, startled. Vertigo washed over her as she was pulled backward out of the vision. It took a moment to realize she had returned to the present.

"What did you see?" asked Colton, her hands still enfolded by his.

Stevie described all she remembered.

"Have you experienced this vision before?"

"Yes, for several months, but this time it had way more detail." The question that had been haunting her burst out unexpectedly. "Who is Shylae?"

His hands dropped away from hers. "That is your given name." A look of awe, confusion, and *Oh, God, please don't let that have been fear* darted over his features.

"A moment, please." Colton rose, his back to her.

What did I do wrong?

After several minutes of stillness, he returned to a seated position in front of her. In a quiet voice, he said, "I beg your forgiveness for my reaction. It is simply that…your abilities are beyond anything ever witnessed—beyond any stories told of the Guardians. Shylae, you are exceptional."

She felt herself blush at the compliment, but had no idea how to respond.

Thankfully, Colton continued, although he seemed to be speaking to himself. "Is it possible that the *Triveatae* is unfolding?"

"Trivia…what?"

"Triveatae, Prophecy. We must not become distracted from your training. What I will tell you for now is that you may have been foretold in the Lorn Prophecy. It is a tenet that one day a Guardian would be born who will be tasked to save and unite our two worlds. Your powers are such that it gives me hope you are that Guardian. Coupled with the fact that you are the first female Guardian in ten generations…"

"Hold up. I'm so not ready for this. I'm only just now adjusting to the whole 'from another dimension' part. The superhero skills are sweet, but a savior? That's a little out there."

"I understand your hesitation. My comment was that it is a possibility, not an absolute. I give you my word that we will discuss this in greater detail, but…" He paused. Then, his tone turned stern. "…we must train.

"First, meditation. You will soon be able to see the Orteh, but before that can occur, you must learn how to feel it, sense its presence. You must master your breath. Slowly inhale through your nose and fill your lungs, then exhale in the same manner, with control. Continue this technique until your mind empties all that flows through it."

He removed from his pouch the leather-bound book she had seen earlier.

"This is the *Din Ashyea*, the Book of Teachings. It is nearly as old as Djenkind." He flipped through the pages, stopping when he came upon a detailed drawing of an orb. He held the book up to her. "This is the Orteh named Tecton. In order to call it forth and connect, you will need to focus on its likeness."

Closing her eyes, she tried to relax her mind. *Think of the Orb…not that I might be mankind and Djen's last hope…oh crap.* Every little creak from the house, Colton's breathing, even the tiniest scent of cigar smoke from years ago, distracted her. She opened one eye a crack to see Colton staring at her, his forehead creased.

"It appears that your focus is weak."

"I don't think I can do this while you're sitting there looking at me. It's a lot of pressure."

A slight nod and Colton rose, heading for the stairs. "I will scout the perimeter. Perhaps my absence will help you to concentrate."

The silence left in the wake of his departure created a void nearly as distracting as his presence. *Focus, damn it.* Stevie slowed her breathing and worked at making the amount of air coming in exactly equal to that going out. It differed from her yogic breathing exercise of increasing the counts. Scanning the basement, she spotted a sliver of sunlight shining through the basement window. As she fixed her eyes upon the little particles of dust that floated in the light, one caught her attention. It sparkled like a diamond.

Shifting focus from counting breaths to the speck, she fell into a trance. All the while, her gaze remained transfixed on the particle.

The fragment of dust transformed. It gained in size, cast out its own light, and began to form into a sphere. The room melted away and the vision overtook her. Nothing existed but her and the glowing ball suspended in front of her.

Inside the orb, liquid swirled and moved as a living thing. Gold in color, the liquid moved in a way that reminded Stevie of a lava lamp, moving and building, then releasing to create another form. Sporadically, arcs of blue lightning would appear within the globe—as though it was the Tesla ball from her science class—charging and electrifying the liquid.

The vision became clearer. The light intensified and the orb began to move as well, spinning, picking up speed, but it did not deviate from its location, tethered by an unseen force.

A presence drew near. A man's voice spoke. "It's working."

Snapped back to reality, she rubbed at her eyes, surprised by the dampness.

"I wish you could see your eyes. Ice blue and shining like a proper Djen." He swooped her into his arms and spun her in a circle.

Stevie couldn't help but laugh at the joy Colton displayed, despite her watery eyes and the burning sensation on her shoulder blade.

"It worked, Shylae. You have mastered your vision."

"What…what happened?" She gasped for air between the laughter. "Colton, you're making me dizzy."

The movement ceased, but her head still swam. She managed to focus on Colton's face, and then he kissed her.

It was a quick peck, like something you'd give your sister, but it altered the nature of their excitement. Stevie looked into her protector's eyes, wondering if he felt the same spark she had. The answer was the twinkle in his eyes and his smile as he bent forward to kiss her again.

Their lips met and parted slightly, tongues dancing playfully. Her entire body trembled. The power of his love surged through her and connected with her soul. The world ceased to exist, leaving only the sensual touch of Colton, the musky scent of earth and fire, the salty taste of his skin, and the pounding in her heart.

They parted briefly and shared a smile. She went back to taste his lips once more. This time the dance was more passionate. She rose and pressed herself against him, the soft, supple leather of his vest contrasting with the rippling, hardened muscles of his back. The sensations overwhelmed her. She threw herself into the embrace, wanting to consume and be consumed by him.

Colton pushed her away. She tried not to show disappointment, but couldn't help it. He seemed to desire her as much as she did him, and yet he resisted.

Her heart sunk into the pit of her stomach. "What? Did I do something wrong?"

"It is not you, my Shylae. I have waited for this moment for nigh on eighteen summers." He sighed and leaned in to take her back into his arms. This time the embrace was gentle and he kissed the top of her head.

"I have been unsure how to explain our connection. We are meant to be."

"I don't understand." His comment made her uneasy.

Colton met her gaze. "In Djen, when we fall in love, it is because the souls speak to each other before the bodies. You and I experienced something beyond this. Something rare and extraordinary, when we first met."

Stevie allowed him to lead her back to their seated positions on the floor.

"Perhaps once or twice in a generation, two souls enter *Bousae-yamae*. It is an event beyond souls speaking…more akin to souls blending."

"But you first met me when I was an infant."

His beautiful smile lit up his face. "It is not a sexual connection. The Bousae-yamae transcends the physical plane. My feelings toward you—as a man toward a woman—did not surface until the last moon turn."

Too stunned to speak, she stared at the man before her. In her heart, her soul, she accepted the truth—they were meant to be together. Call it fate, destiny, or blind luck, but she was in love with him.

"Our newfound passion must be constrained."

Dismayed, she started to protest, but he hushed her with his fingertips on her lips. "We have a lifetime before us to share. Yet, there will be no future if we do not succeed in our quest. This must be our total focus." His eyes twinkled mischievously. "At least, for now."

"Got it. But before we get back to training, is there any other earth-shattering news about me you'd like to share?"

A laugh erupted from Colton. "Nothing immediately comes to mind." Then he took her hands in his. "Shall we get back to your vision?"

How can such strong, callused hands be so gentle?

"Shylae?"

"Sorry…yes, the vision." Refocusing her attention, she noticed a sensation of fuzziness, as though her skin was made of cotton balls. "I'm not sure exactly what I saw in the vision. I remember a clear globe with something gold-ish in it that moved, and there were these blue arcs of—I guess—electricity that seemed to charge the liquid."

"You describe an Orteh," he told her.

"I can't believe the vision came so fast."

"I am pleased, yet not surprised." He stood up and began to pace the room, hand rubbing his smooth chin, brow furrowed. Stevie watched him circle, but remained silent, afraid to interrupt his thoughts. After several minutes, he dropped to his knees in front of her.

"Tonight, after I take my leave, you must practice your meditation. It is clear that solitude aids your sight. While the sun remains in the sky, we will work on breathing."

"Umm…already know how."

"There are dozens of techniques you will need to master to be effective in both meditation and combat. The physical training shall have to wait until we are able to secure a suitable location. I fear that all we may be able to accomplish in this place…" He gestured around the basement. "…is balance, foot placement, and the feel of your weapons."

"By suitable, do you mean outside or inside?"

"Truly, both." His attention moved to the window casement. "Deeper in the mountains, away from the notice of Hundye would be optimal, and it would be helpful to be surrounded by all four elements when attempting to locate Tecton."

Grandfather Barrett's cabin. Stevie spent most summer weekends in the log cabin on the outskirts of Jefferson, nestled deep in the trees on Indian Mountain.

"I know a place we could go. But I'll have to ask my mom first. I wanted you to come to dinner tonight, anyway." Stevie gave a wink. "You can meet Mom—in person—and my friends. With all that backup, it'll be safer to ask her about it then."

"You are certain I should meet your mother at this juncture?"

"Yeah, I'm sure. Besides, she told me to invite you."

Colton smiled. "Well, then, I must not refuse an invitation from the Hundye mother of Shylae. I shall attend, but do not expect my arrival until after it grows dark. Your police soldiers have been looking for me."

"They have? What happened?"

"My informant and I spied the curious one walking around the mountain yesterday."

"Really? Geez, I hope he didn't see us." Stevie pictured Wood sneaking around in a trench coat, watching them jump from tree to tree. She was more amused than fearful at the thought of what his reaction might have been. "Ya know, whateva—I'm sure we can use the cabin, and I doubt the detective will follow us there. I just don't know how Mom's gonna react to me being alone—with you—for weeks."

Chapter 15

Stevie called Jack and Alyssa to ask them to dinner. Jack never turned down a homemade meal, even after Stevie told him she'd be the cook tonight. He hesitantly agreed, but not until being assured that she would limit her skills to grilling the steaks. With his parents rarely around for meals, he seemed to relish the home-cooked dinners and family environment Stevie and her mom provided.

Conversely, Alyssa shared most meals with her parents. It took a bit of prodding, but in the end, she promised to convince her mom to let her skip another dinner at home.

Stevie rummaged through the freezer, thankful there were enough steaks, and then started cleaning the grill.

Her friends arrived around eight thirty and helped set the table. A knock at the kitchen door halted the process. Stevie glanced up, her heart skipping a beat.

Framed by the doorway, Colton stood on the deck. The effect mimicked an archaic painting—the majestic hero in his warrior dress, long black hair flowing away from his face and over his shoulders. The three women let out a collective sigh. Transfixed, Stevie remained as still as her mom and Alyssa, until Jack roughly bumped her as he passed. He faced her long enough to roll his eyes and scowl before opening the door.

This time, Colton had put on a shirt. *Could be coz Mom's here. Good thing, though. Mom and Alyssa would have totally flipped a switch if he'd shown up bare-chested.* Over the blue rough spun shirt was his leather vest—the sides lashed together, the lacings forming a type of lattice, rather than being thread-stitched. Although the cloth of his pants looked to be black muslin, the same leather stitching held together the front and back closures. His hair was unbound, except for a braid here and there decorated with small feathers—it reminded Stevie of an ancient Native American. Gauntlets made of animal hide and dyed black covered his forearms from wrist to elbow. They, too, were held together with lattice work. A belt, on which hung a sword, and a pouch for his tools completed the garb.

If he weren't so damn real, I could see him on the cover of a romance novel.

The moment the sliding door opened, Colton strode in and headed straight for Stevie. He gathered her into his arms. Enveloped in his scent—nature, camp smoke, and musk—his lips brushed her cheek. Heat rose to her face when he whispered huskily in her ear, "My Guardian."

It took an effort to refocus her attention long enough to introduce him to the family. "These are my friends, Jack Snow and Alyssa Brier. And…this is my mom, Jan Barrett."

"Good to finally meet you, Colton," said Jan, separating him from Stevie by taking his arm and escorting him into the dining room. "Why don't you sit here, at the head of the table, so that we can all talk to you together?"

"At your pleasure, Jan Barrett." Colton waited for her to sit down before taking his seat. With her mom taking the chair on the right, Stevie grabbed the one on Colton's left.

"I hope you're hungry," she heard her mom say. "Stevie grilled enough steaks for an army."

Please let that be the only grilling that happens tonight, Stevie prayed silently, but with little hope. She knew her mother all too well.

"Thank you, yes," Colton said with a nod. "I have quite a hunger. I miss the luxury of someone cooking for me."

Jack slid into the seat on Stevie's left. Alyssa hesitated at the foot of the table before finally deciding on the chair next to Jan. The tiny brunette appeared more nervous than usual—jittery. Unable to take her eyes off Colton, she looked down only when he glanced her way.

Jack, on the other hand, made an attempt to act like a grown-up. He sat bolt upright, chest slightly forward, head held high, with a steady glare at the newcomer. Stevie recognized the signs of a beta wolf, trying to be an alpha. The jealousy and actions he exhibited were more comical than his usual wisecracks.

Please don't let me laugh. She smiled instead.

Picking up the plate of steaks, she began to pass it to Colton, but paused. *Steaks? What was I thinking? He's been camping for eighteen years! I should have made spaghetti.* Her worry melted when Colton breathed in the aroma of the seared meat and nodded in approval as he helped himself to a cut of beef. Baked potatoes and fresh salad rounded out the meal.

The usual joking and chatter did not occur. It seemed to Stevie that everyone held their tongue, waiting for Colton to say something between bites. He ate quietly, relishing the dinner, looking up only to smile at Stevie. The first to finish, he laid down his utensils, but did not speak as the others continued to eat.

He must be used to eating in silence, all alone in the woods, but this is seriously weird.

When Jan started in on the questions, Stevie at first appreciated the disruption until she realized, *here we go.*

"So, Colton, I am very curious about this place…Djenrye? How far away is it?"

One brow cocked, Colton glanced at Stevie before he answered. "My apologies for not understanding your question, Jan Barrett. Are you asking how far away as concerns the distance, time, or location? For it is very far in all these matters. It is…in another dimension."

"What I meant, I guess, is distance. How many miles is it from here to the passage that leads to your side?"

"It is in your Canada, next to the sea over which the sun sets."

Jan nodded. "Sounds like British Columbia. How did you get here? I assume you don't drive and I haven't seen a stray horse?"

"Mom, leave Colton alone." Stevie rolled her eyes. "You know that I already told you how fast we can run."

Colton laid his hand on Stevie's arm. "It is fine." He turned back to Jan. "Djen have special gifts that allow us to travel over land, or in the trees, if trees are present. We are not as fast as your sky machines. Yet, we are able to move as swiftly as some of your land cats—at a constant speed. Think of your spotted cheetahs. The burst of speed they employ for the hunt, we are able to maintain from the rising of the sun to its zenith. With a brief respite, Djen who have had greater training may continue until darkness."

Jan's mouth dropped open, but no words came out.

"Shyl…" Colton cleared his throat. "Stevie has the same abilities. It takes me less than half a moon's turn to travel between here and the portal."

Between bites, Jack jumped into the conversation. "So, what's the plan?"

"Right down to business, huh, Jack?" said Stevie, her tone deadpan.

"Pardon me, your grace. Is it so wrong to want to know what's gonna happen to my best friend? You know? Just sayin'."

Ignoring him, she instead turned to her mom. "Colton and I have been discussing where he could train me. The basement ceiling is too low for sword fighting, and, of course, we can't shoot arrows down there. Plus, seriously bad idea to do it outside with the cops sniffing around."

"Just ask whatever it is you need to ask," Jan said, her words clipped.

Stevie glanced at Colton, and then back to her mom. "Do you think Grandpa would let us use his cabin for a couple of weeks?"

"Excuse me?"

Colton stepped in. "It would be safer for Stevie to train away from here. The Rebellion is hunting her and your police soldiers are hunting me. It would be more effective for Stevie to meditate on the Orteh if she were surrounded by the four elements of the earth."

"Wait. I'm getting lost here. What is an Orteh? Swords? Can someone fill me in a little?"

The echo of wood on wood resounded as Colton turned his chair to face Jan directly.

For the next few minutes, the room filled with the hypnotic rumbling tenor of Colton's voice as he set out his reasons for the training. He concluded with, "…and the combination of her newly discovered powers, the threat of the Rebellion, and her current inability to focus completely will be best addressed in an isolated location."

He paused briefly when Jan's eyes filled with tears. "Stevie's safety will be enhanced by mastering her fighting and seer skills," Colton reminded Jan. "For eighteen summers, I have kept Stevie from harm. It is a vow I will never forsake."

Whether from the effect of Colton's voice, the confidence he exuded, or simply exhaustion from processing the events of the past weeks, Stevie's mom nodded, seemingly in acceptance.

Jan's words, however, remained argumentative. "You've protected her all this time. Why does she now have to learn how to use weapons and fight? She's never hurt anything—she's a member of the Wildlife Guardians, for Christ's sake."

"I do not wish to be harsh, Jan Barrett, but you need to accept that these Rebels will not cease their pursuit until they accomplish their task—locating and abducting Stevie. She is not safe... Nor are you." Colton looked at each one in turn. "No one in this world is safe as long as the Rebellion exists."

"I am trying to understand, truly I am." Jan leaned into Colton, tentatively resting her hands on his. "Promise me you'll protect my girl."

Turning his hands palm up, he grasped Jan's. "With my very life, Jan Barrett. With my very life."

A heavy stillness settled over the room for several heartbeats, eventually dissipated by Jan's sigh. Stevie let out a rush of air, not realizing until that moment she had been holding her breath.

Thank God that's over.

Jan straightened her blouse, once again all business. "Still, I'm not comfortable with you two going up there alone, Stevie."

"Then come with us," she pleaded.

"You would be safer, Jan Barrett," added Colton. "Now that the Rebels have located you, discovering your daughter is a certainty."

Jan hesitated. "I can't leave the spa right now. Besides, if the cops are watching the house, they will protect me." She rose from the table to clear away the dishes.

As she started to walk away, Colton grabbed her arm. "Jan Barrett, your safety is more important than your trade. Consider carefully. The police soldiers may not be able to intervene when the Rebels attack again."

Setting the dishes back on the table, she gave Colton a defiant look. "These cops have guns, which make me feel more secure than your primitive weaponry. And they are aware of these men and are keeping an eye on us. If you believe them to be so ineffectual, why do you feel the need to arrive after dark?" She picked up the dishes and left for the kitchen.

Taken aback by her mom's harsh tone, Stevie understood it to be the product of fear and confusion. *Mom feels safer surrounded by what she knows—cops with guns. She's made up her mind.*

Looking around the table at her friends, she asked, "How 'bout you guys?"

Blinking twice and swallowing hard, Alyssa answered with a question. "Us?"

"Yeah. Why don't you two come along? Mom would probably feel better if you were there."

Jack piped up, "Hell, yeah. A bitchin' summer camping va-ca before college starts? I'm in. Besides…" He looked directly at Colton. "…I need to be sure you're okay, Stevie."

Can you say alpha-wannabe? She chuckled to herself. *Jealousy rears its ugly head, as Dad used to say.*

Alyssa remained undecided. "I don't think I can take that much time off. We've been short handed…"

"Come on, girl. You haven't had a summer vacation yet. And you won't get one if you don't put your foot down." Stevie tried to convince her friend.

"You know my folks…my mom…there's no putting my foot down."

Jan returned. Her demeanor had changed. With slumped shoulders, head ever so slightly hung, she appeared ready to surrender. "Stevie, I've thought about this, and you're right, you need somewhere safe to train. I know I can't stop you anyhow, but I won't be going with you. I can't afford to lose the business." Jan hugged Stevie. "I will call your Grandpa Tom later and see if he'd be willing to let you use the cabin."

"Thanks, Mom. Really." It took all of Stevie's will to downplay her excitement about spending the next few weeks in the mountains—with Colton.

"It is settled then," Colton said. "Your friend Jack Snow shall accompany us. Young Alyssa Brier shall remain here. We leave in three sunrises. That will provide time to plan and decide what provisions should be needed."

Stevie left the cleanup to her friends and walked Colton to the door. Stepping onto the deck, he reminded her to practice her meditation, and then turned to give her a long kiss. Goose bumps prickled her arms, whether from the kiss or the cool night air, it did not matter. With passion rising in her, Stevie hungered to deepen the kiss. Colton moved his lips to her ear to whisper that dinner was delicious. Yet, when he pulled back, Stevie saw a sparkle in his eye, a hint that his passion, too, simmered below the surface.

Colton released the embrace and, over the top of Stevie's head, bid the others good night. Her hand slid down to his, fingertips lingering together, extending the touch to the last possible moment before he walked away.

After Colton had left, the rest of the group compiled a list of provisions they would need. Jan called Stevie's grandfather to confirm the use of the cabin, while Stevie told her friends about her day learning to breathe, meditate, and develop her fighting stance. Jack's interest focused on her descriptions of envisioning the Orteh, while descriptions of Stevie's interactions with Colton enraptured Alyssa.

"Wow, Stevie...I keep hearing 'the perfect man'. You are so lucky."

"Seriously. I think I'll puke now." Jack pantomimed sticking his finger down his throat. "Tell me about the swords."

"Yes, please," Alyssa said. Stevie saw a wicked twinkle in her friend's eye and wondered what she really meant.

"He laid out two swords. They were slender and long—about three feet—but had amazing balance. After I learned to hold one properly, it felt like an extension of my arm rather than a separate weapon."

"Sounds a little small. I think I would want something with more heft," Jack said condescendingly.

Alyssa's small voice piped up, "Oh really? I'm pretty sure Colton could kick your ass with a butter knife."

The verbal jousting continued until Stevie decided to call it a night. She had promised to practice her meditation before bed. As she watched her friends leave, she laughed at their jibing each other all the way to their cars.

Alyssa got in the last word, calling out to Jack, "Having sword envy?" before shutting the car door and speeding away.

Up in her room, Stevie sat on the floor to meditate. She concentrated on the Orb, but try as she might, she couldn't clear her mind. Her thoughts whirled around the impending trip. Spending time with Colton, learning about her new abilities, and Djenrye, excited her. A knock came on her door, and she moved to the bed before calling, "Come in."

Jan stuck in her head. "Am I interrupting?"

"No, Mom, I was trying to meditate, but nothing's happening."

Jan entered and joined Stevie on the edge of bed. "Are you sure about this? I mean, going to the cabin. You'll be up there alone with a man you hardly know. And, despite his good intentions, Jack is hardly a bodyguard."

"Yes, I'm sure. I can't explain it, but I trust Colton—with my life."

Her mom remained still and silent. Not a good sign. Stevie rolled her eyes and walked over to her dresser. She ran a brush through her hair, waiting.

A full minute ticked by before Jan spoke. "I guess, as long as you trust him...but I'm having a difficult time understanding why the Djen can't take care of this instead of needing help from a teenager from Golden."

"Mom, you're not listening to me, or Colton, for that matter. I'm not just a teenager, I am a Guardian and that makes me a target. The Rebels will find me, so I have to deal with this now. Don't you think it would be better if I am prepared for when they finally do catch up with me?"

"I'm afraid for you. It's not just the Rebels, I also worry about..."

"Me...being alone with Colton, right?"

"Well, yes. I see the way he looks at you. Up there, with just you and him..."

"And Jack."

"Yes, Jack, the great hero. Seriously, this whole situation could put you in a compromising position."

Annoyed with the snooping, Stevie crossed her arms defiantly. "Don't you trust me?"

"Of course I do. It's him I don't trust."

"Well, for your information, earlier today I was the one that pressured Colton. He had the self-control. Let me put it this way, how many times have you heard the guy tell the girl 'No'?"

"You...pressured him?" Jan shook her head. "At least he was a gentleman." Jan rose and straightened the bedspread. "I won't give you the lecture about being a lady..."

"That's good. I am an adult now."

Sighing, Jan said, "No fighting, okay? I just worry about you." She added, "I guess I better let you get some sleep."

As her mom passed, Stevie reached out and impulsively hugged her. "Love you."

"Love you, too." Jan closed the door.

Crawling under the goose-down spread, she giggled a little about her mom's statements. *Did she really say 'compromising position'? For being such a cool mom, she sure can be nineteen fifties.* Stevie turned out the lamp and stared through the window at the night sky. She had forgotten to return to the meditation. *Oh, well…I'm in bed now and there's always tomorrow.*

Cuddling up with one of her pillows, she pretended it was Colton, and drifted to sleep.

Footsteps in the distance drew Colton's attention. He hoped it was his informant and not that curious police soldier. A woman's voice called out, and he spied Marise coming into view. Her warm smile led him to believe that all was as it should be. She approached and embraced him and together they entered the cave and sat by the fire.

"Any news about the police soldier?" asked Colton as he put another log on the flame.

Marise took a drink from her bota bag. "Not much to report. He went to the saloon and had a few ales, left to purchase food for his evening meal, and returned to his abode."

"He did not leave again?"

"No, I surveyed him through the window. His focus remained on the moving picture box, even as he ate, and then he retired for the night."

He must not have discovered much from his last trek up the mountain, or he would have resumed searching. "This news is good, but I am worried he may yet capture our image."

"I will follow him on the morrow and inform you if he attempts to gain a position to monitor Shylae's home."

Colton nodded. "You have my gratitude for keeping watch. I will leave with Shylae two mornings hence. Until then, I hope to continue training without interruption."

"How does her training progress?"

"She did well for the first session. She managed to glimpse the Orteh in her mind's eye, but failed to see where it is located." He picked up a stick and poked at the embers. "I do have one more request of you, if you will hear it. You know of my plans to take Shylae, and now the boy, Jack Snow, deep into the mountains to train." Colton spoke Jack's name dismissively. "Her Hundye mother refuses to come with us. Would you provide my mind with ease and keep her safe while we are gone? With the Rebels close..."

Marise glanced down to the cave floor and slowly nodded. "It is my hope that I will not encounter them. I am not as adept a fighter as you."

Turning her to face him, Colton spoke. "Marise, you are a strong Warrior. I have complete faith in you and your skills."

She shrugged him off and reached for her pack, withdrawing a chunk of deer jerky and a handful of dark berries. "I will do this for you, Brother, but I much prefer to fight the Rebels in our own land."

"You speak true."

"Are you returning to train in the morn?" Marise bit off a piece of jerky and swallowed it down with another sip from the bota bag. She offered a drink to Colton, but he shook his head.

"Yes," he said. "I pray to the Gods that she sees the Orteh soon—before the Rebels discover her whereabouts. I am curious as to how they found her in this plane, or even learned that she existed."

"I know not. But you, too, have heard the tales of the Rebellion searching for the mystery child."

"Correct. Yet that was Torren, not his men, and he has been slain."

"I have heard that rumor, as well—that death found him at the end of a Rebel's blade. Yet the Council speaks of their fear that the news of his death is but a ruse to allow him to build an army in secret."

"I hope their fears are unfounded, but the increasing number of Rebels in Terra-hun looking for the Guardian, gives me doubt." Colton paused, unaccustomed fear knotting his stomach. "Have you been able to glean any information as to whether or not they still search for a male Guardian?"

Marise nodded. "That is my belief and hope. Yet, with Shylae's mark enlightened, her sex matters not. They will find her, regardless."

"You give word to my concerns. The prophecy…"

The look in her eyes, told him that her thoughts mirrored his. A Guardian who may save both worlds would surely be a precursor to the destruction of the Rebellion. This knowledge would force them to increase their efforts to obtain her, her blood, and her power, exponentially.

Certainty began to grow within Colton that Shylae was the one spoken of in the prophecy—her gender, the first female Guardian born in two thousand winters, her exceptional physical and seer abilities, her expedited connection with the Orteh, despite never being in its presence—far too many signs for mere coincidence.

"I shall take first watch to allow you rest." He stood and swept up his blades. Once secured on his belt, in his boots, and slung over his back, he turned to grab a cloak.

"I require but a short respite," Marise said, crawling under her blanket. "You need sleep as well."

Exiting the cave, he leapt into the nearest tree. Mind racing, he was determined to not allow the Rebels to get within close distance of Shylae. He landed on the cottonwood, the one that had become his watch tower, and honed in on the Guardian's bedroom window. Her light was off. She must be slumbering.

The kiss they had shared earlier surfaced in his thoughts. His lips still felt the pressure of the caress. A smile stretched across his face. *Finally, I will be with her, to love her, to make her my mate.*

Memories of her scent overwhelmed him, and he lost himself in a daydream of their future.

Colton smacked his head hard with the heel of his hand to force himself back to reality. He knew the importance of maintaining control with her. Only by staying the course would they have the life together he envisioned. Besides, without finding and returning the Orteh to Djenrye, there would be no future of which to dream.

Chapter 16

Detective Drake sat on Wood's couch, hunched over the battered laptop on the oak coffee table. It hummed quietly, at home with the cigarette burns, nicks, and other signs of age on the table top. The suspect's face glowed on the screen, casting Sarah Drake's normally attractive face in a sickly green. There was no movement except for her index finger tapping on the mouse as she scanned the other pictures Wood had taken. Two, especially, appeared to pique her interest. She kept returning to them: Stevie opening the back door for the stranger, and one which showed little more than a blur streaked across the yard from the deck to the tree line.

"You say that this is when he left the house?" Drake asked.

"Yeah. I told you already. There's nothing wrong with the camera. He was moving that fast." Wood reached over the top of the laptop and whipped his finger across the screen.

"I thought you were going to video tape the interaction between them?" She looked up.

Wood frowned, hands resting in his pockets, and paced restlessly in front of his partner. "I had planned on it, but there was nowhere to set up without being seen. With the camera, at least I could lie down in the bushes and get better shots of them."

Drake stopped at the clearest picture of the man with the long black hair. "It does look as though Stevie allowed him in without any sign of a struggle or duress, and he is dressed in the strange clothes the Barretts mentioned." She paused, seeming to weigh her next words carefully. "I guess this is sufficient proof to at least challenge Ms. Barrett. When you do, though, remain calm and in control. I don't want to see you go off half-cocked...again."

Choosing not to rise to the jibe, Wood nodded grudgingly. "I plan on talking to Jan at the spa. I'm interested to see what her reaction will be when I show her the pictures. I'd bet my last dollar that she's somehow involved."

"Remember, you get more flies with honey than with vinegar. Careful with the accusations. You need to come across like you are on her side and just concerned about her daughter's welfare."

Slumping into the recliner next to the couch, he grumbled, "Dis isn't my first time around da block, you know. I was interviewing suspects when you were still in high school." He stared vacantly at the blank television on the wall across from him. "But dis whole thing has me befuddled. My spidey senses aren't tinglin', so much as itchin'. Between Jan healing so quickly, Stevie befriending what appears to be her mudda's attacker, and the abilities that both Stevie and dis suspect are showing... I'm beginning to wonder how much Stevie knew about dese men in the first place."

"She appeared genuinely shocked and upset about the assault. No one is that good of an actress. When has any suspect been able to fool both of us?"

"Maybe something's happened to make her forgive them, or maybe she's involved with them...somehow."

"Do you hear yourself? That doesn't make sense. You've no evidence that Stevie knew them beforehand." Drake sighed and rose from the couch. She pursed her lips in a way Wood recognized as deep thought. "Maybe she now trusts this man for some reason. I don't know why, but that's what it seems like to me. And, as far as showing signs of some kind of power, that's a pretty big leap—no pun intended. Have you considered the possibility that your imagination simply got the best of you?"

Wood felt his face grow hot and he rose with his anger. "Bullshit, Drake. I know what I saw. She jumped out of that tree—at least twenty feet down—and bolted for the house in a blur. She traveled at the same speed that caused the pic of the suspect to blur. You haven't seen it with your own eyes, so you don't believe it, but I am telling you, they have powers." He glared at his partner. "I know you don't want to hear this, but I think...no, I believe they are from another world."

Sarah Drake barked out a laugh. "You are losing it, Wood. Another world…seriously? I think you need a psych eval." She snatched her purse from the coffee table. "I'll tell you what, when I see it for myself, I might—and I emphasize might—believe what you're saying. I'm leaving. I promised Cody I'd try and stop by his baseball practice. It is Saturday, you know. You should think about occupying your time with something that doesn't involve creatures from another planet." She stormed out of the living room and toward the front door.

Right on her heels, Wood pleaded, "Come on, Sarah, I need your support in this. You're my partner. Give me a chance…"

She whirled around, barely missing Wood with her purse. "A chance for what? For pulling me into your weird fantasy? I don't think so. I am out of here. Call me when you get it on tape."

"But…aren't you coming with me to the spa?" asked Wood in an innocent, boyish tone.

That knocked the wind out of Drake's sails. She sighed and shook her finger inches from his nose. "Okay, I'll go with you, but no more talk of aliens, and I want you to promise you'll be on your best behavior."

Wood drew an *X* across his chest. "Cross my heart. Thanks for going with me and I promise to be good…Mom."

Detective Drake frowned. "I mean it, James. No more alien talk."

Wood knocked on Jan's office door. She jumped. The paper in her hands fell to the floor.

Jan hurriedly slipped a jacket over her silk camisole, which effectively concealed her arms. Drake gave Wood a barely visible nod. *She's quick – I couldn't get a look at her injuries.*

"Well, if it isn't Golden's finest." Jan stood, leaning over her desk to shake their hands in turn. "Come in…have a seat."

Wood gripped her hand for a long moment to look closely at Jan's face. He found no evidence of her earlier wounds. He looked harder, but could not tell if the damage had been cleverly concealed by make-up or no longer existed.

Drake walked to the couch and sat down. Wood felt her stare.

Disentangling her hand from Wood's, Jan glanced from one detective to the other. "Would you like something to drink?" she asked. "Coffee, tea?"

"Uhh…no thanks, we're fine." Detective Drake responded.

Jan waved at Wood to sit in one of the high-backed chairs.

"Thanks, but I'd rather stand."

"Suit yourself." She repositioned herself behind her desk. "What brings you here today, Detectives?"

Moving to stand next to the couch, Wood never took his eyes off Jan. "You're looking better. Healed up already?"

In response, a forced smile appeared on her face.

"I meant to ask you when we last spoke," Wood continued. "How did you manage to heal so quickly?" Ignoring the nudge on his foot from Drake's heel, he pressed on. "I mean, I'd love to know what sort of magical creams or elixirs you sell here." He gave her a disarming grin but the ice did not melt.

"Look, Detective, I'm the victim here and I don't appreciate your implication."

"Please, Mrs. Barrett… Jan. I am not implying anything. I'm just trying to get to the bottom of this." Wood tried to keep his tone light, but felt his ire rising.

"To the bottom of what, Detective?"

Drake added, "This is crazy, Wood. Leave the woman alone." She rose from the couch as if to say "this interview is over".

"So what's this?" Jan stood as well, but kept the desk between them. "Good cop, bad cop?"

In an attempt to regain control of the situation, Wood placed himself in the doorway, blocking his partner's exit. No one spoke. An uncomfortable minute ticked by before Wood retrieved the laptop from the bag on his shoulder.

"There's no 'good cop/bad cop' scenario. There is, however, something I need you to explain to me…to us." He motioned to his partner. "Please sit back down."

With a loud sigh, Drake returned to the couch. She sat stiffly, arms and legs crossed. Jan remained standing.

"This will only take a moment." He positioned the laptop on the desk with the screen facing Jan.

The room was silent except for the hum of the computer. Jan focused on the screen, her expression changing from placid, to curious, to pale. She slowly lowered herself into the office chair. Rather than words, a rush of air escaped from her lips.

Pointing to the picture of a man standing in front of the sliding glass door at Jan's house, Wood asked, "Would you care to explain why your daughter is inviting this man into your home? A man who fits the description of your attackers."

Without looking up, Jan shook her head. "I have no idea what this is, Detective. Except that, perhaps for the clothes, this does not look like either of the men who attacked me."

With the evidence in front of her, Wood had not expected a denial. "You said you did not get a good look at the men, except for what they wore." He grabbed a notebook from his pocket and flipped it open. "You said they were over six feet, correct?"

"Yes, but…"

"And they wore medieval-styled clothing, correct?"

"Yes, but…"

"Muscular build?"

"Yes, but… Damn it, Detective." Jan's tone rose. "The men who attacked me had brown hair, not black. And I don't even know if this picture is genuine or something you doctored."

"I'm a cop. We don't doctor photos." Wood clicked through the pictures to the ones of Stevie in the tree with the man. "Your daughter seems to know him."

Despite being visibly shaken, Jan remained defiant. "You know what, Detective? I am insulted at your insinuations about me and my daughter. And I'm pretty sure that stalking us is illegal." She lowered her tone, speaking slowly and confidently. "This sounds an awful lot like harassment; harassment of a victim, nonetheless. I'm sure the police chief would like to know about this." And with that, Jan closed the laptop and reached for her office phone. "Would you please give me the number of your boss, or do I have to look it up?" The receiver dangled in her hand.

Wood started to protest, but Drake stopped him. "Ms. Barrett, my apologies that we upset you. Of course you may have the police chief's number, but you must understand we are at a loss here and want answers as much as you."

"Well, you will not find them here. Please leave." Jan replaced the phone in its cradle. "And unless you come back with a warrant, I don't expect to see any more pictures of my house, or my daughter."

"Of course." Drake nodded, retrieving the laptop. Wood was half pushed, half pulled by his partner through the door.

Stomping out of the spa and past Drake, Detective Wood turned his head to ensure that his partner saw the sneer on his face. *How dare she force me out the door? I had Jan Barrett right where I wanted her. When suspects get angry, they get flustered, and that's when their stories start to unravel.*

As she opened the car door, Wood whirled her around to face him. "What the hell was that? Why were you working against me in there?"

"Because you were heading way into left field and your accusations were going to get you into trouble. She could have called the chief. I assume you haven't shown him the pics or told him your alien theory?"

"Maybe it is time to tell him. I think he'd find it intrestin' how a man dat fits de descript of de attackers was welcomed inta de Barretts' home by de daughter. And explain to me how Jan healed so fast? I'm tellin' ya, sometin's amiss and I'm gonna to find de truth, come hell or high wata."

"I don't know what's going on, either, but I think it's a bad idea to run to the chief with some cockamamie notion, especially with your history." Wood tried to respond, but Drake continued. "He will be furious that you're treating the Barretts as suspects. We're supposed to be surveilling the area, not the Barretts. As far as her healing that fast, maybe she's a fast healer. You really want to tell the chief she might be guilty of something because she recovered quickly? Not wise, Dr. Wood."

"Oh… gimme a break! I'll admit I mayave been a little outta line, but come on…you won't admit how strange dis all is?"

Drake shoved him away and slipped into the driver's seat. Wood stormed around the car, slamming the door hard beside him.

Refusing to miss a beat, she launched into a diatribe before he could strap on his seat belt. "No, I don't see any correlation. So she healed up fast. You have no proof of anything, just conjecture. And not only won't it stand up in court, you can't make a case from it."

"Yeah…no tanks to you." He punctuated his anger with his fist against the dashboard.

His partner rolled her eyes as she started the car and pulled out onto the street. He knew she thought he was crazy.

He lit up a smoke.

"Window," was all she said.

Wood rolled down the passenger's side window and leaned out, not so much to keep the smoke away from Drake but to put as much distance as possible between him and her. They said nothing to each other. Wood inhaled, exhaled, and fumed.

The moment the vehicle came to a stop in the police parking lot, Wood shot out of the car and stormed off to the bar. But not before making the effort to slam the car door again—hard.

With their plans to leave the next day, Stevie had hoped to give Colton some good news. Unfortunately, that would not be the case. Despite her efforts over the past two nights, she had been unable to see the Orb. He had remained steadfast in his insistence that she continued to meditate, refusing her explanations that she couldn't just turn it on and off. *Like talking to a brick wall.*

He promised her that Marise, his informant, planned to remain near the house to keep an eye on Jan. Stevie didn't care for Colton's close connection to this woman. *Geez, jealous much?* The jealousy rarely lasted, though. It melted whenever he looked at her.

"Stevie…" Her mom's voice called.

Stevie threw on an old robe over her nightshirt and headed downstairs. She entered the kitchen, barely getting out the word, "Sup?" before seeing Colton standing beside a lithe, dark-haired beauty. Realizing she wore only a ratty terry cloth robe, Stevie turned and made a play for the stairs.

Quick as lighting, Colton caught her. "What am I to think when you take one look at me and retreat in haste?"

She tugged on his arm, trying to make him let go. "I need to get some clothes on."

"You are clothed. I would not expect you to come down otherwise," he said, the hint of a smile playing across his lips. "Please, join us. I wish for you to meet Marise."

"No… I need to get dressed first." Stevie slipped from his grasp and rushed to her room. Throwing on a pair of faded jeans and a black tank top, she took a moment to skim her hair with a brush. *That's more presentable.* She ran down the stairs to find her mom entertaining the visitors in the family room.

Stevie slowed, took a deep breath, and entered with all the composure she could muster. Colton stood and paused to take a long look at her. He seemed to drink her in with his eyes. She floated toward his outstretched hand and allowed herself to be led to Marise.

Marise rose gracefully from the couch. The movements of the woman were cat-like, both graceful and a bit dangerous. When she smiled, however, Stevie was put at ease. Nevertheless, Marise's enthusiastic embrace startled Stevie.

When the feline Warrior released the hug, she remained close enough to brush Stevie's hair away from her face and exclaim, "You are right, Colton, she is beautiful."

Stevie's face grew hot from the compliment.

"I am so honored to finally meet you, Guardian."

Stevie's eyes were drawn to Marise's long black hair and steely blue eyes—so much like Colton's—and wondered if all Djen had the same features. *In that case, are all Guardians fair-haired?*

Marise led Stevie back to the couch, talking to her as if she were an old friend. While Stevie listened to her story about following the detective, Tonka arrived. She must have been on the deck. When Stevie stroked the furry head that came to rest on her lap, it released the smell of fresh grass.

"I heard him speaking into his hand-held machine earlier. His words confided his suspicions, and he spoke of witnessing the two of you." She nodded at Stevie and Colton, who shared a glance.

"It is fortunate we have planned to leave in the morrow," Colton exclaimed. He stood and moved to the window. His back to Stevie, he pushed the curtain aside, as though looking for Detective Wood. He let the material drop back into place. Then he returned to the couch to sit with Stevie.

"I know he's piecing things together," said Jan. "You should have seen him at the spa. He was upset about how fast my injuries healed, and he had pictures of you leaving the house, Colton. I'm sure he's seen both of you use your powers." She waved her hand toward Stevie and Colton.

Grabbing Colton's hand, Stevie hoped his strength would ground her and calm her fears. *He's got pictures? Now what?*

He returned her touch and asked, "Shylae, have you managed to see the Orteh?"

Thankful for the change of subject, but not so much about where it went, Stevie shook her head. "No… I've tried, but nothing is happening."

"I understand the difficulty. This solidifies our need to move the location of your training to the wilderness."

"You know how I feel about all this," Jan began, holding up a hand to stop Stevie from interrupting, "but I've thought it through. Plus, your grandfather has agreed to let you use the cabin for one last vacation with your friends." She then looked directly at Colton. "He does not, however, know that you are bringing a stranger. Let's keep it that way."

"My endless gratitude, Jan Barrett," Colton said as he stood. "The hour is late. Marise and I shall depart to allow Stevie time for one further attempt at meditation before the morrow's travels."

"I'll give you time to say good night to your friends." And with that, Jan called Tonka to her side and left the room.

Encircling Marise and Stevie with his muscular arms, Colton said, "My loves, you give me great pride." He kissed them each in turn.

Stunned, a thought came to Stevie unbidden. *Do men in Djenrye have more than one woman?* She disengaged herself from the embrace.

"What do you mean—exactly—by, 'your loves'?" She tried to keep her expression neutral, but feared it did not mask her unease. Discomfort grew with the ensuing silence. This time, it appeared that the Djen were stunned.

As if on cue, Colton and Marise simultaneously erupted with laughter.

"Okay…what's the joke?"

He took Stevie in his arms, still chuckling. "I cannot believe you thought ill of my declaration of pride in you and Marise." He shook his head. "She is my sister."

Not knowing whether she should be mad or relieved, Stevie softly backhanded Colton's bicep. "Why didn't you tell me? I guess that explains why you two look so much alike." This time she joined in their laughter.

"My deepest apologies for not informing you of our relationship, aforehand. Of course, you could not have known."

When the laughter subsided, Stevie walked the siblings to the glass door. Before parting, Colton bent down and kissed her good night. A proper kiss, this time, not a shy brush of lips.

"You need never worry about my desiring another, Shylae. Before you were old enough to speak, I gave you my soul." He bade her sweet dreams, and with Marise, disappeared into the trees.

Chapter 17

Alone again, Stevie made a cup of tea—a mix of loose leaf chamomile, comfrey, and peppermint. Cupping the mug and breathing in the aroma, she retreated to her room. *One more attempt to see the Orb before morning.*

Cross-legged on the floor, her eyes closed, she tried to relax and breathe as Colton had taught her. Nothing happened. The tickle of the carpet on her legs, every creak of the floorboard underneath, and even the ticking of the clock on her bedside table nibbled at her concentration. The harder she tried to picture the Orb, the more flotsam and jetsam floated through her mind. First Colton... *but what a distraction...* and then her friends, and the talk about the detective.

Frustrated, she opened her eyes and re-situated herself in front of the window. She gazed out into the cloud-covered night sky, thinking about leaving the next day. If they discovered the Orb's location, she would be heading for an adventure. The idea entranced, but saddened, her. To be with Colton on a quest would mean leaving the only home she had ever known.

A lone star twinkled briefly and then was swallowed up again when the clouds reformed. Stevie sat bolt upright at the realization. *In the basement, the sunlight reflecting off the dust particles—that sparkle—it helped me to see the Orb.*

She retrieved a candle and matches from her dresser and returned to the floor. In her excitement, it took several tries to light the wick. She began her breathing technique. She focused on the blue of the fire, assuming it would again shape itself into an Orb as it rose before her. Instead, the flame stretched into a thin vertical beam of light—a crack through which she could glimpse...something. Instinctively, she opened her arms and her mind. The opening widened and grew greater than the span of her arms. She entered into a waking vision.

Stevie stood inside a large cavern. Torches burned in sconces along the walls, giving off light, but little warmth. Shadows moved across the stone floor and a haze of smoke hung in the air. She slipped behind a large boulder worn smooth by eons of water. Groups of men and women gathered here and there, talking amongst themselves. Their clothes revealed them to be Djen.

She listened to the conversations, but could not understand what was being said. She made mental notes of the words to relay to Colton. The language flowed as a gentle stream, dancing over the tongue, every word ending softly.

A voice summoned, "*Octalorei, Kurakaélae.*" In synchronicity, all heads turned to a figure standing on an outcrop at the far end of the cave. Talk ceased.

The crowd surged forward, taking no notice of Stevie. She emerged from her hiding place and moved with the flow of bodies, intrigued by the power the speaker seemed to have over his flock. She tried to remember the words, but it all sounded like gibberish. *He must be their leader, and these must be the Rebels Colton had told me about.*

Slipping through openings in the crowd, she approached the front of the throng. The smell of sweat, leather, and smoke nearly overwhelmed her. The base of the outcrop stopped her—ten feet closer and she would have been at the leader's feet.

He stood above her. She guessed him to be a little over six feet tall. His muscular build, bearing, and the way he positioned himself on the rock made him appear much larger. His strong jaw and chiseled features made her think that he spent few nights alone. In the dim light, she noticed that his eyes were golden rather than blue. When he turned his head to engage the crowd, it seemed to Stevie as though he looked right at her. But he continued to scan the audience without returning her gaze. A draft blew in, moving the long dark hair away from the side of his face. *Did I see pointed ears? And markings at his hairline, continuing down his neck...a tattoo?*

In the singsong language, Stevie did hear two familiar words repeated often and with contempt—Colton and Orteh. The leader finished his speech with a rallying cry. The masses picked up the chant, stabbing their words and their daggers in the air. She managed to memorize the phrase before the vision vanished.

Stevie blinked, trying to adjust to the familiar surroundings of her room. She rushed to the window, calling out, "Colton." Breath held, she strained to hear any stirring in the darkness. Silence. She called out again. Nothing.

Minutes, then an hour ticked by with no sign of her protector. She resigned that she would have to wait until morning to tell him.

Purposely leaving the window open, Stevie curled into bed, her thoughts on Colton. She envisioned the tall muscular body, the heave of his broad chest as he breathed, the raven hair and the way it blew in the wind the first time he entered her sight. Taking in deep breaths, she cleared mind and whispered his name. Warmth spread over her body. Although completely relaxed, every nerve tingled. Her lips did not move, but she called to him, nevertheless.

Rustling sounds from the window stirred her from the bed. She peered out. No fear. Only hope. Colton's beautiful face appeared, smiling at her.

"You called, my Guardian?"

Stevie opened the screen to allow him access. He moved to sit on the bed beside her.

"Wow…that was simply amazing. I wasn't sure you would hear."

The corners of his mouth turned up. "Of course. I can hear the call of your heart far better than your words." He reached for her hand, kissing it softly. "Now. Why did you summon me, my Shylae?"

"I had a vision."

"Of the Orteh?" His voice was tinged with excitement.

"No…that's what I was trying to do, but something else happened." Stevie described the vision. He listened intently, his eyes never leaving hers.

"I heard your name—a lot—and the word Orteh, but I couldn't make out what else they were saying."

"If it was indeed the Rebels, that does not cause me surprise."

"Oh, and at the end of leader's speech, the people started shouting the same words, over and over. It sounded something like, Orteh Hi Lay."

"Orteh Highlae?"

"Yes, that was it. What does that mean?"

"It means Orb of Light."

"Oh. I thought it might have something to do with Tecton, but without knowing the language, I couldn't be sure."

"Perhaps, perhaps not. It is possible the phrase is a form of salute." Colton paused thoughtfully.

"Why didn't they see me?"

"They are not trained to see a walking spirit. Though in a vision state you are able to feel, smell, hear, and often touch your surroundings, it would take another trained in the ways of a seer to detect your presence."

"Cool, but I thought for a sec he, the leader, actually saw me."

"If he did so, he may have been a Mage. Yet a Mage would not have such a following as the Rebellion." He paused, his eyes brightening as if threatening to shine. "Describe this man to me."

"He was about your size, long brown hair, gold eyes. Now, don't laugh...I think he had pointy ears and some kinda tattoo on the side of his face and down his neck."

"Torren," Colton exclaimed, jumping to his feet. "How can it be? It has to be. A confirmation that he lives?" The tenor of his voice frightened Stevie.

"Torren?" asked Stevie. "You mentioned him. But I thought you said he was the former leader of the Rebellion."

Colton stopped pacing to face her. "We believed him to have been slain by his own men."

"He didn't look like a Djen. More like the guys Mom said attacked her."

Offhandedly, he said, "Torren is an Androne Elf. The race is similar to the Djen but for their eyes and skin, which are of a golden hue, and their pointed ears."

"What makes you think that this...this elf is Torren?"

Returning to her side, he answered, "Torren was...is a powerful, charismatic, and driven Androne. It would take his influence to keep the Rebellion searching for a Guardian child that no one believed survived."

"So...if he had died, I would have been safe?" Stevie shivered, appalled that she found the man in her vision attractive.

"I believe that to be true. Torren is cunning and dangerous. Power has twisted the man I once called brother, into my greatest enemy." Colton gazed out the window, silent. After several moments, he looked again at Stevie. "I am pleased that you saw fit to beckon me. I must convey all that you have spoken to Tyré's Mage, immediately." He rose. "I must leave you to rest. We have a long journey on the morrow."

Stevie grasped Colton's extended hands and allowed him to pull her close. The top of her head barely brushed his chin, and she lifted her chin to meet his lips. He moved instead to kiss her forehead.

"I shall miss you tonight, my Shylae." He gazed into her eyes— and her soul. "My hope is that you dream of me, as I do of you. Until the morrow." Then he was gone.

A stream of morning light found its way through the blinds. Stevie waved her hand in front of her face to brush away the intrusion. Through her haze, the realization dawned that there were items left to pack—but first, a hot shower.

She returned to the bedroom, hair in a towel and body cocooned in her comfy robe. Colton's face in the window startled her, and even more so the fact he was drenched. *That's Colorado weather for you. At least it didn't go from morning sunshine to a blizzard.*

"Oh, I see you got a shower, too. The sun was shining when I woke up." Stevie laughed, opening the window wide. Unwrapping her hair, she handed him the damp towel. Even soaked to the skin, he retained the air of a Warrior rather than that of a drowned rat.

"Let me get you another one…you're getting everything wet."
She hurried to the bathroom, returning with a handful of towels, and
tossed them at Colton. Expressing his gratitude, he dried his hair
and situated himself on the floor.

"Thank you, Shylae. Did you have any more visions last night?"

"No. Just that one." She stood facing the mirror on her dresser
so she could watch him in the reflection.

"I still need to pack some things." She replaced combing her
hair with gathering clothes from the closet. An armload of shirts and
jeans were deposited in the bag propped open on her bed.

Colton, still sitting on the floor, commented, "Are you certain
you have packed a sufficient amount of clothing? Perhaps you
would like me to find you a secondary pack."

"Oh…you're so funny. I'm sure your big sense of humor will be
able to carry my bag."

Grinning, Colton rose and approached her, arms outstretched.

"Don't come near me…you'll get me all wet!" He grabbed
Stevie around the waist, picked her up, and threw her on the bed.
The two of them were laughing and Colton shook his hair over her,
showering her with fine droplets. She wriggled out from under him
and managed to get a grip on one of her pillows, which she swung
and connected with Colton's shoulder. The tussle ended at the sound
of Jack's voice floating up from downstairs.

"You're saved." Stevie laughed, holding her weapon in mock
menace.

"And not a moment too soon, my Guardian. I truly feared for
my life."

Stevie wrapped her arms around his neck, cheeks aching from
laughter. "Did you need a hot shower and some dry clothes?"

"Shower? What is this thing that you speak of?" Colton said,
eyes twinkling mischievously.

Stevie wrinkled her nose, playing along. "What do you do to get
clean, wash in a river or something?"

"When I am able. Or I simply roll about in the dirt like your
Tonka."

"Geez, no wonder you smell so earthy."

"This is an unpleasant thing to you?"

"Not at all." She met his kiss halfway. As his mouth covered hers, an intense connection bonded her heart to his.

With a gasp, Stevie pulled away. "We have to go."

She rushed to the bathroom to dry her hair and throw on a little mascara while Colton closed up her bag—making exaggerated groaning noises. She giggled. *My life has changed so dramatically in the last few weeks, but I can't imagine it any other way now.* She felt alive, full of energy and love.

Colton met her at the doorway of her room. "I must ask before we depart. I need to be certain that you harbor no misgivings over leaving…with me?"

"I've never been more sure of anything in my life. Besides, we're only going to the cabin."

"For now." Colton's eyes shone out for a moment. The bag dropped from his grip and he encircled her in his arms once again: the two spun around from the force of the embrace.

"The adventure begins," said Stevie as she took him by the hand and led him down the hall.

Jack stood by the front door, talking with Jan. The conversation ceased when Stevie and Colton stopped at the landing.

"He came in through the window," Stevie said in response to the shocked expression on her mom's face and the dark look from Jack.

Colton remained silent and Stevie wondered if he felt embarrassed or was just being his stoic self. She moved past her mother to hug Jack before ushering him in. "I smell bacon. Thanks, Mom. Breakfast, anyone?"

Jack returned Stevie's hug one-armed, all the while glaring at Colton. He shrugged off Stevie's attempt to slip her arm through his and headed into the kitchen. A knock at the door disrupted the advance. All heads turned to find Alyssa standing on the doorstep, bag in hand, head downcast, feet shuffling.

Stevie ran to her friend and enveloped her in a bear hug. "Are you coming with us?"

Taking a step back, Alyssa pointed at her bag. "If you guys'll still have me. My boss said I can have the time off."

"Don't be a dork. Of course we'll have you. I am so jazzed." She hugged Alyssa again, and arm-in-arm they walked down the hall.

Jan must have continued on, because Stevie heard her voice from the kitchen. "Bacon and eggs are ready."

Breakfast was amazing, despite the silence between Colton and Jack. Afterward, Stevie found herself wandering through the family room while the men loaded the car and Alyssa helped Jan clean up.

Walking around the room, her fingertips lightly caressed familiar objects: over-stuffed chairs, pictures of family, the ornate antique cigarette lighter on the end table, the table itself, paintings of the Rocky Mountains and wildlife. Her hand stopped on the mantle. Her father looked out at her from the last photo they had taken as a family before he died. Since then, it had just been Stevie and her mom, with her dad watching over them. A wave of homesickness washed over her. *Geez, I haven't even left yet.*

Turning around, she saw her mother and Tonka in the doorway. Jan leaned against the frame, arms crossed, eyes teary, watching her. "You'll be back, silly," she said and walked forward to embrace Stevie.

"I know, Mom, but… Who knows what's going to happen after I'm trained?" She reached down to pet her loving companion, who circled around them.

"Whatever does, home will always be here for you."

Stevie returned her mother's embrace, but with a hard squeeze, as if holding onto a life preserver. "I love you so much." Before moving away, she whispered in her mom's ear, "Please take care of yourself. Watch your back and call me every day…okay?"

"I will. Now, come on…everyone's waiting for you."

Chapter 18

As they drove deeper into the mountains, Colton seemed uncharacteristically chatty. He questioned the description of the cabin, the lay of the surroundings, location and distance of the closest neighbors, and the like. Stevie explained that the cabin was bordered by National Forest land, with plenty of acreage and tree cover for privacy, and the closest home was a good mile or more away.

Rolling down the window, Stevie let the cool breeze flow through the car. The rain had ended shortly after they started the drive, leaving everything green, fresh, and sparkling. The air was filled with the scent of pine, wet bark, wild grasses, and flowers. Colton commented how much it smelled like home, prompting Stevie to ask questions of her own.

"Tell us about Djenrye. Is it so very different than here?"

Alyssa moved closer, forearm on the shoulder of the driver's seat. "Yeah, does everyone have superhero powers like you? Are they all Warriors, trained in the art of combat?"

Colton chuckled. "I am not a superhero, little one. And no, all Djen are not Warriors. The life of the Djen is basic and humble. There are families, just like here in Hundye. Most are farmers, craftsmen, hunters, tradesmen; but all the people work together for the good of the city. There is coin for trading outside of each city, but within the towns, barter is common."

"You said basic—how so?" Alyssa asked, leaning so closely her head and shoulders were parallel to Stevie's.

"We have a form of running water within the homes, piped in from the hot pools at higher elevations, but it is not as though one can turn on a metal handle and have water instantly. Every city has a center well, along with wells that have been dug throughout the area. Water is never farther than a few strides from any location."

"Umm, so, no indoor bathrooms?" Stevie asked hesitantly.

"We have rooms in which to bathe, but if I understand your question, there are pots in the sleeping chambers, as well as exterior rooms for privacy in expelling bodily waste."

"Ewww. Seriously?" Stevie wrinkled her nose at Alyssa, who giggled.

"Our machinery is based on living in balance with the earth. We use all that is given us—a deer is hunted for its meat and hide. Even the sinew and bones are used for sewing and tools. Nothing is wasted. It is why, even though the Djenrye culture is much older than Terra-hun, our numbers have not expanded beyond what the planet can provide, nor do we have filth in our air, water, or soil. The Gods do not permit this."

Stevie recalled scenes of Djenrye from her visions. Truly it was a beautiful place, but it sounded as though it could be a hard life as well.

During the exchange, Alyssa made repeated attempts to involve Jack in the conversation, with no success. He either flat out ignored her or shrugged off her efforts with the excuse of being tired. Stevie caught his green eyes in the rearview mirror. His initial excitement about the adventure seemed to have dampened.

"Jack, wassup? You've got this whole hound dog-face thing goin' on."

"Nothing… It's just early for me, that's all." He laid his head against the car door, refusing to say more.

Exchanging a glance with Alyssa, Stevie noticed that Colton remained quiet, declining to engage in the discussion.

They passed a sign reading Bailey in five miles. Stevie suggested they stop to get groceries. Once stocked they were up, she joked about how no one at the store gave Colton a second look.

"That's 'coz they're used to long-haired, feather- and leather-wearing hippies passing through this area," Alyssa said, in a matter-of-fact tone.

Everyone laughed except Colton, who looked confused.

The sun bounced off the trees and grasses, which glistened from the earlier rain. The mountains before them, capped white, were commanding, yet protective. Stevie pointed out a meadow, flush with wildflowers. The reds, purples, greens, and yellows created the look of an impressionist painting—all light and color.

"The evening's meal," Colton called out, pointing to a buck chewing on the spring grass, which ignored the passing cars.

"That's way more than one dinner, C." Stevie punched him jokingly in the arm.

As they crested Kenosha Pass, the landscape of South Park opened before them. Pine trees and canyon walls gave way to an expansive valley. Gentle rolling hills bordered the sixty-plus mile area, behind which fourteen-thousand-foot mountains rose to create a natural backdrop.

South Park had always held a special place in her heart. The freshness of the air, the crisp morning scents here filled her lungs, and the sights saturated her soul.

Arriving in Jefferson, they stopped to fill the tank before turning onto the dirt road that led to the cabin. They traveled another ten miles west off of Highway 285, while Colton expressed his approval of Stevie's choice for the vastness and isolation of the area.

The last few miles to the cabin jostled the party as they traveled over little more than a fire road. Thankful that her Jeep had four-wheel drive, Stevie nevertheless maneuvered the track with long-practiced ease. Pines closed in on all sides, forcing them off the eroded trail to avoid fallen limbs and foot-deep ruts caused by rivulets. The track would have stopped most cars, but created nothing more than a bouncing, rocking motion for the Jeep.

The home Stevie's family had built together came into view over the last rise. A solid, A-frame log cabin nestled into the mountainside, blending into its surroundings. The grassy area bordering the cabin was all that had been manicured. The adjacent growth remained wild and untouched.

"Oh...my..." Alyssa sighed, stepping out of the Jeep. "I'd almost forgotten how awesome this place is."

"An excellent selection. The elements are fully present here. It is as much like Djenrye as anything I have experienced in Terra-hun."

Stevie grabbed a sack of groceries and led the way up the rough-hewn stairs and onto the log deck. She fumbled with the keys while the rest of the party finished unloading the car. A rush of memories washed over her with the opening of the door. The smell of the leather, linseed oil, the musky scent of elk trophies, and an acidic undertone of cleaner greeted her. It brought to life recollections of long winters by the fire with her family. She would curl up in her dad's lap while he and Grandpa told her stories of the woods and the women would fix hot cocoa—with a dash of whiskey for Grandpa.

Her gaze lifted to the vaulted ceiling. The open walkway on the second landing butted against the curve of the stone chimney. A stone hearth dominated the wall at the far end of the recessed living room.

Voices caused Stevie to turn around. Alyssa stood at the entrance, eyes wide, mouth dropped open.

"OMG, Stevie. How come you haven't had us up here for years?"

Stevie moved past her to the kitchen saying, "We haven't used the cabin much since Dad died."

"I love how you call it a 'cabin'." Alyssa nearly snorted. "I'm guessing you think the Titanic was just a boat."

Chuckling, Stevie put away the groceries and nodded at the polished log stairs—wide enough for three or four people to walk side by side. "Colton, you and Jack can take the two bedrooms upstairs. You'll even get your own bathroom." Holding a bag of chips under her chin, her hands full of jars, she pointed with an elbow at the door underneath the upstairs walkway. "Alyssa, we can share the master bedroom."

Colton led the way up the stairs and stopped a few steps onto the open hallway that overlooked the great room. His hands rubbed the smooth wood of the railing and called down, "Feels like home."

"Yeah, but I'm guessing you don't have this in your Djen den," Jack said, sarcasm coloring his tone as he flipped on a light switch. The upstairs brightened. "Voilà, magic!"

"Jack, you have no idea the 'magic' Colton can do." Before either could respond, Stevie winked at her Warrior, grabbed Alyssa, and walked arm in arm to the door under the walkway.

A four-poster bed filled the center of the master bedroom. A smaller fireplace nestled in the far corner, complemented by a bay window that opened to the field behind the cabin.

"This is so awesome. It makes my little fifties home look kinda dinky."

"Seriously, Lissy, I love your house. Your parents fixed it up really cute, and it's comfy-homey."

Alyssa grudgingly agreed, but offered to be adopted by Stevie's grandparents. Stevie laughed and pushed her friend out the door, in the direction of the kitchen, to make sandwiches for the crew.

A bag of lemons, one item Stevie had insisted they buy, became a pitcher of her fabulous lemonade. She carried it out to the deck, Alyssa trailing behind with the sandwiches and chips. Between bites, Colton assured them that the combat training would begin tomorrow, but tonight would be reserved for working with Stevie. She knew what that meant…meditation.

After lunch, Stevie suggested they take a hike around the area to give Colton a feel of the land. Alyssa bounded alongside them and broke the silence by pointing out different flowers, types of conifers, birds, butterflies—pretty much everything. Her enthusiasm was contagious and soon Stevie joined her. Jack tromped silently behind them, while Colton took the lead. His eyes surveyed the land as he commented on how the area could be easily defended. Dusk had begun to settle in when the group returned to the A-frame.

Dinner consisted of burgers on the grill and corn on the cob. Afterward, they kindled a fire in the hearth to take the edge off the evening chill, played cards, and ate Ben and Jerry's Phish Food® ice cream, washed down with hot cocoa. As the evening wore on,

Jack lightened up a bit and nearly returned to his more normal joking self.

"Trump," Jack called victoriously, laying his last card—the ace of spades—over Stevie's queen of hearts. He leapt to his feet, arms lifted in triumph, jibing her, "Whose da man? I'm da man."

Alyssa laughed so hard she snorted, sending Stevie into uncontrolled giggles. The frivolity halted abruptly when Colton rose and announced, "I regret being the one to dampen this entertainment, but the night grows late and Stevie requires time to meditate."

"I know. I know," said Stevie, waving her hands in the air. "But I've tried for the last three nights and the only vision I had didn't show the Orb. Zero. *Nyet. Nada. Bupkis.*"

"There are ancient chants I intend to utilize. They were created by the Gods to connect one's mind and spirit to strengthen both and allow the doorway for visions to open. These are normally spoken in the Djen tongue, but the language is not as important as the meaning and intention behind the words."

As instructed by Colton, Alyssa and Jack sat at the dining room table, which was positioned between the kitchen and the living room. This gave them a view of Stevie, who had situated herself cross-legged directly in front of the fireplace. Before joining her, Colton obtained a pledge of complete silence from both Alyssa and Jack.

Stevie had already begun her focus on the flames. Colton paced behind her, chanting strange yet oddly familiar words, pausing between each one.

"Élan-Vitál—Tecton—Avira—Huana—Borvo."

The air came alive around Stevie. Her senses grew acute. Her skin tingled with the sensations of fire, water, soil, wind. The scents of pine, wild rose, burning hickory, and rushing water—carried in on a breeze—filled her nostrils. The sensations occurred simultaneously, yet she could distinguish each separately. Her hearing sharpened. Colton spoke in a whisper, but to her, the words rang loudly.

"Ty Avira wahaelae. Ty Huana uelahaelae. Ty Borvo aetsilae. Ty Tecton aedulelae. Ty Élan-Vitál aetenudoelae. Ty Greial tsa-amamaelae."

With each syllable, Stevie watched the blue area of the flame rise from the base and become a singular essence. It began to spin, slowly at first, and then picked up speed, as it had done in her basement—a ball of light that transformed into the Orb. It continued to spin as Stevie floated to her feet, arms outstretched. She spread them apart and found herself flying through clouds. The scene below expanded to reveal snowy mountains and cliffs. The view widened to include forests, lakes, and meadows. *Breathtaking.*

Stevie's gaze returned to the mountains. She spied a light twinkling far away, deep within the cover of trees and rock. She struggled to reach it, but the beauty of the landscape distracted her. Below, an imposing white bear drank from a crystal blue lake. On the far side of the mountain, wolves chased down a doe. The scene was as clear to her as if she ran with the pack.

The race excited her, even as her heart went out to the doe. She became lost in the moment, only to be drawn back by the twinkling light still far in the distance. Dark clouds closed in to obscure the glow until she lost sight of it completely. Her eyes desperately searched through the storm clouds for a glimpse or glimmer, but nothing. She cried out, "No!" Her temporal body was pulled back roughly. Lightning flashed through the gloom. A blink and she had returned to the floor of the cabin.

Her friends hovered over her, so close that they nearly knocked heads when she jumped up yelling, "I saw it! I saw it!"

Colton cupped her face, eyes alight with excitement. "Were you able to determine its location?"

"Not exactly—I saw it high up in some mountains. I tried to reach the light, but all of a sudden it got covered by dark clouds, and then I was back here."

Colton released his hold. Furrowed brows replaced his enthusiasm. Without a word, he walked outside to the front porch.

Stevie followed. "What is it? Colton?"

He paused at the wood rail, facing the trees as if deep in thought. She rubbed the back of his vest, running her palm over the smooth leather, patiently waiting. The stars twinkled above them and the leaves of the aspens danced and whispered. A fragrance of lilac floated on the wind and she wondered absently where it had come from.

Moments ticked by before Colton turned to face her. "I need the Din Ashyea." He hurried back into the cabin and retrieved it from its resting place on the chair farthest from the fireplace. With the book balanced in one hand, he flipped through the pages with his other.

Trailing in behind him, Stevie exchanged a glance with her friends, shrugging her shoulders slightly. They seemed to share her puzzlement as to what had suddenly come over Colton.

He stopped at a page, his lips moved as his fingers traced downward. He closed the book quietly and sat heavily in the chair, facing the fire as he spoke, "Shylae, you need to go back into the vision. I fear that the dark clouds are a warning from the Gods signifying the Rebellion's proximity to the Orteh."

"I tried, Colton, but…"

"I understand. Yet…" He opened the book again and pointed to the ancient script. "The Din Ashyea tells us that black clouds in a vision represent 'to cover' or 'to hide. The Rebels could well be on the edge of discerning our intentions, and when they do, they will locate and move the Orteh before we are able."

"But I can't just plop into a vision on a whim. It takes a lot out of me. I feel like I've just ran a marathon."

At this, he rose to face her. In a soft tone, he said, "My apologies, Shylae. With your quick mastery of your abilities, I had forgotten how new all of this is for you. Of course, you must rest tonight." He moved to take Stevie into his arms. "Tomorrow we will try again."

She looked at him, caught in his steely blue eyes.

"My purpose is to guide you, not injure you." The space between them disappeared as his mouth gently kissed her brow.

The following day, Colton attempted to teach them weaponry. Though truly in his element, his pupils were not. He thanked the Gods for the nimbleness of Shylae and Alyssa Brier. They had been trained in the art of gymnastics, which to him sounded much like the evasion skills taught to Djen youth. It developed body awareness and the eye-hand coordination needed for most of the combat training. Jack Snow, however, bordered on hopeless. Colton knew he would need to provide the most basic of instruction for the Hundye boy.

He faced the students, who stood before him in a line. "The weapons I will teach you to use are deadly, more so to you than your enemies if not wielded properly. I have carved and weighted wooden swords to be used during your lessons. The balance and heft is similar to steel. They may break an arm, but will not sever it. The arrows, unfortunately, cannot be altered for practice weapons, and the dagger work will be done with edged blades, as well."

His pause was met with stunned looks and silence. "For your safety and mine, we shall begin with the swords."

Colton divided the group into teams, Jack with Alyssa, and he with Shylae. "The first lesson is to become comfortable with the balance of your sword. It is an extension of your arm. Like this…" Colton held one of the carved swords by the hilt, blade flat, to create a straight line from his elbow to the tip of the wood. Slowly, he uncurled his grip until the entire sword balanced on the tip of his index finger. He winked at Shylae, and with a flick of his wrist, the weapon spun high into the air and caught deftly in his left hand.

"Now you," he said, flipping the sword over to present the hilt to Shylae.

She grinned slyly. Colton had already taught her this maneuver, and her smile told him that she would play along. Hardly a breath passed before she duplicated the motion with smooth precision.

Alyssa squealed and clapped her hands, jumping up and down. "Me next."

Shylae presented the sword to her friend as he had to her, but not with the same result. Alyssa managed the first part of holding the sword in front of her, but when she attempted to balance it on her finger, she swayed this way and that, feet crossing over each other and stumbling to keep hold. It reminded Colton of a Wood Elf who had imbibed too much fermented nectar.

"Excellent effort, little one." Colton laughed, retrieving the weapon to avoid being impaled. "Now you, young Warrior."

Jack grasped the hilt with his right hand and flicked his left hand up behind him, right foot forward, left back. "*En garde,*" he shouted in an accent Colton did not recognize.

Alyssa and Shylae giggled, but Colton did not share their amusement. "No, this is not a game, Jack Snow. Do you wish to learn to wield the sword or continue to play as a child?"

Jack put his head down. "Geez, I was just joshin'…"

"There is no 'Josh'. Only the weapon and the weapon master." Colton nodded to his students. "Now, raise your swords."

The remainder of the day consisted of various drills—how to properly attack without losing balance, high downward swings, short thrusts, low Achilles blows, and, of course, parrying and defensive blocks and strikes.

Shylae's quick study pleased Colton greatly, and he struggled not to show too much favor. Without direction, she developed a move of flipping out of the way of an attack and then coming up behind for the kill.

The little Hundye, Alyssa, showed greater promise at archery than sword fighting. Once Colton had taught her the basics, with barely a pause or breath Alyssa could sight her target, draw the bow, and consistently find the mark nineteen out of twenty times.

Jack, the lanky entertainer, was surprisingly adept with dagger throws. Shylae accredited this to his ability to toss wadded-up homework papers unerringly into the trash can. Although pleased that the students had different strengths that complemented one another, Colton nonetheless became frustrated with their playfulness and lack of serious study. The day's practice ended when Jack begged Colton to stand in front of a tree with an apple on his head. When Colton asked the reasoning, Jack said he wanted to impale the fruit with a dagger.

Alyssa enthusiastically volunteered to be the assistant—going so far as to grab a pinecone and attempt to balance it on her head. Shylae protested behind barely suppressed giggles.

In response, Colton abruptly snatched the pinecone from Alyssa, crushing it in his hand. His frustration boiled just below the surface. "I believe your humor is greater than your skill, Jack Snow. For the health of us all, we are finished for the day."

The days were filled with training and each night Stevie came closer to discovering the Orb's location, but the visions continued to end with the ominous dark clouds. Colton's comment of, "The location of the Orteh must be identified, and swiftly," had become his mantra following each meditation. *As if that's gonna help relax me.*

After narrowing down the type of landscape and the animals that she had seen in her visions, Jack concluded that it must be on the North American continent. "Sounds like Alaska," said Jack confidently.

"If we could pull up some pictures on your laptop…" suggested Stevie.

In response, Jack opened up the browser and began surfing the Internet.

Colton expressed frustration over using the machine. "Shylae has the ability to locate the Orteh without this picture box." He dismissively waved his hand.

"Computer. It's called a computer, Colton." Stevie said. "Let me try this. Maybe looking at the pics will help."

He reluctantly agreed, but chose to read the Din Ashyea rather than joining the teenagers.

At first they had trouble finding good pictures. Nothing looked familiar from the photos of Alaska that Jack was able to pull up. Alyssa suggested looking at British Columbia.

"My folks took me on a cruise up the coastline to Princess Royal Island. See if you can find pictures of that area."

"Seriously, Lissy. Stevie saw a white bear. That had to be polar bear."

"If you read something other than sci-fi/fantasy, you would know about the Spirit Bear." That got everyone's attention. Even Colton looked up from his book. "It is a variant of the black bear. They're only on this one island. A black bear will sometimes have a cub that is born white. They're called Kermode bears."

"That sounds familiar," commented Stevie.

They revised their search for images of the Spirit Bear and Princess Royal Island.

"That's it!" Stevie jumped up so fast her chair flew back and slammed against the wall. "Colton. Come look at this. This is It."

Colton approached, Din Ashyea held open, and squinted at the screen. "A likely place. But, Shylae, that is a large area. You will need to narrow the exact location or we risk losing time searching."

"I know. I know." Stevie refused to let his pragmatism dampen her enthusiasm.

"Do not despair, Shylae. I believe I have located a way to help guide you in the search."

Colton began to read a passage from his book, translating to English as he read. "Help from an eagle will guide the seer in his search."

"What does that mean, exactly?"

"The translation is difficult, but the meaning is that I may be able to join you in your vision." One hand holding the book, the other extended to Stevie, Colton continued. "Come. Sit with me. I will help you see."

Stevie rose and followed him down the two steps to the living room. He held her hands and together they sat on the floor, facing each other.

"I need silence for this to work. Alyssa, would you be so kind as to bring us a candle and the bundle of sage and sweet-grass we picked?"

Alyssa left the room briefly, returning with the requested items. She lit the candle and placed it between Stevie and Colton. Colton took the sage, lighting it with the flame, and then blew gently to extinguish the fire. He waved the smoky bundle between himself and Stevie before handing it back to Alyssa, and asked her to slowly circle them so that they would be enveloped by the haze and fragrance.

Jack sat back, closed the laptop, and watched intently. The smoky-sweet aroma of sage caused Stevie to become lightheaded. She looked at Colton, who nodded back.

"I will be your guide on this journey. You will recognize me as the eagle at your side. The eagle is a creature of keen sight and, as such, may assist you to stay the course. We begin."

Colton's voice took on a melodic quality as he began to chant. This time, he spoke in English. "The air whispers. The water laughs. The fire cackles. The earth gasps. The spirit calls. The Guardian answers."

He repeated the words over and over until, to Stevie's ear, they became one flowing phrase. She dropped her gaze to the candle and began the rhythmic breathing. Stevie called forth Tecton in her mind. Lifting her hands, this time keeping her hold on Colton, she entered the vision.

She found herself over the same valley. Mountains rose on either side of the river below. She moved her head to the right. At her side flew the largest Golden eagle imaginable—a Golden eagle with vivid blue eyes. *Colton.*

The familiar silvery light defining the Orteh twinkled in the distance. Stevie and her guide flew toward it, but as they drew closer, dark clouds began to settle in. Colton's voice spoke in her head. He recited the chant of meditation, fluctuating between English and Djenrye. The clouds thinned as though the words had the power to lift the darkness. The sun beamed on the mountainside.

The reflection of the light caused the sparkle to intensify. Stevie touched the edge of the eagle's wing, and he led her downward to a cascading waterfall surrounded by a forest of Sitka spruce. As their feet touched the ground, the eagle rose to the height of a man and, with a great beat of his wings, transformed into Colton.

Moss hung from the trees and covered the rocks and forest floor. It felt primordial. A palpable scent of mold and humus rose around them, along with the thunderous sound of rushing water. A waterfall rose a good hundred feet above them. It ended, pounding into a crystal blue pool.

Colton moved to Stevie's side. Fingers entwined, as one, they dove into the icy lake. Emerging on the other side of the cascade, Stevie shivered and her teeth chattered as they entered a hidden cavern behind the wall of water.

"Remember, Shylae. This is only a vision. You may see, feel, taste, and smell, but it is with your spirit body, not your physical one. Without leaving this plane, reach your mind back to connect with your material reality."

Stevie clasped Colton's hand and tentatively sought out the cabin in her mind. The warmth blanketed her and when she looked down at her spirit self, she discovered that she was no longer wet or cold.

Colton pointed to a dim light emerging from a dark passageway ahead of them. Following the glow, they moved through the gloom downward. A large cavern opened before them. At its center, a cave pool glimmered. On the far side, stood an urn perched atop a rock pedestal. The light emanated from it. Stevie looked at Colton's face, illuminated by the silver radiance. He nodded and together they flew across the pool to the vessel. She released his hand to remove the lid. The brilliance blinded her for a moment, but she did not look away. Her eyes watered. She gazed deeper into the urn.

The light drew itself in and rose in the form of a globe above the pedestal. It hovered in the air before them and flattened out into the shape of a land mass.

"Look. It's showing us a map to the Orb." Stevie traced a glowing line from the coast on the left side, across several waterways and mountain passes to a spot in the middle of an island. There were no words on the map, but she recognized the land masses and thought the center one might be Princess Royal Island. The light began to dim and she moved back, startled. It faded completely, but in its place a piece of parchment floated downward. Stevie caught it in her hand.

A faint whisper echoed through the cavern. *Hurry!*

Stevie blinked and the cabin came into focus. Colton pulled her to her feet. Her head swam. All strength drained from her limbs. But the exhilaration of her success dumped enough adrenaline into her system to have her jumping up and down.

"What happened? What did you see? Why were your eyes shining?" Alyssa and Jack's questions tumbled over each other and Stevie couldn't tell who asked what.

Stevie stopped abruptly and released her grip on Colton. She held up her hand. There, squeezed tight in her fist, a parchment map.

"What the hell?" Jack took the paper, and opened it. "It's a map."

The last of her energy released, Stevie slumped to the floor. Shaking her head to clear it, she said, "I think I brought that out of my vision." Her voice quavered as she spoke to Colton. "Is that even possible?"

"It is unheard of, but with you Shylae, I am coming to believe little is impossible."

Hovering over Jack's shoulder, Alyssa chatted excitedly about a vision relic made solid. Colton situated himself next to Stevie, drawing her into an embrace. She rested her head on his chest, overcome from the exhaustion of controlling the intense vision.

"It is time for you to rest, my Shylae."

She nodded, trying hard to keep her eyelids from closing. "Water, please," she croaked, surprised at the huskiness of her voice.

The chatter stopped abruptly and Alyssa ran to the kitchen. Jack headed to the table instead of the sink.

"I'm gonna research this." He waved the map in the air. "The landmarks should make it easy to find where this is."

Stevie heard Alyssa opening and closing cabinets, the sound of water running, but it all seemed far away. She yawned and Colton lifted her into his arms, cradled her like a baby, and carried her to the bedroom.

"You have done well, my Guardian. Now it is time for you to sleep to regain your strength. After your rest, tomorrow we need to speak in private."

Stevie could muster little more than a whisper. "About what, Colton?"

"Nothing you should worry about for the moment. Sleep, then talk."

Chapter 19

The sweet smell of maple sausage permeated Stevie's dream to wake her. Sore, but rested, she followed the aroma to the back deck.

"Hey sleepyhead," Alyssa called out cheerfully. "Your timing is perfect."

"Good. I could eat a horse."

"Just sausage and eggs on the menu this morning." Jack chuckled.

"You look well." Colton moved to kiss her on the forehead then guided her to a seat. Alyssa dished up food for everyone and Jack returned with a carton of orange juice, glasses balanced precariously in his hand.

Once the group began eating, Alyssa started in with questions. "That was awesome—the whole chanting, pulling maps out of thin air. Totally magician." She took a quick bite and asked Colton directly, "Was that air whispers chant thing the same as the last time, only in English?"

"You have a good ear, little one. Yes, I translated the words to the Hundye tongue. The words are meant to channel the power of *Ty Asha Vitál*, the Gods, and the Ortehlae. The Gods speak all languages, not just Djen."

"I think I may have narrowed down what place your map is showing," Jack said, his voice an octave higher with excitement. "It looks like the place Alyssa mentioned—you know, the Princess Royal Island in BC."

"Cool. White bears, dude." Stevie shaped her hands into claws. "You gotta show me after breakfast."

The meal passed quickly. Jack was excited to show off the aerial photos he had discovered. Alyssa begged off to clean up, saying that she'd already seen it while Stevie was sleeping.

Jack stood behind Stevie, pointing out the similarity of the photos to the land masses on her map.

"And here," he said, tracing the screen. "This could be used as a trail, but we'll need to pick up some topographic maps to get a better idea of the terrain we'll be crossing."

"Sounds good, Jack. See what you can find online." Stevie high-fived him as she rose. Colton followed Stevie into the cabin, touching her arm and gesturing her to follow him. They entered the master bedroom.

"What, Colton? Is there something wrong?"

He looked frustrated. "I understand your excitement, but there are details we need to discuss about the journey. Will you accompany me on a walk?"

She shrugged her shoulders and said, "Okay…let's go walk-talk then."

As they exited by the front door, Colton wrapped his arm around Stevie's shoulder, pulling her in close. They walked in silence until the cabin passed from sight.

"It's so beautiful out here. Are you feeling romantic?" Stevie nudged Colton playfully in the bicep.

He halted with brows furrowed and shook his head. "I am struggling with the correct words to say to you what I must." He hesitated. "It is not wise for Jack Snow or Alyssa Brier to accompany us on this journey." He faced her fully, his eyes were penetrating.

"Maybe it's because we've had a vision journey together. Maybe 'coz I am starting to read you. But I knew that was what you were going to say." She sighed and kicked at the soft ground with the toe of her boot. "Thing is… I don't know how to tell them. They're gonna be über-disappointed."

"Perhaps I should be the one to explain to your friends. In this manner, they will not be angered with you, only me. On the morrow? After the evening meal?"

By the time they returned to the cabin, Jack and Alyssa had changed into sweats and t-shirts. The day's training consisted of more of the same, with Colton espousing the benefits of muscle memory.

That night, dinner was a quiet and quick affair. Her friends were exhausted and headed to bed without the regular evening card game.

Colton and Stevie cuddled up on the couch, their glasses of wine—pilfered from her grandfather's liquor cabinet—perched on the side table. They watched the fire in silence, relishing the time alone. He kissed her gently on the shoulder. She looked up in response to his husky voice.

"These are the most difficult times for me. I want for nothing more than to hold you in my arms and express my love for you fully."

Stevie moved to his lap, knees on either side of his hips, his face slightly below hers. She leaned forward. Their mouths met. The sensation of flying surged through Stevie's body. Colton laid her down on the couch and slid in next to her. Bodies moving in synchronicity, Colton kissed her neck, his lips descended slowly past her shoulders. They breathed in harmony, but Stevie's mind spun. His fingertips lightly brushed the low edge of her neckline and his mouth moved to her décolletage. She fumbled with the buttons on her blouse, but was stopped with a touch. Undeterred, she wrapped her legs around his and their mouths met again; tongues intertwined, drowning in elation. As they came up for air, Colton's eyes captured hers. She drank in the love she saw there.

"My desire for you is overwhelming. Yet, I know that I cannot—must not—until our task is complete." His eyes twinkled a brilliant blue.

Stevie couldn't help but smile. "I'm gonna regret later what I'm about to say, because I feel the same." She took a deep breath. "I agree. This isn't the right time."

"I love you, Shylae. I have always loved you. My heart, my body, my soul…they belong to you."

"I love you, too, Colton. I can't imagine not having you in my life."

Stevie knew they should separate for the night. She caressed his cheek and found his mouth once more. Before they became lost in each other again, she untangled herself and scouted away to an arm's length. "I should head to bed. I wish that we didn't have to go through all this Rebel stuff. I would love for us to just be together."

It took all of Stevie's willpower to rise from the couch. Colton walked with her to the bedroom door and before she could enter, blanketed her in his arms once again. She laid her head against his chest, breathing him in, not wanting to let go. Though now was not the time, the beating of her heart increased, keeping time with her impatience. She prayed that the right moment would arise soon.

"Good night. May the Goddess of Tranquility watch over your slumber." Colton took a step back, reached for her hand, and gently kissed her palm. "Have no worries, my love, our time shall come, but not this day. When the Orteh is safely returned and the Rebels have been defeated, then we shall profess our love before the Gods. You shall become my mate, my wife. We will finally be as one, forever."

Saturday morning, Colton announced he intended to work solely with Stevie on her powers. During the walk the day before, Colton had said that it was time for her to become comfortable with her abilities. With only a few days left to prepare for the journey, Stevie needed all the time they could afford to grasp what it meant to be Djen. Her abilities needed to become a natural extension of herself.

The agenda was to first practice the basics—the experience of enhanced senses—and then move on to jumping from tree to tree and to the ground running. Colton led Stevie to a quiet place, out of sight and sound of the cabin and the distraction of her friends' training. At the crest of a hill, they climbed onto an outcrop overlooking the valley.

"Calm your mind," Colton whispered, moving behind her. "Allow yourself to completely relax and become one with the nature that surrounds you."

Stevie sat facing the panorama, breathing as he had taught her. She slipped into a meditative state. The breeze flowed over and

through her. The smell of sage, sweet grass, catmint, and larkspur—
a cacophony of scents that were distinct, but at the same time
blended together to create a unique aroma. She opened her eyes. A
bird soared on an updraft, several hundred feet above. Stevie could
literally focus on the bird. Every detail of the Black Kite stood out
as if her eyes were telescopic lenses.

She took in a deep cleansing breath, blew it out slowly, evenly,
and her other senses kicked in—with a vengeance. Laughter floated
off the mountain across from them. A vacationer's dog barked,
branches snapped as elk crashed through the trees, and water
babbled in a brook that had to be at least a hundred yards away. All
these sounds were caught and enhanced by her Djen abilities. The
Black Kite above squawked, the pitch sharp, clear, and loud as if
right next to her.

"This is amazing," Stevie said, breathlessly. "I can't believe
how intense everything is. I can see and hear things miles away, and
the smells—OMG—they are over the top."

Colton smiled, holding out his hand. "Now it is time to work on
running and flying through the trees."

She allowed him to guide her down the rocky slope to the open
field below.

"You will run as fast as you are able—with me at your side—to
the opposite end of this open space. Once there, leap into the trees.
Do not stop, do not hesitate, but continue to go from tree to tree
until you hear me call out to cease. The goal is for the transitions—
from ground to tree, from branch to branch—to be as one
continuous movement." He winked at her. "Shall we begin?"

Filling her lungs and blowing out, she loosened her limbs,
shaking out the tension in her hands, and balanced her weight
between her feet. "Ready."

The meadow rushed by in a blur of color. Stevie imagined
herself a cougar or an elk. The open expanse had to be as long as
several football fields, but she crossed it in seconds. With the tree
line in view, she leapt into the air. Her toes touched the limb of the
nearest tree, and without hesitation, she jumped into the next, and

then the next. Colton had somehow managed to gain on her and led her through the cottonwoods and aspens until they arrived at a grove of smaller pines. He called a halt.

"We cannot jump into those." He pointed at the trees. "See? The limbs are too short and fragile for us. And the pine needles would hurt, especially if the branches broke or bent enough to plunge us to the ground." He laughed. "We will return to our starting point. Do you recall the path?" Stevie nodded and Colton continued, "Once there, stop."

Stevie did as instructed. This time she beat him. At the meadow, she dropped face forward in the grass to catch her breath. In exhilaration, she rolled onto her back, threw her hands up to the sky, and laughed.

When Colton arrived, she was making grass angels and laughing with the uninhibited joy of a child.

He sat beside her. "Very impressive, Shylae. You have proven receptive to your inherent Djen powers. You are ready to move on to the more difficult skills, ones that we have not discussed—cloaking and invisibility."

"Cool." But Stevie did not move. She relished the feel of the grass on her bare arms and legs and thanked the Gods for the foresight to wear shorts instead of sweats.

Colton pulled her to her feet. "First, let us return to the cabin. You will need hydration after your exertion."

Jack and Alyssa were sunning themselves on the deck, a glass of lemonade within arms' reach, the pitcher weeping with condensation on a small table by the door.

"I see you are taking your training seriously," Colton said, but his tone was light.

Ignoring the comment, Alyssa sat up in the Adirondack chair. "Wow, where have you guys been? I was getting worried."

"No need. Colton was helping me to become one with my abilities as a Djen. You should have seen me, Lissy. It was über-amazing."

"What do you mean, become one?" asked Jack. "Totally Buddha-dude? I thought your powers were automatic?"

"In a sense," Colton said. "But Shylae was raised Hundye. She needs to awaken her abilities. How is it you would say—get in touch—with her newly discovered gifts by accepting and understanding them. In this way, they become an unconscious part of her—like breathing or walking—not something she needs to grasp or think about. Next, she will learn how to cloak and become invisible to the Hundye."

"That's gonna be an awesome party trick." Alyssa giggled.

"So I totally get that this training is 'all about Stevie' but I really hoped you'd be back to do more weapons training," whined Jack. "There's only so much Lissy and I can accomplish on our own."

"You are correct, this is about Shylae. She is the priority in the training and must first master her skills before we are able to focus on you and Alyssa."

Alyssa held up her hands. "Don't drag me into this little pissing contest. I'm happy to sit here and enjoy the sunshine."

Colton turned to Stevie. "Once you are finished and ready."

She nodded, gulped the last of her drink, and jumped to her feet. "I'm ready when you are."

They walked to the forest line. He positioned her next to a tall blue spruce. "The first step is to try to feel your connection to this tree."

"What? How am I supposed to do that?"

"Picture your body with the same limbs, the same bark. Look for the details in your mind. The color of the needles, the width of the trunk. See yourself as part of the tree."

Stevie tried to concentrate, but her mind kept seeing her kindergarten teacher saying, "you are the tree…be the tree" while she stood on one leg in front of the class. *Concentrate—yeah, I just feel silly.*

After twenty minutes or so, Colton's patience seemed to be wearing thin. "Shylae, you need to become one with your immediate surroundings. Once it happens and the mental, physical, and emotional draw becomes familiar, you will be able to do it with little effort thereafter. For now, in order to reach that state, you need to concentrate."

Stevie sighed and continued to picture the tree behind her, willing herself not to think of her crazy teacher.

"I don't get it, Colton. This is hard. Did you have to learn this way, too?"

"Yes, we all do. This is not something we are able to accomplish from birth. It is an ability that must be honed and comprehended before it may be manifested."

"I getcha, but…" said Stevie.

Colton's answer was silence.

She continued to practice until her stomach grumbled and her taskmaster finally agreed to break for lunch.

Returning to the deck, they found Jack pointing a wooden sword at Alyssa, asking if she wanted to duel. Alyssa grabbed a training blade and launched herself at Jack, who countered and the two engaged in play fighting to the amusement of Colton and Stevie. Stevie laughed at the two and clapped.

"Excellent footwork," Colton called to the fighters. "Perhaps the coordination of your eyes and hands will improve with practice at providing a meal."

The show helped to ease Stevie's sadness at the thought of telling her friends they would not be coming with Colton and her. They had, after all, willingly come to the cabin to learn how to fight the Rebels. Jack would really be upset, but Stevie hoped Lissy would take it better. She had shown a strength Stevie never expected.

Deciding to enjoy the moment and not dwell on the future, she called to her friends, "Let's get lunch. How 'bout it, guys?"

Jack bowed low to Stevie. "Here, here or there, there. Either way, let's eat."

After a light meal of tuna and fruit, Colton agreed to return to training all of them. Alyssa picked up the bow—she had started calling it her bow—and headed to the border of the woods for target practice.

Jack bounded about, begging to learn more about using the sword. Colton acquiesced and worked with him and Stevie on a variety of strokes, blocks, and thrusts. The Djen expressed an appreciation of Stevie's ability to jump and flip out of the way of an impending attack. She used boulders, tree stumps, fallen logs— anything available—to leap onto and then flip behind her assailant.

Jack, on the other hand, had difficulty blocking and dodging Colton's blows. After several times of being knocked off his feet and suffering mock stab wounds, Jack gave up.

"I'll be over here with Alyssa if ya need me." He jerked his head in the direction of the trees before grabbing a handful of throwing knives. Stevie suppressed a laugh as he wandered off, rubbing his backside.

The training continued until the sun began to set. Tired and grateful, Stevie followed her friends onto the deck.

Alyssa plopped into the nearest chair. "Stevie, I'm thinking about taking a break tomorrow. Ya wanna go into Buena Vista and go shopping?"

"Oh, that sounds great. I'd love to take a break. We've been doing this training nonstop for a week now." She joined her friend. "What do you think, Master?"

Colton ignored the jibe, turning his focus to the trees and then back to Stevie. "I believe it best for you to continue to practice cloaking tomorrow, but you are the Guardian and I do as you wish." He picked up the Din Ashyea. "Tonight, we work on the language of the Djen. We have but a few more sunrises until our return to Golden."

"Weapons training, vision mastery, and now you want me to learn a new language?"

"It is necessary for you to understand the language of your heritage. This knowledge will aid you in understanding what is spoken by the Rebels in your visions."

Nodding her head in agreement, Stevie couldn't help but worry that at some point, she would no longer live up to Colton's expectations. *I couldn't bear for him to be disappointed in me. But, really, I'm only human.*

Chapter 20

Jack and Alyssa offered to prepare dinner. Stevie sat at the dining room table with Colton. He worked with her on several Djen words and phrases. Grateful that he did not push her, she realized she still had a lot to learn. Her mind threatened to overload.

"*Ty Greial ai* Djenrye," Colton said. "That means the Guardian of Djenrye."

The new words perplexed her. She repeated to the best of her ability. "Tie grey owl aye Djenrye."

Colton had her repeat the phrase over and over until her accent and intonations perfectly imitated his.

"Ty Greial ai Highlae…"

"That one's easier," exclaimed Stevie. "I already knew highlae." She smiled with confidence. "Your language rolls over my tongue. It's a song as much as a sentence."

"Yes, it flows softer than your Hundye English." They continued working on several other phrases before being interrupted by Jack's call to eat.

After dinner, Stevie asked Jack and Alyssa if they could talk. Jack looked concerned and Stevie wondered if he had an idea of what was coming, but Alyssa seemed oblivious.

Colton began, "Shylae and I have been in discussions about the journey to find the Orteh."

Jack sat stone-faced, but his legs bounced up and down nervously.

"Shylae, Marise, and I have an advantage as Djen, which you two do not possess. After much thought, I have determined it is far too dangerous for Hundye to accompany us. To put the two of you in harm's way goes against my nature—against everything I believe."

Jack burst from his chair, his finger pointing accusingly at Stevie and Colton. "I knew you would leave us behind," Jack growled. "This was a just waste of time. I should have stayed in Golden."

Stevie moved toward Jack, hoping to calm him. "You being here was not a waste of time. You've both helped and have learned some really important fighting skills. You never know when you might need them."

"What good is that going to do without you?" cried Alyssa.

"Did you forget why we're doing all this?" Stevie asked in exasperation. "The Rebellion could still cause problems back home and Colton and I won't be there to help."

Jack stormed off. The door slammed behind him.

Alyssa sat staring at her hands for several minutes before speaking. "I do understand why we shouldn't go." She looked at Stevie, tears threatening to spill over. "I mean, we don't have powers and this training is new to both of us…"

"That's why it would be too dangerous for you. Besides, you have plans for college."

"I know…it's just… I'll miss you, that's all." Alyssa rushed to Stevie. The girls hugged each other, giving in to tears.

"I get it. You know I do. But Jack's going to need convincing," Alyssa cautioned.

Stevie nodded to her friend. "You're right. I gotta go find Jack."

As she passed Colton, he grabbed her arm. "Shylae, it would be wise to leave Jack be for a while…"

"Colton, let go. He's my friend."

"This much is clear, Shylae, but Jack is a young man…frustrated and wanting more than anything to take my role as your protector. Telling him that he will be left behind is an affront to his manhood."

"No duh, but he's still my friend. He feels dissed. I know how to get him to chill." Stevie turned and ran out the front door, taking the steps two at a time, shouting Jack's name.

After an hour searching through the dark, Stevie gave up, downhearted. Colton's voice drew her back to the cabin.

"What is it?" She panted, mounting the stairs. "Did you find Jack?"

"He returned a few moments ahead of you. He has retreated upstairs. Before you speak with him, there is a woman on the telephone. She professes to be a friend of your mother's."

Bewildered, Stevie hurried to the kitchen and retrieved her cell phone from the counter.

"Hi, Stevie…this is Kate.

"Yeah, Kate, what's up?" *Why is she calling me?* "Is there something wrong?"

"I'm afraid so, sweetie. I'm calling to let you know that your mom is in the hospital."

"Oh my God. Is she okay?" Her heart began to race.

"She's going to be fine. They have her condition listed as serious, but improving."

Struggling to keep her voice calm, Stevie asked, "What happened?"

"All I know is she was attacked at your house by some men. Two police officers were killed. The police managed to shoot one guy—he's dead—the son of a bitch." Kate spit out the words. "But the others got away."

"Tell Mom I'm on my way."

Stevie recalled her mom mentioning at some point Kate being listed on her cell phone as the ICE (In Case of Emergency) contact. *That means Mom was coherent enough to tell Kate to call me.*

They left everything behind but the clothes they were wearing and the weaponry bag. Jack drove the Jeep down the hill. He had apparently gotten over his anger long enough to take the wheel.

Stevie, too distraught to drive, sat in the backseat, Colton's arm around her shoulder, as she repeatedly tried to call the hospital. "Damn it! I can't get a signal."

"Chill, girl." Alyssa reached around from the front seat, patting Stevie's knee. "We'll get there soon. Jack's driving at light speed."

The kindness of her friend did little to alleviate Stevie's fear. Dialing the phone again—this time, Kate's number—she still could not get a dial tone. Colton rubbed her back, but his touch did not relax her.

"How long to St. Anthony's?" Stevie looked out the window, trying to get her bearings, but with no street lights and her sense of time warped by panic, it was useless. Out of nowhere, a thought struck her. "Colton—you can't go to the hospital dressed like that." She leaned forward over the middle console. "Jack, do you have anything that'll fit Colton?"

"Seriously? We left everything at your grandpa's place." He paused for a moment before adding, "I think some of Dad's clothes might fit him. We'll stop by my house first."

It took two hours by the clock, a lifetime by Stevie's figuring, to reach Golden. Jack managed to find a pair of jeans and a sweatshirt that fit Colton, albeit tightly.

By the time the men returned to the car, Stevie had reached Kate on the phone. "Kate has Tonka, and I have Mom's room number. Let's go."

Jack dropped Stevie, Colton, and Alyssa off at the front door and then left to park. After a quick stop at the directory, they ran up the stairs to the second floor in search of the ICU. The desk nurse looked at Stevie's ID before telling her that Jan had been upgraded to stable.

"Family only," the woman in green scrubs said to Alyssa and Colton, frown forming on her face.

"This is my sister and my fiancé," Stevie replied, hurriedly dragging her surprised allies down the hall before Nurse Bureaucracy could stop them.

The handle clicked when Stevie cracked the door open to peer in. Jan appeared to be asleep, hooked up to monitors and an IV. Stevie bit her lip in an attempt to keep from crying out. Jan had a new black eye and cuts covered her face and arms. Her recently healed mouth was split open again and her hair was hidden by a wrapped bandage. Jan's left leg hovered above the bed, enclosed in a cast from ankle to thigh. Stevie moved closer. That's when she saw the stitches in her mother's neck.

"Oh my God," cried Stevie. She turned into Colton's arms. He held her close as they moved into the room. Jack had somehow slipped in behind them, unnoticed until he moved next to her, holding Alyssa's hand.

Jan stirred and opened one eye. She seemed to have a hard time focusing. "Stevie..." she whispered, her hand fluttered up in an attempt to wave. Stevie wanted desperately to hug her mom, but there was too much equipment to maneuver any closer. A wan smile flickered on the corner of Jan's mouth, followed by a grimace.

"Mom, I am so sorry," cried Stevie.

"No, baby." Jan sounded as though she had a mouth full of marbles. "It was my fault..."

"What? No, Mom. How is it your fault?"

"I...should have come with you," mumbled Jan.

"Jan Barrett." Colton moved closer to the bed. "Gracious and beautiful mother of the Guardian, the fault is mine. I should never have left you."

Jack and Alyssa positioned themselves by the window. The ledge was just deep enough to act as a pseudo seat. Colton maneuvered the one chair in the room—a narrow brown vinyl recliner—as close as he could to the bedside. He stood next to Stevie as she sat, holding her mom's hand.

A morphine pump to the right of the bed made it clear that Jan would not be up to answering questions tonight. She faded in and out of consciousness. In a whispered voice, Stevie promised she'd be back first thing in the morning.

The door closed quietly behind them. Stevie choked back her tears as they headed to the stairwell. They passed a hallway, down which she saw Detective Wood running toward her. "Uh-oh," she muttered under her breath. "Detective Wood, isn't it?" asked Stevie, holding out her hand.

The Detective eyed her skeptically. "Yes, Miss Barrett, that's correct." He looked at her friends. "And would these be your siblings and your fiancé?"

"Pardon?"

"According to the night nurse, Jan Barrett had three visitors who claimed to be her two daughters, a son, and a fiancé."

"Oh, that. Really, Detective. You know the condition Mom's in. I needed my friends for support."

Detective Wood gave a dismissive wave of his hand. "No worries. I get it. But…I do need to ask you some questions, if you have a minute?"

Jack moved protectively in front of Stevie. "Detective, she's really tired and upset. Can't you talk to her tomorrow?"

"It will only take a minute." He guided the group into a waiting room off the hallway.

He motioned them to sit down, but Stevie politely shook her head.

"Suit yourselves." Out came the notebook and pen. "First of all, where have you been the past week?"

"At my grandfather's cabin with my friends," said Stevie, too tired to come up with a clever lie and too emotionally beat to ask how he knew she'd been gone.

"I don't know how much you've been told about what happened, but two of my officers are dead."

"Yes, Kate told me."

Jack blurted out, "What the hell has that got to do with Stevie? We weren't here!"

Stevie touched his arm, a silent signal to shut up.

He shrugged her away. "Well?"

"I am not saying Stevie had anything to do with their deaths… Who are you, again?" asked the detective, glaring.

Stevie spoke up. "Jack, that's enough. Look, Detective, I am sorry to hear that your officers were killed, but we don't have any answers. I'm tired. My mom's been attacked—again."

"No answs, huh? I seriously doubt that. The time for games is ova, little Miss. Two cowps—my friends—are dead. Did I mention that Officer Buckna took down one of the suspects before he died? Well, he did. And the coroner is doing an awe-topsy as we speak. He has come up wiff some very strange preliminary findings. What do you know anything about that, Miss Barrett?" A mixture of exhaustion, anger, and frustration clouded the detective's face as he looked from Stevie to Colton.

"No. I don't. If that's all, Detective, I'm going home." Stevie spoke her words in clipped phrases as she headed toward the exit.

"No, you're not," announced Detective Wood. "First of all, your house is a crime scene so you can't go there. Second, I want you to tell me why the dead man in the morgue is dressed like a relic from the past."

Stevie glared up at the man, who blocked her path. He looked more rumpled and road-worn than usual. *Geez, and where did he get that New York accent? I didn't notice it before.* She glanced back at her friends.

Detective Wood pointed a finger at Colton accusingly. "I know you're one of them. I saw you two jumping through da trees like a pair of monkeys." His right hand moved to his holster.

At the gesture, Stevie witnessed a subtle change in Colton. His muscles flexed, stretching the material of his shirt taut. His jaw set and she knew she would need to act fast before things got out of hand.

Stevie crossed her arms. "What are you planning to do? Shoot us? I think you are losing it, Detective. I'm leaving. This conversation is over."

Wood reached to grab her arm as she pushed by him. "I am not finish'd wit you yet…"

Detective Drake entered the room. "Hold up, Wood."

He turned his anger on his partner. "Stay outta dis, Drake."

The female detective positioned herself between Stevie and Wood. She turned to Stevie and asked gently, "Do you have someplace to stay?"

"With Lissy." Stevie reached out to grab her friend's hand.

Drake acknowledged Alyssa with a tip of her head. "She's the one you stayed with after the last incident, isn't she?"

Stevie nodded.

"Okay. Then we already have her information. You get some rest. We'll be in touch tomorrow." Drake placed her hand on Stevie's shoulder as she walked her out to the hallway, her friends in tow.

Wood followed silently, lips tight, teeth clenched, and face red. He stormed past them and out of the building.

Once again on the main road, Stevie pounded her fist on the inside of the car door. "That detective is unbelievable! To accuse me of being involved in my mother's attack. I wanted to strangle him," she blurted out.

Jack added, "I wanted to punch the guy in the nose. Who does he think he is?"

"Well, I am sure that would have made the situation better," Alyssa commented.

"I didn't say I was going to hit him, just that I would have liked to."

Silence hung in the air, broken by Colton, whose gaze had not left the window. "Marise remained behind to be Jan Barrett's protector. Jan Barrett was attacked, imposing the question, what has become of my sister?"

"Oh my gosh, you're right. I totally forgot about Marise," Stevie exclaimed.

Colton turned his head to look at her. "It is my hope that your mother will be able to answer this question."

The moment Jack turned onto Alyssa's street, Colton said, "If you please, stop the vehicle so that I may exit."

"You're not coming with us?"

"I have watched over you since your arrival in Terra-hun. I am aware of the location of your friend's home. Is it your belief that I would be welcome entering through the front door?" Colton hugged Stevie before getting out of the car. "The moment you are settled, I will be at your side."

Colton moved away from the headlights, his image blending into the darkness. Climbing the porch steps, Alyssa warned Stevie and Jack that she had called her mom. "I told her that Jan had been attacked and you needed a place to stay until they cleared your house. She was all okie-dokie on the phone, but be prepared for the freak-out."

Stevie pictured Lian Brier sitting in the kitchen, her expression contorted with worry.

As they entered, the small Chinese woman rushed to her daughter. "Alyssa, what is going on?"

"Mom… I'm okay, we were out of town…remember?"

She pulled back an arm's length. "I know, Alyssa. I just worry. And you two, too, Stevie, Jack. What happen?" Despite twenty years living in the US, Lian had retained a strong Cantonese accent.

Stevie collapsed into the closest kitchen chair. "I don't know, Lian. My mom's in pretty bad shape and she was too doped up to tell us anything." Unable to suppress a yawn, she followed it with, "I hate to be rude, but I'm pretty wiped."

"Okay. Okay," Lian said, her hands fluttering in the air. "All of you sleep. I fix up couch bed down the stairs for Stevie. But Jack?"

Jack exchanged a look with Alyssa. "I don't have my car. Plus, I really don't wanna leave the girls. They're pretty shook up."

Lian sighed. "Okay, Jack. Living room for you."

Stevie headed to the basement. She stepped out of her jeans and crawled under the blanket on the hideaway. Exhausted, but unable to sleep, she decided a hot towel would help her relax.

The Briers' downstairs had been set up as a family room, but could have been easily converted to a small apartment. Alyssa used to joke that her folks would do anything they could to keep her home. The bedroom currently acted as a storage area, leaving guests to sleep on the couch. A full bathroom eliminated the need to head upstairs in the middle of the night.

Stevie sat on the lid of the toilet and covered her face with a hot washcloth. She breathed in the steam. *How could this have happened with the cops right outside? And where was Marise? What happened to her?*

Minutes ticked by on the smiley face clock. The washcloth grew cold, signaling it was time for bed.

The sight of Colton on the couch bed greeted her. She climbed in beside him and curled up in his arms. His warmth and strength comforted her as he caressed her shoulders, back, and arms in silence.

"Did you try to contact Marise?" she murmured, her face buried in his chest.

"Yes, but to no avail." He pulled slightly away from her, enough to gaze at her face-to-face.

Stevie touched his cheek, tracing her fingers down his jaw line and up over his full mouth. "I'm sure we'll find out the whole story. It's just going to take some time."

"Time is a luxury we do not possess, Shylae. It is imperative that we locate and obtain the Orteh before the Rebels conceal it again."

Stevie rolled onto her back, separating from his touch.

"Shylae?"

She turned her head to him. "I don't understand how you can worry about the Orteh with what's going on. It's like you don't care about anything else."

The springs of the couch squeaked when Colton raised himself onto one elbow. "You could not be further from the truth. I care deeply for your mother, for my sister. Yet, I am unable to change what has occurred."

Looking up at the ceiling, she chewed on the inside of her cheek, trying to find the right response. "Right now, I really don't give a damn about the Orteh. I can't leave until I know Mom's gonna be okay and we find Marise."

He leaned back, folding his arm behind his head. This time he spoke to the ceiling as well. "I would not—I am not—asking you to leave. My statement was to emphasize the importance of finding the Orteh quickly, not that we must abandon your mother and Marise in order to do so."

Body still, Stevie turned her head back to him. "I get that. Just give me a day to see what I can find out from Mom."

"A day. To that, I will agree. It will afford me the opportunity to locate Marise."

She rolled back to him and grazed his lips with hers. He drew her to his chest and she fell asleep in his arms.

Chapter 21

Colton rose with the first light of dawn. Loath to leave Shylae, he stood over her prone form. The weak sunlight played across her features. The night before, they had agreed to their separate tasks— Shylae would return to the House of Healing to comfort her mother, and he would continue his search for Marise. They would meet once again when the sun reached its zenith.

Colton bestowed a gentle kiss on his love's forehead and slipped out. He moved silently to avoid unwelcome attention from the Hundye also exiting their homes to attend to their duties. The recollection of the previous evening with Shylae caused him to restructure his priorities. *Yes, the Orteh is of utmost importance, but Shylae spoke true. We need to find out what happened. Neither of us will be able to focus without knowledge of the condition of our loved ones.*

As he left the city, he remained cloaked as a precaution, and sped up the mountain. A careful survey of the area around Shylae's home revealed that no police soldiers lay in wait. He continued on to his camp. By the time he arrived, the sun rays pierced a short distance into the cave. He paused at the mouth to let his eyes adjust to the dark. He feared what he might find.

No movement.

All of Marise's provisions remained in their normal positions. The embers in the fire were cold, scattered across the stone. If Marise had returned the night of the attack, she would have cleared the ashes and laid fresh kindling.

A knot grew in Colton's stomach. *What if the Rebellion overtook her?* Determination replaced anxiety. He tried to reach her again. The past several attempts to contact her with his mind had achieved nothing. Had she been injured, he would still experience a linking. If she were dead, he would feel the loss. No, there was something else—perhaps a power greater than theirs—that blocked the connection.

Again, Colton cleared his mind and called Marise. He searched for her response.

Nothing.

After several attempts, he was left exhausted and unsuccessful. Frustration threatened to overtake him until the realization struck. *Shylae might be able to glimpse my sibling in a vision.*

Attention refocused, breath steady, and mind cleared, he called Shylae for the first time. A spark, a glimmer, and then the connection, so intense it threw him backward. He could smell her scent, feel their bond. He leapt to his feet and rushed from the cave, the need for Shylae spurring him forward.

Stevie sat with her mom most of the morning. Jack and Alyssa played errand boys, retrieving food from the hospital cafeteria, and bringing coffee from the kiosk—anything that was asked of them. Stevie and her friends had tried to find out from Jan what had occurred, but Jan had difficulty speaking. The doctor warned Stevie that her mom's head injury was severe. It would take time for her to fully recover. Although Stevie knew a hug would heal her, that miracle would require explanation. She had no choice but to wait and hope that Jan's condition would improve quickly.

Kate had shown up, offering to take the next watch, so that Jan did not have to wake to an empty room. Stevie thanked her, but remained. Her mom had fallen into another fitful sleep holding Stevie's hand.

"How's my dog?" she whispered to Kate.

"You know Tonka. She's got my cats and the spaniel to play with. Happy as a lark."

Before she could respond to Kate, a vibration hit Stevie. She scanned the room for the source before realizing it came from inside her head. And then, a voice called her name.

No one else seemed to notice. Jack and Alyssa sat side by side, playing with their cell phones, and Kate flitted about the room, straightening the flowers in the vase, wiping down the sink, and reading the get well wishes.

Stevie whispered to her friends, "Did you hear that?"

They looked at her oddly, and shook their heads no. She walked out into the hallway to see who might be calling her, her sandals clicking on the linoleum floor.

Shylae.

It came as a whisper in her ear. She swung her head around quickly, but the hallway was empty.

Shylae.

She recognized Colton's voice. Rushing back into the room, she motioned her friends to follow, and mouthed "thanks" and "see ya soon" to Kate.

After the door to Jan's room closed behind them, Stevie blurted out, "Guys, Colton is calling me."

Alyssa asked, "What are you talking about?" She exchanged a confused glance with Jack.

"This isn't the first time I've experienced telepathy with Colton. Right before we left for the cabin, I had one of my visions and called to him. I didn't think it would work, but was so excited when he showed up. If he's doing the same thing to reach me, he's gotta be desperate."

"But what about your mom?" Alyssa asked, her head nodding toward the door.

"She's in the safest place she can be right now and Kate's watching over her. We need to head back to your house and meet up with Colton."

In the car, Jack flooded Stevie with questions about her telepathic abilities.

"You know the Djen have powers. This must be one of them."

He persisted with more questions.

"Enough!" Stevie yelled. Jack grudgingly let it be.

When they arrived at the house, they found Colton standing inside by the back door.

"How did you get in here..." Alyssa started, but Stevie interrupted by rushing past to hug Colton.

"I heard your call," Stevie said, jumping into his arms.

Colton's eyes shone when he smiled at her, but it was fleeting. He lowered his head as he pulled out a chair. He seemed to be struggling with words.

"What is it, Colton?" He looked up at her, his face dark with concern.

"I cannot contact Marise. I spent the morning in the attempt, but could neither hear, nor feel, her presence." He slumped at the kitchen table, looking defeated.

Stevie moved behind him, her hands on his shoulders. She blamed herself for the disappearance and her mother's attack. If Colton's sister had not stayed behind, two cops would not be dead and she would not be missing. Stevie knew that she had to do something, but what?

As if sensing her distress, Colton laid his hand on hers, his head tilting upward. "Shylae, you are not to blame."

The hell I'm not, she wanted to shout, but instead said, "I can't heal my mom without drawing attention. So I have to let her be in pain. And Marise is missing because she was protecting my mom. Not only is it my fault, I feel helpless." Stevie dropped to her knees beside Colton, burying her head in his lap to hide the flow of tears.

Colton raised her chin. She had no choice but to meet his gaze. "You are not helpless, my Shylae. Your learning has occurred quickly and you have mastered many skills, the strongest being control of your visions. If Marise still lives, perhaps you will be able to locate her."

Stevie sat back on her heels. "I could try," she mumbled. "I don't really know what I am doing."

"For a person who knows not what she is doing, you have already outshone Djen and Guardians who have studied their entire lives. Do not forget, I am here to help you. The Din Ashyea speaks of a Guardian's ability to control the direction of the visions beyond the Ortehlae."

"Okay. We got nothin' to lose." Stevie stood and spoke to Alyssa, "I need a candle." To everyone else she said, "Let's head downstairs. It's as quiet and dark as anyplace."

Stevie took her position on the floor cross-legged and narrowed her focus to the candle flame. Colton's voice flowed as he paced behind her, chanting from the Din Ashyea. As directed, Jack and Alyssa hovered close to the wall and remained silent.

Where are you, Marise? Show me where you are. Stevie's attention centered solely on these thoughts and Colton's chant faded into the background.

A blue light rose from the candle and started to spin. She let it draw her into the familiar trance. Her arms lifted and opened and the vision unfolded before her.

Dirt and pine needles crunched under her feet as she walked. The familiar lay of the land drew her attention to the right—a canyon wall. She followed along its edge. Over the next rise, a ribbon of road wound its way through the hills a good two hundred feet below. A green sign stood out near one of the bends. Squinting, Stevie could make out the words: Pinecliffe eight miles.

Farther up the mountain, movement to her left caught her interest. Two Rebels walked between the trees on what appeared to be a deer trail. They had Marise in tow. Her hands were tied, her eyes covered, and dried blood caked the side of her mouth and arms. Stevie's excitement blanched into fear.

Marise looked faint and had a difficult time keeping up. As they forced her onward, she would trip and stumble, bringing down the wrath of her captors. After a final drop to her knees, Marise did not rise. One of the men kicked her savagely in the side. She fell to the ground, a grunt escaping her. They left her there, casually seating themselves on an outcrop of rocks, laughing and talking in the Djen tongue. Marise was ignored as they retrieved food from their packs and ate. After a few moments, she stilled. Stevie assumed she had passed out. Her chest continued to rise and fall shallowly.

With one more look around to get her bearings, Stevie brought her arms together and returned to Alyssa's basement. Her eyes watered and she swayed from the lightheadedness. "I found her."

Colton pulled her to her feet, hugging her fiercely.

"She's pretty out of it, Colton. They beat her bad."

"You know this place?"

Stevie nodded hesitantly.

"We must make haste..." Colton bolted for the stairs.

"Wait," cried Stevie. "We need a plan."

He stopped at the bottom of the steps. Stevie approached her protector.

"I know you think I'm doing great, but I am totally not ready to fight anyone yet. I can't leave Mom. Jack and Alyssa are even less prepared than me. If you get hurt, I'd have no one from Djenrye to protect or help me."

"Hey, wait a minute," Jack piped in. "I'm with the C-man, here. Let's open a big can of 'whoop ass' on the guys that hurt Jan."

Colton opened his mouth, but Alyssa cut him off. "I may not be the best hand-to-hand person, but I don't have to get close to shoot an arrow."

Stevie held up her hands in defeat. Frustrated, she was still a bit entertained by her best friends' bluster. "Okay, okay, I give. But wouldn't it be better to attack at night—or at dawn? Isn't that when the barbarians attack the gate?"

Jack and Alyssa agreed they should wait until dark.

Colton acquiesced, adding, "I fear we may lose their location."

"With ya, but I assumed I'd enter another vision right before we head out."

Alyssa cocked her head and dashed up the stairs.

"What is it?" Stevie called after her.

"I hear a phone."

The group followed Alyssa, who met them halfway to the kitchen, carrying Stevie's cell. As she held it out, Stevie read the caller ID: Golden Police. Reluctantly grabbing the phone, Stevie rolled her eyes as she answered, "Umm…Hello."

"This is Detective Wood. I would like to talk with you and your boyfriend today."

Stevie mouthed "Detective Wood" to her friends. Into the cell, she said, "Umm…sure. When?"

"I'm in the neighborhood. How about I come to your friend's house right now?" Stevie looked at Colton. "Yeah…I guess. Will Detective Drake be with you?"

"No. She's on another case."

"Okay. We're here. Just one thing—you promise to talk and not accuse?"

The answer was a long sigh on the other end followed by a "Yes."

Stevie hung up. "He's on his way."

As one, Stevie, Alyssa, and Jack jumped up and started straightening the house. Dishes in the washer, the sheets tossed in the hamper, and the couch folded up. Stevie rushed to make a pitcher of iced tea. Colton stood on the sidelines, looking a bit lost. As the flurry of activity began to die down, he moved toward the back door.

"Hold up." Stevie caught him by the arm. "He specifically said he wanted to talk to my boyfriend." She leaned in closer. "And we both know he didn't mean Jack."

At the knock on the door, they all froze. Alyssa primly smoothed the front of her jeans and walked stiffly to the door. She led Detective Wood into the living room, where the rest of the crew had assembled by the couch.

Wood peered at each of them in turn, and then asked to speak with Stevie and her boyfriend alone. Jack and Alyssa waited for a nod from Stevie before leaving for the kitchen.

"May I sit?"

Stevie shrugged her shoulders at the detective, gesturing to the recliner closest to the couch.

"Would you like something to drink, Detective?"

"Sure, water would be good." Stevie hurried to the kitchen, not wanting to leave the men alone for too long. Detective Wood's voice followed her, even though he was directing his scrutiny at Colton.

"What is your name?" asked Wood.

"Colton."

"Colton what?"

"If I understand your query, I am Colton of Tyré."

"And where exactly are you from, Colton?"

"Tyré" The word was drawn out slowly as if Colton were speaking to a child.

Stevie walked back in the room. *Just in the nick of time.* She handed Wood the glass and sat next to Colton on the couch. Silence filled the room, broken by the click of ice cubes in water and swallowing sounds made by the disheveled man in the recliner.

Then he spoke. "Look, I know I came off pretty rough when we last met." He shifted to the edge of the chair, forearms on his knees. "But damn it, I'm tired of dancing around the truth. Two fellow officers—my friends—have been killed. This isn't a game."

"I get that, sir. You need to get that wasn't our fault. We weren't even here. Anything we might be holding back—if we were holding something back, which we aren't, but if we were—it wouldn't help you."

Wood shook his head, causing his brown hair to become more unruly. "I have to disagree. Sometimes things that a victim knows but doesn't think are important turn out to break the case." When neither Stevie nor Colton replied, Wood sat back with a sigh. "I know you think that I can't handle the truth. You're wrong. I have seen a lot of crazy stuff in my day. I need to know what is really going on if I have any hope of getting justice for my fallen friends and …" He paused. "…for your mother."

Again, silence. Wood continued. "Let me tell you a story. A story that will hopefully convince you that I will understand whatever it is you're holding back."

He took another sip of water before speaking. "During my stint with the New York City Police Department, I heard some strange tales on my beat. Folks talked about seeing alien ships in the sky. One guy told me something so odd, I ended up taking vacation time to check it out. You see, back then, rumor had it that Myrtle Beach was a hot spot for UFO sightings."

He paused, whether to gauge a reaction or to decide how much to say, Stevie couldn't tell.

"I bought a fancy camera and camped out on the beach with a dozen or so other curiosity seekers. For two nights, nothing happened. And then…" Another pause. "…around an hour before dawn on the third day, a row of seven orb-shaped lights appeared. They shot from side to side and up and down, performing an involved set of aerial acrobatics. They created the most beautiful designs I'd ever seen…" Wood waved his hands in the air, mimicking the motions. "…flowing figure eights and infinity symbols. And then—they simply vanished."

Stevie wanted to blurt everything out. *Maybe he can help us.* Colton sat stone-faced, silencing her voice.

Wood stood abruptly. His voice increased in volume and he spoke in short, clipped phases. "It's not the first time I saw something…something otherworldly. I realize why you don't want to tell me what is happening. Especially considering your boyfriend." He locked eyes with Colton. Without looking away, he directed his next statement to Stevie. "All I have to do is take him in for questioning."

Under Stevie's hand, the muscles in Colton's thigh grew taut. She feared he would attack the middle-aged officer. *That will surely get him arrested.*

"Detective." Colton's voice took on a menacing low growl. "I am not anything like those of which you speak. I did not attack Jan Barrett."

Wood raised an eyebrow. He dropped back down in the chair, acting as though he were playing with a newly-caught mouse. "Well, then, why haven't you answered my question?"

"Question?"

"Where are you from?"

Stevie reached for Colton's hand.

"I answered your query. I am of the City of Tyré." And then, before Stevie could stop him, he said, "My home is in Djenrye."

She tightened her grip on his hand and felt the blood rush from her face. *I'm gonna faint. I know I'm gonna faint.*

Colton turned to her. "It is his desire to know the truth. Now we will see for ourselves what sort of Hundye he is by what he does with this knowledge."

"Yes, I do want the truth," he said, eagerly at first, before the strangeness of Colton's words seemed to dawn on him. With a look of bewilderment, he asked, "Where did you say?"

"Djenrye." Colton sighed. "I live in a world parallel to this one. The Djen who attacked Jan Barrett bear no resemblance to the beings which you witnessed. They are soldiers of the Rebellion. The attack was an attempt to learn of Shylae's whereabouts… I mean Stevie." He stared at the detective, waiting for his reaction.

Wood's mouth opened and then closed again. To Stevie, he looked like a bass that had been hauled onto a boat. He sat back in the chair with a blank look. *Whatever he expected us to say, I'm pretty sure this wasn't it.*

"You expect me to believe that Stevie is being chased by a group of insurgents from a parallel world? Oh, yeah, and that you're from there as well?"

"You say that you wish to know the truth, and yet you question it…and your own eyes. You saw us in the trees, did you not?"

Wood nodded.

"Look, Detective, Colton was sent to protect me a long time ago, when I was still a baby. I didn't know until recently that I am also from his world, our world, or that I was in danger. When my mom was attacked, Colton revealed himself to me and told me about his—I mean, our—world. He had to warn me."

Wood covered his face with his hands for a moment, and then he peered at Stevie through parted fingers. "So, you're not from around here either." Dropping his hands to his lap, he sighed. "Assuming everything you say is true, why are they after you?"

Instead of responding, Stevie turned her attention to Colton. "What do you think?"

"We have told him this much. For his safety and sanity, it would be best to provide this Hundye police soldier with a full explanation. If..." Colton looked at Wood. "...he will provide an oath to not speak of this to anyone."

Wood dipped his head ever so slightly.

Colton divulged most of the details, with Stevie chiming in now and then to translate Colton's Djenrye words or to expand parts of the story.

The detective listened intently without speaking. He had no questions, no rebuttals. He drank in all they said. He seemed to be a man hungry for truth, and finally satiated.

Colton concluded with, "As it must be obvious to you, Detective, we had to guard this information closely. Not only could the premature exposure of such knowledge place Shylae in danger, but it is a threat to your world."

"A parallel world." Wood no longer appeared to be aware of his surroundings. "And two of its inhabitants are sitting right in front of me."

The tone of his voice had Stevie worried he might be in shock. Wood stood and moved as if in a trance to the living room window, where he remained, staring out without speaking.

Stevie whispered softly to Colton. "So, what now?"

Colton shook his head. He seemed as lost as her. Craning her neck, she saw Jack and Alyssa standing in the passageway between the kitchen and living room, their faces pale. *I hope they're not in shock, too. I'm not sure if I can give CPR to three people.*

After an eternity—actually, ten minutes or so—Wood returned to the recliner. He eased himself down, sighing. "I need a drink."

That broke the spell, at least for Alyssa, who came dashing in with a bottle of scotch. Handing it to Detective Wood, she exclaimed, "Damn. I guess you'll want a glass," and rushed back out.

"So…what are we going to do about this?" he asked Colton.

"We?" Colton responded. "There is no 'we'. At this moment, the Rebels are holding my sister prisoner and I need to free her before she is tortured, or worse. After that task is complete, Shylae and I will locate and retrieve Tecton, the Orteh of which we spoke, and enter Djenrye to return it to its home."

Wood sat back. "Great plan, such as it is. But like it or not, I'm a cop first and a believer second." He retrieved his cell from the tweed jacket and began to dial.

Chapter 22

"No!" Stevie leapt at Detective Wood, clawing for his phone. "You can't get others involved! They won't understand."

Colton rose and spoke in a booming voice. "You gave your oath!"

Wood dodged the grasping fingers and hesitantly lowered the phone. "My oath as a man—not as a cop."

"What part of 'can't tell anyone was unclear to you, Detective?" Jack asked, stomping into the room. "I told you we couldn't trust him."

Ignoring Jack, the detective continued. "You have information that will help me locate the men who killed Buckner and Mitchell. I can't just let that go."

"If you want to be a part of this, you have to." Stevie ran her hands through her long hair, frustrated. "Look, I know you want to get these guys, but so do we."

"It looks like we're at an impasse." Wood sighed, and then seemed to resign himself. "Listen, how about we deal? I'll help you find Colton's sister, which will lead me to the…what did you call them? Rebels? But what about my partner?"

"What about her?" Stevie asked rhetorically. "You have to leave her out of this. If you get someone else involved, it would put more in danger. You have to agree to keep this between us or we will simply disappear. You'll be left with a lot of questions, but no answers. You're gonna look like you've gone crazy."

"Been there, done that," Wood said, defensively. "You're not in the best position to bargain. I have pictures. As far as disappearing—that might work for you and…" He waved at Colton. "…and him, but what about your mom? Your friends? Would you really leave them holding the bag?"

"You're right. It would suck for them."

Alyssa spoke up. "We can take it. Besides..." She looked directly at Wood. "...we don't know anything."

"Vee know notting," Jack added in a bad German accent.

Stevie continued. "In the end, you won't be able to prove anything. And without us, how do you expect to find and catch the men who killed your friends?"

Unscrewing the cap of the whiskey, Wood sat back and tilted the bottle to his lips. Alyssa absently handed him the highball glass she had been holding. He poured a shot and stared at the swirling liquid for a moment. "Uncle. I don't see any other way for both of us to get what we want without joining forces." He leaned forward. "But I've got to warn you, keeping my partner out of this is gonna be tough. She's relentless."

"I got that impression," Stevie said. "All we can do is deal with it when it comes up."

Colton returned to the couch. "Then, Detective Wood. To be clear, as a man—and as a Police Soldier—you give your word?"

Wood sipped at the whiskey. "Agreed. We will work together to apprehend the animals that killed my friends and nearly killed Jan... Mrs. Barrett."

"Punish, yes. Apprehend, no."

"Excuse me?" The detective dangled the glass in his hand.

Colton stood and began to pace the room. "When you confronted us earlier in the House of Healing, you expressed concern over the 'findings' on Jan Barrett's dead attacker. Let us say that you apprehend the Rebels. With these Djen in confinement, at the disposal of your alchemists, tell me how you intend to keep knowledge of Djenrye secret?"

"Yeah," Stevie chimed in. "And, they can cloak themselves. How're you gonna explain that?"

Wood frowned. He ran his hands through his hair, stopping at the back of his neck, rubbing. "Damn it. You're right. Again. But the first problem is the Rebel corpse. The pathologists discovered an anomaly with the blood. They couldn't identify the blood type." The next words he spoke came out slowly. "We've no choice but to remove the body and any samples taken from it."

"Leave this to me. I have—skills—that allow me to accomplish such a task unseen," Colton said.

"You mean cloaked, right?" Wood met Colton's steady gaze. "Okay, so the next problem is the two remaining suspects. You said 'punish', not 'apprehend'?"

"They are Rebels. They attacked the Hundye mother of the Guardian. By our laws, this is treason and must be answered with death."

Wood seemed disinclined to continue his questioning.

Colton must have taken his silence for agreement, because he said, "Then it is settled."

The remainder of the afternoon was passed at Alyssa's kitchen table, with Colton and Wood sketching out the bare bones of the plan to rescue Marise. With the detective and Colton's military training, everyone decided it would be best for them to lead the assault on the Warriors.

"I think Jack should be the driver," Stevie offered. The idea was to free her up to focus on the landscape and give directions.

"I am not driving that old POS Cutlass," Jack complained.

Wood frowned. "That car might be older than you, but it's in better shape."

Before the two could get sidetracked any further, Stevie asked for other options.

Wood said, "Actually, I've got a Chevy Blazer, too."

"Why don't you drive that?" asked Jack.

"Not that it's any of your business, but that beast is a gas hog."

"Enough," Stevie called out. "Can we get back to the matter at hand?"

They all agreed. Turning back to the strategy, once at the location, the detective would approach the camp on foot from the south, Colton from the west—through the treetops. The encroachment from two sides would leave an opening for Alyssa, Jack, and Stevie to rescue Marise.

"I am concerned with the abilities of the Hundye Police Soldier," Colton said to Stevie when Wood left to exchange his Cutlass for the SUV.

"He might not have Djen powers, but he does have a gun. If we catch the Rebels off guard, that should be all he needs," Stevie assured him.

They waited until nightfall to leave. In the interim, Stevie entered another vision to reconnect with Marise's location. Her captors had not moved far from their previous location. It looked as though they were camping in or near an old mine. Confident that she could locate the trail by sight, Stevie was ready to leave.

After thirty minutes on the road Stevie shouted, "Here. Turn in here." The last sign they passed showed Pinecliffe a mile off, but Stevie was insistent. Sure enough, when the headlights shone on the shoulder, the faint outline of tire ruts led into the dark. Jack followed the old fire road until it ended at the edge of a ravine. They left Wood's SUV to set out on foot. Colton and Wood took the lead, with the other three following at a discreet distance. The glow from Wood's flashlight and the blue beacon of Colton's eyes lit the way.

"Are there any caves around here?" asked Alyssa.

Stevie pointed ahead. "If my vision is accurate, about a mile from here there should be an old mine entrance."

"I know the place," added Jack. "But it's blocked off."

"That won't stop them from getting in." Stevie said. "Jack, see if you can catch up to the guys to let them know to head for the mine."

After following for a while, Alyssa and Stevie caught up to find Colton pointing out something to Wood and Jack. A fiery glow flickered in the distance, illuminating the entrance to the mine shaft.

Alyssa whispered to Stevie. "That's gotta be them. You can't camp here—it's not a designated site."

Stevie nodded, and made a shushing sound. Jack waved the girls to join him behind a strand of scrub oak. According to the plan, they would wait for Colton's signal and then move in on the camp. Colton planted a quick kiss on Stevie's cheek and jumped into the trees. As agreed, Wood moved in the opposite direction to circle the camp.

Stevie's Djen abilities allowed her a clear view of the area. Rotting timbers lay on either side of the mine. *Probably removed by the Rebels.* A spot in front had been cleared of debris. She did not see anyone, but a fire blazed in the center of the camp.

A form hovered in the trees above the mine entrance. *Colton.* Rustling in the underbrush to the left could only mean Wood's approach.

It took another five minutes of waiting before a Rebel emerged from the shaft. He wandered around the campsite, staying within the glow of the fire, before sitting down and warming his hands. The long tawny hair braided back to reveal a sun-browned face. Despite the weather-worn skin, he looked to be no more than mid-twenties. As with Colton, this Djen wore a stone pendant around his neck. It flickered in the firelight—red calcite, polished to a high sheen.

Movement on the mountain on the high side of the mine caught Stevie's attention. *Colton.* He must have disturbed the leaves as he balanced on a tree limb roughly twenty feet above. The Rebel rose, head tilted upward in Colton's direction. At that moment, Wood stepped into the light, but not past the entrance's edge. In a low growl, he said, "Freeze."

The Djen turned in the direction of the command. A blur of motion came from above and Colton landed on him, rolling off quickly at the same time he unsheathed his sword from its scabbard. The impact either stunned or knocked the enemy out, because he laid still.

Colton turned as another Rebel rushed at him out of the cave entrance. Pivoting to the side to avoid the strike, Colton used the man's forward momentum against him. As he lunged past, Colton grabbed the nape of his vest, connecting a fist with the enemy's jaw.

The impact whipped the man's head backward. The Rebel's grey-streaked hair flew up as he dropped to the ground. Colton closed the gap. Quick as a cat, the Rebel regained his footing. He charged with a mad vengeance. Once again, a step to the side, a dodge, a turn—Colton propelled the man in a circle and introduced him harshly to a tree. That barely slowed him down. He unsheathed his sword and Colton blocked a downward blow. In a blur of steel and leather, the two Djen fought furiously. Swords slashed, parried, and blocked. The clang of striking metal echoed through the valley.

The other Rebel came to, whether from the sound of ringing steel or the shouting, it did not matter.

Stevie called to her friends, "Now!" And the three rushed toward the melee, sidestepping the detective, who covered the young Rebel with his gun. Stevie and her friends headed toward the mine, but paused in awe. Colton fought with pure elegance, his movements akin to a dance. His last stroke disarmed the combatant. The man fell. His back landed on the forest floor.

Colton growled at the prone form. "*Namea ai Tzak, Ie namae chasea hapae-rú, Ie triyea chasea eh'ankh.*" Then the point of Colton's sword slid into the man's throat.

The dark look in Colton's eyes frightened Stevie more than his action. Grabbing at Wood's arm, she attempted to pull him along into the dark shaft.

He shook his head and motioned to the Rebel at his feet.

In a low voice, Colton said, "He shall not escape. Follow Shylae and find my sister."

Wood holstered his gun and shadowed the teenagers into the mine.

Jack spotted Marise first. His flashlight shone on her limp form, which was tied to a decaying wood beam several steps inside. Stevie hurried to her side to loosen the rope that bound her ice-cold hands. Wood gathered Marise in his arms and carried her out. Alyssa remained behind briefly to look for a blanket to warm the female Warrior.

Outside, true to his word, Colton had not let the Rebel escape. The traitor could not. He lay in a pool of his own blood. Without a look at Stevie, her protector grabbed both bodies by their vests and hauled them into the mine shaft.

Alyssa passed by Colton, her eyes wide but lips silent. She brought the wool cover to the fire and shook it out. Before she could reach Marise, Colton had returned to retrieve his sister from Wood. He sank to the ground.

Colton held Marise close. "Shylae, please…"

Stevie knelt beside the Warriors, wrapping her arms around them. An electricity flowed through her. Sparks of mini-lightning bolts danced over Marise's body. In the light of the fire, the wounds faded.

Wood stood motionless, captivated at the sight. "Whaaaa…"

Colton silenced him with a growl, not releasing his hold on his sister. She stirred, but her eyelids remained closed.

"She will live." Colton looked at Stevie. His eyes shimmered in the firelight. For a moment, she thought she saw tears.

Seconds, then minutes passed. Detective Wood broke the silence. "You can explain all this later. Colton, what about those two you dragged away?" He jerked his head in the direction of the mine.

"They will trouble us no further."

Stevie rose and backed away from her protector. "We can't just leave the bodies. What if they're found?"

Colton stood and placed Marise back in Wood's arms. "You have done well thus far, Police Soldier Wood. Please return my sister to your vehicle. Gently." To Jack he said, "I will need your assistance before the sun rises to return and conceal the dead."

Clearly shaken, Jack said, "I'll drive you, C, but I'm not touching them."

"Agreed."

Stevie reached out to Colton, who took her hand. At the touch, his face softened. They headed back to the vehicle. Alyssa's complexion had paled, and she walked as though in a daze. The trip back to Golden passed in silence, each lost in their thoughts.

Jack was the first to speak. As he turned the SUV onto Washington from Highway 93, he asked, "Where am I headed? We can't go back to Alyssa's. Not with her parents at home."

"We can go to my house." Detective Wood gave Jack directions and he cranked the wheel to the right.

"I need to see Mom soon," Stevie said as the vehicle maneuvered through the narrow streets.

Marise stirred, her eyes fluttered open. Colton helped her to a sitting position. She offered Stevie a faint smile.

"Sister, how are your wounds? Are they healed sufficiently?"

"Yes." She looked again at Stevie. "Thank you, Shylae, for aiding my recovery. As amazing as my brother believes his skills to be, he would have required assistance to heal me so quickly."

"You certainly sound as though you are feeling well." Colton nudged her with his shoulder. "Are you able to remember details of the attack on Jan Barrett?"

She nodded. "I overheard you speaking. It would be my preference to report on the attack to spare Shylae's adoptive mother from having to re-live it." Marise leaned forward to touch Stevie's shoulder. "Your mother was very brave and fought fearlessly."

Stevie pictured her mom scratching, kicking, biting—fighting viciously—with all her strength. "Yeah, my mom can be tough. She doesn't take any crap, especially if she's defending me. I'm sure she didn't go down without a fight."

Turning around from the front seat, Wood asked, "Can we hold off until we get to my house? It's just around the corner."

Jack pulled into the driveway of the modest brick ranch-style home. Wood's front yard had seen better days. Stevie wondered if the detective owned a lawn mower or knew how to use one.

Settled in Wood's living room, Colton and Stevie situated themselves on either side of Marise as she began to recall the attack.

"Are you sure you're ready to talk about it? You're still kinda shaky," Alyssa asked gently.

Marise nodded. "I am fine now, Alyssa Brier. I am back with my brother and our Guardian." She touched Stevie's cheek. "As I started to say, I spent the early evening in the tree closest to Shylae's home and all had been quiet. At moonrise, a light on the door of glass caught my attention. Yet, when I approached and peered inside, I saw no one. After a moment, Shylae's canine rushed at me, barking furiously. This seemed odd, as the animal had never shown me hostility. I slowly opened the door and the canine ran up the stairs and back down again, hackles bristled. Then I heard a scream." Her voice gone hoarse, Marise paused. Alyssa ran to the kitchen to get her water, which Marise accepted gratefully.

After taking a sip, she continued. "I bolted to the upper floor, but the door to Jan Barrett's sleeping chamber was closed. Kicking it in, I came face to face with two Djen Rebels. Unfortunately, there were actually three. Information I only gleaned when the third jumped me from behind as I rushed in."

Colton interrupted. "Coward. He gained the upper hand as a thief, rather than as a true Warrior."

"Agreed, Brother, yet he did overpower me and place me in an immobilizing restraint. The Guardian's mother continued to scream, but she did not cease her fighting. They bound her and attempted to interrogate her. The fools spoke in Djen. I cried out that she did not understand, but my plea was met with kicks and punches. The Rebels continued to beat her and I feared for her life. By the blessings of the Gods, a booming voice stopped the assault. It echoed like the voice of Tzak, the God of Gods."

The detective spoke, his tone wooden. "That was me. I announced our presence over the loudspeaker."

"I thank you for your tenacity and quick action. You saved the life of Jan Barrett. Unfortunately, when the enemy fled, they took me as a hostage. I was unceremoniously bound and thrown over a

Rebel's shoulder." Marise spat. "No better than Jajing." She then continued, speaking directly to Wood. "I know two of your soldiers gave their lives during the Rebels' escape. For this I have deep regret."

She turned to Colton. "Brother, the enemy knew you would come for me, but how were you able to locate us? I never heard your call."

He reached across her lap to grasp Stevie's hand. "You have the Guardian to thank. Her abilities are greater than we could ever have hoped."

She mouthed something to Colton that Stevie could not make out, but it appeared to be "Triveatae." *The Prophecy?*

"You already have my love and loyalty, Guardian. To that, I add my gratitude." Marise pulled Stevie into a hug.

Wood cleared his throat. "I hate to break up your little reunion, but I have to ask." He glared at Colton. "Are we going to kill every suspect we come across? I need to know before we go any further."

"They may have committed crimes in your world, but they are from Djenrye. They must answer to their misdeeds according to our traditions, not yours. This matter has already been addressed. I recall your agreement that you would not be able to cage them. What did you expect was to happen when we confronted them?"

"Understood," Wood responded. "But I am not happy about how that was handled."

"Then this will please you less. We need to speak of the removal of the other Rebel body from the death watcher structure," Colton said.

"Morgue. It's called a morgue." Wood looked around at the rest of the group. "We need to do this soon."

"I have considered the urgency. We should complete the task before the rising of the sun," Colton replied.

The sharp slap of skin on skin had everyone turn to Jack, who had smacked himself on the forehead with the palm of his hand. "Duh, I can't believe I spaced that. I'm in."

"Not so fast, hot shot." Detective Wood grabbed Jack's arm as he moved to the front door. "You're not going. Colton can move quietly and camouflage himself. I can get us into the morgue, but if I'm caught, how will I explain dragging a teenager along with me in the middle of the night?"

"Dude? Really? Who's gonna hack into the computer to delete the info? Anyone here know code? How to break passwords? Hello? Anyone?"

Colton and Wood exchanged a look. Wood released his grip on Jack. "He's right, ya know. I can get us in, but I can barely run my own laptop. Colton, I don't suppose you're any sort of a computer genius?"

Stevie stifled a laugh. "I don't think he can even drive a car. Sounds like Jack's your only hope."

"And don't forget C needs a ride back up the hill to do— whatever it is he's gonna do."

The timid voice of Alyssa broke in. "Should you really be messin' around with the dead? In my family, that's not only sacrilegious, but dangerous. If the soul of the Djen has not found its way home, it could follow you to yours."

The men mirrored each other's expression of disbelief.

Stevie jumped in before anyone could respond. "Alyssa, I get it. But if any souls follow us, I'm sure Colton has something in his book to keep them at bay or banish them. Right, Colton?"

Colton nodded slowly, seeming to pick up the hint. "Of course, little one. The Djen deal with these types of events regularly. I am able to speak honestly when I say that we have never been plagued by a dead soul."

"Are you punkin' me?" Alyssa cocked an eyebrow. "Stevie, help me out here. You know how superstitious my family is. I don't believe everything Mom tells me, but…messin' with the dead?" She shivered noticeably. "That totally freaks me out."

"That's why we're not going, girl." Stevie patted her on the shoulder. "You guys better get a move on. You're wasting time."

Chapter 23

I wish I could have seen Colton when they got back. Stevie had tried to wait up for Colton, Jack, and Detective Wood. After the third time she nodded off, Alyssa refused to stay any longer and dragged Stevie home with her.

It felt as though she had been asleep on Alyssa's pullout couch for less than an hour when her friend gently shook her awake. Lian had asked Alyssa to run some errands for her before noon, leaving Stevie to visit her mom alone.

Stevie yawned as she drove to the hospital. The morning sun warmed the car and, for a moment, she feared she might fall asleep. When she rolled down the window, the blast of cool air perked her up a bit, but she remained distracted. *I'm sure they got out okay—we would have heard something if not—but what the hell did they do with the body...and the other dead Rebels? Then again, do I really wanna know?*

Stevie parked in the visitor lot and headed through the front doors of St. Anthony's. When she reached her mom's room, she found Jan propped up on pillows, watching the morning news.

"Hey, Mom, you're up." Stevie kissed her mother on the cheek and wheeled the hospital recliner close to the bed. Jan's paleness of the day before had been replaced with a flush of color, although the bruises had darkened. And, thankfully, Jan appeared alert.

"You look like you're feeling better."

"I am, but I'd give my good left leg for my cosmetic and hair products." She looked past Stevie with a grin. "Where's everyone else?"

Her eyes focused on her feet, Stevie hesitated long enough for her mother's smile to be replaced by pursed lips and knitted brows.

"I know that look, baby. Talk to me." Jan closed her hand over Stevie's.

"There's a lot going on, Mom. I can't tell you everything right now, but I wanted to stop by and make sure you're okay."

"And…"

"Remember we talked about my needing to leave to find the Orb? Well, the time has come. Sooner than I'd hoped. After your attack and the death of the officers and that Rebel…" Stevie searched her mom's face for a hint of acquiescence. Instead, Jan's color faded to a pasty grey.

"You know how I feel about this, Stevie. I'm scared for you. You don't know how ruthless those men are…" Her voice faded to a whisper.

"Actually, I do. Marise told us all about it. And…she mentioned that you kicked ass." *At least that got a smile.* "I need for you to be strong for me though. I know this is hard, but I promise I'll call keep you updated."

"A phone call isn't the same as you being here. I need to know you're safe."

"Geez, Mom, Colton and Marise will be with me the whole time and this is something I have to do. None of us will be safe until this is finished."

Jan sighed heavily, forcing a wan smile. "You tell those two that if anything happens to you, they'll find out what a bad ass I can really be."

"You got it." Stevie grabbed her mom's hand and sent a quick healing surge, almost a healing hug.

Pulling her hand away, Jan said, "Stop, honey. You know that healing me now is going to raise questions."

Stevie smiled and released her hand. "Yeah, I know, but…how's your head?"

Gingerly touching her bandage-covered brow, Jan said, "Actually, my headache is gone. You're better than ibuprofen."

"Just wanted to make sure your noggin got healed before I left. And…I did a little speed-up on your leg, but it shouldn't be enough to freak out the docs too much."

During the rest of the visit with her mom, she chatted about Tonka, the house—Jan expressed her intention to repaint the kitchen—the weather, when Jan might be released, and the police investigation. Anything and everything, except the matter of Stevie's impending departure.

Hours passed before they got around to discussing what Jan's story would be to the police.

"Just tell them the facts," Stevie offered. "They can't catch you in a lie if you don't tell one."

"What do you think lying by omission is, sweetie?"

"Do you really think that the cops are gonna think to follow a line of questioning involving a parallel dimension?"

Jan actually laughed. It was honest and heartfelt—the kind of laugh Stevie hadn't heard from her mom since the first attack.

Wiping the corner of her eyes with the sheet, Jan said, "Good point. I'll leave it at 'I didn't recognize the men, it happened too fast'."

Relieved, Stevie left to grab lunch from the cafeteria and then stayed with her mother until after two o'clock.

Anxious to see Tonka, Stevie went straight from the hospital to Kate's house. Had all this happened two years ago, the Labrador might have been able to accompany her on the quest. But Tonka was ten years old, and no longer had the stamina for a long journey. Plus, what would Stevie do if Tonka became sick or injured? Nope, it was best to leave her with Kate and say good-bye.

Tonka's ears perked up as Stevie's Jeep pulled into the driveway. The lab jumped, front paws resting on the chain link fence, barking joyfully, tail wagging so hard her entire back end danced. Stevie couldn't help but laugh and leaped the fence easily. Tonka and Stevie chased each other around the yard, dodging and weaving at the last moments—their own version of tag. Laughter and barking blended together as the friends ran and jumped over each other like two puppies. They finally collapsed in the grass, Stevie on her back. Tonka crawled beside her and laid her head on Stevie's thigh. Sitting up, Stevie rubbed the dog's soft fur, paying special attention to the area behind the ears—Tonka's favorite spot. With tears dampening the lab's coat, Stevie whispered, "I love you, old girl. I'll miss you so much. I'll see you soon. Promise."

The drive back to Detective Wood's house proved more difficult than Stevie imagined. She had to constantly wipe away tears with the tail of her t-shirt to clear her vision. Leaving her mom and Tonka weighed heavily on her.

At Wood's, Stevie entered, head hung low. The sight of everyone assembled, except Alyssa, cheered her a bit. If all went well at work, Alyssa should arrive soon. Stevie grabbed a bottle of water from the fridge and joined the group at the kitchen table. "So how'd it go last night? We didn't get a call from the police that you guys were in custody, so I'm guessing…"

"Mission accomplished," Wood said.

A secret look passed between Wood, Colton, and Jack. Stevie wanted more details, but the guys weren't forthcoming. "So…where'd you hide the bodies?"

Again, that look. This time between Colton and Jack.

Colton spoke up. "Jack Snow and I took the enemy's corpse to the mountains. He lies with his fellow traitors. The three Rebels will not be discovered."

Clearly, Stevie would not be able to get anything more from him. A slight shrug and she changed the subject. "Hmm, well, then, what's the plan for finding for the Orb?"

"The journey should begin by sunrise after next. Marise and I have planned out the route according to the map you brought back from your vision. The remainder of this day and the morrow will be spent gathering provisions." Colton extracted a slip of paper from his jeans pocket. "Here is the list Marise and I discussed. This should be sufficient for three people for half a moon cycle. If provisions fall short, we will hunt."

"Whoa, cowboy. Three?" Wood broke in. "How do you figure? I count four—you, your sis, Stevie, and me."

Jack chimed in. "Am I the only one who can do math here? I'm counting five. Colton, Marise, Stevie, the cop, and me."

Then everyone spoke at once. Colton and Marise argued with Wood, Wood argued with Jack, and Jack argued with everyone.

Stevie threw her hands in the air in frustration. "Hey. Quiet!" And, surprisingly, they were. "Wood, use your brains. You have a job; you're a cop. And Jack, really? We already talked about this. Did you both forget you don't have powers? Even if we let you come, you'd never be able to keep up."

"I wouldn't miss this for the world," Wood stated. "Besides, I can help in other ways. You have no idea how far flashing a badge can get you and how much trouble it can get you out of."

"I understand your exaggerated view of your capabilities, yet you have a companion soldier to whom you must answer." Colton's voice had an edge to it. "Another question begs consideration. How do you propose to keep up—to follow us through the trees?"

Wood grinned. "I've already thought this through. First, I have an SUV. You don't need to be leaping through the trees like monkeys, we can drive. Second, I have a gun, a badge, and a plan."

"So, what's your plan?" Stevie crossed her arms.

"You're gonna love this." Detective Wood tapped a cigarette from the pack in his jacket, lit it, and took a long drag. "The chief got wind of all the extra hours I've been putting in on your case. I let it slip to one of my patrol guys about the unsanctioned surveillance I've been doing and over beers, told another I was gonna kill the guys when I caught them."

That's not stretching the truth much. Out loud she said, "Seriously? How's that gonna help?"

"If all goes according to plan, I'll be pulled off the case." He paused. "He wants to see me in his office first thing in the morning."

"Then what?" Stevie shook her head.

"I'm hoping to be put on administrative leave due to stress and exhaustion. That'll mean a couple of weeks off work."

"You know you're nuts." Stevie laughed.

Wood gave a mischievous wink. "That would have been my second ploy. Luckily, I didn't have to use it."

Jack did not join in the humor. "I'm glad you all are enjoying this, but what about me? You guys need me. I'm your resident hacker. You'll need my expertise. Who else can read a true satellite map…not just GPS? Which one of you knows how to get direct satellite access to the Internet when we're in the middle of Nowhere, British Columbia?"

The sound of the front door shutting echoed into the kitchen. Alyssa appeared, tossing her purse on the couch. "What did I miss?"

Everyone around the table looked at each other and laughed.

"What's so funny?"

"It's nothing really, Lissy," Stevie said, still giggling. "Wood and Jack are trying to convince us why they should go on the trip."

Alyssa eased herself into the closest chair. "You mean I'd be the only one staying here?"

Carefully surveying her friend's expression, Stevie said, "We haven't decided on Jack yet, and besides, I need you to be here to watch over Mom and Tonka."

Her friend nodded hesitantly. "Yeah… I guess we could watch each other's back…'specially since no one else knows wassup with all this."

The creak of a chair turned Stevie's attention to Marise.

She had risen and placed her arm around Alyssa's shoulder. "You are a very brave Hundye to remain. May we rely on you to be our informant for the Rebel activity on this plane?"

Alyssa turned her chin up to Marise and nodded.

"Great. That's all well and good, but I'm still here." Jack waved his arms over his head.

"Jack…" Stevie started, but Wood interrupted.

"I never thought I'd be on this guy's side, but he's right about the electronic hocus-pocus stuff. This guy's a whiz."

Stevie sent Colton a pleading look. Colton confirmed. "You may accompany us, Jack Snow, but under the strict conditions that you follow my commands without argument. Without hesitation or…" At this, Colton paused. "…inappropriate humor."

"Ahh, shucks, Dad." Jack smirked.

Colton stood abruptly, knocking the kitchen chair backward. He slammed both fists on the table. The room went silent. His voice tight with anger, he said through a clenched jaw, "Such a comment is exactly to what I was referring. This is neither a game nor a childish adventure. Your lives are in danger. Both our worlds are on the brink of catastrophe. Have you so quickly forgotten what my sister and Jan Barrett have had to endure?"

Jack drew back and then lowered his gaze. "I have not forgotten," he whispered.

"Okay," Wood broke in. "Now, can we get back to business?"

"How 'bout tomorrow we get clothes for these two?" Stevie tossed her head in the direction of Colton and Marise. "And provisions for the mountains."

During dinner, the group reviewed the route and firmed up their plans. On the home front, Wood said he would call in some favors to keep Jan and Alyssa under guard. He pointed out that Stevie needed a viable excuse for leaving town with Jan still hospitalized. She agreed to call her mom the next day and see if the two of them could come up with a ruse that would satisfy the cops.

Plans completed, pizza cleared, beers and sodas chilled and opened—Wood not being the sort to keep a good bottle of wine on hand—and dibs called for the comfortable spots in the living room, Stevie asked to hear more about Djenrye.

Colton began, "The best place to start a tale is at the beginning. The history of Djenrye starts with the story of Lorn, The First Keeper of The Prophecy.

"Before the Djen were awakened, they were much like your Hundye ancestors. They lived in concert with the land, taking only what they needed, returning all they could, and moving with the seasons and the herds. One night, Lorn, a great hunter in his tribe, awoke to a bright light. It filled his tent as though it were midday. A voice spoke to Lorn, professing to be a messenger of the Gods, and commanded him to counsel with Tzak, God of Gods. More than a skilled hunter, Lorn had proven to be not only the bravest of his people, but their chosen leader. For this reason, he went with the messenger willingly."

As Colton paused, all eyes were on him—even Marise, who must have known the story since childhood. "They rose into the heavens and entered into the God plane. It appeared much the same as our world, yet the colors were luminescent, clearer, as though the trees themselves were made of amber with leaves of emerald and jade. Lorn moved down a forest path and came upon a clearing within which stood an ancient stone chair. Seated on the throne, a shimmering image held court. He appeared as a man, but Lorn knew him to be Tzak. He had a golden beard, and hair flowed past his waist, and his outline shifted slightly as though he were made of a substance other than skin and bones.

"To his left rested a large intricately bound book, near the size of a small child. The cover had been inlaid with stones representing the four elements. In his right hand—a diamond sphere. It, like Tzak, shimmered and shifted, tricking the eye so that Lorn could not truly describe it when he returned to his people.

"Tzak spoke to Lorn in a voice that shook the trees, yet did not hurt the ears. He instructed Lorn as to what would be Ty Djen's purpose from that point forward."

Silence. Stevie and her friends held their breath, waiting for him to continue.

Colton looked at each one in turn. "The remainder of the tale I shall save for another night. Dawn comes soon and we must rest."

A collective cry went up. "No…" Stevie begged. "We want to hear more."

"The Prophecy of Lorn is lengthy and is told to Djen children over the span of many seasons. You will hear it all, I promise, but not this night. We have much to do on the morrow."

"But, when?" Alyssa whined.

"After we have dined next evening. Will that suffice?" Everyone agreed, and split off—Jack and Alyssa to their respective homes, and the three Djen to the spare room and couch. Stevie pouted. She wanted Colton to share the extra room with her, but Wood would not hear of it.

"Wow, now you're old-fashioned? You sound like my mom. I am eighteen, you know. An adult under the law."

"Not under my roof. I don't care if you're twenty-five, you're not married. Go to bed."

Marise took Stevie's arm and maneuvered her toward the spare room. Stevie turned at the last moment to see Wood hand Colton bedding and point emphatically at the couch. Stevie sighed. *Man, it's going to be a sucky night. I miss him already.*

Taking off their outer clothes, the young women climbed into bed. Stevie knew she should get some sleep, but everything ran simultaneously through her mind—the shopping tomorrow, calling her mom to devise a lie, Wood putting on a performance to convince his boss to place him on administrative leave. The lies made her nervous. The cops made her nervous. The whole thing made her nervous—even without the Rebels being added in.

Chapter 24

After an hour chatting with her mom on the phone, Stevie hung up. Their plot to fool the cops was no-frills. In her mom's words, KISS—Keep it Simple, Stupid.

They had decided that the excuse for Stevie leaving would be to visit her aunt and uncle in Toronto, Canada. Jan did not have to be a great actress to convince the cops of her desire to keep her daughter safe. It sounded good. But they'd have to wait and see if it could be pulled off.

Marise entered the living room, dressed in a well-worn t-shirt with "Why did God make Cops?" on the front. She had untucked her pants from her boots to conceal them. Stevie asked Marise to turn around and started laughing when she read the back, "So that Firemen can have heroes, too."

Marise gave a quizzical look. "Is this Hundye humor? I do not understand."

Stevie tried to explain, but the joke was lost on Marise. "Never mind. It's not important."

Colton looked a little better. At least Wood's borrowed clothes did not look out of place on him—only ill fitting.

"This so proves my point. You two really need new clothes."

On the way to the mall, she called the bank to check her account. She doubted the Djen had money. Even if they did have something to barter, she did not want to try and explain the value of a Djen coin.

Colton asked about the story she and Jan planned to tell to allow Stevie to leave town without suspicion.

After her explanation, Colton asked, "And you are certain the police soldiers will not attempt to track you?"

"Why would they? It's not like I have anything to do with the investigation. I wasn't around when the attacks happened."

"What of Wood's partner, Detective Sarah Drake? Will she not question your departure?"

"That's Wood's gig. As far as I know, she's the only one Wood's confided in, at least about me."

Colton retreated into his own thoughts. His silence bothered Stevie more than his questions, but for now she needed to let it go. There was too much to do.

Shopping with Djen was an experience Stevie would not soon forget. Colton and Marise wandered into the wrong changing rooms. *At least they're using them.* Stevie waffled between laughter and embarrassment the first time Colton began undressing in the aisle to try on a pair of jeans. *Thank God Marise got the hint before taking off her shirt.* Stevie smiled anxiously at the other shoppers, explaining, "They're from France."

"*Oui,*" Marise added, eyes twinkling.

Three hundred dollars later, the threesome headed back to the Jeep. Stevie's cell rang. *Jack.*

"I've just picked up Alyssa. Wanna meet for breakfast?"

"Your timing's perfect. We just finished. How 'bout the diner by school?"

With the plans set, Stevie, Colton, and Marise arrived first and grabbed a table. Worried that she hadn't heard from Wood, Stevie excused herself to make a call. It didn't take long. Instead of Wood, an electronic voice came over the line asking her to leave a message. She did. Returning to the booth, she found that that Jack and Alyssa had slipped in.

They ordered drinks while Jack boasted that he had already packed, including the computer gear, and would be ready to go at an instant's notice.

"I told my folks that I'm going on a writing trip. A Jack Kerouac sorta thing. My dad thought I was nuts. I said I wanted to be alone to do research for a book I have in mind."

"Seriously? Did they buy it?" asked Alyssa.

"Yeah. Told me to call every day and let 'em know I was okay."

"That is awesome." At this, Alyssa dropped her gaze to her root beer. "I still kinda wish I could come."

Before anyone else could respond, Marise reached across the table and laid her hand over Alyssa's. "You wield a great deal of responsibility, agreeing to be a sentinel during our absence. Do not think of your role as a minor one."

"Forget not your station as Jan Barrett's guardian," Colton joined in. "And as caregiver of the Guardian's faithful canine companion."

At this Alyssa laughed. "Geez, C, I love the way you talk."

Stevie sipped her Coke. "I hate to change the subject, but…Jack, I hope you're planning on pitching in some moola. Our little shopping spree set me back."

"No worries, Doll. My dad gave me spending money and my bank account's flush."

As they were about to order breakfast, Stevie's phone rang.

"Hey, Wood," she answered. "Everything go okay?"

"I'll fill you in when I see you. Where are you guys?"

"The diner by Golden High. See ya soon." To her friends she said, "Wood's on his way. Let's wait to order."

Wood entered five minutes later. The waitress returned the moment he pulled up a chair. He asked for iced tea and then looked at the group. Waiting until all eyes were on him, he sighed and relayed the basics of the morning. "Well, the chief did what I expected. Told me I was working too hard, becoming obsessed over the case, and that he was placing me on administrative leave. Of course, I argued with him, even created a scene and stormed out of his office. Drake caught me as I left, but I brushed her off. I was so jazzed, I didn't think I'd be able to keep up the pissed-off pretense in front of her. She let it go—for now, but we'll see."

The waitress brought Wood's tea and took the food order. Wood waited until she left before continuing. "Anyway, Drake knows me too well. In the ten years we've been partners, I've always gotten a little obsessed over my cases. And she knows how important this case has been to me. Not sure she's gonna buy my leaving."

"Let's hope for the best," Stevie said. "Now, back to the plan. We still have to get the food and camping gear. Wood, I hope you're planning on pitching in." She rubbed her thumb on the tips of her forefingers.

"Of course. I wouldn't expect you to pay for everything. I may only get a cop's wage, but I've got a little squirreled away for a rainy day. And, young lady, it looks like it's gonna pour."

The food arrived, turning the exchange from talking to chewing. After breakfast, the group went their separate ways, agreeing to meet at Wood's house after the supplies were bought and the coolers packed.

Stevie helped haul the last of the coolers into the back of the detective's SUV. With a little direction from Jack, they'd managed to fill the vehicle and still leave room for the five travelers. "I'm gonna need to go to my house to grab some clothes and stuff," Stevie said.

"No problem, I'll come with you," Wood offered. "The investigators should be done by now, but just in case..."

The ring of a cell phone had everyone grabbing at pockets and purses. Colton and Marise looked on with amused expressions.

"It's me," the detective said. "Hey, Drake."

Wood rolled his eyes, interjecting the occasional, "Uh huh," "K," and "Sure," all the while looking at Stevie. "That's fine. I'll meet you over at the Post in about an hour."

After he hung up, he explained that his partner wanted to meet to discuss the safety of Jan and Alyssa. "Don't worry, I'll get all the job stuff taken care of and meet you guys back here." Wood turned and headed to the house. "Umm, Stevie, can I talk to you alone for a sec?"

"Ah…sure."

Stevie followed the detective. Once inside the front door, he said, "I wanted to fill you in on the police investigation without everyone around. I don't want to worry them. After I spoke with the chief and Drake, the chief—Henderson—called me into his office to ask about the missing body and the test results. Apparently, the front desk guy remembered seeing me the night of the body's disappearance."

"Crap. Does your boss suspect you?"

"He didn't say so directly. He grilled me about my whereabouts that night, if I saw anyone suspicious, and why I was at the morgue. The usual."

"And?"

"I told him I wanted to get more information on the results and find out if the pathologist had drawn any conclusions about the suspect's origins. But no one was there, so I left. I did tell him that the doors to the examination room were locked and I didn't see anything out of the ordinary. That's not my main concern, though." Wood paused to shake a smoke out of the pack he withdrew from his pocket. "Drake's been texting and leaving me voicemails since my meeting with the chief. She wants to know what's up."

Stevie stood silently, trying to come up with ideas on what to do next. "So what now?"

"There is a very real possibility that Drake might tail me. I'm gonna wait and see what she has to say when we meet before I get my shorts in a knot."

Entering the VFW ahead of Drake, Wood positioned himself on his favorite stool. The bartender acknowledged him with a nod. In short order, a beer and a shot of whiskey were set down in front of him on the scarred, polished wood. Half a swallow into the beer, Detective Drake appeared at his side. Her arms were folded across her chest, her eyes squinted and full of suspicion.

"Hey Drake…pull up a seat." He patted the stool next to him. "I'm buyin'."

His partner sat down with an audible huff and ordered a Salty Dog, minus the salt.

The VFW had started to fill with locals. Laughter, the smell of freshly popped corn, and the smooth country sound of Alan Jackson filled the air, but the space between the detectives remained tense.

The blonde officer kept her green eyes focused on the drink in front of her, fiddling with the stir stick, "Okay, Wood…it's time for the truth."

The detective conjured up the most innocent voice he could muster. "I have no idea what you're talking about." He moved to put his arm around her shoulder, but she shrugged him off.

Now she met his gaze. "Do I look stupid to you, Wood? I mean, do you really think I'd buy that bullshit you fed the chief? What the hell's really going on here?"

Instead of responding immediately, Wood took a swig of his beer. Outwardly he remained calm, but his mind raced through all the options. Twenty years as a cop had honed his skill of quickly reviewing and checking off all potential outcomes to come to the best conclusion. *Drake is not going to easily believe any lie I concoct. She's a pit bull when it comes to this stuff. She won't let it go.*

"You remember the first case we worked together?"

"Geez, really? The one you almost lost your job over? What's that got to do with it?"

"Bear with me. We solved that one because of my beliefs in the metaphysical and supernatural, along with my mundane knowledge of Wicca and other alternative religions. The other cops, including Chief Henderson and you—remember?—thought that the killer was a witch, but in fact turned out to be a religious zealot. If it hadn't been for my involvement and willingness to see beyond the obvious, we never would have caught the bad guy."

"True. I had your back on that one, even after you called in one of the witches…"

"Wiccans."

"Wiccans…whatever…to give a Tarot reading on the suspect."

"And it was accurate."

"She gave us hints and clues that could have been interpreted any number of different ways." Drake's volume increased. She downed the rest of her drink and slammed it on the bar.

Wood waited. Years of working with his partner had taught him to let her come to a conclusion on her own. He tossed back the shot and finished most of his beer before Detective Drake's shoulders dropped and her teeth unclenched.

"Okay, uncle. I admit that the way you interpreted those hints led us to the last murder in time to prevent it."

Wood examined her face to be sure of her acquiescence or for a hint that she might be baiting him. Her skeptical nature might still make it hard for her to handle the truth. *And what if I tell her everything? What will she do with that information? Will she cover for me? For that matter, if I continue to lie, will she cover for me?*

He turned to stare blankly at the liquor bottles lining the back of the bar, contemplating what to say next. Finishing his beer in one swallow, he motioned to the bartender for another round and offered, "Come on, partner. Let's go out to the patio... I need a smoke." He headed for the side door, but caught a glimpse of Drake rolling her eyes as she rose to follow.

The cover over the patio, the worn wood decking, and the cross breeze kept the area cool and comfortable. Luckily, a table in the far corner was vacant and Drake took the seat opposite him.

Wood lit a cigarette, took in a drag, and did his best to ignore his partner's glare. He waited for the drinks to arrive before starting. "I'll tell you what, Sarah." He met her piercing green eyes. "If you ever believed in me—I mean the cop and the man you know me to be—then I need you to trust me now." He took another drag, followed it with a swig of beer, and waited for an answer.

"Of course I believe in you. Haven't I always had your back, even when I thought you were crazy? How could you question my loyalty?"

"It's true...you have always been a good partner."

"Well, then why don't you trust me?"

Wood hesitated, squinting as he spoke. "Shit. This is difficult. You are so skeptical…a good balance for me. But, for this moment, I need you to keep an open mind."

"About?"

If I tell her the truth, I'm going to have to convince her with more than just words. "I'm not crazy, you know."

"I know, just maybe a little eccentric—but open." She sipped her drink, finally giving him a smile. Wood knew he had her. It was now or never.

"Well, I guess the only thing left is a little show and tell." He downed the last of the beer as he rose from the bench.

"What are you saying?" She stood slowly, her expression both puzzled and, yes, Wood did see a bit of excitement. "Are we going somewhere?"

Wood turned around and grinned. "Yup."

Chapter 25

Detective Wood turned in to the paved driveway. He noted Drake's puzzled expression. Under other circumstances, he might have laughed, but nervousness tempered his humor. There had been a lot of surprises over the past few days. Wood worried that this one might be too much for Colton. But what other choice did he have?

"Why are we at your house?" asked Drake as she stepped out of the car.

"The answer to what's going on is here."

She closed the door and leaned against the roof of the old Cutlass, ignoring the dirt that dusted her forearms. "What do you mean?"

"Follow me, but you have to promise to withhold your judgment."

In response, Sarah cocked an eyebrow, but followed him to the front porch. Before they could enter, the screen door swung open to reveal an angry blonde teenager. Stevie's reaction did not hold a candle to the vibes radiating from his partner.

"What the hell are you doing?" Stevie demanded, glaring at Wood.

He smiled wanly, choosing to take the direct approach. "Detective Drake wants to know the truth and we're going to give it to her."

"Have you lost your mind? You promised!"

Wood braced himself against Stevie's attempt to bar the entrance.

Unmoving, he stared down at her. "Let us in. My partner will figure it out eventually, or come up with some form of what she thinks is the truth. Full disclosure is better—safer."

Drake interrupted. "What is Stevie Barrett doing here? Why are you letting her stop you from entering your own home?"

"I'll 'splain everything once we're inside." Wood stared Stevie down until she gave way, saying nothing.

Wood entered the house, the women in tow. He spotted Colton at the dining table and walked directly to him, breath held, then released. "Colton. This is my partner, Detective Drake."

Drake moved to Wood's side, hand extended. The gesture went unanswered. Instead, Wood received a stony glare.

"You pledged to tell no one." The Djen's voice boomed, rage reverberating off the walls.

"She needs to be filled in on this. She can be trusted."

The expression on his partner's face was a mixture of shock and anger. Wood tried to see the scene from her point of view. The two Djen wore jeans and t-shirts, but the clothes did little to hide the differences—the striking blue pupils encircled in black, the easy manner in which they stood and moved. Even Stevie now possessed a grace and confidence absent from the people he'd met in his lifetime.

Colton stormed away from the detectives. Stevie followed him into the kitchen, murmuring quietly. She paused long enough to look over her shoulder at Wood and shoot him a death stare.

"Isn't he one of the suspects?" asked Drake, her nails digging into his bicep.

"Ow! That really hurts." He peeled back the perfectly manicured fingers. "I told you your answers were here. Let's hit them one question at a time." The detective motioned his partner to sit on the couch. He hovered between rooms, waiting for Stevie and Colton to return. That's when he noticed Jack and Marise at the computer desk at the far corner of the living room.

"Crap. I didn't even see you guys. Drake, you remember Stevie's friend, Jack? And this is Colton's sister, Marise."

The raven haired beauty nodded. An errant strand of hair played across her forehead. Wood's eyes followed the line of her face down the side of her neck, and to her collarbone. *She does create a certain awe.*

"Another one? Seriously? Are there any others—perhaps hiding in a closet? What's going on here, Wood?"

"Just give Colton a minute to calm down and then we'll talk." Wood nervously checked the time on his cell phone.

Alyssa strolled out of the kitchen, diet soda in hand. "Hi," she said as she dragged a chair next to the couch. "I don't know if you remember me. I'm Alyssa." Looking back at Wood, she added, "Colton and Stevie are talking, they'll be out soon... I think." The pop and fizz of the opened can spoke to the ensuing silence.

Wood inched closer to the kitchen. "I'm getting a beer. Anyone else?"

Jack piped in, "I'd love one."

"Think again, Scooter. I'll get you a soda." He left the four of them to stare at each other.

A few minutes later Wood re-entered, carrying a beer, a cola, and several bottles of water. Stevie and Colton were a few steps behind him. Colton sat stiffly in the recliner and Stevie positioned herself on the floor, leaning against his legs.

Wood cleared his throat. "Colton, I know that I promised not to get anyone else involved, but I know my partner. She's determined. She won't let this go. They call her 'Pit Bull' at the station."

"With lipstick," Drake added tersely.

Colton grunted in response.

"Okay, be mad, be frustrated, be...whatever. The bottom line is she's seen you and your sister—in the flesh. It's too late to turn back." He threw up his hands. "Give me a break. You're the one who told me the truth without consulting the others. Remember?"

"Quit talking in circles and tell me what's going on, or I'm leaving," Drake's volume increased with each word.

"Colton?" Detective Wood took the slight nod from the Djen as a sign to dive in.

"I originally had this guy pegged as a suspect, but now I know that he wasn't involved."

"How do you know? Because you're buds? Talked football over a beer? And why are Stevie and her friends here?"

"Damn it. Give me a minute ta 'splain widdout interruptin'." Wood sat down next to Drake. "You know I've been staking out Stevie and Colton over the past several days. I've learned the whole story. It's gonna take you down the rabbit hole, Alice, and calls for something stronger than water." He asked Alyssa, "Would you please grab the bottle and shot glasses from the counter?"

Drake cocked an eyebrow. "Whiskey? If you're planning on telling me that these two are from another planet, I swear, I'll..."

"We are not from another planet." Colton growled. "We are from Djenrye, a world in another dimension, parallel to this one."

Drake's mouth dropped open. "Wh..wh..what did he say?" She looked at Wood.

"He said they're from another world, parallel to this one." All trace of Wood's accent had disappeared.

"You are pulling my leg...right?"

"If I were to pull on an appendage of yours, you would know it," Colton answered.

Stevie spoke up. "Look, Detective Drake, it's a long story, but the bottom line is that Colton didn't hurt my Mom. He didn't kill those officers. The men who did are the enemy."

"So, now you're protecting him...why?" Detective Drake asked. Her volume had lowered, but her voice gained a sharp edge. "Because he's your boyfriend?"

"No." Stevie sighed and leaned forward. "Because I am one of them. I didn't know before."

"Shit." Drake stood. Wood grabbed her arm to prevent her from marching out.

Colton's anger seemed to have faded. He approached the detective. "Detective Sarah Drake, I understand your confusion. It may be abated if you would be so patient as to allow me to relay the entire story. It would be unwise for you leave with vague half-truths."

Detective Drake plopped back down. "This better be good, mister."

It took an hour for Colton to complete his explanation, including their impending departure for Washington and the lie to cover Stevie's leaving. Marise remained at the computer desk, uncharacteristically stoic. *I'm guessing being the younger sibling, she's giving her brother a chance to hang himself before jumping in.*

"I hope this aids your understanding of the necessity for our subterfuge," Colton concluded.

The clock on the living room wall broke the silence intermittently. *Tick. Tick. Tick.*

Drake, who had remained motionless during the entire telling, finally said, "That was a lovely little story. And you've managed to explain all the oddities away. I guess having a seasoned officer as your ghost writer came in handy." Before anyone could respond, she continued, "Now. I only have one question. Where the hell is your proof?"

"You want proof?" Stevie jumped to her feet, hands clenched into fists, and eyes shone a vivid blue. The light bounced off the wall behind Drake.

The cropped blonde head turned from Stevie to the wall and then back. Drake began slowly, "Well, that's new." Then, with confidence, said, "Some eye novelty. Did you get those contacts at the magic store?"

"Contacts don't do this." Stevie crossed her arms in defiance, the light dimming. "And I don't wear them, anyway."

"Perhaps, my good Police Soldier, you can arrive at a logical explanation for this?" And then Colton was gone. All that remained a shimmer of smoke.

Wood witnessed something he never had before—Drake fainted. He lunged toward her, but Colton beat him, un-camouflaging as he caught Drake's limp body, and then easing her to the floor.

Alyssa rushed into the fray, bottle of whiskey in hand. Wood grabbed it, pulled the cap off, and waved the opening in front of

Drake's nose, spilling some of the liquid on her face. She woke sputtering.

"Damn it, Wood. Get that away from me." Drake sat up, flailing at her partner. "What the hell is going on?" This time when she looked at Colton, she appeared frightened.

Colton knelt, ignoring it when she flinched away from him. "I showed you an ability that Djen have, to cloak by bending the light around them. Stevie has not yet mastered the skill, but she will, in time."

Wood and Jack moved in to help the detective up onto the couch. The rest of the party stepped back. Even Jack managed to refrain from wisecracks.

With shaky hands, Drake reached for one of the glasses Alyssa had set on the coffee table. "I think I'll take that shot now."

Grinning, Wood filled her glass and then his. She downed the golden liquid in one gulp and motioned for another.

Stevie spoke up. "Sorry 'bout that, but you did ask for proof."

The female detective ran her fingers through her short hair. "Yes. Yes, I did." She rose unsteadily. "Would you excuse me for a moment?" and nearly tripped over Stevie's feet, heading for the bathroom.

She returned after a few moments, patting her damp face with a towel.

"Feeling better?" Wood asked.

"I don't know how to react to all of this." Drake helped herself to another shot. "Part of me thinks this is a bad dream and the other part wants to know more."

Wood nodded. "That's how I felt." *And how I felt after turning a blind eye to Colton and Jack disposing of the dead Rebels in the mountains.* Colton had left that part of the tale out and Wood was grateful. He hoped that they had buried the men deep enough and far enough in the mountains that the bodies would never be found.

As he stood to stretch his back and legs, Wood asked, "So, partner. Now is the moment of truth. With everything you've heard and seen tonight, can I count on you to cover for me over the next few weeks?"

Her green eyes blinked. "I can't believe you'd ask. Haven't I always had your back? Give me time for this to sink in, though, or I'll come off just as crazy as you."

"I hear ya. How 'bout dinner? Nothing like a good steak to make you feel normal. Jack..." He opened his wallet. "...here's forty bucks. Do me proud."

Jack grabbed the twenties and headed out the door, Alyssa in tow. "Be back in a flash."

Stevie offered to start the grill. She sat on the rickety top step of the deck, waiting for the coals to turn white. The wind rustled the leaves and took her thoughts back to the first time she saw Colton outside her bedroom window. The longing to be alone with him came back in a flood. She felt as though she had known him her whole life, yet she knew so little about him.

A creak of wood and Colton was beside her. His arm slipped around her waist and she let herself be pulled close, tipping her head upward to kiss his cheek.

"I waited for you to return. What keeps you out here in solitude?" he asked, lips brushing her brow.

She gazed at him. "I was thinking how I need time with you—just you—to listen to your stories and be together."

"I feel as you do, my Shylae. This is not how I imagined our beginning to be."

She leaned her head on his shoulder and the two of them stared at the stars beginning to emerge on the horizon. The realization that it would be a long while before they could be intimate caused her eyes to tear. She wiped them away, trying not to let Colton see, and got up to start dinner.

Colton grabbed her arm as she moved away. "Tonight, after the evening meal, perhaps you and I may find a place of privacy."

She touched his face in agreement. *That's it.* She pointed her finger up, signaling that an idea had come to her. He looked at her with curiosity and followed her through the French doors.

"Detective Drake, can I talk to you for a minute?" Stevie asked as she entered the kitchen.

Drake looked past Wood, who sat with his back to Stevie. "Sure, what is it?"

Stevie motioned Drake into the living room with a jerk of her head. Once out of earshot, she asked, "Umm, don't take this wrong, but can I go home?"

Drake looked puzzled. "I think the evidence is gathered, but…with everything that's going on, why would you want to?"

Stevie leaned in conspiratorially and whispered in the detective's ear, "I need some time alone with Colton."

With a crease of her brow, Drake said, "I'm still trying to wrap my head around all this. You and your crew have told me to accept things I never would have believed. And now…you want to spend the night with this virtual stranger?"

Embarrassed, Stevie professed, "It's not what you're thinking. It's just…well…with all that's happened, we need privacy…you know…to talk."

Drake patted her on the back. "I'm not keen on the idea, but I'm not your mother. You are an adult. Let me call and see if the house has been cleared." She wandered down the hall, cell phone in hand.

Colton stood in the doorway. *Of course. With his Djen abilities, he heard everything.* Stevie gave a sly grin and he came to her, enveloping her in his arms.

"You are a clever one. I cannot wait to lie with you at my side." His eyes twinkled.

Wood had not been pleased with the pronouncement that Stevie and Colton would not be spending the night at his house again. He wanted everyone in one place, arguing that it would be safer and make their exit in the morning quicker. Drake sided with Stevie. After a bit of back and forth, Wood finally acquiesced.

Once the dinner dishes had been cleared, Alyssa hovered in the kitchen to start the coffee. A beer in hand, Wood and the rest of the group settled in the living room.

"Before you two leave, Colton promised to finish the Prophecy of Lorn," Alyssa called from the other room.

Colton cleared his throat. "In truth, I do not know the Prophecy itself. Only those descended from Lorn have that knowledge. We are told the story of how the Prophecy and the Ortehlae came to our people."

Alyssa entered with cups and the coffee pot. "That's okay. The 'Tale of Lorn' is good enough for me." She smiled.

"Me too," Stevie piped in, followed by a resounding "me three", "me four", and "you betcha."

Colton chuckled and began. "If I recall correctly, I ended the story with Lorn standing before Tzak.

"Lorn was in awe of all that surrounded him. He knelt before the God. Tzak spoke to him, 'Rise, child of Djenrye, for I have summoned you to perform a great task.' Tzak motioned for Lorn to sit at his side. As Lorn stared at the knoll, a stone chair—near the height of Tzak's throne—materialized, along with an imposing dais. The Great Being lifted the book…"

Alyssa whispered to Stevie, "Book?"

"Intricately bound, the size of a child, on his left side…remember?"

"Oh, yeah."

"…as though it weighed nothing and placed it open before Lorn.

"'This is the *Din Saeklae*, the Book of the Prophecy. It speaks to the future of Djenrye, of Terra-hun, and of the planet upon which they both reside.'"

Marise interjected, "And that is also when Tzak spoke to Lorn of the dual planes existing in the same space."

Colton silenced her with a look. "Do you wish to relay the telling?"

"My apologies, Brother."

"Then, to continue…Tzak explained that the Din Saeklae, as any great book, has a beginning and an end. Lorn quaked in terror. 'An end?' he asked the God of Gods.

"'Yes, Lorn,' Tzak replied. 'But not all endings are final. Some signal new beginnings. The one foretold herein should be feared only if it comes to pass. Yet, it may be prevented. This is why I have called you forth, to place the knowledge of this Prophecy with you and your descendants in the hope that you may rewrite the ending.'

"And with that, the great book emitted a blinding light and the pages flipped quickly, one by one, as if caught by a strong gale. Yet, no wind stirred. Lorn could not see, but his mind filled with images and knowledge. When the last page turned, the book closed itself, and it vanished in one last brilliant burst. Lorn's head burned, but his thoughts were clear. He had become the keeper of the Prophecy." Colton paused for the length of a heartbeat.

Jack blurted out, "Dude. Seriously. Tell me that's not the end."

Colton smiled. "No, young Jack. That is not all there is to the telling. As I informed you at the beginning, this story is told over a Djen's entire childhood. My version must be brief as we cannot afford the time for me to relay its entirety in detail." Colton took a drink from his flask, and then continued. "The Prophecy may only be passed to Lorn's heir and his or her heir's heir at the time of death. This was the gift given to Lorn.

"Tzak further instructed Lorn to choose three Djen from his tribe to go out and establish the three tribes of Djenrye. 'They are to be the first Guardians of the Ortehlae. To them I give a similar gift. Solely with the blood of each Guardian's firstborn may the Ortehlae be accessed to maintain balance.'

"Then Tzak made a fluid gesture with his left hand and the five Ortehlae materialized, hovering above the dais. He relayed to Lorn the properties each Orteh represented, what they controlled, as well as their interdependence.

"'For if one is removed from its sisters and brothers, the balance will be broken and all may be thrown into chaos. It is not akin to breaking the link in a chain, but rather a string in a web. All is connected—the Ortehlae to each other, to the Djen, to the Hundye, to the planes, to the planet.'

"To house the Ortehlae, the Gods erected a great hall, known as Raile Ai Highlae. In the Hundye tongue, the Hall of Light."

"And they lived happily ever after," Jack concluded.

"I wish I could end with that statement, but unfortunately, there have been wars in Djenrye, as within your dimension. Despite our conflicts, the Djen and the Guardians have successfully maintained the balance of our shared planet. Until now. This is where the Djen history ends, and our story begins."

Stevie jumped to her feet. "Not to state the obvious, but that's why finding the Orteh and returning it to…what is it you said? Its sisters and brothers…is so frickin' important. The balance cannot be re-established without that happening—with or without using my blood to control it or the others. Right?"

"You are correct, Shylae—but never forget that you are an important piece to this puzzle. As a Guardian, you are more than a mere keeper of the Ortehlae. Your presence near Raile Ai Highlae keeps everything in balance."

Chapter 26

Djenrye
Present Day

Firelight bounced off the cavern walls, shimmering as it glinted across pockets of condensation. The men huddled around a campfire, which created shadows of dancing giants on the earth and stones behind them. The earthen floor muffled Warrior Teig's entrance, yet Torren heard every step. Respect, mingled with fear, sent the Warrior down on one knee, head bowed, before the Leader of the Rebellion.

Torren looked down at his young recruit, biding his time until the man showed signs of discomfort. Only then did Torren speak. "You may stand, Teig. What is your news?"

Teig rose to full height, still half a head shorter than the Leader, yet his eyes remained downcast. "Sorcerer Entek has arrived. He awaits entry at your word."

"Send him to my private chamber." Torren left the great room to move down a cold, damp tunnel, lit with torches set in sconces. The sides gave way at irregular intervals to separate rooms—soldiers' quarters, supplies, food storage, eating and cooking areas, and armory—dug by hand, tools…and dark magic. Magic so sinister Torren heard the soldiers' whispers of their fear to enter many of the rooms.

The head of the Rebellion continued down the makeshift hallway until it ended at his private chamber. A frame of black oak, pounded into the sandstone walls, supported a thick door made from the same wood. This afforded Torren solitude and security. A series of incantations and gestures, taught to him by a Mage he had promised to free, opened the door. *Death is one form of freedom. The Mage should have been more specific with his bargaining.*

Inside, a fire in the center of the room remained lit at all times. *Another accommodating gesture from the Mage.*

Torren positioned himself at the end of the sturdy oak table, which had a full view of the door. His feather bed, hidden behind a wall of silk, was to his right. Beyond that, concealed by a tapestry, a secondary exit.

As Torren waited for the prospective strategist to arrive, he filled a silver mug with ale and plucked an apple from the bowl next to the pitcher. He savored the fruit, kept sweet and crisp by the cool storage. *Little luxuries can be found even in exile.* The apple raised, Torren forwent the next bite when the door swung open. *Damn sorcerer.* But Torren kept the thought to himself.

Entek entered. Layered robes, embroidered with intricate runes unknown to Torren, flowed over the sorcerer's feet, giving the illusion that he floated, rather than walked. Torren watched the ageless man. His braided black hair draped down his back, fingers were entwined in front of him, the long milky white nails overlapped to the wrist. The man stopped before Torren in a rustle of silk. He nodded once, a slight sardonic smile cracked the edge of his mouth, and colored lights flickered from the depths of his dark eyes.

Torren motioned Entek to join him at the table, but the sorcerer chose instead to glide to the fire and gaze into the flames.

Restraining a retort at the rudeness, Torren poured a cup of ale for his guest and brought both mugs to the fire. Before positioning himself on the other side of the blaze, Torren set the drink beside Entek. The alchemist swayed slightly from side to side, his eyes in a narrow slit. A low hum reverberated from him. The flames rose and danced in harmony with the vibrations. Torren forced himself to wait patiently for the end of the meditation.

"What is the purpose for your summons of me, Torren, Leader of the Rebels?" With the words, the fire diminished to a low burn.

A spasm of nerves, a skipped heartbeat, a caught breath. Torren had waited for this moment for five moon phases. He knew that

Entek had traveled a thousand miles from his home in Dangrial for this meeting. Torren thought carefully how he would answer.

To summon a sorcerer is to invite dark and dangerous power. Despite the peril, Torren craved any advantage that could be gained against his opposition—the leaders of the three cities and their Warriors. Aid from one skilled in the dark arts could be a means to take control of Djenrye and the Ortehlae.

"I summoned you to join the Rebellion. It is said that your art as a conjurer is strong and your hatred of our common enemy even stronger. I have gathered information that may be of benefit to both our causes: yours—annihilation of the council, and mine—control of the Ortehlae and the destruction of Terra-hun. To join forces will ensure the achievement of our goals. Together, we will be the new leaders of Djenrye."

Entek stared at Torren for a few moments, and then a sound emerged from his throat. At first a low growl, it erupted into full-blown laughter.

Hot anger coursed through Torren's body. His eyes flashed gold across the room and washed the sorcerer in a yellow glow. "Would you explain to me what you find amusing about conquering Djenrye together?" His voice rose, bellowing off the walls. "Do you not desire this?"

Entek's laughter ceased, but the occasional snicker escaped. "Certainly, I welcome a sweeping change born of destruction. I have waited many winters for the Rebellion to reach the necessary point of power." Entek paused for a moment and the ale-filled cup drifted up into his hand. "Yet, you have shown me nothing new since the time of Dekren. You remain as children playing at the game of insurrection. You have neither the wits nor the means to overthrow a system that was put in place millennia ago...by the Gods themselves."

"Do not be blinded by the mistakes of my predecessor." Torren stormed to the table to refill his cup. "I have created an organized army of Warriors from Dekren's scattered bands of men. Our base camp is well stocked and has gone undetected for a generation." The ale disappeared in a single swallow, long enough to suppress Torren's outrage. In a steadier tone, he continued. "We have recently discovered the whereabouts of the missing Guardian. We are closing in on the location of the Orteh hidden by Dekren before his death. We will soon have them both in our grip. All that will be left is to bring them back to Djenrye."

"Are you a fool or a liar?" Entek asked, the words oozing from his lips. "I have searched since the death of the last Guardian for his successor—to no avail. It can only mean that the child did not survive. As for the Orteh, it too is lost to our world, or it would have shown itself in my visions."

"I am neither fool nor liar. Both of the things you greatly desire have been hidden in Terra-hun. The mark has come into enlightenment and we followed the call." Torren hesitated, carefully choosing the next words. "The one obstacle that may prove troublesome is Colton, son of Kamm. He has stood watch over the Guardian these many long seasons. But he cannot hide him much longer."

"This Colton is protecting him?" Entek's nails stroked his jaw line. He stared at the embers, rather than Torren. "I require a space to conjure. If the mark is enlightened, my incantations and dark sorceries will locate not only the Guardian, but also the Orteh. The bond between them gains strength, one from the other. But I require privacy. Have you a chamber fit for my needs?"

Then Torren made a gesture that surprised him as much as it seemed to shock Entek—he bowed. "At once."

Entek called back as he walked toward the exit. "And once you have the two treasures?"

"They will be brought back here. I am Androne. My abilities may not be as encompassing as the Djen, but my determination is far greater. With your aid, I will annihilate Phraile Highlae and enter Ty Raile untouched. I will perform the Guardian ritual and take over the Ortehlae."

Entek stopped and turned to face Torren; his hand floated back to his face. The unnaturally long nails were unnerving.

"There is a way for you to gain your own power, but it is as painful as it is dangerous. An aligning of the planets occurs as we speak. It will create a river of dark power greater than any of us have ever seen or experienced. To tap into this source would make an Androne stronger than any Djen. Near as strong as the Magi, without the need for lifelong training and practice. However…it comes with a price."

"Which is?"

"Your answer would be dependent on my ability to control the flow of the energy and the number of times that energy is tapped. Multiple attempts could result in madness, or in death. The overriding philosophy is restraint. You must proceed cautiously. This could be the path for which you have been searching."

An answer…a way to finally reach the goals so long unattainable.

"We have a room previously used as a sanctum. It is quite spacious and the men are reluctant to approach. A Mage occupied it…and suffered an untimely death within. My men will send for your books and assistants."

"And…my chambers? I require a place of rest and study for these tasks."

"The fight has taken many Warriors, leaving several vacant rooms. You may choose the one you find most suitable." Torren called for Teig, who entered immediately. "Take Entek to the late Mage's chamber and bring him his apprentices." The soldier nodded and escorted the sorcerer out the door.

Torren picked up the forgotten apple and bit a chunk out of it. The juice ran down his chin. The honey flavor tasted almost as sweet as his impending victory. He paced back and forth, unable to remain still. Lifelong yearnings of leading the Djen, of ending the other world, of taking control of the planet, were coming to fruition. He could feel it deep in his bones.

Chapter 27

Entering her house by the back door, a musty, stale smell assaulted Stevie. She looked at the footprint-shaped bits of mud, grass, and debris crisscrossing the hardwood floor and carpet.

"They couldn't clean up their mess?" she asked rhetorically. Colton shrugged and they proceeded through each room to open windows and light scented candles. Once the air began to clear, Stevie and Colton moved to the front porch. The feeling of being violated caused her skin to prickle and sullied her earlier excitement.

Despite the weather, the chalked outlines where the Rebel and the police officers had fallen, along with remnants of crime scene tape, were still visible. *Clean the carpet, remove the tape, wash away the chalk—but home's never gonna feel the same. People died here.* A sob escaped her throat.

Without a word, Colton pulled her close. She wept against his chest as he ran his hand through her hair.

"Colton," she said her words in hiccups. "Why did this have to happen?"

"My Shylae… Would that I could have prevented all of this and kept you innocent of the ugliness of our war. Had the circumstances been different, you and I would be joined by now, living together in Phraile Highlae, raising our children. Me guarding you, and you guarding the world. Yet we must wait for that future and hold out hope."

She looked up at him. He wore his Warrior's face on the surface, but beneath, she glimpsed a deep empathy and love. "It's not your fault, Colton. You didn't create this…and without you, Mom and I would be dead by now."

His grip tightened. He whispered softly, "My life would have ended with yours, Shylae. You are my world."

His mouth found hers, soft and sweet. Their love merged, flowing through her, washing away her dismay. Her pulse quickened, the energy rushed into every fiber of her soul, filling her completely.

Breathless, their lips parted reluctantly.

"Let us make this right for your mother. I will assist you in returning the home to its rightful condition. When Jan Barrett returns, it will be the home she remembered."

Stevie gave him a quick last hug and they set to work.

Tired and overwhelmed from hours of drudgery, Stevie and Colton headed upstairs for the night. Colton changed into a pair of pajama bottoms borrowed from Wood, and Stevie headed to the bathroom. She waited for the room to get nice and steamy before climbing into the shower.

Eyes closed, Stevie let the hot water pulsate over her tired muscles, especially her shoulders. The spray washed away the stress and opened her mind. Without warning, her mark began to burn. Every nerve tingled and Stevie felt lightheaded—signs of an impending vision.

Bracing herself against the tiled wall, the scene around her changed to that of a cave. It looked to be the same passage from her earlier vision. The torches in sconces were familiar and water dripped down the earthen wall.

Alone, she headed toward a glow at the far end of the tunnel and found herself standing at the mouth of the cave. After a cautious peek through the opening, she remembered that she could not be seen. Stevie exited onto an outcropping of stone. Cliffs rose from both sides and mountains stretched as far as she could see. The moist, warm air settled on her skin. Raptors of all kinds flew overhead. To her right, a waterfall raged over a crevasse between two cliffs, ending at a river hundreds of feet below.

Voices to her left caught her attention. The man Colton had called Torren was speaking with a sinister- looking man, who must have come out of the cave behind her. *How did I not notice him before?*

They spoke to each other in the Djen language, and she thought she recognized the words Orteh, Colton, and—at this, her heart sank—a bastardized version of Colorado. The man in the robes did most of the talking, with Torren staring stoically out at the canyon. When the robed man walked away, the expression of the supposed leader changed from stone to anger or, more accurately, to rage.

He raised his fists to the sky and bellowed "Colton!" He shouted the name again, and the cliff walls answered with wave upon wave of echoes. Torren tore a huge rock from the cliffside and held it above his head, grunting loudly, the muscles and veins standing out on his biceps and shoulders. He heaved the boulder into the canyon, crying out "Colton" once again.

Out of breath, his hands and muscles still clenched, he leaned back against the mountainside. He ground his teeth, and the light from his eyes illuminated the shadows across the valley in gold. It unnerved Stevie. His raspy breath steadied. Torren straightened his leather vest, and moved down the path. Shortly after he passed out of sight, that same booming voice echoed up from below. The sounds of scrambling feet followed, indicating Torren was barking orders.

Unable to follow the noises, her vision ended as abruptly as it had started.

The shower, still hot, meant that the vision had taken no more than a few minutes. Stevie finished washing and rushed to tell Colton what she had seen.

She ran into the bedroom, wrapped only in a towel. As she shook Colton awake, her loose hair splattered him with water. It took Colton's wide-eyed expression and the sensual grin that spread across his face for her to realize she had forgotten to put on her robe. Her face hot from embarrassment—and maybe a bit of desire—she hurriedly threw on her old terry cloth standby and told Colton of her entire vision.

When she finished, Colton shook his head. "Shylae, my pardon, but I could not focus my mind on your words after being awoken by such a lovely sight. Please repeat the details of your vision again."

Heat rising to her face again, Stevie slapped him hard on the arm. "Oh you…"

The second telling seemed to hold his attention. After Stevie repeated the story, Colton paused for a moment and then started to laugh.

"What's so funny?" Stevie asked, taken aback.

"Do you not see, Shylae? You have borne witness to Torren being informed of the death of his Warriors—all of the Warriors he sent after you. His anger is to be rejoiced, not feared. It confirms his humiliation."

Continuing to laugh, he sat up and motioned for Stevie to sit with him. His eyes sparkled as she moved closer. Before she could speak, he flipped her on her back. His mouth found hers in celebration and triumph. His kiss became urgent, wanting, and he lowered his body on top of hers. Passion filled her as his lips moved down her neck and over her shoulders. Stevie's breathing intensified, her robe fell open, and she pulled him closer, their bodies moving in sync.

Their lips met again and this time his kiss was soft and alluring, his tongue running against her bottom lip, sucking it in and then finding hers. As their tongues danced, his hands moved to her thighs with a gentle caress. He slipped them under her hips, tugging her closer. Stevie wanted to give herself to him—right here, right now—but she knew this wasn't the time for them to come together as one.

Colton must have felt it, too. He slowly pulled back, barely enough to allow him to put a layer of material between them. He covered her with the robe and rolled to her side, facing her, stroking her jaw line.

"You are so beautiful, my Shylae." He reached for her hand and kissed each finger in turn. "But this is not the time…"

"I know…" she murmured, her lips brushing his cheek. Reluctant to move away, Stevie forced herself to sit up. She rubbed her face and ran her hands through her long hair.

"I'm going to put on some PJs. Thick—flannel—shapeless ones."

As her feet touched the floor, Colton grabbed her. "I love you. You must know, more than anything, I wish to show you my love."

Stevie smiled. "Ditto. Hey, if you can wait, I can, too."

He released her and eased himself back on the bed.

"I'll be a minute. At least tonight we can sleep in each other's arms."

His legs crossed, he stared into the flames, willing his mind to open. The sounds of the men in the camp gnawed at the corner of his thoughts. He ignored their words. Torren's eyes watered, but he remained unblinking. His heart pounded with anger at Entek's discovery of the Guardian. Moments earlier, Torren had been informed that Entek had a vision—a vision of Shylae. *A female Guardian. After ten generations. How is this possible? Is the Prophecy more than the ramblings of an inbred sect?* He breathed in slowly to calm his rage. When his pulse, his mind, and the flames synchronized, he allowed his eyes to close.

"Colton…Colton…" he whispered, concentrating on the message he wanted to send. Torren fell into a deep trance, reaching out for his nemesis. *This will surely unnerve him. An unsettled opponent is easier to defeat.*

"I am coming…" His voice was monotone, edged with threat. He held up his arms. His muscles and resolve tightened. When he opened his eyes, again, the gold light shone brighter than the flames. The heat of the fire caused his eyes to water.

"I am the demon in your nightmares. I am the death on the battlefield. I am the darkness of forever. I am coming, Colton, I am coming for you…" He repeated the message, over and over, until the rage inside him intensified to an inferno.

Then he changed the words. "I know your secrets. I know who you protect. The Guardian lives. I now know—the Guardian…is female. She is named…Shylae.

"I will drain her and you will watch. You will see her life flow away and the power become mine." He paused, letting the message permeate Colton's dreams. "You know that you cannot stop it. Then, in the depths of your dismay and despair, will I kill you." As he continued repeating the message, images of their childhood flickered at the edge of his thoughts.

He recalled the friendship he had shared with Colton—play-fighting with swords, swimming in the lake, dreaming of being Warriors. They were brothers in arms, best of friends; fighting for the same goals, the same people. *Then you discarded me after my father's death.*

He refocused on the present, but summoned those memories to reach Colton. *I found a new family in the Rebellion.*

"You are my enemy now. No longer my brother. No longer my comrade. I come for the Guardian—and you." He drove the last of the thought outward with all his strength. Exhausted, he leaned back, and breathed slowly and deeply, satisfied the message had been received.

Colton bolted upright. Stevie, awakened by the movement, sat up.

"What is it, Colton?"

He shook his head. "It cannot be…"

In the weeks that Stevie had known him, she had witnessed many moods and emotions—far more than anyone else—but this was new. He rose and began pacing, his muscles taunt, clenching and unclenching his fists, breathing raggedly.

"What's wrong? What 'can't be'?" She watched him pace. "Talk to me, Colton. Were you dreaming?"

"I was asleep. Yes...no... I do not know. It did not feel as a dream." He returned to the edge of the bed, holding his face in his hands. "This extends beyond the realm of possible."

"What's not possible? What's going on?" She moved closer, touching his leg. "Talk to me," she pleaded. He met her gaze. The muscle in his jaw tightened.

When he spoke, it was through clenched teeth. "Torren has sent me a message. I do not know how he was able to accomplish this, but he did."

"Wait. I thought you told me the Djen could call each other with their minds."

Colton turned and the morning sun coming through the window cast a light across his face.

"He is not Djen. He is Androne. He should not be able to reach anyone with his thoughts. And to be able to enter my dreams? This is not even a feat of which the Magi are capable. He has broken through a barrier...somehow..." His voice trailed off, eyes staring at the sunbeam on the carpet at their feet.

Stevie didn't know what to do. She didn't understand half of what the Djen, or the Androne were capable of, but she knew that for Colton to be this upset, something was very wrong. She reached out to give whatever reassurance she could. Her touch made him start.

Colton grabbed Stevie's hand, practically pulling her off the bed. "Make haste. We must leave. Immediately."

Unnerved, she grabbed clothes out of the closet, giving little more than a cursory thought to what she packed. In minutes, she and Colton were rushing for the stairs.

At the bottom, he stopped and turned to her. "I did not mean to frighten you." He paused and smiled wanly. "We will be fine. I will keep you safe, but you must trust me."

Stevie returned the smile, willing hers to look more hopeful. "Of course I trust you...with my life." She touched his face. "I'm just confused."

"I understand. For that you have my apology. There is much I need to tell you, but our time is short...far shorter than I had expected. I am able to tell you this—Torren is far stronger than I could have anticipated. He not only sent me a message with his thought, he reached into my mind and drew me into his. I could see him sitting in front of a fire."

Stevie shivered uncontrollably. "What was the message?"

"It was filled with hate, with rage, with revenge." His voice dripped with disgust.

"What was the message?" Stevie asked, again, fearing the answer.

Colton would not meet her gaze. Instead, he looked past her, at the front door. "He is coming to kill us," he whispered.

Stevie grabbed both sides of his face, forcing him to look at her. "Tell me the rest. I know that there's more."

For a moment, he looked as though he might confess, but then his face softened and he smiled. "No...that is all," he said simply.

"We've come too far for this bullshit. Don't lie to me."

"I do not speak mistruths. It is only...Torren comes for us, and he knows of you. It is more than knowing the Guardian's existence. He knows your name and that you are here in Terra-hun. How he could have possibly gained this knowledge is a mystery."

Stevie moved slowly toward the door, staring straight ahead. "How powerful is he?" she asked, trying to keep her voice steady.

Colton stopped and faced her. "Do not worry, my love. He will never touch you. I will not allow that to happen." He kissed her on the forehead. "He is strong, but I am stronger. I am a greater Warrior, and I have something besides power for which to fight."

With nothing more to say, they left the house, hand in hand.

Chapter 28

The truck packed, Wood waited impatiently for Stevie and Colton to return. Distracted by thoughts of the night before, he was thankful that his partner had agreed to cover for them. Drake would ensure that Alyssa and Jan would be in a safe location. He worried less about Jan. Strength, stubbornness, and classic beauty—all wrapped up in one package. *Maybe when all this is over, I'll ask her to dinner.* And there was Alyssa. She showed inner strength, but still seemed fragile to him.

The rumble of the Jeep could be heard before Stevie and Colton came into view. Wood waved as they parked in the driveway, relieved that they wouldn't be getting a late start. Stevie seemed shaken as she exited the Jeep, but there was something else. *She's grown years in this past week. Her beauty rivals that of Colton's sister.*

"Stevie?"

"Good morning," she said, and then looked past him.

He touched Stevie's arm. "What's going on?"

"Oh…it's really nothing. Colton had a dream last night and it kinda freaked me out…" She trailed off. Wood looked to Colton for an answer.

"I will explain at another time," he said and sidestepped Wood.

Stevie and Colton entered the house first, with Wood trailing behind. Marise and Jack looked to be nearly finished packing the cooler. The detective noted that Stevie visibly relaxed in the presence of her friend.

She called out, "Ready to go, Jack?"

Jack's big grin elicited a smile from Stevie as he walked over and hugged her.

"Morning, Stevie… Hell, yes, I'm ready," said Jack.

A sigh escaped from Marise. "He has been ready since dawn."

Stevie laughed. "You brought your passport, right? Wood?"

Jack patted his jacket pocket. "Right here, Baby Girl. And I saw Wood stick his in his backpack." He sidled closer to Stevie and in a stage whisper, said, "And it has a truly horrible picture."

Ignoring the jibe, Wood placed his hand on Colton's shoulder and maneuvered him farther into the kitchen. "Colton here had a dream he needs to tell us about."

The Warrior's look hardened. "I told you it is a discussion for another time. Let us begin the journey."

His tone ended any further query, and the group quickly loaded the remaining items into Wood's SUV.

On the way out of Golden, Stevie asked to stop for Starbucks. This led to a heated argument between her and Wood about the merits of lattes over convenience store coffee.

"We have to gas up anyway. Why make the extra stop?" asked Wood, defiantly.

Stevie refused to give in, ending the disagreement with "...because the Guardian said so."

This brought a chuckle, even from Colton.

Once out of city traffic and well on their way, Wood explained his discussions with Drake the previous evening.

"She promised to regularly check in on Alyssa and Jan and keep me informed about how the case is—or isn't—progressing. She also swore to keep my 'vacation spot' secret."

"Seriously, Detective—you're certain this isn't gonna affect your job when all this is done?" Stevie asked, genuinely worried at the career risks the detective was taking.

"No worries, Stevie. Most of the cops in my department already think I'm too intense and a bit nuts. They're probably glad to have me outta their hair. I doubt it will add up to more than cop-gossip." He laughed. "As for anyone figuring out what I'm really doing, we'll have a lot more to worry about than my job. Can you spell, FBI?"

"Why would the Feds get involved?" Stevie asked.

Jack answered before Wood. "Girl, haven't you heard about Roswell, the Kecksburg Incident, or the sightings by military pilots? It's not Wood's fear that this will all go public, it's the cover-up that the government is gonna have to implement to make people think the truth is a hoax. And cover-up usually means no witnesses."

"Geez, Jack. Paranoid?"

Wood cleared his throat. "Stevie, Jack is right on the mark here. I've seen the Feds in action, and it's not always pretty." He broke the ensuing silence with a reassurance. "The only time we'll need to worry is when we actually get to Princess Royal Island. If the Golden PD really wants to look for me, that's where I'll end up leaving a trail."

"How so?" Stevie asked, grateful for the turn in the conversation.

"We're gonna need to rent a boat to get to the island. Even with cash, they'll want to see some sort of identification and they may require a credit card to ensure we don't run off with or damage the boat."

"Why can't I use my ID?"

"If it's like renting a car, they require you to be twenty-five years old. Regardless, our cards or IDs will be plugged into the system. And you, young lady, are supposed to be with your aunt in Canada."

Jack piped up, "Try this one on—I can have my dad call ahead and rent the boat. My folks are loaded and he travels all over the world. His info being pinged won't raise any suspicions."

"Your dad would do that, Jack?" Stevie asked, amazed. Jack's down-to-earth attitude made her forget sometimes that he "comes from money", as her mom would say.

"Babe, you're the one who always calls me spoiled. Hell, yeah, he would. Especially if I tell him it's research for my book. I'm the golden boy who got accepted to DU on a scholarship…remember?"

"Damn, Jack. Glad you came," Wood replied.

They drove in silence for a few minutes, and Stevie realized Marise had not participated in the discussions; a common characteristic of Colton, but not his sister. She nudged the female Warrior. "What's wrong? You're so quiet."

Marise directed her gaze out the window rather than Stevie. "My brother has been on edge and has pointedly not spoken of his dream. It worries me."

Stevie noticed Wood's look in the rearview mirror, which was directed at Colton.

The detective took the initiative. "Okay, Colton, fess up. Now you've got everyone worried."

Colton's tone was neutral, but Stevie noticed his body tense as he attempted to downplay the experience.

"I dreamt of Torren sitting before a fire…he sent me a message."

Marise gasped audibly. "You said dream, but it sounds akin to how we communicate…at least during waking. How is it possible for Torren to accomplish this? What did he say?"

"It was nothing—the usual empty threats by the Rebellion. Childish taunts. Do not worry, my sister. It frightened Shylae, but you and I know it means nothing."

"The message itself is inconsequential, yes. But he is showing a power he cannot possess. This is the real threat, Brother."

"I hear your concern, but do not share it. He will be defeated."

Marise refused to let the matter go. "And what was the message?"

Colton sighed, took a deep breath, and admitted, "That Torren himself is hunting us, and that he will personally kill the Guardian."

"Back up a few steps, will ya?" Detective Wood interjected. "Who the hell is Torren? What are you talkin' about?"

"Torren is the leader of the Rebellion, and an enemy of both Terra-hun and Djenrye. I have known him my entire life. We grew up together in Tyré. His father was a Master Warrior, trainer of all the new soldiers, and personal guard of Hayden."

Jack cocked an eyebrow. "And Hayden is who?"

"Patience, Jack Snow, there is much to tell and I will attempt to explain succinctly…if you cease interruptions," Colton continued.

"Hayden is, or I should say was, one of the Guardians. He and his family disappeared during the Jajing war. But that is another story. Torren and I grew to manhood together. As children, we were more akin to brothers than friends, despite his being an Androne Elf and my being Djen. But the death of his father during the Jajing war, twisted Torren's sensibilities. He became bitter and desperate, no longer content to serve the Guardians." He looked at Stevie, his eyes clear but pained. When he spoke, his voice lowered. "It was then that we had a…a falling out. He felt I deserted him. A glimmer of truth, as I could no longer comprehend this longing of his for power and control. He chose to join the Rebel uprising and changed from my brother to my enemy."

Colton paused for a moment, appearing to gather his thoughts. "We heard rumors of Torren's death for many years, but it clearly was not so."

Marise nodded. "I did manage to contact Esalon." She turned to Jack and the detective to explain, "He is Tyré's assigned Mage." Then she continued, "He will inform the Council that Torren lives."

"So they'll send in the cavalry?" Jack asked. "You know, the guys on horseback who come in at the last minute to save the day?"

Colton shook his head. "That is a useless wish. Open war between the Rebels and the Djen on this plane cannot occur."

Chastised, Jack kept silent.

"Torren's newly found strength and powers emphasize our need to practice when we are not actually traveling. Shylae, your visionary skills must be used to determine the extent of Torren's advancement."

"Sounds like we need to look for a camping area off the beaten path," Stevie suggested. "When we stop for dinner tonight, let's ask around."

All but Wood agreed. "I don't want this trip to get too stretched out. I was under the impression we need to get to the Orb as soon as possible."

"You are correct, but if we approach the enemy unprepared, we are certain to fail," Marise cautioned.

Not wanting to argue on either side, Stevie chose to change the subject and grabbed the atlas off the floor. "Hey, Wood... I'm getting hungry. Laramie, Wyoming, about half an hour ahead. How 'bout we stop there for breakfast?"

Jack tugged at his shirt. "Yeah... I could use some sustenance. I'm wasting away."

"You, I'm ignoring," Wood grunted. "You always want to eat..."

Stevie couldn't help laughing.

The attempt to defend himself made it worse. "Hey, this body didn't get perfect by chance. You gotta feed the machine." Jack flexed his bicep.

Wood shook his head. "If I say yes, will you shut up?"

Jack's head bobbed up and down, reminding Stevie of her Labrador.

"I need to top the tank off, anyway. We should be able to go at least three hundred miles between fill-ups, and I don't want to stop all the time."

Feverishly tapping on his iPad, Jack called out suggestions. They settled on Shari's Restaurant off Interstate 80.

Breakfast came and went quickly, with a friendly waitress, few patrons, and good food. Colton and Marise ordered steak and eggs—steak bloody, eggs well cooked. Jack and Wood originally opted for bacon, eggs, and pancakes (with whipped cream), until Colton glared at them.

"If you eat such a concoction, your training shall consist of nothing more than how to hold down your meal."

Wood changed his order to mirror the Warriors', but Jack simply pouted.

Colton must have taken that as agreement, for he told the waitress, "The young man will have the same."

The two looked so different to Stevie. Jack slumped in his seat, and Colton sat proud and tall. *The boy and the soldier. I bet Colton will whip these two into shape whether they like it or not.* She hid her grin behind her napkin.

Heading back to the SUV, Wood announced loudly that he needed a nap. There was a quick shuffle and the final seating resulted in Stevie driving, Colton up front, Jack and Wood in the back, and Marise positioning herself between the two front seats.

"Aren't your legs gonna get sore, squatting like that?" Stevie asked Marise.

Colton chuckled. "I once bore witness to my sister holding that position from sunrise to nightfall, surveying her prey. When the time came to act, she bounded on the enemy with unmatched speed and agility."

"All of which you taught me, Brother." Marise spoke of the time they were children, how Colton instructed her in a variety of fighting arts and the proper use of the bow. "With which I became far more skilled than he," Marise added with a wink. "He spent what time he had protecting me and keeping me near him, all the while teaching me how not to rely on his protection."

"Torren had a hand in your training, as well. The manner in which you trailed us reminded me of the wolf cubs Father kept as pets," Colton said.

"And I must admit to an infatuation with Torren when I was a child."

Stevie gasped. "For real?"

"He did not come into this world a wicked man. He stood taller than Colton when we were children, and his age being greater than ours, he grew into adulthood sooner. He had a face pleasing to the eye…and still does, by all accounts."

Stevie felt her head nod slightly before she could stop herself. The flash of—is that jealousy?—in Colton's eyes told her that he noticed the movement.

"Oh, Shylae. I daydreamed of being his mate and having the most beautiful Androne/Djen offspring. Colton teased me endlessly about it, but…" Marise touched Colton's shoulder. "He was kind enough not to do so in front of Torren. They were inseparable, with me constantly at their heels."

Stevie glimpsed a wistful smile, which contrasted sharply to Colton's stony expression.

They drove for a time in silence, punctuated by Jack tapping on the iPad or a soft snore coming from the detective. Stevie noticed the sky darkening. "It looks like it wants to rain. I hope it moves on."

Jack grumbled from the back. "I agree...It would be major Suckville if we had to camp in the rain."

The female Warrior leaned forward, pointing at the windshield and smiling. "Look. Over there. A rainbow."

Stevie glimpsed Colton reach over to touch his sister's face.

"Leave it to you to see the positive," he said.

After four hours on the road, Stevie begged for a bathroom break. Jack checked his tablet for the closest stop and located Evanston, Wyoming—right off of the highway and just a few miles from the Utah border.

Twenty minutes later, they exited off the highway and into the first gas station on the right. The group piled out of the car to stretch their legs and Jack rummaged in the coolers.

"Okay, Stevie, I know we're in 'training' mode, but you coulda packed at least one soda." He closed the cooler lid and headed into the convenience store, his tablet tucked under his arm.

When Stevie entered to pay for the fuel, she found Jack engaged in a lively conversation with the teenage clerk. The tablet rested on the counter between them, her friend tapping on the screen and asking questions, such as "Any camping in this area?" and "Which roads did you say were washed out?"

Back in the SUV, Jack relayed his findings to the group. "So, I found a National Forest—Uinta-Wasach National Forest—on the satellite map and was asking Josh—the guy at the counter—about camping. Well, check this out... The campgrounds are technically open, but several of the fire roads have been washed out."

"So?" Wood asked.

"That means we can camp in an area with no one else around. Assuming, of course, that this beater can handle the roads."

"If the road is passable for the rangers, my Blazer can make it," Wood said confidently.

Colton craned around in his seat to face Jack. "Is this area which you have located on your picture slate truly isolated? And will we be able to reach the site by nightfall?"

"Totally."

Over the next couple of hours, Colton grilled the detective on his weapons training.

"I was in the military," Wood assured him. "And, of course, my police training. We're required to test at the range twice a year, but I'm there several times a week."

"Range? Is that a type of auditorium to practice hand-to-hand combat?"

Wood shook his head. "No. A firing range. For guns. But if you're asking about close fighting, I just said I was in the military. A Marine, as a matter of fact—Hoo Rah. I can disarm, disable, or kill an opponent with no other weapon but my hands." His tone made it clear that he wasn't talking smack.

Stevie caught the look of newfound respect from Colton.

Wood added, "Just so ya know, I might not have experience with a sword, but I'm a quick learner."

"You have allayed my concerns, Detective Wood. Tonight we will concentrate on learning the skill of swords. Tomorrow, the skill of the bow," Colton said.

"Excellent," Wood said. "I've bow hunted with my brother in New York, and twice bagged a doe."

"This is a good thing, but remember, my friend, the Rebels shoot back," said Colton. "Jack Snow. You are the one who will need to focus to improve your training."

"Hey…" whined Jack. "I've been reading up on sword maneuvers. It's just that I'm not used to the weight."

Colton laughed. "Reading is something to improve your mind, but it will not teach you how to wield a sword. Only with practice may you achieve skill. After we have finished the evening meal, sword training shall commence. Marise is an excellent teacher and has trained the best Warriors in Tyré. Shylae, your sole task is to concentrate on your visions."

"Do not worry," Marise said to Jack and Wood, her tone sugary sweet. "I will be gentle with the two of you...this time."

True to Jack's satellite images, they managed to locate a decent site in a dry clearing. With plenty of daylight left, Jack helped Colton set up the tents, Stevie and Marise gathered kindling for the campfire, and Wood pulled out a propane stove to start dinner and coffee for the cold night ahead.

The smell of sage and roasted pig called everyone to dinner. A hearty meal of sausage, corn on the cob, beans, and shepherd's bread, followed by campfire coffee, had Stevie thinking of sleep, not training.

Colton, however, began to pull weapons from his pack. "It is time to begin. Jack, you found us an excellent location—quiet and desolate. Shylae, we will leave you to concentrate."

The men followed Colton and Marise into the woods. Stevie stared at the fire, listening to the sounds of her companions as they moved farther away. As the familiar sphere rose from the flames, but before completely losing herself in the vision, she heard Colton's voice in the distance.

"Everyone, hold your sword thusly. Feel the weight. It is an extension of your arm, not a separate object. Good. The training will now begin..."

Chapter 29

Soaring over mountain ranges, Stevie spied a pass she recognized from her previous vision at the cabin. A path appeared on her right, roughly an equal distance between the peak and the river that wound its way through the valley below. From her vantage point, she could make out three people hiking up the trail. She willed herself closer, and discovered the people were Colton, Marise and herself. The physical Stevie looked up and seemed to wave. *She—I mean, I—can see me?*

A familiar light caught her attention. Though faint, its sparkle created an unmistakable glimmer. She raced toward it. As she drew closer, dark clouds threatened to extinguish the light. She willed herself to fly faster before it completely faded.

Without warning, the light shot upward and, in an instant, was gone altogether. *What the hell?* Confusion threw Stevie out of her vision. The smoke from the fire caught in her throat. She sputtered, "Colton... I need you."

Colton came crashing through the woods, the rest of the party on his heels.

"Shylae, are you injured?"

Coughing, she waved at the particles stubbornly trying to enter her nose. "Except for smoke inhalation, I'm fine...physically, but something really weird happened in my vision."

"Weird?" Jack asked. "Sci-fi weird or horror-movie weird?"

Stevie glared at her friend, choosing not to answer. Instead, she explained to Colton the odd way the light disappeared.

Her protector looked perplexed and retrieved the Din Ashyea, flipping pages back and forth as he scanned the text. After a time, he closed the cover slowly. "I could locate nothing to explain this strange occurrence." The feathers in his hair quivered as he shook his head back and forth. "The meaning behind the dark clouds appears to be as before. Lacking better direction, I fear that the sudden and swift disappearance may foretell the Rebels capturing the Orteh before we are able."

Marise came up beside Colton. "I interpret the meaning to reflect the Orteh's exit from this plane. Would that not make sense?"

Colton's eyes brightened. "It does indeed. If the Rebellion manages to obtain the Orteh prior to our arrival, they will have completed the first phase of the destruction of Terra-hun." Darkness crossed his features. He took Stevie's hands into his. "They cannot accomplish their goal without you. They will return to Djenrye, either with you as their captive, or they will lure you to them."

"No. We have to get to it first," she whispered.

"That's the plan." Jack and Wood spoke in chorus.

Stevie had forgotten they were there. Her focus had been intently on the brother and sister, and on Djenrye.

The thought of going to her home world frightened her—it seemed to have little in common with the world she had known her whole life. What if it was too strange and she couldn't adjust? *Would Colton return to this plane with me to live life as a Hundye? Could he?* The dilemma created discomfort.

Colton's fingers stroked her cheek, bringing her back to the present.

"Do you feel able to re-enter a vision to find Torren?" he asked.

"I don't know… I mean, I'm up for it. I just don't know if I can. The only times I saw him were not by choice."

"I understand, my Shylae," said Colton. "But we need you to make the attempt. It would be of great help to know whether he is still in Djenrye or has crossed into this plane."

Stevie sighed and returned her attention to the fire. *At least the smoke isn't blowing in my face any more.*

Willing forth the trance, she sat silently, breathing slowly, deeply and focused on calling forth a vision to show her Torren. Sap from one of the logs crackled and spit. The sound startled her, but she willed herself beyond it.

Refusing to be distracted by the movement behind her, she nonetheless felt Colton touch her shoulder as he seated himself beside her. The resulting contact opened a vision before her. The fire began to fade, and then brightened again—no longer the same campfire as in Utah.

Men sat on trampled ground in front of a fire pit. Horses whinnied in the shadows beyond the flames. Stevie noticed lights flitting around them. *Too bright for fireflies, and, OMG, they're different colors!*

Before she managed a closer look, she realized Torren sat at her left side. Oblivious to her presence, he gazed into the fire, a stick in his hand, rolling one of the logs through the embers. His closeness unnerved Stevie. The aroma of musk, mixed with scents of the trail—horse, dust, leather—filled her nostrils. *Except for the horse odor, he smells like Colton.*

She rose quickly and moved behind him. Looking around, she couldn't determine if Torren and his men were in Djenrye or the human world. From Colton's descriptions, the two planes were similar. The same pine trees creating the forest, and the same night sounds of crickets and birds. An owl hooted from the dark, and she walked toward it and away from the camp. The Rebels' voices faded behind her. She lowered herself onto the nearest boulder and asked the vision to show her more.

The scene changed. The sun had come up and Stevie now looked down on the woods rather than through them. A group of mounted men, bearing the insignia of the Rebellion— two black gloved hands holding the Orteh, Élan-Vitál—passed through a marshy area. The horses' hooves left imprints on the damp ground cover. Stevie recognized the look of moss when the permafrost melts from shows she had watched on nature channels. *Alaska, maybe?*

Beyond the thawing tundra, silhouettes of mountains rose in the distance—the direction in which the Rebels were headed. The flutter of butterfly wings caused her head to turn and her focus to move away from the riders.

A light moved from her peripheral vision to directly in front of her. She stared at it and discovered the glow came from what she could only describe as a tiny girl with wings. The cheerful, pixie-like features turned into a smile, and a miniature hand waved in greeting. Stevie giggled with delight, which seemed to draw more lights to her. *Faeries? Toto, I don't think we're in Golden any more.* She closed her eyes and willed herself out of the vision.

Stevie explained all she had seen to her friends. Colton confirmed that Djenrye do have creatures that the Hundye call "faeries". "The area which you described could only be the Crey Moors near the Westnoch Mountains."

Marise agreed. "The Moors are still a good several sunrises from the portal."

Colton rose, pulling Stevie to her feet. "This is excellent news. Torren is still in Djenrye. Now, let us discover if Jack Snow and James Wood will be of any use to us with swords."

"Slave driver," Jack said, sullenly.

Ignoring the jibe, Colton passed Stevie her short sword. Marise partnered with her to spar. Despite being a quick learner, Stevie was prone to announcing her moves by mouthing "thrust, retreat, pivot, jab, lunge." Marise pointed this out, laughing. Stevie took the advantage and managed an excellent parry. "Ah...ha!" yelled Stevie.

Disarmed and backed against a tree, the point of Stevie's sword at her throat, Marise yielded. "Excellent move, my Guardian," declared Marise, her hands held out in submission.

Stevie dropped her weapon and pulled Marise to her. Hugging, grinning, and laughing at her success.

Colton joined in the embrace. "I cannot express my joy, Shylae. Master swordsmen have never disarmed my sister, yet you did." He then turned to the other two. "Which of you is now ready to fight?"

Jack jumped to his feet, arm raised in the air. "Pick me. Pick me!"

Colton handed him Marise's sword, and then retrieved his claymore.

"Dude. Seriously? You're giving me a girl's sword?" Jack looked from the short sword to the claymore and back in disbelief. "I am feeling very inadequate right now."

"After you have mastered the weight and balance of the smaller weapon, you may move on to something larger." Colton patted his blade.

"How 'bout I just borrow Wood's gun?"

"I have witnessed your…" Colton cleared his throat. "…skills, with a gun. Tell me what do you intend to do with such a thing? Throw it at me?"

"Don't joke about it," said Jack. "I have a great throwing arm. It could be lethal."

"Unless your intention is to throw your sword at your enemy, that will not help you in a fight," Colton replied. "Weapon up!" He raised the claymore over his head, the tip pointed toward Jack.

"Whoa! I really don't want to fight, Colton," Jack whined.

In response, Colton lunged. Jack's first move resulted in tripping over his own feet and landing hard on the ground.

"Rise and fight. You need to exchange blows with me if you ever hope to defeat the enemy."

Jack fell at least three times before he actually began a decent sparring session. Once the laughter died down, he regained his sense of balance and quickly developed a feel for the blade—even managing a few good jabs.

From Stevie's training with Colton, she knew he was holding back. *Maybe because tech-boy is taking the training more seriously.* Regardless, in less than ten minutes, her friend became noticeably tired.

Colton waved Wood over to take Jack's place. "You need to look at sword-play as a form of dance. First, you must know your partner. Swing the blade a bit to gain an understanding. Use your weight behind it, but do not overextend. Balance is a key component of the dance."

Wood nodded and swung the blade in a large arc several times, first to his left and then to his right.

"You look like a natural," Stevie commented.

"I watch a lot of sword and sorcery movies." Wood admitted sheepishly.

A quick tutoring on basic offensive and defensive moves, and then Colton shouted, "Weapon up!" He attacked.

Wood blocked the first blow, turned quickly, and blocked a low thrust. The concepts seemed to come to him quickly and his stance became confident. As did Jack, Wood managed a few good thrusts, at one point slashing Colton's sleeve, but not close enough to draw blood.

The moon had risen, but the light was not sufficient to work on archery and knives. Colton called an end to the training, and the group gathered around the fire.

"How many sunrises shall we see before we arrive at the City of Seattle?" asked Colton.

Wood rubbed the stubble on his chin. "My best guess is we'll have to spend one more night camping." An idea must have come to mind, because Wood jumped to his feet saying, "Hey, I brought a little surprise for us. That is, if you're interested."

Heads bobbed and Wood headed to his tent. A bottle of whiskey was in his hand when he returned.

"I thought it was sodas for the kids," Jack said, reaching for the liquor.

"If you don't shut up, it will be," Wood retorted.

Stevie punched her friend hard in the arm and took the proffered drink. She poured a little in her coffee and the bottle was passed to Colton, Marise, and finally, Jack.

Despite the burn as it went down her throat, the drink warmed Stevie. *Thank God for cream and sugar.*

After Jack tried to get a second helping and instead received a pop in the back of his head from Wood, the group settled down.

Marise brought out several blankets and Stevie begged to know more about the faeries.

Colton obliged. "There are a few creatures in our world of which humans have created fables."

"So, do you have leprechauns and dragons—things like that?" asked Stevie.

"No…those creatures are truly imaginary. The Hundye myths and children's stories speak of faeries, wizards, and elves, as well. These beings do exist." Colton went on to explain about the Faugns—a half man/woman, half animal of many types, the Wood Elves—a distant cousin of the Androne race, but smaller, shy, and peaceful, who mostly keep to themselves, and the Jajing—a warring race of intelligent beasts who had been exiled across the Nibiruin Sea after the last Djen/Jajing war.

Marise's smile at Colton's telling entranced Stevie nearly as much as Colton's stories themselves. The love between the two of them shone clearly.

Fascination replaced Stevie's uncertainty and reduced the fear of her lost homeland. *Djenrye certainly sounds fascinating. But will it be just a place to visit, or will I want to live there?*

Stevie woke to the sound of her name. Rolling out of her sleeping bag, she peeked through the open flap in the tent.

"It is time to awaken, Shylae," Colton said, as he busied himself packing up the gear.

Throwing on a pair of jeans and a sweatshirt, she left the warm tent.

The morning was cool, almost crisp. Dew covered the forest floor, trees, rocks—a billion tiny diamonds sparkling in the dawn sun. Stevie pulled the poles out of the ground and worked with Colton to dismantle the tents.

"You are a godsend," Stevie said to Marise, who had arrived with two cups of coffee. Taking a moment to inhale the rich smoky aroma, she sipped the liquid. Stevie loved camping—always had. The bird songs, the babbling sounds of water from a brook nearby, and leaves rustling in the breeze. She breathed it all in, stretched languidly, and then got back to work. Camping might be a pleasure, but the long ride ahead seemed arduous. The one bright spot was that they knew Torren was still in Djenrye...but on his way to this side of the portal. Time was of the essence.

After hiking back to the SUV, Wood offered to take the first shift driving. Marise joined him up front while everyone else piled into the back seat. Stevie ended up stuck in the middle between Jack and Colton. *Geez, I know they'd rather sit by me than each other, but I'd like a window view, too.*

"So, Jack, where are we headed?" asked Wood as he turned the ignition.

"You're gonna go back on Blacksmith Fork Canyon Road to East Park. There you'll take a right on Main Street—which becomes Nibley Road..."

"How 'bout you tell me as we go?" Wood said, and then drove out of the park.

A couple hours on the road and they stopped in Burley, Idaho, for gas and breakfast. They managed another three hours before pulling into a little station in Ontario, Oregon, for gas and snacks. This time Stevie and Colton took the front, leaving Wood and Marise with Jack.

"Hey, guys. When do I get to drive, or at least sit shotgun? I've been stuck back here for the last six hours and it's getting mighty cramped," Jack said.

"What? And miss your scintillating backseat driving?" Stevie responded. "How much further to Seattle, whiny-boy?"

"Drive time, at least nine hours...but we are gonna stop for food, right? So, figure at least ten."

Stevie glanced at Colton. "It'd be a long haul, but we could make Seattle tonight. Whatcha think?"

Colton gazed out at the road for a moment. "One more evening of weapons training is necessary. Anything we are able to do to prepare would be beneficial."

"It's up to you again, tech-boy. Can you find us our next campsite between here and Seattle?"

Jack responded with brooding silence.

"All right. At the next stop you can ride shotgun," Stevie acceded.

"Do I look stupid to you? That's when we stop to camp." Jack did not give Stevie time to answer before he continued. "How 'bout I drive first thing tomorrow. Then you've got a deal."

"Geez, Jack, what are we, in junior high? Okay. Okay. You get the first shift. Now will you please tell me where the hell I should be going?"

His fingers flew over the iPad for several moments and then Jack called out, "Found it. Whitman National Forest. It should be about two and a half hours to the ranger station."

"Excellent," Marise chimed in. "That will give us ample sunlight for practice and another hearty meal prepared by James Wood."

Wood saluted. "I end up in charge of the Chuck Wagon. Ya'll just call me 'Cookie'," the detective replied, with a terrible attempt at a western accent.

That afternoon, they arranged a dispersed camping at the ranger station. The site had the isolation they needed and luckily, campfires were allowed.

Marise took the lead in training. The group worked mostly on bow skills, and Wood remained true to his word.

"Good, but not as good as Alyssa," Jack said, after the detective shot a quiver of arrows. "She hit the bull's-eye nine out of ten times."

Wood handed the bow to Jack. "I need to start dinner, but not before you show me your impressive skills."

Instead of hitting the target, Jack managed to annihilate the mountainside behind it. He redeemed himself with knife throwing, but Wood left to cook burgers before the bragging began.

"Who da man?" Jack crowed after successfully impaling the heart of his target with all six of his throwing knives.

Dusk arrived before Stevie and the rest of the group returned to camp.

"Timing's perfect," Wood called out.

The rest of the evening remained uneventful. Instead of tales of Djenrye, Wood regaled the group with cop stories. At one point, he had Jack laughing so hard he snorted coffee through his nose.

They had a good night's rest, then eight more hours of drive time—including stops for auto and people fuel. They arrived in Seattle, Washington, a little after two in the afternoon.

Chapter 30

By the time they arrived in Seattle, finished training, and had dinner, the boat rentals had closed. They didn't lie down until after midnight. The motel rooms were small, but the beds were more comfortable than the cold, hard ground. Stevie was so tired, it took no more than food and a bed for her to instantly fall asleep.

Despite her exhaustion, she tossed and turned. It seemed only a few seconds had gone by when a knock on the door woke her. Marise padded across the carpet and Stevie heard a click, the squeak of a hinge, and faint voices. She rolled onto her stomach, putting the pillow over her head to muffle the sounds.

"Shylae." Colton's voice whispered in her ear.

She moved her pillow away enough to squint at him. Somehow, while she slept, the Sahara Desert had slipped under her eyelids. His outline seemed surreal, but then he began to shake her awake. She let him pull her to a sitting position. Blinking, her voice faint and cracked, she asked, "What time is it?"

Marise answered, "It is before dawn. We need to rise before the sun. There is much to do."

Stevie glanced toward the window. "But it's still dark out, I want to go back to sleep," she said, trying to lie back down. Colton slipped his arm behind her back and righted her again. She collapsed against him.

"No, Shylae." He shook her again, less gently. "We must practice before we leave and break the night's fast. Nourishment and movement will revive you."

Stevie crawled off the bed sluggishly.

"I need to wash up first," she muttered. "I'll meet you at the truck." She stumbled to the bathroom, her mind a fog.

Colton caught her and before leaving, kissed her on the forehead. "Make haste, my love."

Stevie glimpsed Marise following him out the motel door. *Damn it. How is it she's so awake and put together already?*

By the time Stevie met the rest of the group downstairs, she felt nearly human. *Eye drops and a hot shower can do wonders. Now, for coffee.*

While they ate in the little breakfast area at the motel, Jack made small talk with the staff and several locals to find a good place to practice. Stevie, amused at his ruse of telling the folks they were practicing for a movie, said to him, "So now you're a movie star, too?"

"When ya got it, ya got it," Jack replied, all grins and bravado.

Bellies and thermoses full, they drove to an area in the woods a few miles outside of Seattle. The directions were easy to follow and the terrain deserted and level—as promised. Small droplets splattered across the windshield as they exited the truck.

Colton looked at the sky. "Let us make haste before the rain impedes us too greatly."

Marise jumped from her seat, energetic and cheerful as usual. "Brother, the elements smile on us. These neophytes must learn to do battle in all types of weather. The Gods know this and have blessed us with this opportunity." She raised her hand, either to feel the air, thank the Gods, or from joy, Stevie could not tell which.

Colton set up a target to continue the bow training and Marise instructed them in her technique, hitting the bull's-eye every time.

Wood took the opportunity to question the female Warrior on how she drew her bow. "I didn't mention this yesterday, because you did not correct me on my form. Why do you draw the back of your hand to your cheek rather than the palm?"

"It is how the Djen have always drawn. We find it improves our aim and allows a greater pull without as much effort."

Wood changed his draw to mimic Marise. To everyone's surprise, he still managed a bull's-eye four out of five tries.

"Okay, Warrior Queen. I'm sold. That was amazing. My brother is gonna flip the next time we go bow hunting."

"Exceptional shooting," exclaimed Colton. "Now your turn, young Snow."

Jack took the offered bow, snatched an arrow from the grouping stuck in the ground, aimed, drew, and released. Bull's-eye! Everyone clapped and yelled with delight as Jack continued to loose the arrows.

With nothing more to shoot, Jack turned to his audience and made a swooping bow. "You were wrong, C. I've been reading up on stances and focus. I guess you can learn to fight from a book," he said, a grin spreading across his features.

"I stand corrected... I am pleased to see the change in your position toward training. You are developing a Warrior's focus." Colton patted the young man on the back.

Although Stevie held her own in the archery, she excelled at knife throwing, hitting whatever area of the tree Colton instructed. Her protector grinned with pride, making her cheeks flush. After a couple dozen throws, he retrieved a small axe from his bag of tricks.

"Now this," Colton said, pointing the handle at her.

Stevie missed the pine entirely on her first throw. Her smug expression and confident stance melted, but for little more than a moment. The flicker at the corner of Colton's mouth gave her determination. She flipped the axe several times, catching the handle in her left and then right hand...getting a feel for the weight. The next throw landed precisely where she intended. Arms crossed, eyebrow cocked, she turned to Colton, daring him to make a snide comment. He diplomatically remained silent.

As the training progressed, excitement filled the group. Every event saw improvement in their skills, creating confidence and accelerating the training. The sun peeked out directly above them before slipping back into the darkening clouds. Wood stopped his parry with Marise. He looked from the sky to his watch.

"It's time to get moving. And I need to eat. I'm starving," Wood said, rubbing his stomach.

In no time, the weapons were packed and the crew headed back to the city for lunch. On the drive back, the rain returned. Not quite a downpour, but harder than the earlier sprinkles. Soon, Wood had to turn on the wipers and defroster to clear the foggy windshield.

"I don't know how these people live here," Wood said, brooding. "I miss the Colorado sunshine."

Stevie looked out the window. "It's kind of pretty, though. I don't think I have ever seen this much green in a forest," she exclaimed. "Are we gonna get the boat after lunch?"

Wood shook his head. "I don't know. I guess it takes several days to get to Princess Royal Island. I was thinking maybe we should charter a small plane instead."

Jack chimed in from the front seat. "Try five days... Wood's got a point. I just got off the phone with my dad and they aren't going to let us captain the boat ourselves, after all."

Stevie looked at Wood's reflection in the rearview mirror, but his eyes remained glued to the road. "But don't Colton and Marise need IDs?"

Marise answered, "Worry not. Have you so quickly forgotten the Djen ability to make ourselves unseen?"

"Hang on, guys. It's a bit more complicated than that," Jack added. "The only way into the island is by water."

"What do you mean, we have to take a boat?" asked Stevie.

"Naw...there's got to be a puddle jumper we can charter. Jack, check around and see if we can get on one of those," said Detective Wood.

"Hey, there's a place we can eat lunch." Stevie pointed to a mom and pop restaurant and they pulled in. Once seated, Jack continued to research the best and least conspicuous way to get to Princess Royal Island.

Colton ordered broiled chicken and salads for everyone. Jack grumbled that he'd rather have a burger and fries, but ended up settling for the chicken. When the plates had been cleared and they were finishing their drinks, Jack went over what he had found.

"There are no direct flights from Seattle to Princess Royal. Most of the island and surrounding areas are protected by the native peoples because of the white bears. It looks like our best bet is to go to one of the villages and see who we can talk to about giving us permission go in the protected areas."

"What?" said Stevie. "That's crazy! They aren't going to let us on that island alone. How are we going to do this?"

"Cool your jets, Baby Doll. From what I've come up with, it looks like we can land a chartered flight from Port Hardy into Bella Bella. The pictures show it to be a pretty hoppin' seaside town. Hey—they even have a coffee shop and Visitors' Center." Jack held up his iPad for everyone to see.

"Unless anyone has a better idea, that's as good a plan as any," Wood said. "How far to Port Hardy?"

"That's the über-bummer part. Looks like a good ten hours from Seattle, and only if we drive straight through—gas and snack stops only."

"It's doable," Wood said. "As long as everyone's careful about eating in the car."

Stevie barked out a laugh. "Now you're worried about us messin' up your ride?"

"I'm just saying…"

"Got it, Police Soldier Wood." Jack gave a smart salute.

Wood's retort, which Stevie had no doubt would zing Jack, was interrupted by the ring of a cell phone.

"That's me," she announced. "It's Mom."

Stevie left the restaurant to talk to her mom, and they chatted for several minutes.

"So how's the trip so far?" Jan asked. "And the weather? I saw on the news it's been raining. Are you doing okay?"

"Everything's copacetic," Stevie assured her. "It's actually been pretty cool."

"You know, Tonka really misses you…"

Holding back a sigh, Stevie said, "I miss her, too. Give her lots of love and treats for me. K?" Before her mom could expand the guilt-trip, Stevie asked, "Can I talk to Lissy real quick?"

"I heard most of the conversation, Stevie." Alyssa switched to a whisper. "Geez, your mom turns the receiver up high."

Stevie laughed and Alyssa continued.

"So...how is everyone? How's Jack? Has he said anything about being homesick or...missing me?"

Stevie chuckled to herself. She knew that Lissy had had a crush on Jack for—well—ever, but she'd never considered that the feeling was mutual. *There seems to be somethin' up...some sorta spark this last week or so.*

In her most casual voice, Stevie asked, "Girl, what's up between you and Jack?"

Silence.

"Come on, Lissy. I'm your BFF. You can tell me." The sound of a door closing came through the receiver.

"Well, when Colton came into the picture, Jack was totally bummin'. Part of it was this mysterious handsome man in your life. But mainly 'coz he was afraid our BFF triangle would be broken. He felt like it was getting pretty FUBAR, and I guess wanted to know that nothing could come between the three of us."

"I had no idea. But what's that got to do with you two?"

"Chill. I'm gettin' there. Me and Jack spent a couple of late nights when we talked till nearly dawn. I wanted him to know everything was okay. One night, the discussion changed from the three of us to the two of us...I mean, Jack and me."

"Get out." Stevie exclaimed.

"Yeah, I know. Blew me away. He got me to fess up I that I'd a crush on him since we were kids, and—wait for it—he told me that he had been thinking about me, well, romantically, the past couple of months."

Stevie could almost hear Alyssa blushing. "And...girl? I'm dying here. Spill."

"That's pretty much it. We kissed and decided to try dating... That part came before we knew about the trip."

"Wow. Wait...you kissed?" Stevie's cheeks hurt from grinning. *It's about frickin time!*

"Okay, now I'm getting embarrassed. Don't you dare tell Jack I told you. We're kinda waiting for everyone to get back before we…we come outta the closet on our relationship."

"My lips are sealed, GF. To totally change the subject, how's house arrest treating ya?"

"I hate it. All I do is sit in this motel room with your mom and watch TV. Detective Drake won't even let me get on the computer. Like the Djen know how to track me with an IP address." Alyssa's voice became shrill. A couple of seconds passed before she went on. "Drake said it shouldn't be much longer…at least for me. There's been zippo signs of anyone prowling around my house, or yours, for that matter."

"Colton's probably right that the Rebellion knows we've left Golden. My guess is that they're not gonna send anyone else there to hunt for us."

"OMG, I hope not. The sooner I'm back home, the better the chance your mom and I won't kill each other."

"Speaking of mom's, how're your parents holding up with this?"

Alyssa sighed. "They're doing okay, just mom calls me almost every hour, worried. She wants me home but knows I am safe here."

"I'm sure you will be soon."

Stevie said her good-byes and returned to the table, giggling. She filled in the group with the small talk and news…of course leaving out Lissy's confession. "Wood, have you talked to Drake at all?"

"Yeah, we spoke this morning. She's thinking Alyssa can be cut loose within the next couple of days. Jan, however, is gonna need to stay under Drake's watchful eye a little longer. The last time we thought your mom was safe… Well, let's just say we don't want to take any chances."

"Prudent decision, Police Soldier…my pardon, Detective Wood," Colton responded. "Upon returning to Djenrye, we will dispatch a Warrior to protect Jan Barrett from the shadows, much as I have done for Shylae."

"I hate to break up this little shindig," Jack interjected. "But if we wanna get to Port Hardy in time to charter a plane for Bella Bella, we better *vámonos*."

Despite their best efforts, it was well after dark when they arrived in Port Hardy. There were no puddle jumpers to Bella Bella until morning, so they went to a motel for the night. Stevie was concerned about the money situation. So far, they had managed to pay for everything in cash and split the food and gas three ways. But now, the expense of chartering a plane, renting a boat, and buying provisions for their time on the island loomed before them.

Only a couple of options remained. Either they would need to use Wood's or someone else's credit card, or Stevie would have to make the phone call in the morning—a plea to her mom to wire money. Not a fun conversation, but it might be a necessary one.

Stevie fell into a dreamless sleep the moment her head hit the pillow. She did not stir until Marise woke her around seven o'clock in the morning. Marise let Stevie have the shower first, which turned out to be a good thing. Apparently, Marise had never used a Hundye shower before. Hot running water and liquid shampoo were a novelty to her.

The thin bathroom door did little to deafen her exclamations. The expressions of "By the Gods!" and oohs and aahs made Stevie giggle.

"Shylae. The falling water is growing cold. How do I increase the temperature again?"

A full-blown laugh escaped Stevie. "You can't. The hot water has run out. That's what happens when you take a forty-five minute shower."

When Stevie heard the water stop, she left the room to give Marise privacy and to grab a cup of coffee from the lobby. She met the guys there, who must have had the same idea. On seeing Colton's damp hair, she asked if he had showered as well.

"A marvelous invention of the Hundye. I will speak to our architects about having one of those installed in the palace upon our return. Far more refreshing than a hot bath."

"Way," Stevie replied. "But you're gonna have to work with your alchemists on the whole liquid shampoo and conditioner thing, too."

Colton smiled and gave a low bow. "As you command, my Guardian."

She answered him with a smack on his bicep.

"Hey, you two," Jack interjected. "Leave the wisecracks to the professionals. Besides, if you can't play nice, the detective here won't let you play at all." He winked.

Before returning to the room, Stevie excused herself to call her mom. She had the speech worked out in her head as she dialed. Jan, however, managed to surprise Stevie.

Halfway through the explanation, Jan simply said, "Cut to the chase, baby. How much do you need?"

That's a first. Usually, I'd have a better chance of winning the lottery than getting money from Mom.

The next few minutes Stevie spent with the front desk person and her mom on the line to arrange wiring the funds. With the money situation resolved, the group packed up and headed to the ticket office.

Wood, Jack, and Stevie bought three tickets on a chartered flight. They had time to kill before the ten o'clock departure, so they joined Colton and Marise for breakfast and shopping. Stevie hunted for a poncho and Jack bought a pair of gloves and a box of those little chemical hand-warmer packets.

After the extra items had been packed, and before heading into the airport terminal, Colton and Marise made themselves invisible— a trick Stevie longed to master. *Soon, I hope.*

The ticket agent, a twenty-something blonde, had been won over by Jack almost immediately. She informed the group—Jack, actually, the rest just listened—that they would be traveling in a

Cessna Caravan. It could hold up to ten people, including forty-four pounds of luggage per passenger.

Stevie was relieved to see seven seats unoccupied. *At least Colton and Marise won't have to stand in the shadows and dodge the other passengers.*

The plane took off for Bella Bella.

After the Cessna gained altitude and leveled off, Stevie watched the pilot to see if she noticed the extra invisible weight, but both she and her co-pilot seemed oblivious.

The twenty-minute flight consisted of small talk and Colton murmuring in her ear about the view from the air.

"At no time in my life have I imagined seeing such a sight in material form as experienced in meditation."

Mesmerized, he whispered to her his awe at the magnificence of the sun on the ocean and how it sparkled when the light hit the peaks of the waves. The plane flew close to the shore, and evergreens and leafed-out deciduous trees blanketed the inland, with little beaches along the coast caressed by soft waves.

Stevie called out, "Look. I think that's Bella Bella." She pointed to a small island in the middle of two bigger ones. The pilot, whose name turned out to be Sarah—*like Detective Drake*—congratulated Stevie on being the first passenger ever to recognize the land mass from that distance.

"That's where several of the original Heiltsuk villages were located. The town of Bella Bella is to the west, your left, on Campbell Island." The pilot radioed air tower control and asked for clearance to circle Bella Bella and Campbell Islands before landing. After she received the all clear, she turned to Stevie with a wink. "Just to give you one last view, since I don't have a door prize for your sharp vision."

After the scenic detour, the plane set down in Queen Charlotte Sound.

Stevie positioned herself to be the first person at the door. She stretched out her arms and breathed in the salty air. Her goal was to block the exit to give Colton and Marise time to sneak out unconstrained. Wood and Jack both gave Stevie a wink as they exited a few seconds later.

Once the luggage was unloaded, Wood suggested they head straight for the Visitors' Center. "It's only a few blocks up Waglisla Street. That's where Jack thinks we can get info on a boat rental…right?"

Jack nodded in agreement. "And…it has a café. Anyone else hungry?"

"Seriously?" Stevie asked. "We only ate a couple of hours ago."

"Do I have to go over the whole growing boy thing again?"

This time, Colton's voice interrupted the verbal sparring. "If you are not careful, Jack Snow, you will find yourself growing out rather than up."

Stevie's friend squeaked, startled by the disembodied voice.

"Geez, Colton. I forgot you were there," Jack said. "The pilot and her trusty sidekick are outta sight. Would you and your sis please re-assemble yourselves?"

Stevie noted the shallow prints left in the soft ground as Colton and Marise moved to the nearest building. They emerged around the corner, visible again.

Finding the Visitors' Center was easy and Wood dragged Jack along with him to the boat rental side. Stevie could hear Jack complaining that he was hungry and she called back that they'd save him a seat.

With the coffee ordered, Wood and Jack returned.

"Hey, we've got good news and bad. Whatcha want first?"

"Bad news," Stevie, Colton, and Marise said in unison.

"There are no boats."

On the verge of tears, Stevie managed to choke out, "After we've come this far?"

Jack jumped in. "Chill, Baby Doll. We found a guy who'll rent us his boat for a great price."

"He overheard us talking to the rental gal and caught us outside," Wood interrupted. "Apparently, the tourist season's been slow and he needs the money. So bad, in fact, that he's willing to let us take it up the coast without him. Of course, I had to give him tons of information about me so he felt safe doing that, but once he saw I was a detective, he seemed to come around."

"That, and," Jack interrupted, "the couple hundred you slipped him."

"Yeah, but that extra money also bought us an excellent topographical map," Wood finished.

"Next time, just give me the good news, K?" said Stevie. She grabbed her bag and drink and headed for the door, calling over her shoulder, "Let's go."

They found the boat at the docks. To Stevie, it looked like a yacht. Not at all what she had expected.

"So here she is, kids. A thirty-five-foot fiberglass Glasscraft. This little baby can sleep five comfortably, has indoor bathroom facilities, and a small galley. Makes me feel kinda bad for the guy not having any charters this week." Wood spoke like a man conducting a tour, pointing out little nuances that made no sense to Stevie, who had lived her entire life in a landlocked state. "It has a two-hundred-seventy-horsepower motor manufactured by…"

Stevie hated to dampen his enthusiasm, but the sooner they left the better. "Umm, we should probably dump our stuff and get supplies if we wanna head out before dark."

"That would be 'stow' your stuff, young lady," Wood said with a smile. "But you're right. Let's make a provision run and get this little baby outward bound."

Chapter 31

Stevie stood on the bow, holding firm to the railing to keep her balance as the boat rocked in the ocean waves. The sound of the water slapping the nearby shore mesmerized her and the salty spray blew her hair back from her face. The view was spectacular. Clouds from the recent storm blanketed the mountaintops and blue sky peeked out here and there.

A black bear emerged onto the beach from the mossy tree line that separated the shore from the rain forest. The animal lumbered down the beach and stopped at the water's edge. It buried its muzzle in the sand, and then raised its head at the sound of the approaching boat. The bear reared up on his hind legs, nose in the air, as if trying to catch their scent.

It watched them pass by. Stevie could not take her eyes off the beast. He differed from the black bears she had seen in Colorado, being much larger—enormous, in fact. Although, to be fair, this happened to be the first time she had seen one up close, well, other than at the Denver Zoo.

Stevie looked behind her through the glass into the bridge at Jack. He gave her a thumbs-up, indicating that he had seen the bear.

Since their departure from Bella Bella, Wood had done most of the piloting. He agreed to give up the wheel only after repeatedly running Jack through drills. Jack appeared completely at home on the bridge. Before going below, Wood confided to Stevie that Jack seemed to be a natural, with a connection to the water. Of course, he made her promise not to tell Jack—his ego didn't need any more stroking.

Colton maneuvered himself beside Stevie, slipping his arm around her shoulder. "We have arrived, Shylae." He bent over and kissed her head. "I understand that our companion is looking for a safer place to go on shore."

"I hope we get to see a spirit bear...wouldn't that be awesome?"

His eyes sparkled as he leaned in, his lips brushed her cheek. "Yes, that would be a wondrous sight," Colton whispered. He straightened. "Would you care to break your fast before we assemble the provisions for our trek?"

Stevie followed him below deck. Wood stood at the stove, removing bacon from the frying pan. "Morning," he said as he set the crispy strips on a paper plate. "Are you ready for your long hike?"

Colton nodded. "All that is left is sustenance and to pack what we require for the journey."

Marise walked into the galley and made a direct line to the coffee. Her cup filled, she sat at the small table. "Good morning," she murmured, sipping the steamy liquid. She yawned and leaned against the wall.

"Morning," said Stevie. "Did you sleep well?"

"Yes. I did not even dream last night. The boat rocked me to sleep."

"That's a far cry from the first day, when you and Colton spent most of your time at the railing."

Marise glared at her. "We Djen do not ride on the water. We prefer the ground or trees. Yet, we are an adaptable people. It simply took time for us to get our—what term did you use, Detective?—oh yes, 'sea legs'."

Jack walked in, but he bypassed the coffee to head directly for the bacon. A sharp slap rang through the cabin. All eyes went to Jack, who held his hand.

"Hey...that hurt," Jack complained to Wood. "I just wanted one piece. I'm starving."

Wood growled back, "You can wait until breakfast is ready, like everyone else. I assume you dropped the anchor?"

"Of course. Whatcha you think? I'm an idiot?" Jack rubbed his hand.

Stevie laughed. "Come, on Jack. Sit with me and stay outta trouble."

Jack slunk over to the table. He filled a glass with orange juice. "Why do I have to stay here with him? He's grumpy."

"Did the big man hurt your wittle hand?" Stevie teased, giving him her best pout. "You'll be okay, Bro. You and Wood won't be stuck on the boat. He said you'd be going to hunt and explore during the day. At least you'll have a bed to sleep in. I'll be sleeping on the ground for the next few nights."

"True. Guess it sucks to be you, huh?" Jack reached over for an orange and began to peel it. "Still, I wish I was going with you guys. I'm gonna miss all the fun."

"Fun, Jack Snow? This journey will not be a leisure excursion. We will be moving over unmapped lands, wherein are dangerous animals. We will carry little food, and if necessary we will forage or hunt. If we are unsuccessful, we will go hungry." Colton patted Jack on the back. "And truly, my young friend, are you able to convince me you would enjoy the exertion and the lack of sustenance?"

"You've got a point."

Wood set the bacon and scrambled eggs on the table. "Come on, eat. I need to steer us to a proper place for you to go ashore." As he headed to the deck, he said, "I'll be back soon…save me something to eat. That means you, Jack."

After breakfast, Stevie, Colton, and Marise loaded the backpacks until they were close to bursting. Wood had located a good spot to drop anchor, close enough for a short ride in one of the inflatable dinghies but far enough out to avoid running aground.

Colton noted, "Removed from the Rebels and other animals."

Their packs secure, the three Djen said good-bye and reminded Wood to keep his walkie-talkie close. On Princess Island, they had only each other to rely on.

The drizzle had abated, for the moment, and the morning sun warmed the air. Colton dragged the dinghy inland, far from the high-tide line. As they entered the woods, strands of hanging moss dampened their hair. They moved through the old-growth hemlock and cedar forest. Their footprints quickly filled with water, and just as quickly, the spongy ground absorbed it, leaving few signs of their passing.

They walked uphill steadily for what Stevie guessed was half an hour or so. Awestruck by the primordial forest enfolding her, her nostrils filled with the heady scent of salt air, earth, and mold. The colors and textures of green created a blanket of growth. At times, the area became so dense it was nearly claustrophobic. She had never in her life seen such lush landscape.

The scene opened to reveal a small clearing on the edge of a precipice. A panorama of mountains spread before them, untouched for millennia. A cold breeze blew in from snow-covered peaks, chilling Stevie's neck. It seemed surreal to walk out of a rainforest into a mountain range.

Across the chasm, Stevie spotted a doe eating grass, its ears flicking at insects. At the simple beauty, homesickness rushed in unbidden. She recalled the does and fawns who would breakfast on her mom's flowers most mornings. Stevie's heart ached for her mother, for Alyssa, and for the home she grew up in. Wiping at the onslaught of tears, she reminded herself of the importance of the quest and tried to refocus on the Orb's call.

Colton broke the silence. "Lead on, my Guardian. We must not tarry."

The connection Stevie had made with the Orteh now pulled her toward it. Inner knowledge of the path drew her forward. Lessening or strengthening of the bond let her know if she turned the wrong direction.

She lifted her chin, sensing the Orteh. *I bet I look like that black bear on the shore.* "That way," she said, pointing right. They followed the faint sign of a deer trail up the hill.

The path wound around the next precipice and, for a time, meandered downward.

Marise asked, "Are you certain we are on the right trail?"

An eagle's cry, high overhead, interrupted her answer. Stevie squinted into the sun, watching the outline of the majestic raptor. *I know what you see.* She remembered her earlier vision. Without hesitation, she waved at the bird, knowing she was waving at herself.

"Why do you giggle so?" asked Marise.

"Nothing. It's just me." Which made Stevie laugh even more.

The brother and sister glanced at each other and shook their heads, but remained silent.

They continued on, Stevie occasionally stopping to sense the direction. She asked for a water break and a bite of food.

Colton acquiesced, but after a few brief moments he expressed a desire to continue. "I must ask, Shylae, are you winded, or would you like to exert one of your newfound abilities?"

"I'm good, Colton. Whatcha got in mind?"

"If you are able, I would ask that we increase our speed. With the heavy burden you carry and as a neophyte in our ways, Marise and I agree not to move at a pace greater than you can manage."

"I'm game if you two are. I'll let you know if I need to stop or slow down." She tried to keep the excitement out of her voice. A chance to flex her newly discovered skills without prying eyes about...well, that'd be a blast.

The three Djen began to run. At first, it seemed to Stevie as though they were simply jogging, not nearly the speed she had managed at the cabin with Colton. Then she saw the wolves, higher up the mountain, led by a beautiful white male. The animals ran alongside them. Even jogging, Stevie and her friends quickly outdistanced the pack. She turned back to see that the white wolf had stopped. It dipped its head toward her, perhaps conceding the race, and turned to disappear into the woods with its kin.

The Djen ran with wind in their hair, the sights streaming by. Stevie leapt across a twenty-five-foot-wide river as she would have previously jumped a creek. Her breathing remained steady for the first hours, but became short as the sun lowered in the east. The Orteh pulled her, called to her, and she wanted to continue, but her strength waned.

"I have to rest. I'm getting winded."

"We have covered a good distance. This is an acceptable area to set up camp." Colton removed his pack and began unloading the tent.

"Thanks. I don't think I'd be able to handle that canyon without food and rest."

Marise winked at Stevie. "Truly, Guardian? It is little more than the length of five horses, muzzle to tail."

Stevie did a quick calculation in her head. "Thirty feet? Are you outta your mind?" She approached the edge of the canyon. It was a long, long way down. "What if I found out I could only jump four horses...in mid-jump?"

Marise and Colton both laughed, but Colton assured her. "After we have supped and rested for the night, you will practice on solid ground before making such a leap. Do not let my sister tease you."

By the time the tent had been raised and dinner finished, Stevie's muscles reminded her that she had not yet become used to running as a Djen. The fire warmed her a bit, but could not completely eliminate the damp of the night. She huddled closer.

"Colton, do you think I should try to see where Torren is again?"

"It seems as though you are able to read my mind. It would be of great benefit to gain additional knowledge of the activities of the Rebellion."

Marise placed a blanket around Stevie's shoulders. Warm and relaxed, Stevie heard Colton chanting behind her. She called forth her visions.

She found herself again in a cave, but not the same one as before. Light flickered at the far end of the passage and she moved toward it. The glow came from one of the walls of the cave, and it shimmered. *The portal.* Two men emerged from the flowing substance. They stepped aside and more men came through—ten in total, including Torren.

They appeared well provisioned, with full packs slung over their shoulders, and torches in hand, ready to be lit. It was night when they left the cave. Stevie followed closely behind, watching as they scouted for a place to camp. The ground was frozen below her feet. Pools of water formed in the crevices of the rocks. Patches of white remained under bushes and the north side of boulders. *Good thing I'm only here in spirit, or they'd be able to see my breath.*

Torren had stopped at the entrance of the cave, facing the interior. He seemed to be in deep thought. A far-away expression shadowed his features. He stood tall and proud, much like Colton, but with a hint of arrogance. Ochre covered the hollows of his eyes. Slash marks and golden circles decorated his chest and arms. His eyes seemed brighter, more intense, with black war paint around them. And then he snapped out of whatever held his thoughts. Torren strode to his men.

He seated himself by the comfort of the fire and left his men to set up camp. One of his soldiers approached with a mug and then backed away, bowing. As far as Stevie could tell, the men raised one tent, clearly meant for Torren. They appeared to be settling in for the night. With nothing more to see, Stevie decided to do the same.

In a blink, she returned. "Well, he's come through the portal. Where is it?" Stevie asked Colton.

"It is not far from here," he said. "The span of two sunsets, if one travels at the speed of a Hundye on foot."

Marise asked, "What did you see?"

"They set up camp by the portal, and Torren is wearing war paint." Stevie paused. "He stopped and just stared at the portal for a while. It was kinda creepy."

"Is it conceivable that Torren was telepathically contacting someone?" Colton asked his sister.

Marise looked up at him. "Considering the manner in which Shylae described him, I would agree."

"Who do you think he was contacting?" Stevie asked, chewing the side of her lip.

Pulling her close, Colton consoled her. "Worry not, my love. He may have been contacting his men on the other side. The Rebels may be near, but we are between them and the Orteh."

"How do you know that?"

"I have gone through the portal many times. I know its location. And you know the location of the Orteh."

Marise spoke up. "Brother, does it seem to you as though Torren is obtaining power from some source other than training and natural ability?"

"This possibility has weighed heavily on my mind. Yet, I do not know what source could be feeding him. Nor do I have knowledge of how his new power will affect our ability to protect the Ortehlae." Colton's eyebrows drew together.

"We are at an impasse. Perhaps we need another's insight on this matter. Esalon?" Marise offered.

Stevie perked up. "Esalon? I remember you mentioned that name before. He's some kinda Prime Minister or something of Tyré, right?"

Marise grinned. "Or something…"

"Esalon is the Mage of Tyré." Colton explained. "He is a counselor, consultant, and healer, among his many duties. Esalon is the one who taught me how to assist in a vision and how to contact him when I am in need."

"It appears that we are in need now, Brother," Marise said solemnly. "I recommend you attempt contact tonight."

Colton agreed. He rose and moved from the fire, closer to the edge of the canyon. There he sat, with his focus across the expanse. Stevie followed him and watched as the steely blue of his eyes began to glow. The beams cut through the darkness.

He held his fingers to his temples and began a chant Stevie had not heard before. Colton seemed to be chanting on the intake of each breath. Five, ten, then fifteen minutes passed. Stevie grew antsy, wanting to know if Colton had reached Esalon. Another ten minutes and the light dimmed. His eyes returned to normal. Without a word, he rose and returned to the fire, Stevie trailing along behind.

"Wassup? What did he say? What happened?" She questioned him each step.

Once Stevie could clearly see his features in the firelight, she shut up. He looked worried.

Marise offered Colton a flask and told Stevie, "This type of communication is extremely trying. You must give him a moment to gain his strength and gather his thoughts."

After a couple of sips, Colton began. "Esalon spoke to me of the alignment of the planets. The power such an event brings is concentrated, and can be dangerous. With dark sorcery, this power could be tapped." He paused for another drink before continuing. "Esalon spoke of the alignment being the only source Torren could be utilizing to gain abilities normally unattainable by an Androne."

"Dark sorcery. Is it his belief that Torren is in league with one of the Dangrial Sorcerers?" asked Marise, the slightest quaver in her voice.

This time, Colton took a hearty swig. "He spoke of the only sorcerer strong enough or mad enough to attempt such a feat— Entek."

Marise gasped, causing Stevie to jump.

"But why? How? Entek has never meddled in the affairs of the Djen or the Rebellion. For Torren to gain him as an ally…" Marise began.

"…would mean open war between the Rebellion and our people. A war in which we might not be victorious," Colton finished.

For a time, all that could be heard were the chirping of insects and the howling of wolves.

"What if Esalon could help us to tap into this power as well?" Marise asked. She held up a hand to stop Colton's protest. "Hear me out, Brother. Such a sacrifice could turn the outcome of war to our advantage."

"Hold up, you two," said Stevie. "What sacrifice? What danger? I don't want to lose either one of you."

Marise moved closer and grasped Stevie's hand, looking at her directly. "The power is vast and dark. If done without caution, the person receiving the power could go mad."

Stevie jerked her hand away. "What? Is that why Torren is so evil? Is this causing him to go insane?"

Colton nodded. "Perhaps, but it would only have increased a dark evil already inside him." He drew Stevie close and wrapped his arms around her. "I fear that we must consider this course of action if we discover Torren has indeed allied with Entek."

"I don't want you going crazy, Colton. It's not worth it."

"If it comes to that, Esalon will ensure we control the flow of power I intake. He is a wise Mage, far more advanced in the art of conjuring than Entek shall ever hope to be."

"I hope you're right, Colton." *Because if you're not, I could lose everything—you, the human race, and both our worlds.*

Chapter 32

The *drip, drip* of condensation from the trees onto the tent woke Colton. He unzipped the flap and peered out. The clouds were an ominous gray, obscuring the distant mountain peaks. He sat back and gently shook Shylae and his sister awake. "The rain has begun," he told them. Their faces exhibited frustration. He thought of Marise's earlier words "The Gods are smiling on us to afford us fresh water."

"This should be fun," Shylae mumbled, poking her head out of the tent. "Now what?"

"Now, we get wet. There is nothing to do, but continue on," said Colton.

Marise shoved Shylae playfully, knocking her over. "Do you fear melting, my Guardian? Colton and I have traveled in such weather many times and yet we remain."

"Thanks for the understanding, Marise." Shylae said pushing her back. "I think I'll live."

Marise started the coffee on the portable metal burner. Colton watched his sister with admiration. *I must admit that there are some Hundye inventions that have proven useful.*

Once the coffee had warmed, the three moved to sit at the base of a tree. Mist clung to them, instantly dampening their outer clothes. Clouds settled over the landscape. The rain felt akin to walking through water, but without the weight. It took all of Colton's focus to see the individual drops within the fog.

Shylae rustled through her pack. She presented a water-repelling garment to his sister and donned one herself. Colton did not wish to wear the noisy, bright-yellow coat, choosing instead his oiled cloak.

In the distance mountain peaks rose above the cloud cover. It took further focus to make out the details of the landscape through the mist. The colors vibrant below the obscuring fog—a multitude of every shade of green and brown.

"It's beautiful, isn't it?" commented Shylae.

"Yes, but dangerous for one not adept in maneuvering wet terrain," said Colton.

In an attempt to keep everything as dry as possible, packing took longer than usual. Stevie took the opportunity to contact Wood by walkie-talkie.

"Hey, stranger," said Wood. "We're doing good. Haven't seen a soul since you left. Over."

"How's Jack holding up? Any complaints? Over."

Wood's laugh boomed through the receiver. "You know, the usual. But he did manage to bag a small doe the first night here, so we've been eating well. How 'bout you, guys? Over."

"Still eating trail food. We haven't had time to hunt, but we're making progress. We're thinkin' we'll reach the Orb by tomorrow morning. Over."

"Keep us informed, Stevie. Over and Out."

Once they were packed and ready to go, they headed out. With direction from Shylae, Colton led the way over slippery rock, moss-laden stones, and mud, which threatened to suck his boots from his feet. They moved swiftly at first but the weather and terrain seemed to dampen his Guardian's earlier determination.

After a few hours, the mist turned into a torrent, forcing Colton to find shelter. He spied an alcove that had been kept dry by a large overhang.

As they waited for the storm to pass, they wet their thirst and Colton passed around the bag of trail mix. When he handed it to Shylae, it slipped through her fingers and she collapsed to the ground.

"A vision," she whispered.

Shylae's eyes brightened and shone out into the downpour. She turned her head to face the interior of the rocks. Colton cradled her as she grasped him, every muscle tense. Then her body went slack.

Colton held his love. Her breathing remained steady and slow yet barely audible. He counted each breath. At ten, Shylae stirred and looked intently into his eyes, her tears streaming.

"I saw him," she said. "Torren and his men, running toward the Orb, the Orteh."

Shylae drank from the bota bag offered by Marise and then continued. "Torren was grinning. It was an awful, evil grin—triumphant somehow. I saw the trail. Rocky and damp, but not wet. When they came to an outcropping, they jumped over it. It was twenty feet high and they vaulted it like it was nothing. On the other side, the ground dipped and there was a lake and the waterfall—the one from before. Torren motioned his men to go into the water." She grabbed Colton's cloak in both hands. "It wasn't raining. Maybe the vision is of the future." She hurried on, excitedly. "One by one they dove into the pool and swam under the fall…"

"And?" Marise queried.

"And nothing. That's where the vision ended."

"Let us hope this is a vision of the future," Colton said. "The past is set, but our future may be changed."

It took Shylae mere moments to regain her composure. *She continues to amazes me with her resilience and abilities.* To Shylae, he said, "We need to increase our pace, if you are able."

"Let's get going. I'm not gonna let that bastard beat us." This time, Shylae led the way.

Stevie scanned the horizon and lifted her head to breathe in the moist air.

Colton commented, "The storm has moved on. Unless you have us change direction, it is likely we shall stay dry until we camp."

Handing the bota bag to Colton, Stevie asked, "How far do you think we've gone?"

"That depends on how much further we have to go." He smiled at her.

"Ha ha. I'm guessing we've hit fifteen miles so far today. The pull of the Orb is stronger now. I can't imagine it's much farther. A few more miles before sundown, and then a hop, skip, and a jump in the morning."

Both Colton and Marise turned to her quizzically.

"It means a short distance." Stevie chuckled.

During the last part of the day's trek, the clouds parted to reveal a crystal-blue sky. The sun beamed down on them. Stevie, although grateful for the warmth, cursed and swatted at the multitude of flying insects the heat brought out.

Within the hour, they found a likely campsite near a glacier lake, set up the tent and started a fire. Marise proved her skills at finding dry wood, while Stevie helped Colton prepare sandwiches of pita bread and jerky. The bread was soggy and the meat had taken on an unpleasant texture of re-hydration. With only coffee to warm them, they huddled around the campfire, their clothes drying on their skin. Conversation was non-existent.

While Marise and Colton sipped their coffee, Stevie spoke up. "I think I should try to see what's up with the Rebels."

Stevie moved closer to the flame. As she stared into the sparks that shot out from the the campfire, the vision overtook her. But this time was different. Overcome by a new sensation, she seemed to be levitating. Looking down, she saw her body lying prone on the ground. Colton and Marise had rushed to her side. She wanted to let them know that she was all right, but the pull of the Orteh forced her on into the wilderness.

A voice in the Djenrye tongue ebbed and flowed around her as she soared above the tree tops. She struggled to recall the words Colton had taught her. Confusion set in. She fought unsuccessfully to understand.

The force pulling her forward lessened as she approached a campsite. Until that moment, she had not fully realized her lack of control in this spirit form. She was a leaf blown about in the wind; her movements were under control of the Orteh.

She had not traveled far, maybe a few miles. The men below wore Djen clothing—all leather and steel. *The Rebellion. I need to warn Colton and Marise. How did they get here so quick?*

She dropped lower to the camp. Torren warmed himself by the fire, eating his fish, drinking his ale, and laughing with his men. Anger welled up inside her. *He's so confident and arrogant, he makes me sick.*

The conversation was fragmented. She could hardly make out any words. Once or twice she heard Orteh, but nothing else she recognized. Then came the disembodied voice again. This time it spoke in English.

"Shylae…Shylae, they are coming…You must not tarry…The Orteh…"

Stevie looked around. "Who are you? I can hear you but I don't see you," she whispered.

"It is my mind that is near. My form remains in Djenrye. I am Esalon of Tyré."

"You're the Mage Colton contacted."

"Correct, Shylae. I felt your vision quest. Colton did not exaggerate the strength of your abilities. I was compelled to show you how close the Rebels are to your encampment."

"What is Torren planning? You must help me understand." Her attention returned to the three men who now stood in front of Torren.

"He speaks of the proximity of your camp. His men are to attack before the midpoint of the night. He intends to kill your protectors, capture you, and retrieve the Orteh." Esalon's words came in a whisper. "Be warned, my Guardian. He has the power to see you, even in this form." The voice boomed. "You must make haste to warn Colton and Marise."

Stevie fought to hold contact with Esalon. The voice faded. She tried to return to her body. Instead, a falling sensation overcame her.

She screamed.

Torren looked up, golden eyes burned into hers.

He sees me.

Her downward plummet ended with a painful impact on the forest floor.

Colton shook Shylae but the vision held her fast. Her mark had shone through her jacket. Marise arrived beside him with a wet cloth for Shylae's forehead.

"Why will she not awaken?" Marise asked. Her tone edged with confusion and fear.

"I know not. Never have I seen this happen." Colton took Shylae's hand in his. "Come back to me, my love," he whispered, leaning in close. "I am lost without you."

Marise overturned Colton's pack in an effort to retrieve the Din Ashyea. "Perhaps this holds an answer?"

Taking the offered book, Colton held it near the fire to read the words. He scanned the pages. His fingers came to rest on a passage. *This must be it—'Out of body trance'.*

"Did you find something?" asked Marise.

"The Din Ashyea speaks of long experienced seers having gained the knowledge of separating their spirits from their bodies." He paused and gazed at Shylae.

"Yet she should not have such ability." Marise stroked Shylae's arm.

"A Mage or Sorcerer must be present in order to accomplish the trance, and we have neither here."

Colton began to flip through the pages once more. "I will read further. Perhaps I can find an answer on how to bring her out of this state."

In the firelight, Colton combed through the book. The lilting sound of Marise humming a Djenrye children's song drifted in the wind.

"There is a ritual." He held up the book. "We need certain herbs."

Marise moved to his side and peered over his shoulder. Her braid struck his back when she shook her head. "Hold, Brother. We do not know how this separation is affecting her. Time may be of the essence. Perhaps you should try to contact Esalon."

Colton felt cold. "Why did I not consider that option?" Angry at himself for missing the obvious, he focused on reaching out for Esalon. Mind clear, the image of an old man—white beard and hair flowing to his waist, came into focus.

"My Lord, Colton? What is it you wish of me?" A voice spoke in Colton's ear.

"Shylae slumbers as the dead. The vision she entered will not release her."

"I fear the fault is mine for Shylae's state," Esalon whispered.

"How is that possible?" asked Colton.

"It was I who pulled her spirit from her body. The spirit journey was required for her to understand Torren's proximity and plans. Her strength led me to believe she would be able to reunite her body and spirit unaided."

"Then, why has she not returned? You are of the Magi! How could you be so careless?" Colton's anger roiled, but he quelled it, fearing loss of the connection.

"I will do what I can to aid Shylae. You must focus your energies on Torren's impending attack."

"Attack?" This, Colton spoke out loud, breaking his connection with the Mage.

"What is wrong?" Marise asked instinctively retrieving her sword.

"Torren and his men plan to ambush us. Place Shylae in the tent and make ready for battle."

Stevie tried to move but could not. She could feel the cold damp ground beneath her and tried to focus on the night sky, but a dark shape blocked the stars.

"Welcome back," the shape said.

Torren. Stevie could see his face clearly now and the smug look he wore. Panic engulfed her. She tried to back away, return to the sky, anything. But fear restrained her. She could see she was still at Torren's camp. Alone.

"I see you." His lips curled into a smile. "I am stronger than your worst fears or those of your servant boy." Then he laughed.

Stevie felt naked and defenseless but would not give him the satisfaction of a response.

"I hope you were able to say good-bye before you left." Torren sneered. "That whelp and his sister will die."

He crouched over Stevie's prone ethereal form. "When I return to my camp with your body, I believe I shall have a bit fun before reuniting it with your spirit." Torren grinned. "Do not worry, young Guardian. You will not feel a thing."

Anger gave Stevie strength and some control.

She sat up.

"You freakin' ass!" she yelled.

"Direct your venom at the Mage. He left you in this state." As he stood, he added, "Left you with no idea how to reconnect. Pity." He turned away dismissively.

"Come back here, you dick," Stevie cried. She watched him disappear into the forest, his men at his heels. Terrified, Stevie forced her spirit to stand. She tried to run after them but her ethereal body would not respond.

"Esalon!" she called out. "I need you. Why don't you answer me?" Not knowing what else to do, she returned to the ground and calmed herself. Desperate to warn Colton, she used what energy she had to reach Esalon. She received silence in return.

A Rebel Warrior broke through the trees. Colton looked to his sword, but the axe was closer. Colton dove for it. In one smooth motion, he grasped the handle, rolled onto his side, and threw the axe. It sank deep into the man's chest.

An angry roar preceded Torren's entrance into the clearing. Simultaneously, two Warriors rushed in. One veered for Marise, who met him with her sword drawn.

Colton regained his footing and his claymore. He charged Torren, but another Rebel blocked the assault. Colton swung hard, connecting solidly with the other's blade. Steel rang out, overpowering the mundane sounds of the night.

Torren joined in the melee. Colton battled them both—a block, a thrust, a duck, a dodge. Despite his efforts, the enemy gained the upper hand. Colton caught a glimpse of his sister through the flurry of strikes. She had fallen, pinned by a mountain of a man. His hands were locked around her neck. She struggled, but appeared to be losing consciousness.

Rage spurred Colton, unleashing his full fury. He disarmed the lesser threat, who stumbled backward into the fire pit. Colton turned his attention to Torren, barely registering the screams of the burning man who ran into the forest.

Each strike landed solid, blade on blade. Colton threw his weight into every blow. Sparks flew from the swords with each connection. Veins protruded on Torren's tense arms. Colton would give him no leave to counter, only block.

Torren gave ground.

Colton pinned him against a tree.

"I yield," he cried out.

The uncharacteristic surrender took Colton by surprise. Torren had an opening to counter-parry, but did not. Colton pressed forward striking Torren's wrist with the sword hilt, and simultaneously punched the Rebel leader squarely in the face. Torren crumpled to the ground.

Colton rushed to his sister's aid but Marise no longer struggled. The Rebel released the grip on her throat to meet Colton's attack. Colton fought with the fury of a man possessed. He did not see the steel nor feel the blows. His only desire was to avenge his sister.

The sword seemed to move on its own. The murderer fell back. Colton raised the claymore for the killing strike, but a sharp pain seized him. His legs buckled and he collapsed to the ground. As he fell, he saw Torren towering over him, blood dripping from a dagger.

Colton knew the blood was his own.

Chapter 33

Stevie wandered disembodied through the forest, unable to discern the direction to the campsite. Time had no meaning in this form, but it seemed as though hours had passed. Her mind searched for Esalon. From the darkness, she heard a faint voice. She stopped. "Esalon…is that you?" She listened.

"Shylae…"

"Esalon. You left me. Alone…"

"I beg your forgiveness, my Guardian. I was certain you could return without my aid."

"Obviously not. Hurry up. I need to get back…The Rebels…Colton…"

"It is not that simple. The separation has lingered too long. A spell must be performed to enable your return."

Stevie heard the regret in his voice, but her frustration left no room for compassion. "Damn it, Esalon. What kinda Mage are you? I need to get back to Colton. Which way do I go?"

"I understand your urgency. I must leave you briefly to collect the materials for the conjuring. You are moving in the correct direction. I will contact you soon…" The voice faded with the last word.

"Esalon? Esalon? Damn it. Alone again." Stevie continued toward the camp, but she struggled with her spirit form.

An owl hooted somewhere above her—death's harbinger. With a prayer for Colton and Marise's safety, she continued the slow movement forward.

Torren entered the tent. Shylae's physical body rested on the ground, her chest rose and fell with each shallow breath. Her beauty took him aback. *She looks so like her mother.*

He removed his sword belt and lowered himself beside the prone form. *Serene. Such fine features.* As he studied Shylae's face and allowed his gaze to move down her body, he pictured Carlynn's face as it looked the last time he had seen her.

His body tingled and he lost himself in memories of the last encounter with Carlynn. *I wonder if Shylae's eyes shine as brightly as her mother's when she is terrified?* The idea of draining the exquisite creature before him, looking into her eyes as her life slipped away, seeing, feeling her terror, filled Torren with a desire and lust he had not felt in over a decade.

Unable to contain himself any longer, he reached for Shylae. With a curse, he drew back his hand. The shock left his fingers numb.

"What?" He moved to touch her again. This time, a painful electric current surged through his body. It took a moment for his twitching to cease. He roared. "A spell protects her!" He stormed out of the tent.

The men approached. "My lord?" They dropped to one knee.

He kicked one over with his boot, stomping the ground as he paced. The men held their tongues until Torren's fury had subsided.

Torren returned to the tent and held his hands out over the girl, chanting words meant to lift the spell. Wave after wave of energy repelled him. The spell was too strong.

Angry and frustrated, he grabbed his weapons and returned to his men.

"Only a Mage could have set a spell I cannot remove." He ordered his men, "We shall gather our provisions. We leave for the Orteh at first light."

The Rebel who had dispatched Marise asked, "And what of the Guardian's body, my lord? It cannot be touched, but if she awakens…"

"Do not take me for a fool, Lucun. She seems unable to return to her form. Her spirit roams the hills." Torren stopped and looked back in the tent. "After such a time, she will need my help to awaken. After you and the men have packed camp, you will return here to stand guard while we retrieve the Orteh."

Lucun looked at the fallen Djen Warriors. "And them?"

Torren walked over to Colton's body. He stared down at the motionless form. With his boot, he pushed the fallen Djen on his side. Satisfied, Torren snorted. "Do you fear the dead? They are not a concern. Not any more." Without another word, Torren led the way back into the woods.

Stevie floated to a ridge not far from her camp. It took a great effort to stop. She listened for Esalon. *I continued off this cliff, would I survive? Would I float down like a leaf or get caught in the wind and drift away?* Either possibility chilled her. Thankfully, Esalon's whisper distracted her from the morbid thoughts.

"Shylae?"

"Esalon…are you ready?"

"I am… First, you must be made aware of what will occur when you return to..." He paused. "When you awaken, your limbs will be heavy and pained. It will be difficult to move, but you must move quickly."

"Why? What's going on?"

"Torren and his men have infiltrated the camp and engaged your protectors. Colton and Marise are both grievously injured. You must heal them immediately, or they shall not survive."

"Then stop talking and help me."

Esalon's chant filled her mind. It grew in volume and strength to become a living thing. It lifted her spirit off the ridge. A tingling sensation started in her stomach and spread through the rest of her. It overtook her, much like the first time she had a waking vision. This time, however, rather than being pulled back, she was propelled forward. The forest rushed by. She caught a mere glimpse of her body before being forcefully thrown in.

Nausea, not pain or heaviness, was her first sensation. Her eyes would not open. Her arms and hands lay unresponsive, like stones. *Wiggle your toes, anything.* But her mind would not connect to her body. She prayed silently to whomever, whatever would listen. *Help me move… I must save my love…*

For whom the bell tolls. That's what this reminds me of. The long ago practice of cords placed in coffins, tied to a bell above ground, in case the dead woke up after being buried. The sense of urgency and fear compelled her to concentrate harder.

There was wetness at the corner of her eyes. *I'm crying. I can feel the tears.*

Then pain—a wonderful pain. Her hand clenched. She willed her eyes to open. The lids cramped, but she managed a small squint. Her arm next, flopped to the side. It bumped what could have been a bota bag. Her control returning, Stevie reached for the object and managed a drink. More spilled on the sleeping bag than trickled into her mouth. The water helped to revive her. Crawling on her hands and knees, the blessed agony of the movement sharply cut through her fog and she emerged from the tent.

Marise's body lay within a few feet. The distance might as well have been a mile. The pain of each flexing muscle was overwhelming, as if rigor mortis had set in. Yet, determination pushed her on. Reaching Marise, Stevie embraced the still figure.

"Please let her be alive." Stevie sobbed. Not knowing their names, she nonetheless prayed to the Djen Gods. "Please, I beg you." An invisible energy surrounded her and Marise. She felt its presence. Marise's eyes fluttered and she began to choke and sputter. She gasped for air and grabbed at her throat, clawing at the injury. She stopped abruptly. Marise breathed in deeply and opened her eyes.

Oh, thank God…

Leaning on each other, Marise and Stevie managed to sit up.

"Thank you, my sister," she croaked.

Then, Stevie saw Colton. Scarlet saturated the ground around him. "Take me to him," she sobbed. *Please, don't let it be too late!*

Supporting each other, Marise and Stevie stumbled forward. Crying, they collapsed next to Colton's body. As they turned him over, the women placed their hands on the wound and prayed.

Stevie mouthed the words that Marise spoke until she could confidently join in. An energy surge poured from Stevie and joined with Marise's. A vortex formed about them. The wind picked up and created a protective whirling cone, with the three of them at its center. The energy flowed into Colton at the site of the wound, creating an elemental suture. The speed at which it disappeared into his body gave the impression of water rushing down a recently opened chasm. The blood remained, the only evidence of the injury.

Marise leaned in and, with Stevie, embraced Colton.

He gasped.

The women pulled back and Colton opened his eyes.

"It's working," whispered Stevie. "Oh, thank God. You're alive." She bent forward, covering his mouth with hers.

Marise interrupted the kiss. "We must sit him up."

Together, they slipped their hands under Colton's armpits and tried to lift him. The forest spun around Stevie and she collapsed.

"Come, my love." Colton propped himself up on his elbow. He pulled her to him. "You expended far too much energy on saving our lives. Let us help you now."

After a few minutes, Stevie thought she could manage to move closer to the fire, which had died down to a few scattered embers but gave off a semblance of heat. Stevie gratefully accepted the water Colton offered when he sat next to her.

"I thought I lost you." Stevie hugged him.

Colton wiped away her tears, his calloused hands a welcome comfort.

"My feelings earlier were as yours are now, when we could not rouse you from your trance." His mouth found hers.

Marise cleared her throat. "How do you fare, Guardian?"

Stevie stood and stretched her limbs, flexed and relaxed her muscles. "I'm still kinda wobbly, but at least the pain is gone. And..." She balanced on one leg and then the other. "...my coordination is coming back."

"Excellent," Colton exclaimed.

He rose and surveyed the camp. Two Rebel bodies remained. One had fallen near the clearing's edge, motionless and smelling of burnt flesh. The other had an axe protruding from his chest. They looked to be dead.

"Torren," Colton growled. "We must make haste. We cannot allow them to reach the Orteh before us." He glanced back at Stevie. "The luxury of time for you to properly heal is not ours. With your sanction, Marise and I will return a portion of the energy you gave us."

"But wait," Stevie protested. "What will that do to you?"

"Worry not, Shylae. It will not impede us." He turned her shoulders so that she faced him. "I know of no Djen that has ever healed two people close to death. At least, not one that survived. You have great strength. Yet, even a Guardian with your abilities has limitations."

The siblings enveloped Stevie. Colton laid his hand on the top of her head. The Djen words he and Marise recited created a tapestry of sound. A prickly sensation surged through Stevie's body. Her muscles relaxed, the joints loosened.

"Wow. I feel like I just woke up from a good night's sleep. Refreshed."

"Then we are ready." Colton clasped Stevie's hand. "Does the pull of the Orteh continue?"

"It's stronger than ever." Stevie took the lead, with Colton and Marise close on her heels.

The Orteh's hold guided Stevie. When she veered in the wrong direction, she would teeter backward from the absence of the dragging force. In this manner, the path became clear with every step.

Stevie ran, without giving thought to her footing. The ground blurred beneath their feet. An inner certainty assured no more stumbles. They had run several miles when the pull abruptly ceased. Stevie swayed on a cliff's edge. Far below was a pool, fed by a waterfall—the one from her vision that hid the Orb's hiding place.

Colton spoke behind her. "Shylae, you hesitate."

Stevie closed her eyes, trying to reestablish the connection.

"I can't sense the Orb. I think we're too late."

The look of anguish on Colton's face was more than Stevie could bear. "Let's go see, at least," she said.

Marise dove off the cliff first. For a moment, her form hung gracefully in the air. Then she plummeted downward, disappearing into the pool below. Stevie and Colton followed, hand in hand. The shock of the frigid water took Stevie's breath. They had sunk deeper into the pool than she expected. Determination made her legs kick all the harder. When she broke the surface, she was on the other side of the waterfall, a rock platform before her.

Emerging from the water, shivers rocked Stevie. Colton and Marise stood, facing two different tunnels.

Colton touched Stevie on the shoulder. "Movement will warm you."

Stevie nodded and looked around. "I don't have a clue which tunnel to take."

Pointing to the passage on the right, Colton said, "Marise, follow that pathway. Shylae and I shall investigate the other."

They lost sight and sound of Marise at the first bend. After a few more feet, she and Colton came to a dead end. Retracing their steps, they found a fissure hidden in the shadows to their left. It took a moment to squeeze through, but the other end opened to reveal a lake. The surface of the water reflected blue. Stevie had become so used to the ability that she did not realize until that moment she and Colton had been lighting the way with the glow of their eyes.

They scanned the cavern frantically, thoroughly, for any sign of the Orb. Tears dimmed her eyes. "It's not here."

Colton wrapped his arms around her. "I am sorry, my love," he murmured. "All is not yet lost."

"But Torren has the Orb."

"We may still be able to intercept the Rebels before they reach the portal... They could not have outpaced us by too great a distance."

Her hope and determination renewed, Stevie grabbed his hand and led the way back to the tunnel. "Let's hurry...we might catch up to them."

They met up with Marise at the mouth of the cave.

"It appears as though you fared no better than I," said Marise. A frown tugged at the corners of her mouth. "Are you certain we are in the correct location?"

"Positive," Stevie said. "We found the lake."

"The Rebellion preceded us to the Orteh, but they shall not do so with the portal," Colton said confidently. Without another word, he dove into the water. The women followed suit.

They scaled the precipice that bordered the pool. At the top, Colton and Marise paused briefly to scan the ground.

"The Rebels travel east," Marise said, pointing back the way they had approached. She followed the footprints for about one hundred feet. "I see no further ground signs," Marise said.

"They must have taken to the trees..." In a blur, Colton ascended to the top of the closest pine.

Moments later, he called down, "Torren is proceeding with little caution, but much of the evidence of his movements has dissipated." Colton jumped down next to Stevie.

"My best guess is that Torren left our camp before dawn. He thinks we're dead, so of course he's not worried," Stevie surmised.

"I believe he would not have left your body there, Shylae. He requires you to complete his plans. Yet, his direction away from our camp is peculiar," said Colton.

They raced back to camp. Stevie refused to let Colton's words dampen the giddiness she felt. Despite all that had happened, they still had a chance of beating those bastards to the portal. And then she saw the body.

The Rebel they had thought dead had managed to crawl to the entrance of her tent. The hair on the back of his head had been burned away, revealing raw, blistered skin, cracked and oozing. The leather vest, or what remained of it, had adhered to his back, making it difficult to distinguish burned skin from animal hide. The moan that escaped from his lips upon her approach startled Stevie. *How is he still alive?*

Colton passed her, kneeling next to the Rebel. "Marise, Shylae, assist me. I believe we may still be able to heal him."

Her mouth agape and eyes wide, Marise stared at Colton. "Have you lost your wits, Brother?" she exclaimed. "What sorcery has overtaken you to inspire such folly?"

"He may be privy to the course Torren and his men are taking. We need any information he is able to provide."

Turning him over, Colton called for a rope, which Marise hastily retrieved from her pack. The moans increased in volume and frequency as Colton secured the man's hands and feet.

Stevie steeled herself and joined Colton and Marise, already in the process of healing the dying man.

The wounds closed, leaving the charred rags hanging on his form. Stevie noted that the healing did nothing to return the hair to his head.

Colton positioned himself in front of the Rebel soldier, knife at his throat, waiting for a sign of consciousness. The Warrior stopped moaning. His eyes flickered open, widening when they met Colton's gaze.

"*Namae ai Élan-Vitál,*" he sputtered. "*Hyne ar, Torren?*"

Stevie could not make out his last question, except for the name "Torren."

"The fate of your leader is the least of your concerns." Colton growled.

"*Eamá chasea whynae le nudo?*" Fear sparkled in the captive's eyes.

"You will provide me answers as to Torren's next move." Colton pressed in the edge of the blade.

The Warrior winced. When he spoke, it was in clipped English and his voice quavered. "He have Tecton Orteh. He demand *chasean eh'ankh*, your death, and *redul Ty Greial*…grab the Guardian." He looked at Stevie.

Pressing the knife harder, Colton regained the man's attention. "You speak of old information. Torren already believes he has achieved my end. What is his intention on returning for Shylae?"

"He knows you live. Lucun returned, found you had fled."

"They left you to die," Colton hissed. He removed the blade from the Rebel's throat and sat back. "We may well have lost our advantage." To Stevie and Marise he called, "Pack quickly. I need to dispatch this traitor."

The captive struggled to a sitting position, raising his bound hands to his chest. "I beg. *Eh eh'ankh le*, no kill me. *Namae ai Élan-Vitál. Namae ai Tzak.* Torren *eh okih*, no friend, no brother." And then his pleas changed entirely into the Djen tongue.

Stevie could not mistake the look of disbelief on Colton and Marise's faces. "What did he say?"

"He begs for mercy," Marise answered. "He claims that he became a Rebel not by choice, but through extortion. They threatened his family."

"*Le hyrl Greial Shylae whynae,*" the Rebel concluded.

"And…" Marise sneered, "…he pledges his allegiance to you, the Guardian."

Colton leaned in close to the turncoat. "Why should we now trust you?"

"I speak truth. Torren *eh'ankh*, he kill my brother," he pleaded to Colton.

Colton looked over at his sister and Stevie. "This is not a decision I am able to make alone. If we free him, all of our lives could be in peril."

Stevie knelt down, putting her hand on his forehead. She commanded, "Look at me." The man's distress engulfed her. She knew it to be real. "We can trust him."

"I will only agree to this…" Marise said, "…if he is kept under guard at all times."

"That's fine, but I know he is telling the truth. I can feel it," said Stevie.

Colton untied the rope around the man's ankles. "Do you know the path Torren will take to the portal, Traitor?"

Standing, the former Rebel said, "I will lead you. And," he added, "…Namae Eli, not Traitor."

Chapter 34

Eli turned to Stevie and knelt. "Rumors spread of the lost *Greial*, Guardian, child." He lowered his head, his voice submissive, "*Le* rejoice in their truth. *Le hyrl chasea whynae.*"

Stevie did not know how to respond. All she could think of was to incline her head and go help Marise pack.

Marise nodded in Eli's direction. "He pledges his allegiance to you."

"Okay. That felt weird," Stevie said.

"Guardian…he is still on one knee."

Horrified, Stevie turned back to Eli and waved for him to rise.

The band moved quickly through the forest. Eli carried Stevie's pack, despite her protest and his hands being bound. He said something to Stevie that Marise translated as "It is my honor to serve you, Guardian."

The female Warrior held tight to the rope leashing Eli, and Colton stayed close at their side, pushing their new ally forward each time he turned to look at or speak to Stevie.

They had been running for hours when Marise called a halt. She dropped into her normal squat and ran her hands over the ground. When she stood, she scanned the horizon silently. Her brow furrowed. "The tracks of the Rebellion change course here. Brother, tell me, do you recognize those peaks?"

Colton looked in the direction Marise pointed. "They head back to shore. Their path will intersect with the police soldier and Jack Snow."

"What?" Stevie asked. "Are you saying Torren and his men are heading for the boat?"

"It appears to be so." Then Colton spoke to Eli. "Tell me if Torren knows of our water craft."

The former Rebel flinched away from the harsh tone. "*Yi.* Torren visioned it the night past."

Marise jerked hard on the rope, pulling Eli off his feet. She towered over him, cursing. "*Ka-chet*," she spat. "This you could not tell us before? Are you still loyal to Torren?" She drew back her arm to strike.

Before the blow landed, Stevie commanded, "Stop!"

Marching over to Eli, she helped him to his feet. "Marise, I have told you and Colton I believe Eli. I trust him. If I am to be your Guardian, you will respect that and treat him with dignity."

Marise lowered her head. "Le hyrl chasea whynae."

Turning to Eli, Stevie softened her voice. "Tell me. Why didn't you mention this before?"

"Not important." Eli shrugged and then pointed at where the tracks changed direction. "Before, Torren head to portal."

Fixating on the direction, Stevie took off in a run. Colton caught up to her quickly.

"I feel your fear, Shylae. Yet, you must have sustenance. Your abilities are young and your stamina is not at its full potential."

Reluctantly, she returned to Marise and Eli. An outcropping of rock provided a shaded, grassy nook. Stevie dug in her pack, removing the two-way radio, in the process jostling Eli.

Marise intervened, untying Eli and releasing his burden. She motioned him to sit while Stevie made her call. It took several attempts before Jack's voice crackled through the speaker.

"Hey. It's Jack. Over."

"Hey back," Stevie said. "Is Wood around? I need to let him know what's up."

There was a long pause before Jack chided her. "You're supposed to say 'Over.' No, he's on land attempting to hunt. Over." Jack snickered.

"What? Oh, never mind. Listen up. We think the Rebels are heading your way. Please keep your guard up. Over."

"Say what? Over."

"It's a long story, but we should reach you by morning. Please stay on the boat. Over."

"Try telling Wood that. He said he only likes being on the boat when we're moving. There's nothing to do when we're docked. Over."

"Damn it. You'll be safer on the water. The boat's way more defensible. Over."

"Wow, girl. You're starting to sound like a real Warrior. Maybe if I put it that way, Wood'll listen to me. I'll have him call when he gets back. Over."

"K, sounds good. But keep your eyes peeled. Over and out."

Anxious to get going, Stevie forced herself to sit down and grab a bite of food. She watched Marise's attempt to treat Eli with some respect. She handed him the bota bag, speaking a Djen word. Rather than taking a drink, he walked to Stevie, the bag held out in front of him. Out of nowhere, Colton snatched it away, offering it to Stevie himself.

"What's going on with you?" She looked into Colton's eyes for some hint of his behavior.

"I apologize for any slight I may have given. I will do as you wish, but he has not earned my trust." Colton glared at Eli before returning his attention to Stevie. "Additionally, I am troubled by the events of last night. Why did Esalon expel you from your body and then leave you in peril, unable to return? How was Torren able to see your spirit form?"

Marise approached as Colton lowered himself to sit beside Stevie. A furrow creased the female Warrior's brow.

Stevie looked at the siblings. "You're not thinking Esalon did that on purpose, are you?"

Colton shook his head. "I... No. I do not believe that is the case. Esalon is many things, but not a traitor." He paused. "I must communicate with him tonight and query his intention."

"Tonight? I thought we'd push on to reach the shore by morning," Stevie said.

Marise and Colton exchanged a look. "We will require a short rest to regain our strength, but we will travel through the night."

Rope in hand, Marise approached Eli, but Stevie stepped between them.

"Leave him untied. It's just slowing us down."

Reluctantly, Marise wound the rope and secured it to her pack. As she did, she fixed Eli with a glare. "Do not thwart the Guardian's trust in you. If you run, you will find an arrow in your back."

At dusk, they found an area suitable for a few hours' rest. Stevie concentrated on helping Colton gather tinder. Pictures floated in her mind of Wood trying unsuccessfully to fight off the Rebels with a sword. She cringed. "What if Torren and his men get to the boat before we do? I'm really worried."

"There is naught we can do at the moment. We must increase our pace in the hope of overtaking the Rebels."

While Stevie and Colton built and lit a fire, Marise disappeared with Eli to fish for dinner. They returned with three fat salmon.

Colton remained silent during much of the meal.

Stevie asked, "What's bugging you?"

When he looked up, he seemed to gaze past, rather than at, Stevie. Blinking, he refocused on her face and smiled wanly. "The sooner I contact Esalon, the sooner my concerns will be allayed…or affirmed." He stood and moved a few steps from the fire, presumably to meditate.

Stevie helped Eli clean up the plates. Outside the glow of the campfire, she could make out the blue beams from Colton's eyes. She listened for any sign that he had made contact with Esalon.

A rush of static from her pocket interrupted her. It was followed by the rumble of Wood's voice.

"Stevie, are you there?"

She snatched it, cranking the volume knob to the left, praying the noise had not disrupted Colton.

"Yes, Wood. I'm here," she said, in a low voice.

"What's going on? Over."

"Long story. Bad news. The Rebels got the Orb. We're on our way back to you, but the glitch is, so are the bad guys. You need to stay on the boat until we get there. Way more defensible, ya know? Over."

The loud sigh emanated through the speaker. "How did all this happen? Over."

"Like I said, long story and I don't want to waste the batteries. We're gonna need them for tomorrow. Just trust me. They're headed your way. Over."

"All right, but you be careful, too. Check in with us early tomorrow. Over."

"Okay. Over and out."

As she released the switch, Colton emerged into the firelight. He grabbed the bota bag and took a long swallow. His movements and breathing had relaxed, especially compared to the last several hours. "Was that the voice of Detective Wood?"

"Yeah." Stevie took a drink from the offered bag before continuing. "Did you get hold of Esalon?"

He nodded. "I contacted him, yes. Join me at the fire and I will relay what he imparted."

Metal plates clanked as Marise and Eli stowed them in a pack. It took a few moments before they joined Stevie and Colton.

"I heard you have news, Brother."

"Esalon explained the reasoning for his actions, and I believe they ring true."

"How so?" Marise queried.

"He had been observing our progress and chose to lead Shylae in a spirit walk. He thought her able to locate the Rebel camp and return to inform us of their close proximity. Esalon avowed his belief in the Guardian's mastery, but he overestimated her abilities."

"Ya think?" Stevie crossed her arms in a huff.

"I believe his sincerity, my love. He has proven himself time and again to be a good friend and a wise counselor." Colton placed his arm around Stevie.

"And what of Torren's powers?" Marise asked.

"That is the part of Esalon's tale which greatly concerns me. With the impending planetary alignment, Torren's power—indeed, all magic—is magnified."

"If he speaks true," Marise added, "why do we wait to utilize this…this energy?"

A mirthless laugh escaped Colton. "Sister, we are too alike. I asked the same. In return, Esalon spoke to the dangers of such a venture—madness or death. We must be patient. The attempt of such a feat requires the assistance of a Mage."

"Then we remain in agreement? You will allow Esalon to aid you in this undertaking?"

Colton nodded.

Stevie sat silently, chewing on her lower lip. *I don't like this… I don't like it at all.*

A Kermode bear. Although anxious to get to her friends, Stevie and the other Djen stood as still as stone. It was the first break they'd taken since the night before and she was thankful that Eli spotted the animal.

The bear hovered at the bank of a stream, white fur reflecting in the sunlight. With a speed Stevie did not expect, the bear leapt into the water. It emerged, head shaking side to side, the swaying motion continuing down its body, throwing off a shower of water. A salmon dangled from its jaws.

Stevie took advantage of the moment to gaze at the surrounding beauty. Mountains and cliffs peeked through the tops of the Sitka spruces and pines. Moss hung everywhere in the primeval forest.

Colton whispered, "We must keep moving and leave the creature to its feast."

Stevie sighed. Colton stroked her cheek and she knew he understood her disappointment.

Marise pointed to a rise across the stream. "We need to get to the higher ground. This muck hinders our every movement."

Looking upward, Eli asked, "To the trees?"

Colton shook his head. "They drip with slippery moss. One misjudged step and injury is inevitable."

An hour later, Stevie found herself hugging a cliff wall. Her balance and agility improved every day, but she was not prepared to take on a two-hundred-foot drop. The mountain goat trail they followed intermittently narrowed from a foot-wide path to a few inches; from level ground, to a sharp slope, to rocky steps. She cautiously mimicked Colton's moves—*left foot here, on the granite outcrop. Grab the root for stability. Right foot there, wedged into a cleft.* The procession and focus stopped when Stevie's radio crackled to life. Startled, she lost a handhold and teetered backwards. Colton caught her by the wrist and steadied her.

"Wood to Stevie. Are you there? Come in. Over."

She turned to brace her back against the cliff, her heels dug into the ground. Releasing her held breath, she asked Marise to retrieve the radio from Eli's pack.

"Your timing really sucks. Over." She clutched the radio.

"You were supposed to call. Got worried. Over," said Wood.

Stevie huffed at an errant strand of hair which had fallen into her eyes. "We're fine. Just hanging onto the side of a cliff like a bunch of spiders so that we can chat with you."

"Oh...." said Wood. "Oh, shit... How about you call me when you're in a less precarious situation?"

"Good idea. Best guess—around one o'clock." She looked to Colton for affirmation. "We should be on lower ground by then."

Stevie handed the radio back to Marise and took a deep breath. "Well, this is fun. Let's get moving." She motioned Colton forward.

"Your balance is improving, yet you remain unsure of yourself," he said, his face breaking into a grin. "Consider this training to prepare you for the cliffs we will climb in Djenrye."

"Peachy. Can't wait," Stevie responded.

By the time the path widened, Stevie's fingers had begun to cramp. At the next bend, the mountain leveled out and they stood on a rock plateau. The view made her forget her pain.

The valley below stretched on for miles. A crisscrossing of streams, pools, and rivers broke up the dense green background. From their vantage point, the trees became an indistinguishable mass of foliage. Everything appeared connected and cocooned together.

Colton spotted another animal trail along a tributary, which led to the valley floor. Marise and Eli brought up the rear.

As they approached, Marise pointed out a flat area next to a pool. "There. Boot prints. The Rebels passed this way, and not long ago."

"How far ahead do you think they are?" asked Stevie.

Colton moved to the pool. "It is hard to say. Perhaps a few hours."

"I'll call Wood," exclaimed Stevie, retrieving the two-way radio. "Jack, Wood, you there? Over."

Silence.

She tried again, but there was no response. After the third attempt, she threw the radio to Eli. "We gotta go. Now!"

Through a break in the trees Stevie spotted the boat. The deck was empty, the anchor line visible. She rushed forward onto the beach.

Chaos.

A wrecked cooler rested on its side against a tree trunk. The lid had been wrenched off and laid a few feet away. Empty beer bottles, some broken, littered the ground. A mound of ice was melting into the sand, indicating that whatever happened, it had occurred recently.

Contents of a backpack were strewn about. A partially dressed salmon had been placed on a rock, neglected by all except the insects and carrion birds.

"What the…" Stevie exclaimed, clutching at Marise.

Marise dropped into a crouch. Her fingers traced an indentation in the sand. "Signs of an attack."

"Here…" Colton cried out. Stevie and Marise rushed to his side at the edge of the water.

"Blood." He dipped his finger in a sticky crimson substance smeared across the surface of a boulder. He sniffed and then tasted it. "Human blood. I know not whether it is from Police Soldier Wood or Jack Snow."

Stevie's heart sank. *Oh please, oh please, let them be alive.*

Eli's call from the other side of the small beach pierced her pain. He stood over a dead Rebel Warrior. Blood congealed in the man's hair and created a scarlet halo in the sand.

"Ka-chet!" Eli kicked the body. Scratches covered the man's chest and arms, the cloth of his breeches shredded and torn.

Colton moved Eli aside. "You know this one?"

"Kardaen. No better than a Jajing." He spat.

Colton knelt down to examine the wounds. "There is bark and other debris in the abrasions," he muttered. He looked up at the trees. "He fell from there." Colton pointed to a Sequoia a few feet away. Returning his attention to the body, he poked his finger into the puncture in the Rebel's chest. "Not the work of an arrow. This is from a bullet."

"Jack!" Stevie called. "Wood!" She couldn't quell the sick feeling in the pit of her stomach. "What are we gonna do if they're dead?"

Colton pulled her into his arms. "Do not imagine scenarios of panic until we know more."

After a few moments, Stevie managed to calm down. The Djen split up to search the area.

Chapter 35

Colton retrieved the dinghy he had beached above the high-tide line. It was a tight fit with all four of the Djen in the little boat, but they managed the short distance to the yacht without sinking or capsizing.

The first one on the boat, Stevie scanned the deck. The chest lids were open and the life vests had been pulled out. She nearly tripped over one and saw two others bobbing in the water on the starboard side.

Marise and Colton led the way into the salon. It was in disarray. The Rebels appeared to have searched every room.

Returning to the deck, Stevie asked, "What were they looking for?"

"Supplies, weapons, enemies," Eli responded.

With no further clues to be found, Colton suggested that they return to shore to bury the Rebel's body. As he and Marise lowered themselves into the dinghy, Eli called out.

"Hundye." He pointed to the beach.

The shape of the figure looked familiar to Stevie. "I think that's Wood."

Without waiting for a command, Marise dove into the water. Colton called her back. "Return to the small boat, Sister. He appears injured."

Chewing her lip, Stevie paced the bow, squinting into the darkening night. The dinghy approached after what seemed like an hour. Marise leapt on board and together she and Colton helped Wood onto the yacht. The left side of his shirt and shorts were covered in blood, as was his forehead. Otherwise, there were no visible wounds.

Stevie grabbed Wood's shirt. "Where's Jack?"

Weak, but conscious, Wood was led into the salon. "We were ambushed. Last I saw, Jack was on the yacht."

As they entered, Wood limped over to the liquor cabinet and retrieved a bottle. Unscrewing the cap, he took a long swig. "I was on shore cleaning the salmon when they attacked. I heard what I thought was a bear coming out of the trees. It turned out to be the Rebels." Wood took another drink of whiskey, coughed, and looked at Colton. "Boy, you Djen can move fast—I hardly had time to pull my gun before they were on me. I got one shot off, but it went high. I missed them all."

"Not all," Stevie said. "You hit one in the trees."

"Good." Wood's eyes narrowed. "At least I got one."

"But what about Jack…" Stevie was unable to finish the sentence. A vision came on—fast.

She saw moving torches on a mountain. Rebel shadows bounced off the trees. Jack, hands tied behind his back, mouth covered with a cloth, stumbling up the path. He was intermittently pushed and dragged. There was fear in his eyes—but there was nothing Stevie could do.

"Where are you?" she called, but her voice only whispered. The area did not look familiar. Darkness hindered her perception. She willed herself back to the boat.

"I saw Jack." Stevie allowed Eli and Colton to help her to a chair. "He's alive. Scared, but alive. We have to go after him."

"Do not worry, my love." Colton's brows knitted. "They had opportunity enough to end his life, if that was their desire. They hold him as trade. To attempt rescue is to willingly enter a trap."

"I don't care. We have to go after him."

Colton slid in beside her. "And we will. We will get young Jack back—undamaged."

"And your plan, Brother?"

"Ambush them near the portal. We number them one to one. And we have an advantage they do not. We have a Guardian, a police soldier and his gun."

"Well," Wood said, "despite Marise healing me on the beach, I'm pretty wiped. I'm gonna need to rest."

"But, Jack..." Stevie pleaded.

"Think it through," Wood said. "It's night. I can't maneuver the boat in the dark, not in these shallows, and not when I don't have any idea where we're going." He switched his drink to water. Taking a deep drink, he rose from his seat and paced. "Plus, we've got to have a plan. I'm not going in there blind. Not against those guys."

Eli joined the discussion. "I traveled as a Rebel for two summers. Torren's tactics I know."

Colton rose and clasped the Djen's forearm, who returned the gesture. "It is agreed and bound. Let us retire for a time. We leave before the night is half past."

"I'm hearing midnight." Wood shook his head. "Did you not hear me? I can't steer without light."

The room became awash in a blue glow. Stevie looked at the shining eyes of Colton and Marise, and then back to the detective's shocked expression.

"Light enough for your taste?" Marise asked. Then, a blink, and the salon dimmed.

"Forgot. Got it. I'm still gonna eat and catch a little shut-eye." Wood rose, but stopped in front of Eli, who stood at the doorway into the galley. "And who are you?"

"This is Eli." Colton stepped between the men. "He has joined in our fight against Torren."

"Right..." Wood drew out the word, keeping his eyes on Eli. "He dresses like a Rebel, walks like a Rebel, smells like a Rebel. Must be a duck."

Colton cleared his throat. "Not a Duck. Not a Rebel. He is Djen. We found him near death at our campsite. Shylae, my sister, and I healed him. We have heard his story and the means by which he was conscripted into the Rebellion and of the ruthlessness of Torren. Shylae trusts him fully. I trust the judgment of the Guardian."

Colton's focus moved from the detective to the former Rebel. "He proves himself each day."

Marise added. "He has given us no reason to believe the trust is misplaced."

Wood looked from Marise to Colton to Stevie and, finally at Eli. "I am afraid it's gonna take more than just hanging around and not killing us in our sleep to gain my trust. But, I'm willing to see how it goes. Eli, welcome." Wood offered his hand.

Eli clasped Wood's forearm. A look of confusion crossed the detective's features, then he clasped Eli's forearm in return. "I guess that's how they do it in Djenrye, huh?"

The ex-Rebel smiled. "My gratitude. You shall see. I want to stop Torren."

Crisis averted, Colton returned to Stevie and kissed her on the cheek. "Let us go find something to break our fast. A bit of nourishment will help to allay your fears. Then rest."

Right. Like I'm going to get any sleep. But she knew it was hopeless to try to convince her friends to leave now. Jack would just have to hang on until they could rescue him. *And we will rescue him. I won't let that bastard kill Jack. No matter what. Even if it means giving myself up. And I will, with or without Colton's agreement.*

Short of an hour in bed, Stevie woke in a cold sweat. She hadn't had the nightmare since she met Colton and learned the truth of her family's past. Running through the forest, in fear for her life, dodging arrows—she shuddered at the residual memory. Quietly, she slipped into the center of the salon, hoping to find the room empty. She grabbed a book from the shelf. Scanning the first few pages, she tossed it on a lounge chair and began to pace.

Marise wandered into the room fully dressed, with her hair neatly braided.

"You're still up?" Stevie asked.

"I was attending to other matters." Marise sat down and Stevie joined her.

"So…besides you, what's up?"

Marise sighed. "Know that I trust my brother's judgment, but I do not trust the Magi. They are tricky and cunning and secret their true motives." Marise paused. "I contacted my father to request his diligence with Esalon. They are in each other's company most days. I informed my father of the Magi's missteps and it gave him pause as well."

I don't think I completely trust Esalon, either. Stevie kept the thought to herself. Instead, she asked, "Don't the Magi have more powers than us?"

Marise shook her head. "Not greater than you, my Guardian. Your innate power eclipses even that of the sorcerers. Once you have gained full awareness, there is no telling what you will be able to accomplish. The Magi know how to read the stars and planets, and see signs and portents in nature, but these are not true visions— only interpretations."

"So why do the Djen rely on them?"

An expression flickered across Marise's face, as though she had had the same thought at one time. And then it was gone. "The Mage, Esalon, holds influence over the Council. Colton will require his aid to convince Manem, the Supreme Leader, of the need to take the fight to the Rebellion."

"Convince him? Don't they want to put an end to Torren and his so-called Rebellion?" asked Stevie.

"That would be the obvious direction. Yet, for the past generation, the Rebellion has been little more than a rumor. The fight they wage has been one of insurgency and indirect attack. Until my brother and I discovered Torren on this side, the Council thought him dead."

"Still, once they know, won't they step up?"

"The matter is not as simple as convincing the Council that the Rebellion and Torren are a true threat. The hostilities with the Jajing left the Djen with fewer fighters. It takes a generation to rebuild an army such as we once had. And Manem is a..." Marise paused. A look of contempt flickered over her face. "Manem has grown weary of war—as have the Djen."

Stevie sat back. *I'd swear she was about to call that Manem guy a coward.* She was worried. Stevie had never considered that they might not get help from other Djen. It had been difficult enough for her and her small group to fight Torren and the men he brought into this world. *How can the Council expect us to win once we are faced with the full force of the Rebellion? Even with two warriors, a Guardian, and a Rebel turncoat, four Djen aren't gonna be able to defeat hundreds of insurgents.*

Anxious and exhausted, there was nothing left to do but sleep. It was what it was. Worrying would not change the outcome. Stevie stretched and told Marise she was heading back to bed.

As she closed the door to the cabin, Colton stirred. The moonlight enhanced his form as it caressed the muscles in his arms and shoulders. Stifling the urge to wake him, she slipped under the sheet, fully dressed, and curled up against his back. They had a long day ahead, with the promise of more trying days before this would all be over. The last sound she heard before drifting into a dreamless sleep was the boat's engine rumbling to life.

Chapter 36

A strong wind rocked Stevie as she walked onto the deck. Stars sparkled above her. She kept one hand on Colton's arm and the other on the railing as they continued to the bow. Marise had positioned herself at the head rail. The blue beacons from her eyes scanned the dark water for snags and obstructions. She raised her arm in the air and motioned to the left. The yacht made a slight correction to port.

Rather than join Marise in the worst of the wind, Stevie veered off to the cockpit, dragging Colton with her. Wood stood at the helm. The creases at the corners of his hazel eyes looked deeper in the dim light. Or perhaps the long days and twice being on the brink of death made him look tired. As had become his norm, his hair had been combed by only his fingers.

"What time is it?" Stevie asked.

He let one hand off the wheel to look at his watch. "Four a.m. give or take."

"I thought we'd be there by now." She walked to the captain's table. A nautical map was spread across the top. "Where are we?"

Pointing in her general direction, he said, "See where I've marked the Fiordland Recreation Area?"

"Yeah."

"Follow the Mathieson Channel down until it meets the ocean. Right about there is Milbanke Sound. We've just passed that…"

Stevie followed the thick blue line downward with her finger.

"Now move your finger up north again. Okay, see the Perceval Narrows? We've just entered there."

"I know little of water distance. Will we land by dawn?" Colton asked, studying the lines and curves on the paper.

"If Marise keeps us off the rocks—which by the way, she's become a natural at—we'll drop anchor in Kynoch Inlet by morning."

Stevie nodded. "I can't see hanging out here the entire time." She looked up at Colton. "Wanna head back down?"

In response, he led the way out of the cockpit and down the stairs. When he moved to turn on a light in the salon, Stevie touched his arm. "Leave it. I kinda just want to sit in the dark for a bit."

They cuddled together on the loveseat, comfortable in the silence.

In an effort to keep her mind off worries about Jack, Stevie thought of the stories Colton and Marise had told her of Djenrye. The amenities she took for granted in this world did not exist there. No hot running water, no electricity—which meant no TV, no radio, no computers. Worst of all, no Starbucks. *God, I hope they at least know about coffee.*

Her nerves were on edge. Thoughts of going to another world, even though she was born there, did little to calm her agitation. *Buck it up, girl. You're the Guardian.* The idea initially terrified her, but now had become a part of her.

"What musings have you so intently occupied, Shylae?" Colton whispered.

"I'm thinking about my role as a Guardian. What exactly does that mean? It's gotta be more than the fairy-tale princess thing."

Either her eyes had adjusted to the dark or dawn was approaching. She could see a smile crease her protector's lips.

"From what I know of Hundye fairy tales, you are no princess, my love. A Guardian is not a figurehead. The role entails active interaction not only with the Council, but with the people, the Ortehlae, and the Gods."

"What?" Stevie sat up straight. *This is a new one.* "You keep telling me your Gods are not a form of myth—that they're real. But you mean really-real?"

"Correct. Not all are able to see or speak to the Gods. It is not like the Hundye priests, who speak to a spirit or idea. The Supreme Leader, Manem, converses directly with the Gods."

"You actually mean 'beings', right? Physical, touchable Gods?"

Colton sighed heavily. "I am not privileged to that knowledge, so my answers and insight are not exact. When we go to Djenrye, you will have the opportunity to speak with Manem. I do know that the Gods do not visit us. Manem, and Djen who are called, go to the plane of the Gods."

"You mean like in the Lorn story?"

"Yes."

Stevie's head spun. The idea of God in the flesh was difficult to comprehend. *And what would I say to him—her—it?* "So, outside of chatting up the Gods, what else will I do?"

"You are a protector of the people, the Ortehlae, and the balance of both worlds. You will continue to train for combat and to hone your mental skills. Your duties and connection with the Ortehlae will leave you little time to lounge about, being waited on hand and foot by servants."

The tone was serious, but Stevie noticed the room had turned a soft blue—lighted by eyes that were not quite glowing, but definitely sparkling. She snuggled closer to him. "But I'll have time for you."

Colton shifted on the loveseat and enfolded Stevie in his strong arms. "I will be at your side. Forever. My love." The words ended with his mouth covering hers.

Marise's voice interrupted the embrace. "We arrive at our destination."

Up on deck, Stevie was surprised by the height of the granite cliffs bordering the channel. The sky had lightened above her, but the boat remained in deep shadow.

Eli waved to her from inside the cockpit. Stevie left Colton to rejoin his sister at the bow. "Hi, Eli. Getting the hang of boating?"

He greeted her with a smile. "Police Soldier Wood has been instructional."

Wood shrugged. "He has the enthusiasm of a little kid. I'm finding it hard not to like him."

As he steered into the Kynoch Inlet, Wood slid open the window in front of the wheel and called to the Djen Warriors, "See anything that looks low enough to hike into?"

"There," Colton called back. He pointed to a bay on his left, around which the cliffs leveled off. All but Wood headed below to stow their gear and pack what would be needed for the trek.

Maneuvering the yacht as close to land as he deemed safe, Wood dropped anchor. Colton, Marise, and Stevie were the first to take the dinghy to land. While Colton and Stevie waited on a narrow strip of rocky sand, Marise ferried Eli and Wood to shore.

"I have not approached the portal from this direction. We need to move to higher ground to get our bearings." Colton and Eli consulted in the Djen tongue, pointing and gesturing away from the water. Stevie let them take the lead. She followed them up a faint trail, which meandered up the nearest cliff.

Two hours later, they reached the summit. Beyond it spread an expansive valley. It looked deceptively serene, but Stevie's recent experience traveling the islands taught her it would be swampy and boggy. They would need to skirt the edge, but there, the dense forest and deadfall would be no easier. Eli said something to Colton to draw his gaze northeastward.

"Do you see that peak?" Colton asked Stevie. It looked to be miles away. "That is our destination."

Behind the mountain, dark clouds rolled in, as if drawn by the mountain itself. Stevie stared at the monolith in awe. Even at this distance, she could see its snowy cap towering above the rest of the range.

Colton picked up the pace, but kept it at what Stevie had started to think of as "Hundye speed". Even so, Wood struggled to keep up. They needed to hurry to have any hope of setting up camp before the rain and the night fell.

They covered five miles of rough terrain—downed trees, slippery moss, hidden holes, and muck that sucked at their boots.

Above the valley, they came to a river that flowed from the mountain to which they headed. Along it, they stumbled onto a pair of black bears. Skirting them cost another mile of travel.

As dusk approached, Colton located a flat, open area under tree cover and close to a small waterfall. It was a halfway decent spot to pitch the tents.

"Colton, Marise," Stevie called out. "Which Gods should I thank for holding off the rain until we set up camp?"

Eli answered, "All of them, Guardian. All." They laughed—a welcome release of the tension and worry.

Marise set up the portable propane stove as the first rain drops hit. Colton and Eli raised the lightweight blue nylon tarp. It created a makeshift pavilion under which they ate dinner.

After the meal, with coffee in hand, Wood began the discussion on how to ambush Torren. "Maybe we can use Eli to infiltrate the Rebel camp? You know, as a Trojan horse sort of thing."

Stevie quickly shot that idea down. "Guys, did you forget that Torren's powers are way wicked strong now? I'm pretty sure he'd see right through that and probably kill Eli. And then he'd know we're close." She shook her head. "Why don't we just sneak in and grab Jack? There are only four of them now. We could take 'em."

"I appreciate your enthusiasm, Guardian. However…" Marise started.

Colton finished the thought. "…it is likely Torren has sent for additional men. Young Jack will slow them down, yet I anticipate Torren shall nonetheless arrive at the portal before us. We must attack before they break camp." He sipped the warm coffee.

During the discussion, Marise turned to Eli and translated parts with Djenrye words. At the mention of Rebels on the other side of the portal, Eli nodded. "More Rebels are coming."

Options were tossed around, but nothing anyone could agree on.

"I think it's time for me to see where the Rebels are and what Torren's up to," Stevie said. "I wanna make sure Jack's okay."

Stevie sat cross-legged in the center of the group. Her thoughts focused on the endless rhythm of the waterfall. Colton began chanting. She entered a vision.

Enveloped in darkness, Stevie was unsure of her location. The sliver of the waning moon did not create enough light to guide her.

Sounds in the distance.

Her mind moved through the trees until the glow of a fire joined the voices. She had arrived at the Rebellion campsite.

Torren sat in front of the blaze, eyes closed, chanting. Not far from where he meditated, she spied Jack, tied to a tree. His back rested against the trunk—his chest rose and fell rhythmically. His face was swollen, and there was blood dried on his forehead from a jagged cut. *But he's alive.*

Before leaving the vision, Stevie took count of the men at the scene: Torren meditating, two of his men playing some sort of game with runes—*where's the fourth?* The answer came in a rustle from the tree where Jack was bound. The lookout shifted in the uppermost branches. Relieved that there were no signs of other Rebels, she began to pull back.

Then Torren rose.

An evil grin cracked his features. Stevie waited. He sauntered to his men, saying something Djen-ish, causing them to laugh. One of the men moved toward Jack. Torren stopped him with a slap across the shoulders. With a disapproving shake of his leader's head, the man sat back down. Torren returned to the fire, Stevie assumed, to continue his meditation. Instead, he locked his focus on her.

"I feel you…my young Guardian. I know you are watching," he whispered. "I know you're coming for your friend. I'm waiting." He began to laugh.

The sound of Torren's taunts echoed in Stevie's mind when she emerged from the vision. She still felt him. His coldness, his madness, left a coppery taste of fear.

"Shylae. You are shivering." Colton covered her with a jacket, rubbing her arms.

"He really is evil!" she exclaimed. "I don't mean like comic-book evil. I mean really, really nasty 'I'm gonna kill babies' kinda evil. I could feel it, Colton. Like a living energy radiating off of him. And, he saw—he sensed—me again. He taunted me."

"That is not the Androne I grew up with—the one I thought of as *Okih*, a Brother. I know not what journey led him into this madness."

A cup of coffee was in Stevie's hand. She had no idea how it got there. The whiff of alcohol mingled with steam told her it must have been Wood. A hearty gulp warmed her enough to convey the rest of the vision.

"Jack's alive, barely. Torren has three men with him."

"By dawn, he will call more men to this side of the portal," Colton said. "It is then he will attempt to barter Jack for the Guardian."

Wood stabbed out his smoke, set down his mug, and rose from the small boulder where he sat. "I think we should get some sleep. We've got miles to travel before hitting the portal. And we're still going to have to come up with a plan before we get there."

Stoking the fire, Marise announced, "I will take the first watch. We may have no fear of Rebels, but the bears could be active."

Eli piped up, "I relieve Marise."

Wood nodded. "Yeah, let's do it in two-hour intervals. I'll set the alarm on my watch and wake you, Eli."

Marise climbed into the nearest ancient fir, while the rest headed for their tents.

Stevie felt a tug on her sleeve. It was Wood, motioning her to follow. He led her to the edge of the camp and sat down. Shaking a cigarette out of the pack, he crumpled the wrapper.

"Whatever we do, we gotta do it soon." He held up the cigarette between his fingers. "I only have one more pack and there are miles between us and the nearest convenience store."

"Is that what you wanted to talk to me about?" Stevie asked.

"No. Not exactly." He lit the smoke. "I just want to tell you, you remind me of my daughter. Hell, you've kind of grown on me."

Stevie smiled. *He's cute when he's sincere.*

"I want you to know," Wood continued, "I've seen a change in you. Not just with this whole Djen-awakening thing. You've grown strong and sure of yourself."

"Uh...thanks," Stevie mumbled. She'd gotten used to the Djen complimenting her and treating her with respect, but it felt a little awkward coming from Wood.

"Your mom—Jan—would be proud of the woman you've become in this short time. I was just getting to know her before we left. I think she might have even been starting to kinda like me. Be assured, if anything happens to you—or you end up going to Djenrye—I promise I'll keep Jan safe."

He won't look me in the eye when he says Mom's name. What's up with that?

Impulsively, she hugged the detective. "Thank you." She meant it with all her heart.

The trek to the portal had been the hardest hike so far. The damp and cold did little to improve Stevie's mood. Her stomach lurched with every step. Her nerves were on edge at the thought of facing Torren again.

The path Colton followed crisscrossed rough terrain, but always climbed upward. Huge fallen logs interrupted the trail and had to be skirted or scrambled over. Small creeks and river-sized waterways hid slimy rocks that threatened to break their ankles each time they crossed. Dense curtains of moss and foliage hung from the trees, and they were forced to cut their way through. The hard freezes and humid conditions had heaved the soil, making it uneven and treacherous. In the wilds of British Columbia, the wildlife presented a further obstacle. Black bears, wolves, and the occasional grizzly required frequent direction changes.

When they emerged from the densest area, Stevie could see the summit through the trees. The monolith appeared even more imposing close up, with its snowcapped peak and jagged cliffs.

Seriously? She bumped into Colton, who was in the process of pulling off his pack.

"We are close." He shaded his eyes as he looked up. "The portal is hidden there."

Marise said, "It was not bears growling the last league." She patted her stomach. "I would be grateful for a little sustenance before the climb."

"Shylae," Colton said, "you should call forth another vision once we are closer to the portal. We need to know exactly where the Rebels are stationed, how many there are, and anything that may aid us in gaining the element of surprise."

Stevie gazed over at him between sips of water. She nodded.

"Brother, I have seen no sign of the enemy. They are either very clever at hiding their passage, or they did not come this way."

Eli approached Marise and spoke in Djen.

"He says," Marise translated, "that the path he traveled was on the far side of the mountain. I do not know the Hundye name…we call the mountain *Wankurá*. On the other side is where he believes they will camp."

Between bites of trail mix, Wood asked, "How much farther?"

Colton pointed to a path about a half mile ahead. It looked to be little more than a goat trail disappearing into the trees. "We travel that path for another league and then we will be in close proximity to the portal."

Stevie followed the route with her eyes. It seemed to go on forever, winding up the side of the mountain. She sighed. "I need to eat something." She located the wheat crackers and raisins from the side pocket of her backpack.

After the quick break, as usual, Colton was first on his feet. "A meager meal, but enough to sustain us until the evening."

"I will scout ahead. The enemy may yet send one to discover our position," Marise said, moving quickly toward the mountain.

Right on her heels, Eli called out, "*Le* join you."

"Man," Wood said, watching the two Djen disappear over a ridge. "I can't get over how fast you guys can move."

Before Stevie could finish her jerky, Colton and Wood resumed hiking. Hurriedly pulling on her pack, she caught up to them. Blessed with a smile from Colton, she slipped her hand into his and continued on with the man who loved her more than his own life.

It was near dusk when Marise and Eli returned with news.

"It is as Eli recalled. The enemy took the same path they used when they entered this world. They are a league away on the far side of the mountain. The entrance to the cave of the portal stands between them and us."

Colton followed Marise to a granite overhang half a mile farther up the trail. Below the outcrop, a hollow provided an excellent campsite. The dry ground had been protected from the elements.

"There is sufficient tree cover. It may be possible to build a small fire to keep out the night chill," Colton noted.

Eli and Marise set off to gather whatever dry kindling they could find. Stevie unpacked the propane stove and sorted through the remaining provisions in hopes of finding something suitable for a meal. Eli must have seen her frustration when he returned with the firewood. He set down his bundle and dug through his pack, emerging with several large cans of stew.

"I found these on water craft. It has meat picture. Is this edible?"

Stevie hugged the former Rebel and thanked him profusely. "This is way more than edible. With the crackers and dried fruit, we might just be able to fix a real dinner." Her elation increased when, after surveying the site, Colton pronounced that a fire could be safely lit.

With her belly full and the coffee brewing, Stevie prepared for her vision. Although she no longer needed tools or assistance to enter, she acquiesced to Colton chanting behind her.

The scene opened before her of a camp similar to theirs. Hidden under a similar overhang, the enemy also had a fire going. Relieved to see that there were no more Rebels other than the original four, she searched for Jack.

Tied to a tree, barely recognizable by his swollen features, the Rebels had left him one arm free to eat what looked like a bit of stale bread. When he raised the bread to his mouth, his arm shook as though he had no strength left.

A soldier approached, loudly addressing Jack in the Djenrye language, and then laughed. The soldier cuffed Jack on the shoulder. Jack cowered. As if the action offended him, he slapped the bread from Jack's hand. Stevie watched helplessly, frustrated at her inability to intervene.

Thankfully, another Rebel came to Jack's aid. The man cursed the other, smacking him on the back of his head as though he were an ill-behaved child. The second Rebel retrieved Jack's meager dinner, brushed the dirt from the bread, and handed it to him.

Torren arrived. *That's my cue to leave.* She glimpsed him berating the two soldiers, and then she was looking at Colton.

"He's still alive. And I didn't see any more Rebels."

"Good news indeed," Colton replied.

She clutched Colton's vest in both hands. "We need to hurry though. I don't know how much longer Jack can hold up."

Chapter 37

Stevie worried about Jack. The likelihood of his surviving another night was slim—almost as slim as their chances to get back the Orb. *Jack or the Orb... I hope I don't have to choose between them.*

The crackle and pop of the fire broke the silence that had settled over the camp. Her comrades were focused on preparing for battle.

The sound of metal grating on stone filled the circle. Light danced off Stevie's sword when Colton held it near the fire. Turning it this way and that, he ran the whetstone over the edge two more times before handing the weapon to Stevie. Then, retrieving his own blade, he repeated the process. *Whish, whish, whish*—until that sword, too, bore a razor's edge.

Marise's attention focused on her bow. She tested the tension by drawing, releasing, and then tightening the string until it met her needs. Moving to the arrows, she counted her stock. She held each one in front of her so that her eye traveled down the shaft. Seemingly satisfied, she placed them in the quiver.

Wood checked his ammunition. He squinted through the smoke that curled up from the cigarette dangling in his mouth. He filled each magazine and dropped the remaining bullets into his pockets. "Damn," Stevie heard him mutter. "I wish I'd brought the cleaning kit."

Sword laid across his lap, Colton motioned the group to move closer. "It is time." He nodded to Eli, who turned, moved away from the firelight, and melded into the dark.

Earlier, the group had agreed that Eli should scout ahead. A single Djen had a better chance of slipping in close. Stevie, with the help of Marise's translation, had made Eli promise to make it his initial priority to get Jack safely away. But first, Eli would gain a vantage point in the trees and report to Colton.

"How?" Stevie had asked.

"You will understand soon, my Guardian," Marise had told her.

The remainder of the group would attack from three sides, each taking the closest Rebel soldier.

"Sister, you and Wood head to the campsite. Detective…" Colton fixed the man with his steely blue eyes. "…the enemy you are about to face is Djen. They can hear you breathe before you see them. Follow Marise carefully. Step where she steps and you have a chance of approaching them unnoticed."

Wood opened his mouth as if to respond, but nodded instead.

"As in our last encounter with the Rebellion, the moment Marise signals, you will come out—what is that expression Jack used?"

Marise grinned. "Guns blazing." Her blue eyes did not quite glow, but they did sparkle.

"If I'm understanding our positions…" Wood used a stick to draw Xs in the dirt. "…Colton and Stevie will be within my line of fire. I can't risk hitting one of you."

"Aim high. Once you sight my brother and the Guardian, you may direct your aim at the insurgents," Marise suggested. "Yet, I would take the accuracy of my bow over your bullets." Her mouth curled in a mischievous smile.

Stevie looked at Marise with admiration. *A true Warrior. Excited and ready for battle. And I'm scared shitless.*

"Wha…?" A vision flooded Stevie's mind. Her viewpoint was skewed, as if seeing it through someone else's eyes. The Rebel campsite seemed to be beneath her. Then, the voice of Eli echoed in her thoughts.

"Did you hear that?" She looked to the Warriors.

"It is as I said. Eli reports back," Marise clarified.

Two other voices rang in her head—Marise and Colton. She stared at them, but their lips did not move. "And you can see the camp, too…right?"

The voices ceased.

"You see through Eli's eyes?" Marise's mouth dropped open.

"I'm guessing that part's not normal, huh?"

"We do not see the camp," Colton said. "We merely hear Eli." He tapped his temple. "He reports it is time."

"What the hell are you guys talking about?" Wood asked.

"Don't worry about it." Stevie patted the detective on the shoulder. "We'll explain later."

Marise clasped Colton's forearm and slapped him hard on the back with her other hand. "To battle, Brother."

On her way out of camp with Wood, she pulled Stevie to her. "And you—my Guardian, my sister—take great care, and fight well."

Stevie watched them disappear into the darkness and then asked Colton, "What do you need me to do?"

"My sister spoke true. You might have to fight, my love. I hoped to keep you safe in the trees, but it will take all of us to retrieve the Orteh and young Jack Snow."

She nodded, determined. "I want to fight. I'm not some airhead princess in a tower waiting to be rescued."

He put his hand on the side of her face and leaned in to kiss her. The taste of his mouth was sweet and sent a tingle through her entire body. *Will it always feel like this?*

They parted and he gazed into her eyes. "You are a strong fighter." He smiled. "But you have another task."

"Meaning?"

"While Eli rescues Jack, you will purloin the Orteh and return here."

The possibility of spoiling Torren's plans excited Stevie, but the elation was short-lived. "Uh, how am I gonna find it? I doubt they've left it sitting out."

"You are tied to the Orteh. See it now in your mind. It will call you."

"I haven't felt anything since Torren got a hold of it."

"His power is strong. It is possible he has found a way to shield it from you. You must accept your legacy. Your strength is greater than anything Torren may concoct. Trust in yourself."

If Colton is so certain, I have to believe, too.

Closing her eyes, she took a deep breath. Her mind reached out for the Orb. A chasm of emptiness lay before her. Then a glimmer. A push. The nothingness gave way. The Orb broke through. Torren's safeguards defeated, the light rose before her. It spun, growing larger. The lightning within became more intense. Stevie opened her arms to it. She and the Orb became one.

Surrounded in light, Stevie was pulled forward. In a split second, she stood inside a tent. On the ground in front of her sat an intricately carved chest, the grooves worn smooth. The oak had the look of centuries of handling—a soft sheen that no amount of polishing could replicate. The leather and metal straps securing the lid were weathered, but looked sturdy enough, as did the lock. Runes adorned the box. Light seeped in and out of them, merging with her.

The chest was solid, nearly the size of a footlocker. It looked too heavy to carry. *And those symbols…maybe some kinda spell?*

The light began to fade. Stevie looked frantically around the tent for a key. Besides the chest, the enclosure contained a small table and bedding. Seeing no key, she proceeded to leave her vision, but a moaning drew her back. A still figure was wrapped in the blankets. The moan ceased and the figure rolled over. The covers slipped from his face. *Jack!*

He looked barely alive. He coughed. Blood trickled out of his mouth. He didn't wipe it away—either too weak or too resigned. Her heart ached. She approached him. Her thoughts—a whisper in his ear, "We're coming for you, Jack…we won't leave you, I promise."

Darkness enfolded Stevie. The disconnection from the Orb—the light—left her chilled. Then, the scene before her brightened. She had returned to her campsite.

After explaining what she had seen to Colton, he asked, "Are you able to recall the symbols that were upon the chest?"

Stevie grabbed a stick and began scratching in the dirt. "These are all I remember."

ᛟ   ᚼ   ᚠ   ᚳ

"Powerful indeed. Esalon had shown me two of these as part of a ritual. One signifies protection—the other, concealment. Without the aid of a Mage, I am uncertain how to open the chest."

"We'll figure it out when we get there," Stevie said, with more confidence than she felt. "I'll have the Orb in my hands tonight."

This seemed to satisfy Colton. She slipped her pack over one shoulder and took his hand. "To the trees, my love."

In one leap, they landed in the limbs of a Sitka spruce. From there, they ran swiftly, tree to tree. Below them, the ground sped by in a blur. Boulders, fallen logs, and moss-laden tracts blended together. They traveled three miles around the mountain pass before Colton spied firelight.

Dropping to the ground, Stevie pointed out Eli's position. Camouflaged in a tree, he was a quarter way around the clearing. Colton nodded, and in turn, jerked his head in the direction of the tent opposite their position. The largest in the area, it was clearly Torren's. Wood crouched behind it and Marise perched in the spruce in between. A four-point strike. They had the camp surrounded.

"He wasn't there before," Stevie whispered to Colton, pointing to the guard in front of the tent. Firelight flickered over the sentinel's bare chest and arms, accentuating his muscular build. The smooth skin evidenced his youth. Blonde-brown hair braided tightly, eyes focused straight ahead, expressionless face—reminded Stevie of the Queen's Guard at Buckingham Palace.

"We must place our faith in Eli or Wood dispatching him. There is nothing we are able to do from our position."

"Agreed. I'm sure Eli's seen him." Stevie signaled Wood with an owl hoot and hand gesture.

At the sound, Eli slipped out of the tree and crept along the outskirts of the clearing. At that moment, five new Rebels walked into the circle of light, between Marise and Wood's positions.

Stevie looked at Colton. They were now outnumbered. No matter. They had come too far to turn back.

Torren emerged from his tent, addressing the newcomers. He barked a question in the Djen language. A bald, battle-scarred Rebel answered, waving his arm toward the east.

Colton whispered to Stevie, "More are coming from the portal."

Eli's shadow, on the far side of the shelter, disappeared as he ducked into the tent. A single shot shattered the calm. All heads turned toward the sound. Torren's young guard collapsed, blood coursing from his back and chest. Then chaos ensued.

Torren screamed at his troops, *"Redul chasean tahka! Beyea ty Greial! Eh'ankh ty payharu!"*

Stevie and Colton stood, loosing arrows. Colton shouted beside Stevie, "He orders them to kill all but the Guardian." Stevie caught sight of Eli carrying Jack on his shoulders before they slipped into the forest.

Several of the Rebels rushed toward Wood. Others scattered. Muzzle flashes lit the oiled silk of the tent as Wood shot into the air. His attackers slowed. He aimed, now with a purpose, and two of the Rebels fell. The third ran in the opposite direction. The detective moved closer to Marise.

Arrows struck and downed a newcomer. He pitched backward, bringing another Rebel into view. A trail of raven black hair flicked behind him. Stevie watched Marise's blade turn crimson as it opened his throat. Before the body slid to the ground, Marise attacked the next closest insurgent. She pushed him deeper into camp.

A laugh escaped Stevie. In her wildest dreams, she had never expected to be exhilarated by battle. Throwing the bow aside, she led the charge. Rather than run, she leapt high into the air, Colton an arm's length behind her. They dropped into the middle of the skirmish. Their swords, unsheathed, caught the glow of the campfire, adding cold silver to the blue which shone from their eyes.

The shooting had stopped.

"Go!" Colton yelled.

Stevie dashed around Colton, dodging strikes. Moving low, she skirted the smaller tents, trying to keep out of sight. Between strikes, Stevie watched Torren head straight for Wood.

Slamming in another magazine, the detective aimed the gun at Torren and got off one last shot. Blood trickled down the back of the Rebel Leader's shoulder, but the wound did not slow him. With Djen speed, he struck the gun from Wood's hand. Instinct or panic caused him to head-butt the Androne. The force stunned Torren long enough for Wood to break away into the forest. The last thing Stevie saw before slipping into the tent was Torren on Wood's heels. The fighter in Stevie screamed for her to follow, but she could not. The Orb was her priority.

The chest glowed as she approached. She made quick work of the leather straps, but the lid would not budge. Her attempts to lift the chest failed. *I can't drag this with me.*

She stood, arms crossed, frustrated to have come so close and perhaps fail. Unsheathing her knife, she knelt down to pry the lock. All she managed to do was splinter a good blade. *Brute strength isn't gonna do it.*

The light from the runes began to pulsate. Standing, Stevie took a step back from the chest. Closing her eyes, she reopened herself to the Orteh. The familiar pull returned, but gently—as a child pulling on her sleeve.

A whisper—a thought—an impression. The Orb beckoned her to call the Djen gods.

"As the last Guardian, the last of my line, I ask for your help. Tell me what I need to do. If this is my destiny, help me fulfill it."

The draw of the Orteh gained in intensity. Energy and light flowed from the chest and into her solar plexus. It filled her, flooding her limbs. Opening her arms wide, she accepted the power. The energy moved through the Orteh to her, blending. She became the Orteh, and so much more. Her life force stretched to the sky and rooted itself deep into the earth. The tent glowed blue and gold from her eyes and her mark. She created the light. She *was* the light.

The power surged. First warm, then growing hotter. Stevie felt she would burst into flames. She threw her head back and words flowed from her. Words she didn't know. It was no longer the Orb. The power of the Gods filled her.

She had become the Guardian.

"Seihi le ty tenae—Ty Highlae ai Élan-Vitál —Le Ty Shylae— Bousae-yamae graoch—Bousae-yamae gramein—Ty Asha Vitál aetaenudo—Ty Greial tsa-amamaelae."

The Djen words created their own power. The sides of the tent bowed out as she repeated them over and over. The chest before her rose, suspended by the force of her will. The lock melted away. The lid flew open. The energy coursed out of her in a whirlwind and was gone.

Stevie collapsed to the ground. A dull thud sounded as the chest did the same. She crawled to the box and peered inside. A deep purple cloth, covered in runes, nestled within. She gingerly removed the fabric. It slipped off, exposing the light of the Orteh. The glow intensified as she held it in her hands. It had little weight. She had expected it to be heavier. The pull she experienced earlier gave way to a morphing of energy.

Two essences became one.

The words returned to her, but this time in the language of the Hundye.

She whispered, the Orteh held out before her. "Show me the path—The Light of Élan-Vitál —I am the Bringer of Light—Joined in Blood—Joined by Birth—The Gods Call—The Guardian Answers."

Stevie felt her sense of being slipping. A longing to give in and be one with the Orteh, countered by a voice in her head—Run. What occurred could not have gone unnoticed. The Orteh broke the connection. The link remained, but less intense. She slipped the Orteh inside her backpack and secured it on her shoulders. She ran. Adrenaline and Djen abilities propelled her forward. She cast a glimpse behind for pursuers. A fiery glow in the forest background illuminated the trees. A memory caught her by surprise. *My dream?*

Despite their girth, neither of the two men Colton fought would have been a match for him on their own. But together, they proved troublesome adversaries. Between strikes, Colton spied Shylae slipping into the largest tent. The bald one did, as well. Before the man could cry out a warning, Colton parried a blow and slid his sword cleanly through the man's throat. The warning became a gurgle as the traitor collapsed.

Marise seemed to be weakening, but she held her ground. Colton recognized the Warrior she fought as the same one who had choked her near death. He would not interfere. Marise would have her vengeance. A light diverted his attention to the tent. It now glowed.

The Rebel he fought saw it, too. Around him, the sounds of fighting dimmed as the light intensified. It would have been a perfect time to take down his enemy. But he could not. With the glow came warmth. Not only on his exterior, but in his soul. A memory of being wrapped in his mother's arms came, unbidden. He managed a glance around him and saw all had ceased fighting. They seemed mesmerized by whatever was happening inside the tent. Then the voice spoke, inside and outside his head. *Shylae? The Gods? Both?*

He wanted to run to her, but he could not move. His legs ignored his commands. And then, it all stopped. An instant before he resumed his attack, Colton glimpsed a sight of his love dashing away. He quickly dispatched his opponent before the Djen regained his senses, opening him up from shoulder to hip.

Praying to the Gods for her safety, Colton called out, "Marise, I leave to aid the Guardian."

His sister's voice came from behind him. "Go. I shall shortly end this dance and join you."

Shylae moved quickly. After the first glimpse, Colton lost sight of her. Being forced to follow her tracks was slowing him down. A short distance out, he spotted Eli slipping between the trees.

"*Okih.* Did Shylae cross your path?"

"*Eh Greial,*" Eli responded. "Jack *ar* safe. *Hine* sleeps."

"Go to my sister. She fights well, but is weakening."

Without question, Eli rushed past Colton and toward the Rebel camp, his earlier caution abandoned.

Colton ran to the aid of his love.

Having dispatched the old Hundye with the loud and dangerous weapon, Torren returned to his camp. He stepped over the bodies of his men. All that remained were the female Warrior and Torren's second at arms, Lucun. *The Djen bitch still fights.* A look around the site revealed that the reinforcements had not yet arrived from the portal. *What delays them?*

Torren rushed into his tent. No hostage. No Guardian. *No Orteh!*

The rip at the back let in the blackness of night. Torren ducked through it. The ground before him glowed gold from his eyes as he scanned the area. There were two sets of prints. One moved south, perpendicular to the direction of the portal. The impressions were deep. *A Djen male. Carrying something heavy. Colton?*

The other prints were smaller and the stride long. Torren focused his mind on the girl's path. He sensed the Orteh, but the direction was erratic.

No time to wait. If he wished to capture the Guardian and the Orteh together, he would need his reinforcements. And the portal was close.

Moving swiftly through the dark, he intercepted his men halfway between the portal and camp. Torren loosed his anger and frustration upon them. "*Ka-chet!* You walk with the sloth of lovers on a night stroll. What hindered your arrival?"

Several of his soldiers began to speak, but he cut off their babble. "I will entertain no excuses. The Guardian escaped with the Orteh. She runs alone." Torren motioned to the west. "You four..." He pointed to his swiftest runners. "...find our prizes and return them to me. The rest of you—this way."

Stevie ran as fast as she could and soon realized she was lost. There were no sounds around her other than her own breathing. *Damn it, girl. Stop!*

She slumped against the nearest tree. It took her a minute to get her bearings. The moon cast her shadow in front, rather than behind her. Turning, she glimpsed the top of the mountain, snow sparkling in the faint light. *Damn it, this is the wrong way.* She had been moving west, but the camp was south of Torren's.

She took a sip of water. *Time to change course and hope everyone made it back to camp.* She repacked and started to rise. An arrow embedded itself in the tree, directly above her head. Ducking and dodging, Stevie took off at a full run. The direction was all wrong. But to go south meant to invite danger.

Arrows flew all about her. The densely packed trees took a majority of the damage, but her arms and legs stung from a multitude of glancing blows.

She tripped on a tree root, caught her balance, and forged ahead, driven by the instinct for survival. Her legs pumped hard. She dodged left, and then right, as an arrow whistled past her shoulder into the dark. Even with her speed, the pursuers were gaining. The large trunk of a Sitka spruce caught her eye. She darted behind it for cover, struggling to catch her breath.

They seemed to be coming from several directions. She was running for her life—at night—in the woods. An enemy chased her, shooting arrows. The sensation of déjà vu engulfed her. *This is my dream.*

Hope replaced fear.

The dream that Stevie had for months—months before ever meeting Colton, ever knowing of Djenrye or Guardians or the Androne—the dream had been a vision. Colton would soon find her.

As she again changed directions, an arrow struck within an inch of her hand. A shot of adrenaline pushed her onward.

A small clearing, no more than twenty feet across, opened before Stevie. As she entered, a Rebel warrior rushed in from the opposite side. She darted to the right, but another insurgent blocked her way. One by one, they came into view. Stevie stopped running. She was surrounded.

Chapter 38

The scene that greeted Torren and his reinforcements was not what he had expected. Blood saturated the ground. Lucun still stood, but was only now in the process of dispatching Colton's sister. On her backside, disarmed, Lucun towered over her. His sword was poised in the air to strike. Torren laughed at the sight.

Lucun glanced in Torren's direction, a smirk curling at the corners of his mouth.

It turned to a grimace.

Instead of delivering the death blow, Lucun's sword dropped to the ground beside the female. The soldier pitched forward, bringing the traitor Eli into view. A knife protruded from Lucun's back.

Eli clasped Marise's wrist and pulled her to her feet. As they turned to run, Torren ripped an axe from a fallen Warrior next to him and loosed it at the defector. The weapon imbedded itself in Eli's back. The traitor lunged forward from the impact. Marise turned to catch him, but he was dead before he hit the ground.

Marise met Torren's eyes. Her face contorted with shock and anger. For a moment, Torren thought she would attack him. Instead, she ran for the trees.

"Do not stand around like women at the washing well," he belted out to his men. "You three—go after her!"

"Hand me the Orteh," commanded the first Rebel who had entered the clearing.

Stevie glared. Unsheathing her sword, she took a fighting stance. "How about you come and get it."

This seemed to amuse him. He smirked, unsheathed his sword in turn, and waved to his companions to stay back.

Stevie lunged, taking the offensive. He blocked the worst of the strike, but blood trickled from the slash to his forearm. His eyes opened wide, but Stevie knew he would not underestimate her again.

The Rebel swung high. She dodged to the right and tried to somersault out of the way, but the pack hindered her movements. Removing it was not an option. She needed to change her fighting style. Rather than reverting to flipping out of the way, she had to meet the assault head on. Unfortunately, the Rebel was larger and stronger, making it difficult to get the upper hand.

With the next parry, his eyes were no longer on her. He looked past and gave a slight tilt of his head. Before she could react, Stevie's arms were seized from behind.

The adversary before her grinned, moved forward, and plucked the sword from her hand. Stevie struggled against the vice-like grips. She kicked, spit, and cursed, but the Rebels held her firm.

Three more insurgents entered the clearing. The tallest one spoke a series of words. Stevie managed to catch Marise's name, but little else.

The Rebel she had been sparring with replied in the Hundye language. "We have our prizes. Let us return them to Torren."

He wants me to know what I'm in for. Stevie was not afraid. She was angry. The thought that these men believed they could intimidate her was insulting. As her anger grew, a burning sensation raised from her shoulder blade. She looked around, turning the trees blue. Her eyes shone out with renewed brilliance. A familiar sensation rose from her core. The power—of the Orteh—of the Gods.

She heard a voice in her head, "Leave me. If they capture us both, the Rebels will have all. Apart, they cannot triumph."

"No. I can't," Stevie said and renewed her struggles. A glow from behind—*my pack?*—lit the faces of the Djen who held her arms. Their grips slackened. A sudden tingling in her limbs. She willed it transferred to the Djen. Eyes wide, they released her. They took a step back. In sync, they bowed their heads and knelt.

That's weird. Too shocked to react, she could only stare down at the two Djen. The light began to fade.

The one she had fought shouted at the others, *"Redul Ty Greial!"*

Four Rebels rushed Stevie. Someone cried out, *"Teklae tyea,"* and the pack was ripped from her shoulders. Her soul felt torn in two. She cried out from the pain. "NO!"

The wrenching fell away as one of the Rebels fled into the forest, her pack clutched to his chest. The voice in her head grew fainter. "Fear not. We cannot be truly parted." A tear slipped down her cheek. *Colton, where are you?*

The two who had been kneeling stood off to the side. They had not joined in, but they had not aided Stevie, either.

Held steadfast by four Djen, she let her body go slack, as though all fight had gone out of her. They dragged her forward. Stevie waited for them to loosen their grip ever so slightly. At the edge of the clearing, they did just that.

Coiling the muscles in her legs, she pushed against the forest floor. Flipping up and behind the Rebels, she landed in a crouch. Rising, she whipped her heel out, connecting with the outside of one of her captor's knees. It bent inward in an impossible angle. He dropped, screaming, to the ground.

She pulled a knife from her belt. All she needed was an opening in the circle. She heard a grunt and a thud behind her. She risked a glance over her shoulder.

Colton! A dead Rebel lay at his feet.

"May I offer my assistance, Guardian?" He grinned, opening his arms wide.

"It's about time!"

Colton grabbed Stevie's hand. "Shall we?" His head cocked upward. Together, they leapt into the nearest tree.

The men on the ground stood dumbfounded. Without a pause, she and Colton took off. As they ran from tree to tree, Stevie caught sight of her protector, still smiling.

From the sounds behind them, she guessed one or two of the Rebels had screwed up enough courage to give chase. *Good luck.* She and Colton quickly outdistanced their pursuers.

The trees ended. A sheer drop halted their progress. Forced to a slower pace, Colton balanced his way along the edge of the cliff, with Stevie close behind. He stepped onto a narrow path that led down the granite face. She lost sight of Colton behind a group of pines tenuously attached to crevices in the rock. When she maneuvered past them, a hand lashed out and pulled her into darkness.

The entrance of the cave was narrow, but Stevie crawled behind Colton. Several feet in, they came to an opening large enough for them to stand. He wrapped himself around Stevie and whispered in her ear to be silent.

There they stood, in an embrace that in another time and another place would have been perfect. For now, it was one of caution and quiet.

Torren watched his men throw the last of the wood into the fire and pack up camp. Dawn would break soon. He paced like a caged cat, waiting for the rest of his men to return. He was confident that one group would bear the Guardian and the Orteh—the other, a dead Marise.

Nerves twitching, Torren's thoughts returned to how it would feel to be infused with the Guardian's power. She had proven to be far more powerful than her predecessors. *Could she truly herald the Prophecy?* A female Guardian, the first in ten generations, with an innate connection with the Gods and the Orteh. *What occurred in my tent? How did she shatter the spell Entek conjured to seal the chest?*

He had stopped pacing—chewing on his thoughts as he would a stale bit of jerky. He straightened, his mind clear again. *No matter.*

The Guardian will be mine. The Orteh will be mine. The Power will be mine.

At the sound of movement, Torren slipped into the shadows, his hand hovering over his sword hilt. Five of his soldiers entered the camp—two of the three he had sent after Marise, and three of the four he had sent after the Guardian.

Torren moved back into the light of the fire. "Where are the others?"

The remaining pursuers of the female Warrior took a step back. "Marise, daughter of Kamm, eluded us. We heard signs of battle and joined Nei'lik and his soldiers to capture the Orteh."

Nei'lik dropped to one knee. "My lord." Head remaining bowed, the seasoned Warrior presented a backpack.

Torren ripped open the pack, removing his prize. "This offering is all that has saved your worthless lives." He gestured at his man to stand. "Now you may present me the Guardian."

Nei'lik flinched and took half a step back before answering. "Colton, son of Kamm, escaped with her. Toiber and Adrek gave chase, but lost them. The Guardian is more skilled and her abilities greater than we anticipated."

"*Kat-chet!* Fools and simpletons surround me!" Torren ranted and raged, striking Nei'lik with the back of his hand. The blow dropped the man to the ground. Rebels scattered as he stomped around the site. "I should kill you all!" He pointed to the bodies littering the camp. Flies that had begun to gather in the pools surrounding the fallen rose in swarms as Torren kicked the dead. "Add you to the pile with these other worthless dogs!"

As if a switch flipped, Torren calmed.

"It is no matter. We have squandered enough time in this plane. The Orteh is ours." In response to the stunned expressions from the men, he said, "The son of Kamm is sworn to retrieve it. He will most certainly bring his precious Guardian with him. We will capture the girl in Djenrye."

Torren ordered the last of the tents and weapons be gathered. When his men attempted to bury the fallen, he stopped them.

"Leave them for the carrion eaters." He turned to leave, knowing his men would follow.

At the portal, Torren waited as, one by one, his men passed back to their world. Adrek, the last to enter, carried the chest containing the Orteh.

"Halt," Torren commanded. "Leave that with me."

Torren opened the chest and removed the Orteh. With his back to the portal, he summoned all his control to suppress the anger which threatened to burst anew. He held the sphere out before him. His lips formed into a sly grin. And then he turned and entered Djenrye.

In the dim light of the cavern, Colton whispered, "We need to get back, now."

They crept out of the cave, straining to hear sounds of footsteps or voices. Nothing. Certain that they were safe, for the moment, at least, Stevie began to cry.

Pulling her into his arms, Colton said, "Fear not, my love. They no longer pursue us."

"I lost the Orteh. It spoke to me. Told me to let it go," she hiccupped through her tears.

"But you are safe. It is as it should be. Do not twice guess the reasons."

His strong hands encircled her face, encouraging Stevie to look up into Colton's eyes. "You put your hopes and faith in me and I have failed. Not just you, but our people, and the Hundye."

A gentle laugh escaped Colton. "You have done nothing to show my belief in you to be misguided. Torren has the Orteh, but without you, it is useless to him. Quakes and storms are ineffective to him if he cannot control them." His soft lips met hers, pausing there for a moment before pulling back. "We will continue our hunt. With your power, we will not be defeated."

Determination won out over dejection. Stevie decided Torren would not get away with all he had done. *The Orteh and I will be reunited and Torren will pay for his crimes.* She started in the direction of Torren's camp, but Colton stopped her.

"I have to find out what happened to everyone. We can't leave them behind," Stevie said.

"Eli crossed my path when I searched for you. Young Jack Snow is safe and resting, although injured. I am certain Eli and Marise have dispatched the last of Torren's men. We may see for ourselves, if that is your wish."

Stevie suggested they take to the ground. If the Rebels still searched for them, they would be looking in the trees. After a short distance, the scent of pine intermingled with charred wood. *We must be getting close.* It was the last thought Stevie had before her energy was forcefully extracted, as though the remaining connection to the Orteh had been shredded. The forest floor rushed up to meet her. Her head struck a rock and she cascaded into a vision.

Stevie blinked a couple of times, seeing Colton's face haloed by stars, his voice in a panic.

"Shylae… Shylae… What is wrong?" He knelt beside her. His body was warm as he cradled her in his arms.

"Ow." Stevie gingerly touched the bump on her head. "I had a vision. Actually, it felt more like a vision had me."

Colton helped her to stand. "What did you witness?"

"Torren. He passed through the portal with the Orteh."

"Are you certain it was in his possession?"

Stevie wanted to cry—or curse, or scream—at the Rebel leader's arrogance. Instead, she stated, "Oh yeah. He held it up for me to see."

For a moment, Colton stood silently. Then he seemed to have made up his mind. "Pursuing the Rebellion at this point would be madness. We cannot overpower Torren and his men alone. We must locate Eli, Marise, and Detective Wood. And then join Jack Snow at our camp."

They smelled the enemy camp before they saw it. The reek of death enveloped them. Blood, sweat, and feces blended into a nauseating stench.

Entering the clearing, Stevie spotted Marise. The Warrior crouched beside a fallen figure, her back to them. Colton ran to his sister's side, calling her name, but Stevie hesitated. Marise's hoarse chant, spoken through a raw throat, signaled something very bad.

"I could not heal him." Her voice was a low growl of grief and pain. "He saved my life. I could not save his."

Approaching slowly, Stevie saw that the body was Eli. He lay where he had fallen, face down, an axe protruding between his shoulder blades. Stunned, she asked, "What? How?"

"Torren. Eli appeared and killed my opponent." Marise's words came in clips, anger tinting the anguish. "Before the Rebel hit the ground, Torren's axe cleaved my savior."

The blood rushed out of Stevie's face. She could not make herself look at the Djen she had thought of as a friend. Anger boiled up, burning out the shock and sorrow. "I will kill that bastard!" Stevie screamed.

"He will answer for his actions. You have my word." Colton pulled her close, positioning himself so as to block her line of sight. "We must leave for camp. Eli would not have returned until Jack Snow was safe."

Stevie pushed Colton away. "Wood! I saw Torren chasing him in that direction." She pointed northeast, roughly where Torren's tent had stood.

Colton picked up the trail easily. Soon, the group came upon the detective. He had managed to crawl under the brush, face down in the moss. He had not been able to completely conceal himself. Stevie spotted his shoes sticking out of a pile of leaves. They removed the debris to reveal a knife jutting from the small of the detective's back.

Stevie reached for the blade, but Colton stopped her. "Leave it. The weapon has sealed the wound. It is all that prevents the blood from flowing out."

While Stevie watched anxiously, Colton bent over their friend, gently turning him on his side. First he placed his fingers on Wood's neck, then his wrists, and finally, laid his hands over the detective's chest. "He lives, but his energy is tenuous and threatens to leave this world." Meeting Stevie's look, Colton said, "Come."

The three Djen knelt beside the detective. The women gathered Wood into their arms. Colton waited for Stevie's nod. In one fluid movement, he extracted the knife and added his embrace to the fold.

A light washed over the four. It coalesced and spun above Wood, creating a whirlpool which funneled into the wound. Stevie felt the combined electricity. The intensity was greater than when she and Marise had healed Colton. Detective Wood glowed. His skin pulsated.

The gash sealed, but they did not lessen their hold until the light began to fade. Wood's hand twitched. He opened his eyes and sucked in air.

Colton helped the man to a sitting position.

"Man. That was some fight. What?" he asked. "What are you all looking at?"

"You're alive!" said Stevie as she reached over and hugged him.

Wood smiled and returned the hug. "Darling, I have no idea what you're talking about. The last thing I remember was killing me a few bad guys, and then running through the woods. I think I must have fallen and hit my head, coz the next thing I know, you're all standing around me. "

"You didn't fall. Torren stabbed you in the back. You nearly died...again," Stevie told him.

"Damn...really? Well, ya hadda know you coulda not ditch me dat easy." He struggled to his feet, playing up his New York accent.

Marise helped him walk back to Torren's camp.

Surveying the scene, Wood spoke. "The last thing I remember, Eli was rescuing Jack...I think. You three were kicking some serious Rebel ass." He moved his head this way and that, apparently searching. "So, where are Eli and Jack?"

Marise turned away.

Colton replied, "Eli is dead."

"He was a hero," Stevie said, tears welling. "He saved Marise…"

"I am shamed at not having trusted him," Colton spoke, his tone somber. "He will be honored."

"We need to bury him," Marise said.

"Agreed," Wood said. "We need to bury all of them."

"What about Jack? He needs our healing, too."

"Shylae speaks wisely," Marise said. "The dead can wait."

Arriving at their campsite, no one saw any sign of Jack. Stevie ran to the women's tent, Colton to the men's, and Marise and Wood searched the outskirts of the clearing.

"Any luck?" Wood's voice rang out. The responses of "nothing" and calls of Jack's name echoed through the dark.

A shape moved at the back of the women's tent. Wavy brown hair peeked out from under the blankets, followed by Jack's swollen features. His breathing came easier than in her vision.

She called her friends, "I found him."

The approach of dawn signaled renewed hope. After the long, trying night, the group felt joy in being alive. Although saddened at the loss of Eli, Colton called him Okih.

Torren's capture of the Orteh could have brought despair, but Stevie said, "It's only a setback, not a defeat. It will be returned to its rightful place."

Marise further reminded everyone that Colton had done as he had sworn. "The Guardian is alive and safe and will soon return to Phraile Highlae."

"And Jack lives," Wood chimed in. "Another day to be a pain in my ass."

With his bruises faded by healing, the swelling down, and a full belly, Jack made a quick comeback. "Yeah, that does give me a reason to live."

During breakfast, discussion of how the men had hidden the bodies was kept to a minimum. The exception being the assurance to Marise by her brother that "Eli was buried in the manner that ensures swift travel to the God plane."

All joking aside, Jack seemed reluctant to discuss what had happened. "Those guys had a knack for inflicting pain without killing you. And I gotta tell you, there were a couple of times I wanted them to."

"Don't say that," Stevie said. "I saw you in my visions. I watched over you."

A look crossed his face—*of what? Sorrow, shame, sadness...love?* Stevie couldn't decide. Rather than press Jack to give more details, she hugged him for the hundredth time. "I am so happy that you're okay... I don't know what I would have done without my best friend."

He hugged her back, lingering. Then, in Jack-fashion, said, "Yeah...who would pick on you if I wasn't around?"

"Alyssa!" She ran for the satellite phone. "We haven't called home since landing on Princess Royal. Mom and Alyssa must be panicking."

Jack stopped laughing. "You're right. They're probably freaked. Why haven't you checked in?"

"I was waiting to call her until I knew you were okay. And then we had to rescue you. I was a little busy."

"Okay. Okay. Now would be good, though," said Jack.

Stevie and Jack talked to both Jan and Alyssa and gave them a quick update on the past several days—the sanitized version. Stevie left out the part about Eli and about Jack being captured. She tried to break the news gently that she wouldn't be returning to Golden, at least not right away.

"You can't come home first..." Jan's voice wavered. "...to give me a proper goodbye?"

"I didn't plan it this way, Mom. But we have to act now." Stevie paused. "Take care of Tonka for me. I love you and I'll see you soon."

Jan said, "I love you," and then began to cry.

Handing the phone to Wood, Stevie whispered, "Can you talk to her? It breaks my heart to hear her cry like that."

"Jan," Wood said, "How are you holding up?" A pause. "Glad to hear that." Another pause. "No, Jan. You don't need to worry about Stevie. She has turned into a very capable, amazing young woman."

The conversation went on like that until Stevie was certain Wood had calmed her mom. Stevie completely tuned out when he asked to speak to Drake. He'd give details later.

"You're up," Wood said, handing the phone to Jack. "Alyssa's on the line for you."

"What did Drake have to say?" Stevie asked.

"Apparently, her new partner is a bigger pain than me. She's struggling to keep him from calling the FBI. If I don't get back soon, I'll have to either deal with the Feds' involvement or Drake shooting the new guy."

"I guess I didn't think they'd give her a new partner."

"Yeah, he's digging into all the weird stuff pretty deep. The missing body, the strange DNA...we missed the sample the crime unit had sent off for further testing." Wood rubbed the back of his neck. "It's gonna be a shit-storm when I return."

The light did little to hinder the group's sleep. They agreed that they needed to rest before heading their separate ways. When Stevie rose, the sun had reached its peak—half the day was gone. For the last time, Marise made coffee to wash down the remaining food. The provisions were packed in silence. It was time to go.

Stevie hugged Wood. "Thank you for helping us...you truly are a Warrior." Her cheeks were wet with tears. In his ear, she whispered, "I know you'll keep my mom safe."

Wood held on to her. "I'll miss you all. Thanks for letting me be a part of your journey. Hurry back to us, Stevie...and when you do, you better be prepared to tell me everything about Djenrye. And, at the very least, maybe a summer invite?"

Patting Wood on the back, Colton said, "When the Orteh has been secured and the Guardian has claimed her birthright, then we will have peace and you may see the beauty of our home."

Stevie stepped past the men and went to Jack. She pulled him close. "I will miss you so much… You were so brave. I'd be proud to have you fight at my side any time. My best friend."

Jack's tears sprinkled Stevie's face as he bent over her. And then he kissed her on the lips, lingering. "Take care of yourself. I want you to come back soon. And with stories of how you annihilated that puke."

As they parted, Colton shocked Stevie—and certainly Jack and Wood—when he grasped the men in a bear hug. "Thank you, Brothers, for all you have done. I swear on my honor, on my life, I shall keep Shylae safe."

Standing with Colton and Marise on either side, Stevie watched her Hundye friends walk down the path, toward the boat and away from her. Before she lost sight of them, Stevie saw Jack stop and wave good-bye.

Holding back her tears, Stevie turned away from the sight, knowing it was time to move toward her future. She would miss Jack so much. He had always been there for her. The thought of his not joining them broke her heart. She knew she had to first learn how to be a Djen and a Guardian before she could let him into their world. When Djenrye was safer, she would send for him. For now, it was time to see her new home.

Stevie faced the portal, mesmerized. The colors were intoxicating— how they separated, reformed, and intertwined. It took only a few drops of her blood to open it. But it didn't look open, only changed—the colors blended into one, that of an ocean after a storm.

When I walk through, will it feel different?

Memories of Djenrye from her visions and dreams comforted her. *I was raised in this world, but Djenrye is home.* And—there was Colton. He stood beside her, staring at her rather than the portal. Her feelings for him reflected in his eyes.

"Are you ready, my love?" he asked.

"I am," Marise piped in. "And I am anxious to be back in our world. I will see you two on the other side." With that, she disappeared through the portal.

Only two Djen remained in Terra-hun.

"I have dreamed of this moment since I first became your protector."

Stevie stood on her tiptoes to kiss him. "I've loved you all my life. I just didn't know it."

"And I as well. My Shylae." He embraced her, completing the kiss she had begun.

They could no longer delay. Colton held out his hand. Stevie intertwined her fingers with his and, as one, they stepped through the portal...

To be continued in Book II of the Lorn Prophecy: Lore

DICTIONARY OF DJEN WORDS AND PHRASES

Djen-rye Word	Pronunciation	Plural	English Word / Description
aedul	ā-dyül	aedulelae	gasp
aetaenudo	ă-tā'-nü-dō	aetenudoelae	call
aetsi	ā-tsē'	Aetsilae	crackle
ai	ī		of
Androne	An-drôn	Ty Androne	Androne - a race in Djenrye (cousin of the Wood Elves)
Anreo	Ăn'-rō	Ty Anreo	Elf
ar	är		is
Asha Vitál	Ăsha Vē'-töl		Gods (referring to all gods as one)
ashlil	ăsh-līl	Ashlilae	Run, to run, a runner
Avira	Ăvēr-ă		Orb of the Air / Wind, Currents, weather Stone: Opal City: Plates Warriors: Bow-men/women
aviranal	ăvēr-ă-năl	Aviranal	air
beyea	bē-yē-ā		watch / watch out / watch for
borvadé	bôr-vä-dā'	borvadalae	flame
borval	bôr-väl'	borvalae	fire
Borvo	bôr-vō'		Orb of Fire / volcanoes, lightening Stone: Red Calcite City: Teskna Ta Warriors: Magi (fight w/magic)
Bousae-yamae	Büsz-ā'-yä-mä'		Soul connection/ blending that occurs at sight/ meeting with a true soul-mate. Rare.
chasea	Cha-sā		you

Dictionary of Djen Words and Phrases to English

Djen-rye Word	Pronunciation	Plural	English Word / Description
chasean	Cha-sā-än		your (possessive)
chatea	sha tā'	chataelae	chant
clor	klôr	Clorlae	burn
Dangrial	Daŋ-grīāl (r is rolled)		The city in Djenrye where the sorcerers reside
Din Ashyea	dĭn ă-shā		Book of knowledge / Ancient Book of the Djen
Din Saeklae	dĭn sāk~klā'		Book of Prophecy / Given to Lorn by Tzak
Djen	Zhĕn	Ty Djen	Djen, beings altered by the Gods
Djenrye	Zhĕn-rī		Djenrye, world parallel to earth
eh	ĕ		no
eh'ankh	ĕ-änk	eh'ankhlae	death
ehtae	eh-tā'		not
Élan-Vitál	ē-lăn' vē'-töl		Orb of the Spirit that Connects All Stone: Diamond City: All - Djenrye & Terra-hun Warriors: Guardians
Faugn	fôn	Ty Faugn	Faugn, a race in Djenrye (cousin of the Jajing)
fwuwae	fū-wā'		meet (as in a greeting - meet a friend)
glyt	glīt	Glytlae	Grant
gramein	grā-myān		birth
graoch	grā-äk		blood
graochomae	grā-äk~ō'mā		Blood Cycle (moon cycle/ ~28 days)
Greial	grāy~yĕl	Greiallae	Guardian
grinih	grĭn~nī	grinihlae	suspect

Djen-rye Word	Pronunciation	Plural	English Word / Description
Halle	hāl	Ty Halle	House of Learning, Worship, a Holy Place (there is no exact translation to English)
hapae-rú	ha-pā-rū'	hapae-rúlae	traitor - one who sells his/her services
highlae	hī'-lā	Ty highlae / plural same as singular	light - formal, spiritual connotation
highlea	hī'-lē	highlealae	light - mundane usage
hine	hīn-eh		he
hir	her		we
Huana	hyü-an-ă		Orb of the Water / Oceans, streams Stone: Blue Agate City: Tyré Warriors: Sailors (like the Coast Guard)
huanae	hyü-an-ā	huanaelae	water
Hundye		Ty Hundye	Human (Exact translation - Children of the Earth)
hy	hī		judge / proclaim
hycre	hī-kreh		would
hyne	hī-ne		where
hyrl	hərl		Will
hyt	hīt		find
ilha alon	īl-hë ălŏn		warrior tattoos - permanent or not
Jajing	Zhā-zhĭŋ	Ty Jajing	A beast-like race (cousin of the Faugn)
ka-chet	ka-chĕtt'		curse word - no exact translation
kala	kă-lă		trash
Kurakaé	Kŏ-rā-Kā	Kurakaélae	Warrior / Soldier / Resistance fighters

Dictionary of Djen Words and Phrases to English

Djen-rye Word	Pronunciation	Plural	English Word / Description
Le	leh		I
meahine	mē-hīn-eh	meahinelae	male
meashine	mē-shīn-eh	meashinelae	female
namea	nă-mā'		name (i.e., I name you / I call you)
nighete	nī~yĕ'-the		never
octalorei	äk-tă'-lô-rā		hear me or attention (a command)
Okih	Ō-kī	Okihlae	Friend, Brother, Sister, Comrade (term to define not only kindred but close friend)
omaka	ōma-ka	omakalae	year, or more precisely one full complete cycle of all the seasons
Orteh	Ôr-teh'	Ortehlae	Orb
paeharu	pā-hă-rū	paeharulae	enemy
Paehatesna	Pā-hă-tehs-nă	Ty Paehatesna	Sorcerer
Phraile Highlae	Frāl Hī-lā		A capital city in Djenrye
Plates	Plāts		A capital city in Djenrye
ra	ră		and
Radii Mene	Rā'-dē Mēn-ĕh		Orteh room in the Hall of Light
raile	rāl		hall
Raile ai Highlae	Rāl ā Hī-lā		Hall of Light
rajea	rä-zhē	Rajealae	realm
redul	rä-dyül		grab or grasp / forcefully
saeni	sā-nī		pregnant, pregancy
shine	shīn-eh		she
shurb	sherb	shurblae	drink (beverage)-noun

Djen-rye Word	Pronunciation	Plural	English Word / Description
Shylae	Shī-lā		Shylae (means bringer of light)
tahka	täh-kä	Tahkalae	weapon (commonly sword)
Tecton	tĕk-tän		Orb of the Earth / Techtonic Plates Stone: Green Courmaline City: Phraile Highlae Warriors: Swordsmen/women
tectrea	tĕk-trā'-yă	tectrealae	earth / planet, ground
teklae	tĕk-lā'		separate, remove, take away
tenae	tĕn-ā'	Tenaelae	path
Terra-hun	Tĕr-ă-hŭn	Ty Terra-hun	Human plane
Tesknata	Tesk~nä-tä		Mage singular
Tesknata	tesk~nä-tä	Ty Tesknata	Magi (plural of Mage)
toch	Täk	Tochlae	tree (same as wood)
toch	Täk	Tochlae	wood (same as tree)
Toch Anreo	Täk Ăn'-rō	Ty Toch Anreo	Wood Elves (cousin to Androne)
toch ashlile	täk ash-lī-leh	tochlae ashlile	tree-runner
Triveatae	Trĭv~vē-atā		Prophecy (i.e. Lorn Prophecy)
triyea	trī-yē'	Ty triyea	sentence (i.e., judgement)
tsa-amamae	tsă-ă-mă-mā'	tsa-amamaelae	answer
ty	tī		the

Dictionary of Djen Words and Phrases to English

Djen-rye Word	Pronunciation	Plural	English Word / Description
Ty Tesknata Halle	tī' tesk~nä-tä hāl		Magi House of Learning
tyea	tī-ā		them
Tyré	Tī-rē'		A capital city in Djenrye
Tyrénian	Tī-rē'-nē-ĕn	Tyrénianlae	A citizen of Tyré
uelahae	yū-lă-hā'	uelahaelae	laugh
wahae	wă-hā	wahaelae	whisper
wanajae	wănă-zhā	wanajaelae	Entryway / doorway / passage
Wanaji mánae	Wän~nä-zhjē măn-ā'	Ty Wanaji mánae	Portal (spirit walk)
Wanku	wän-kü'	wankulae	Mountain
Wankurá	wän-kü-ră'	Ty Wankurá	Mountain (name of the one that holds a portal)
whynae	hwī-nā'	whynaelae	wish
yi	yē		yes

Chants

Meditation Chant

The air whispers	Ty Avira wahaelae
The water laughs	Ty Huana uelahaelae
The fire crackles	Ty Borvo aetsilae
The earth gasps	Ty Tecton aedulelae
The spirit calls	Ty Élan-Vitál aetenudoelae
The Guardian answers	Ty Greial tsa-amamaelae

Shylae's call to the Gods

Show me the path	Seihi le ty tenae
The light of Élan-Vitál	Ty Highlae ai Élan-Vitál
I am the Bringer of the Light	Le Ty Shylae
Joined in Blood	Bousae-yamae Graoch
Joined by Birth	Bousae-yamae Gramein
The Gods Call	Ty Asha Vi'tal Aetaenudo
The Guardian Answers	Ty Greial tsa-amamaelae

Phrases

In the name of Tzak	Namae ai Tzak
I name you traitor	Ie namae chasea hapae-rú
I sentence you to die (Strict translation - I sentence you death)	Triyea chasean eh'ankh
In the name of Élan-Vitál	Namae ai Élan-Vitál
Grab your weapons	Redule chasean tahka
Watch for the guardian	Beyea ty Greial
Death to / kill the enemy	eh'ankh ty pay-ha-ru
A pledge of loyalty - "I will do as you wish" or "as you command" (Strict translation - I will you wish)	Le hyrl chasea whynae

ABOUT THE AUTHORS

Lisa Fender

I have the complete joy of living in Golden Colorado with its splendid mountains and awesome views! I have two adult children and two beautiful grandchildren, and of course, my dog Branch (a Yellow Lab mix). I am married to the most amazing and supportive man on the planet and have a wonderful and helpful sister, whom if it wasn't for her, I would not be this far with my book! I am so grateful to her and to some of my wonderful friends that have encouraged me along this journey of writing a novel.

Toni Burns

I am blessed to live in the most beautiful state in the U.S., and doubly blessed to be near my entire family – my two grown kids, my sister, her children and grandchildren, my mom, my husband's folks, sister, and nephew. I am happily married to a loving and supportive husband, and we have two wonderful dogs – Daisy (our Malamute-Shepherd) and Studley (our Newfoundland-Labrador). I feel very fortunate to have been invited on Stevie's journey by my sister as the writing of this amazing story has brought us closer together, not only as sisters but as friends.

We LOVE hearing from our fans!
Please feel free to contact us at:

LisaFender8160@gmail.com / ToniBurns8160@gmail.com
www.LisaFender.com
www.Facebook.com/FableBookI
www.Twitter.com/LisaFender1

CPSIA information can be obtained at www.ICGtesting.com
Printed in the USA
LVOW11s0935021213

363510LV00002B/253/P